Till We Meet Again

Penelope J. Stokes

Tyndale House Publishers, Inc.
WHEATON, ILLINOIS

Visit Tyndale's exciting Web site at www.tyndale.com

Scripture quotations are taken from the *Holy Bible,* King James Version.

Library of Congress Cataloging-in-Publication Data

Stokes, Penelope, J.
  Till we meet again / Penelope J. Stokes.
    p. cm. — (Faith on the home front ; 2)
  ISBN 0-8423-0852-0 (sc)
  1. World War, 1939-1945—Mississippi—Fiction. I. Title. II. Series: Stokes, Penelope J.
Faith on the home front ; 2.
PS3569.T6219T55 1997
813'.54—dc21
                                                   96-45608

Printed in the United States of America

04 03 02 01 00 99 98 97
 9   8   7   6   5   4   3   2   1

To my parents,

who gave me roots and wings.

ACKNOWLEDGMENTS

Many thanks are due to many people for their particular contributions to this book:

My parents, Jim and Betty Stokes, who first lived the story and then gave me permission to write it;

Bill McCarthy, whose experiences in a German prison camp brought reality to the work;

Dan Balow, who trustingly sent me priceless research materials from the forties;

Judith Markham, who corrects, encourages, and refines with the touch of a master.

And special thanks to my family and friends, who continue to endure my obsessions with grace and goodwill.

CONTENTS

PART ONE

Gathering Dreams / AUTUMN 1944

PART TWO

Shining Star / CHRISTMAS 1944

PART THREE
Winter Chill / JANUARY 1945

PART FOUR
Easter Song / MARCH 1945

ONE

Gathering Dreams

AUTUMN 1944

1

⋆ ⋆ ⋆

Resurrection of a Dream

Eden, Mississippi
Autumn 1944

Libba Coltrain stood in the drizzling rain, idly watching the drops of water soak into her good black linen suit. She should be listening to the minister, she supposed, but after twenty minutes of accolades inside the church and another ten minutes here at the graveside, she had just about had her fill of hearing what a fine, upstanding man her father had been. Robinson Coltrain, honored deacon of the Presbyterian church. Robinson Coltrain, benefactor of the poor. Robinson Coltrain, model citizen of Eden.

Robinson Coltrain, liar! her mind shouted. *Robinson Coltrain, thief! How could he do such a thing?* she wondered. *How?*

Libba twisted a white handkerchief between her gloved hands, and her eyes darted to her mother's puffy, tearstained face. Poor Mama. It was too much for her, losing her husband so suddenly and finding out at the same time what a dishonorable, despicable person he was. A woman like Mama should at least have the comfort of burying her husband in peace, believing the best of him.

Libba's fingers groped inside her handbag, stroking the cache of letters tied with a faded ribbon. Letters from Sergeant James Lincoln Winsom—from France, and from the hospital in England. Letters her father had deliberately hidden from her. She never let them out of her possession now that she had them back.

She had believed Link was dead, shot down at the front and buried in an unmarked grave. Even now, the pain washed over her in a wave, reminding her of the searing grief, the emptiness, the sense of loss. And Daddy had left her to this agony, hiding Link's letters and letting her believe that the man she loved and wanted to marry had died.

Rage welled up in Libba's soul, and even the shuddering sobs coming from her mother could not assuage her anger toward her father. It was a righteous punishment, Libba thought—dying of a heart attack, alone in his office, with Link's letters in a strongbox beside him. She imagined her father going to his office every day, locking his door, reading the letters, gloating over his treasure. She could almost see the sneering look on his face—that expression that always meant he had won, had gained control over someone weaker than himself.

Daddy had almost succeeded in tearing her dreams apart. Almost, but not quite. Link was alive and was being transferred to Kennedy General in Memphis. For all Daddy's manipulations and machinations, he could no longer stop her from seeing him. From loving him. From marrying him. Finally, once and for all, Daddy had lost.

Like a minor electrical shock, the awareness jabbed at Libba that she was glad—really glad—her father was dead. He was out of her life forever. She supposed she should forgive him, but she couldn't. Her only regret was that she would never have the chance to confront him for what he had done to her.

Her gaze rested on the deep hole dug straight and square in the ground, on the raw mound of earth beside the casket. Rivulets of red clay ran down the mound into the grave, like the blood she had seen in her dreams for weeks. Tears sprang to her eyes—tears of pain and relief, tears of physical weariness and emotional exhaustion. Libba caught her mother's gaze, and Mama gave her a brief, wan smile. Maybe she thought Libba's tears were signs of grief over her father's death. Well, let her think that if it helped. It was a small concession, the least she could do to give Mama a little support.

When the pastor uttered the final "Amen" and came over to shake Mama's hand, Libba breathed a sigh. It was over. Finally and completely over.

Or so she thought.

★ ★ ★

Within minutes after the funeral, the house was filled with people milling about and murmuring in low tones, offering sandwiches and sympathy, cake and condolences. Half the town of Eden turned out, most of them related by blood or marriage to one or the other of Libba's parents.

Just when Libba thought she would scream if another person hugged her and told her how sad it was for a girl so young to lose her precious father, her cousins Willie and Mabel Rae appeared at her elbow.

"Let's go sit down," Willie suggested, taking Libba by the arm and steering her to the sofa.

Mabel followed with a plate heaped high with sandwiches, potato salad, and chocolate cake. "Have something to eat, Cousin," she said. "You need to keep your strength up."

The absurdity of the statement, coupled with the enormous quantity of food Mabel thrust into her face, struck Libba as oddly funny, and she began to laugh. "Right, Mabel," she giggled. "Chocolate will cure anything."

Mabel's round face widened in a sheepish grin, and she struggled for composure. "I just thought—"

Libba lifted a forkful of potato salad in salute. "You just thought that since Daddy is finally out of the way, we should celebrate!"

"Hush, Libba," Willie warned, looking about apprehensively. "Somebody will hear you. You wouldn't want people to think—"

"That I don't mourn my dear departed father?" Libba grimaced. "Of course not. We have to keep up appearances, you know."

Willie sat down beside Libba and put an arm around her. "I'm not thinking about appearances," she whispered. "I'm thinking about Aunt Olivia."

Libba sobered. "Mama." She turned to look at Willie and saw in her eyes an expression of unutterable sorrow. Willie was right. She knew what grief was all about—after all, she had lost both her brother, Charlie, and her sweetheart, Owen Slaughter, to this terrible war. She was more serious now, and more sensitive. The experience had deepened her, but much of the light and life of the old Willie had dimmed.

Libba patted Willie's work-roughened hand and smiled. "You're right, Willie," she murmured. "No matter how I feel, I'll try to keep it to myself. For Mama's sake."

"Stork and Madge Simpson are here," Mabel Rae said brightly, pointing to the other side of the room. "With Mickey."

Good old Stork, Libba thought as she looked across the room toward Link's best friend. Stork had been with Link when he was wounded. His arm was still in a sling from the bullet he had taken, but he appeared to be the happiest man on earth. Finally reunited with his wife and baby son, Stork had taken to fatherhood immediately, and his obvious love for Madge warmed Libba's heart. Madge deserved to be happy, Libba mused. She had certainly become a good friend to Libba since she came to Eden a few months ago.

Libba handed the plate back to Mabel Rae and got up off the couch, then carefully threaded her way through the crowd toward her mother. Mama was smiling at last, bouncing little Mickey Simpson up and down and making faces at him. Thelma Breckinridge, owner of the Paradise Garden Cafe, stood beside Mama with a comforting hand on her arm.

Suddenly, as if a heavy weight had lifted from her shoulders, Libba realized that Mama would be all right. She wouldn't have to worry about money—Daddy had seen to that, at least. And here in Eden she was surrounded by people who cared about her—friends, relatives, and loved ones who would look out for her, keep her busy, not let her get too lonely. . . .

Libba stopped in her tracks as she became aware of the direction her thoughts were taking her. The timing was bad, she knew. She ought to be here, helping Mama deal with her grief and with all the complications Daddy's death would bring for the business and for their personal lives. But she had to leave. Link was coming home—to the army hospital in Memphis. He had sent a telegram asking for her to come there. That last compelling line—*Love, Link*—tugged at her, drawing her. She had to be near him, to give their relationship a chance. She didn't know how she would manage it—living in Memphis by herself; she only knew that if she didn't go, she would regret it for the rest of her life.

Tentatively, Libba approached her mother and gave her a kiss on the cheek. "We need to talk, Mama," she whispered.

Her mother's smile faded as she handed Mickey back to Stork. She extracted herself from the group and clung to Libba's arm as they walked through the kitchen to the enclosed back porch. All along the way, friends and relatives stopped them to offer their sympathy, to give a hug or a kiss or a pat on the back, to remind Olivia Coltrain how fortunate she was to have a loving, supportive daughter like Libba. And the farther they went, the more rotten Libba felt.

At last Mama closed the porch door behind them and sank down onto the love seat. "Come sit, honey." She patted the space beside her. "You must be exhausted. I know I am."

Libba edged onto the small sofa but kept her eyes averted from her mother's. "I guess so, Mama. I'm—I don't know—emotionally wrung out."

"A lot has happened in the past few days," Mama sighed. "It's been draining for all of us."

Libba turned and took her mother's hand, looking intently into her eyes. "Will you be all right, Mama? I mean, you and Daddy were married for so long, and—"

Tears filled her mother's eyes, and Libba willed herself not to turn away. "Libba," her mother said softly, "there are a lot of things you never knew about your father, and some I wish you never had to find out. I won't go into details—my mother taught me not to speak ill of the dead. Suffice it to say that life with your father was not always as . . . ah, idyllic . . . as I wished it might have been." Mama closed her eyes and sighed.

Libba watched, fascinated, as a kind of cloud passed over her mother's features. When Mama opened her eyes again, a look that Libba could only identify as *relief* hovered briefly in her gaze, then flitted away.

"In the early days of our marriage, when we were struggling to get the hardware business off the ground, we had a few good years. But even then our relationship wasn't based on honesty. We—" She paused, seeming to consider the wisdom of continuing. "But that's another story. Perhaps I'll tell you about it someday."

Libba wanted to shake her and shout, *Tell me now—I need to know!* But she kept silent and waited. A delicate balance was developing here, the transition from the parent-child relationship to the confidence of friends. Libba didn't want to take the chance of the door slamming shut.

"Anyway," her mother went on after a moment, "when your father did . . . what he did . . . to you, hiding your letters and all, I was shocked, of course, but I wasn't really surprised. When I thought about it, I realized that it was just the sort of thing Robinson would do to try to maintain control over you—the kind of thing he was perfectly capable of doing."

"But you defended him!" Libba gasped. "You always told me—"

Mama interrupted her with a shrug. "He was my husband."

"And he was my *father.*" Libba felt her breath catch in her throat. "He had no right to let me believe that the man I loved was dead."

"No, he didn't." Mama faced her squarely, her chin thrust out. "He was wrong—and it was a terrible thing for him to do. If I had known about it, I would have stood up to him. You must believe that."

A rush of pity swept over Libba—sympathy for what her mother must have endured all these years. "I know," she said quietly. "I believe you, Mama."

Olivia Coltrain's fingers trembled as she brushed back errant strands of faded auburn hair. "But now it's over," she said resolutely. "Your daddy is gone. And you and I have to get on with our lives."

Libba's head snapped up. "What do you mean?"

Gently, Mama took Libba's handbag and opened it. She withdrew the packet of Link's letters and stroked them tenderly. "Someone's waiting for you in Memphis, Libba. Someone very special. You have to go."

"Go?" Libba choked on the word. For all her determination to find Link, she hadn't expected this. Oddly, she felt abandoned, rejected. "You want me to leave?"

Mama took her hand and squeezed it. "Of course I don't want you to leave. But this is important—to you, to your young man, to your future together. And it won't be forever."

"But how?" Libba frowned and shook her head. "I don't have any money, Mama. And neither do you until Daddy's estate is released. There's no way I can just pick up and leave—"

Libba stopped suddenly. Her mother was gazing at her with a strange expression, a half smile mixed with love and amusement. "What happened to all that faith?" she asked quietly.

"What?"

Mama shook her head. "Your faith, Libba—this new experience with the reality of God you've been telling us about for months now. Have you been praying about this?"

Libba gulped. "Well, sort of. I've been so caught up in what's happened since I found out Link was alive that I haven't had time to figure out what to do—"

Mama gave a low laugh. "You know *what* to do, Daughter. We just have to figure out *how*—"

In the hallway beyond the kitchen, the telephone rang, and Libba jumped up. "No, I'll get it," her mother said, rising and going toward the door. "You think about this. I'll be back in a minute."

Libba sat, stunned, as thoughts collided and spun in her mind. So . . . her mother wasn't ignorant of her father's true nature after all. She knew. And she felt some sort of relief at his passing as well. It was *freedom* Libba had seen on her mother's face in that unguarded moment—liberty, at last, from the domineering control of a man determined to have his own way at any cost.

A shudder ran up her spine, raising goose bumps on her arms. Libba didn't have the faintest idea how this would all turn out with Link, and she hadn't a clue how she was going to manage getting to Memphis and staying there until she found him and gave their relationship another try. This wouldn't be one of the carefree shopping trips to the big city she and Mama used to take. The way the army did things, it might take weeks for Link to get to Kennedy General. She would have to get a job, find a place to live . . . and Memphis was a huge, scary place for a girl to be in alone.

Libba closed her eyes and tried to pray, but her mind wouldn't settle. The buzz of conversation from the mourners in the living room filled her ears, and she could hear her mother on the telephone in the hall, talking in a subdued voice.

Then gradually, before she realized what was happening, silence descended over Libba—a deep quietness, in which the darkness behind her closed eyelids enveloped her like an embrace. The fear and apprehension melted away, replaced by an assurance of—of what? She didn't know. She only felt, illogical as it might seem, that everything was going to be all right.

She opened her eyes to find her mother standing in front of her, arms crossed. Libba blinked, trying to bring her mind into focus.

"Who was it?" she mumbled. "On the telephone?"

Mama smiled. "It was the one-and-only Magnolia Cooley—your Great-Aunt Mag."

"Your mother's sister!" Libba shook her head. "You haven't heard from her in years."

"I know. I only met her once, when you were about five, although she sends a Christmas card every year or so. She heard about Robinson's death and called to offer her condolences."

"That was nice." Libba frowned, puzzled at her mother's expression—a cat-with-a-canary look if ever she had seen one. "What's wrong, Mama? What else did Aunt Mag have to say?"

Mama's eyes glinted with amusement, and she put a forefinger to her lips. "Well, she said her arthritis is bothering her a lot these days—she's over eighty, you know. She wants to find some young girl who can come live in the house with her, to help with housework and look out for her. Do a little cooking, that kind of thing."

"I suppose she shouldn't have too much trouble finding someone in Atlanta for that kind of work."

Libba's mother began to laugh. "She doesn't live in Atlanta anymore, honey. It seems that six or seven years ago, she moved—" Mama paused. "To Memphis."

Libba's heart began to thud against her rib cage. Was it possible? She hadn't even taken the time to pray specifically, and yet here was the answer, staring her in the face. She jumped up and threw her arms around her mother. "You can't be serious!"

"I'm perfectly serious, dear. She lives off Getwell, about four blocks from the army hospital."

Libba's mind raced. She had seen Great-Aunt Magnolia only that one time, when she was a little girl. She barely remembered the meeting. But Aunt Mag was family, and she represented the opportunity Libba needed—a place to stay, where she wouldn't be alone.

"But what about you, Mama?"

Her mother smiled. "I'll be fine, dear. I'm certainly capable of taking care of myself."

Libba looked into her mother's eyes and knew she was telling the truth. She *was* fine—perhaps better than she had been in years. Despite the weariness in her face and the sagging lines of grief at the corners of her mouth, there seemed to be more life in her than Libba had ever seen.

Libba's dream fanned to a flame in her heart—the dream of Link Winsom, of their life together. For the first time in months, she gave herself over to the joy and wonder of it. Daddy had tried to kill her dream, but he hadn't succeeded. God, somehow, had made a way through the darkness. Resurrection out of death.

"It's all right if I go?" Libba asked eagerly.

Her mother nodded.

"Then let's call Aunt Mag—now!" She pushed past Mama and began to move toward the hallway.

"That won't be necessary," Mama said, turning Libba around and cupping her cheek with a gentle hand. "I told her you'd come on the first bus Monday morning."

2

★ ★ ★

Farewells

Mabel Rae Coltrain stood in the kitchen of her parents' aging farmhouse and stared dejectedly at her sister. Willie looked as shabby and worn as the house itself, her strawberry blonde hair in a tangle of curls, her apron spattered with flour and pie filling, her shoulders stooped like an old woman's.

Rae had always figured that when this scene finally played out, she would be the one left standing in the kitchen while Willie went off into the sunset with her Prince Charming. Mabel Rae never expected to fall in love and get married, never anticipated that anyone would love her and want her—certainly not anyone like dashing Andrew Laporte, who at this moment was sitting in the living room making small talk with her father.

Drew was so incredibly handsome, with his dark hair and broad shoulders and dimples you could get lost in. It seemed unnatural, somehow, that the groom should be that much prettier than the bride. Mabel Rae—or Rae, as Drew called her— was still self-conscious about being seen with him, constantly aware of her dumpy figure, her round, moonish face, her nondescript brown hair. But Drew, bless him, didn't seem to notice. He thought she was beautiful . . . and he made her feel that way. He looked at her with a love that melted all her apprehensions and set her soul on fire. With him, she thought, she could do anything, be anything—

Rae drew her attention back to Willie, still standing by the sink with her hands stuffed in her apron pockets. Willie's Prince Charming, Sergeant Owen Slaughter, was dead, killed at the front in a German ambush. When Willie and Owen met at a USO dance and fell in love, Mabel Rae had been jealous and ecstatic all at the same time. Willie deserved to be loved by such a delightful man—dear, dependable Willie, who had always been the rock of the family.

Now Willie was staying home to take care of the farm, and Mabel Rae was about to go flitting off to New Orleans to meet Drew Laporte's high-society family. Never in a million years had she dreamed it would turn out this way.

"I—I don't know what to say, Willie," she stammered, taking a step in her sister's direction. "I hate to leave you here alone, with all this work, and Mama and Daddy in such a state—"

Willie smiled wanly and made a dismissive gesture with her hand. "They've taken the news of Charlie's death pretty hard," she said with a shrug. "But I expect they'll come around eventually."

Mabel Rae raised one eyebrow. When their brother had been wounded in General Patton's siege on Sicily, the family had expected he would be sent home as soon as he was well enough. But for some reason they still didn't understand, Charlie ended up back on the front, this time in France. *Missing—presumed dead,* the army said. Since that fateful day when postmistress Charity Grevis brought the telegram to the door, William and Bess Coltrain had gone downhill noticeably. Daddy could barely get around to do the chores and feed the animals, and Mama spent most of her time sitting in the swing on the front porch, staring out over the fields. They tried to be happy over Mabel Rae's engagement, of course, but they couldn't quite manage it. Their hearts were with their son, dead on the battlefields of Europe.

And to make matters worse, the news of Owen Slaughter's death had come at the same time—a double grief for Willie.

She was holding up well, of course. Willie always did. She made a point of being strong for everybody else. But Rae knew her sister, and she suspected that Willie's fortitude was, at least in part, a facade—an external structure designed to keep the inner Willie from completely falling apart. Willie was going through the motions, keeping life running from day to day, but behind her eyes lay a haunted, empty expression—the look of a woman who had nothing left to live for.

"I wish I could stay," Rae sighed. "Maybe Drew and I could postpone our trip—"

"You'll do no such thing, Mabel Rae Coltrain!" Willie said, suddenly flaring to life. "Now, you listen to me! Andrew Laporte is waiting out there to take you to meet his parents. When you get back, we'll work on planning an April wedding. But for now you will go, and you will have a wonderful time."

"Is that an order?" Rae giggled.

Willie's face relaxed into a grin. "That's an order. But—" She paused, and a flash of pain shot out from her eyes. "Don't you go forgetting us. . . . Write and tell us all about it."

"Oh, Willie!" Mabel Rae's tears fell on Willie's shoulder as she swept her sister into a fierce embrace. "I'll miss you so much. Thank you for everything."

"For what?" Willie said gruffly.

"For being the best sister anyone could ever have," Rae choked out. She pushed Willie back and looked into her eyes. "I love you."

"You love me now," Willie quipped. "But wait till you see the apple pie you've got all over your nice suit." She brushed at the flour sticking to Mabel Rae's front, then pointed over her shoulder at the door that joined the kitchen and the living room. "I believe somebody's waiting for you."

Rae turned and saw Drew standing in the doorway, his wide shoulders grazing both sides of the doorframe.

"I hate to break this up, sweetheart, but we've got a train to catch."

Rae looked from Drew to Willie and back again. Willie was her sister and her best friend. But Drew was her love, her soul mate, soon to be her husband. It was the way of the world, saying good-bye. As difficult as it might seem, she knew she had to go, had to trust and leave Willie and her parents and Libba and all the other people she loved in Eden in the hands of a caring God.

She picked up her train case from the kitchen table, kissed Willie on the cheek, and took Drew's hand. "Good-bye, Willie. I'll pray for you. And I'll write every day."

"You will not," Willie countered. "You'll be far too busy. But write when you can."

Rae and Drew started for the door.

"Drew?"

They turned to see Willie brandishing a flour-covered rolling pin. "Take good care of her," she said, glaring fiercely at him. "Or you'll have me to answer to."

★ ★ ★

When Mabel Rae and her Lieutenant Andrew Laporte had shut the door behind them, Willie sank down at the kitchen table and put her head in her hands. Had they stayed another minute, she would have lost her composure completely. As it was, her hands were trembling, and tears burned at her eyes. She swallowed hard, cleared her throat, and swallowed again.

Willie Coltrain had never felt so alone. Come to think of it, she had never *been* alone—not really. Always, someone had been there—Mabel Rae, Charlie, and more recently Libba, Madge Simpson, and Thelma Breckinridge. These friends—family, really—had surrounded her with a safe haven, with love, and sometimes, since news of Owen's death, simply with noise and commotion that distracted her from the pain. Now Mabel Rae was gone off to New Orleans to meet her future in-laws. Libba was leaving for Memphis on Monday, hoping to be reunited with Link. Madge would be caught up with her husband and baby, and Thelma, the surrogate grandmother, would be right in the middle of it.

And where would Willie be? Here, in this cold tomb of a house, with her parents wandering about like the living dead. No one to talk to, no one to laugh with . . . if she ever felt like laughing again. No one to understand. Just silence. Silence and emptiness.

Barrenness. That was it—the word Willie had been searching for to describe her life, the term that had eluded her. Images of a wilderness cascaded through her mind, a desert where nothing grew and no living thing survived. Certain women in the Bible were described as barren—aged, shriveled-apple women who begged God to take away their shame and open their wombs. But Willie's barrenness went far beyond the loss of the children she and Owen Slaughter might have had. It penetrated her very soul and made a hollow wasteland of her heart.

Willie slammed her hand viciously on the hard wood tabletop. Against her will, tears welled up and spilled over. After a minute or two of fighting them, she gave in and cried—great wracking sobs of anger, frustration, and loneliness. Losing Owen was bad enough. Did she have to be stripped of everything else, too? Did she have to say good-bye to her sister, her friends, her sense of purpose, all at once? It was too much for one person to bear.

Then let me bear it.

The words seeped into her consciousness like the trickle from an underground spring. Willie was only vaguely aware of the change at first, but the gentle encouragement penetrated the grief-baked soil of her heart. Gradually her tears subsided, and she took a deep breath.

Stop trying to be strong, child. Let me bear your pain.

She heard the words clearly this time, deep within her parched spirit. Words of comfort and hope. Words of power and promise. The problem was, she didn't know how to do it . . . how to let God—or anyone, for that matter—bear her pain. She was the capable one, the one others depended upon. But just the suggestion that someone else might be willing to shoulder the burden made her feel a little better.

Willie sat up and pushed her hair away from her face. Owen and Charlie were still dead. Mabel Rae was gone, and Libba would be in Memphis for weeks, if not months. Her parents still wandered about like zombies, depending on her to keep the farm running. Nothing had changed.

Except that—somehow—she no longer felt so terribly alone.

She got up and went back to the counter where her unfinished piecrust lay waiting. She picked up the rolling pin and began to work, humming softly to herself.

For the first time in months, Willie Coltrain sensed a glimmer of hope. She only prayed it would be enough.

3

☆ ☆ ☆

Monday in Paradise

Olivia Coltrain stood on the gravel in front of the Paradise Garden Cafe and waved good-bye to Libba. She shaded her eyes against the morning light and watched as the bus rounded the curve in the highway. When it was out of sight, she pulled open the door of the cafe and went in.

Olivia hadn't spent much time at the Paradise Garden. Robinson had always been adamant about avoiding "that Breckinridge woman," as if Thelma had some kind of communicable disease that would turn anyone she touched into white trash in the blink of an eye. Olivia knew the stories about Thelma, of course; in a town like Eden, precious little was kept secret. The woman had lived a pretty wild life years ago, according to all accounts. Then suddenly she up and got herself engaged to a Yankee named Roundtree or Raintree, or something odd like that, and became the picture of propriety.

Or she tried to. But despite her best efforts, Thelma's attempt to rewrite her reputation failed—at least in polite society. The Yankee left her, practically at the altar, and instead of leaving town like a self-respecting woman scorned, Thelma Breckinridge plopped herself squarely down in Eden to stay. But why, if she wanted to fit in and be accepted, did she insist on dyeing her hair with that horrible henna? And why did she let that crazy old war veteran Harlan Brownlee hang around the place? He acted like he belonged there, playing that rickety old piano and bothering the customers with his stories about the last Great War.

Oh, yes, Olivia knew all about Thelma Breckinridge, and she had been duly warned to keep her distance. The problem was, Olivia liked Thelma.

The woman seemed to have something special, some quality about her that generated trust. All the young people seemed drawn to her—Willie and Mabel Rae, that nice Simpson boy and his sweet wife, Madge—even her own daughter, Libba. And although Olivia couldn't help being a little jealous over the fact that Thelma had been the person her daughter had confided in during the past few difficult months, she knew deep down that Thelma Breckinridge had been a godsend for Libba, and she was grateful.

"Morning, Miss 'Livia." From his perch on the piano bench, Harlan Brownlee waved a greeting as Olivia entered the cafe.

"Good morning, Harlan," Olivia responded politely, not meeting his eyes.

"Call me Ivory, Miss 'Livia," he said with a cackling laugh. "Everybody does."

"All right, then . . . Ivory." Olivia settled at a table near the window and tried not to notice as Ivory Brownlee shuffled over from the piano to stand beside her. He waited for a moment until she looked up. "What is it, Harlan . . . I mean, Ivory?"

His watery old eyes met hers with a sympathetic look, and he reached out a clawlike hand to pat her back. "I'm sorry about Mr. Robinson dyin' like that," he said. "Must be terrible hard on a fine lady like yourself.'

Taken aback by this unexpected show of compassion, Olivia swallowed with difficulty and blinked. "Why, thank you, Ivory," she said quietly. "That's very thoughtful of you."

"You doing all right, Miss 'Livia?" he asked intently. "I can play something special for you, to make you feel better." His eyes lit up, and his mouth opened wide in a grin that showed every missing tooth. "How 'bout 'Moonlight Serenade'? It's nice and soothing."

"That would be lovely, Ivory. It's one of my favorites."

Olivia watched as the old man ambled back to the piano and began to play. Even on the ancient, rickety upright he played masterfully, moving from "Moonlight Serenade" to "Moonlight Sonata" without hesitation. Evidently he was partial to moonlight, Olivia mused, even if it was seven-thirty in the morning.

★ ★ ★

Behind the counter, Thelma nodded to Olivia Coltrain and waited for her fresh coffee to brew. She smiled to herself as she watched the woman visibly warm to Ivory's show of sympathy.

Olivia Coltrain wore her liberty like a mantle, thought Thelma. She looked tired but . . . *free.* No longer did she go around with her shoulders stooped and her eyes to the ground like a whipped puppy. Ever since her husband's death, she had walked straighter, held her head up, and looked people in the eye.

Thelma wasn't one to rejoice over anyone's death—least of all a man like Robinson Coltrain, whose eternal destiny was, in her opinion, gravely in doubt. She wasn't in a position to judge the state of a man's heart, of course; she left that to the only One who knew all hearts and was capable of administering both justice and grace. But from everything she could see, the man had lived for himself alone, reveling in his ability to exercise control, even domination, over those weaker than himself. She doubted things would go easy for him in the presence of the Almighty. Perhaps his daughter's newfound faith had exerted some influence over him before his sudden demise, but Thelma had no way of knowing. All anyone could do now was entrust him to the mercy of God.

Still, Thelma couldn't help observing that everyone within Robinson Coltrain's orbit, particularly his wife and daughter, seemed more relieved than heartbroken over his unexpected departure from this life. Olivia had appeared shaken at the funeral, but the shock alone would be enough to do that. She had willingly sent Libba off to Memphis, and she now seemed perfectly content to sit in the Paradise Garden, a place where she had rarely set foot unless it was absolutely necessary, and listen to Ivory Brownlee play the piano.

Thelma shrugged. *People do change,* she thought, remembering the growth that had taken place in Libba Coltrain over the past year. *Better late than not at all.*

With a coffeepot and two cups in hand, she made her way over to Olivia's table and took a seat across from her. "Hey there, hon," she said, pouring both cups full and setting the pot on the table. "Care for some company?"

Olivia looked up and smiled, and Thelma noticed how much her green eyes resembled her daughter's. "Certainly, Thelma," the woman said smoothly. "Do sit down."

Thelma started to remark that she was already sitting, but she held her tongue. She suppressed a smile and patted the woman's hand. "How are you holding up, Olivia? This must be difficult for you."

If Olivia Coltrain was offended by Thelma's use of her Christian name, she gave no indication. In these parts, her position in society demanded that she be addressed as "Mrs. Coltrain," or at the very least, "Miss Olivia." But Thelma Breckinridge had never been one to accede to the unreasonable expectations of society, and she didn't intend to start now. They were practically the same age, after all, and the very notion of Olivia's being

Thelma's superior went against every belief Thelma held about the equality of all people in the eyes of God.

Besides, up close, Robinson Coltrain's widow looked like a woman who could use a friend. The strain of the past few days showed on her face, and there was something behind that expression—something troubling. Something besides grief and strain and physical exhaustion.

Thelma sat back and sipped her coffee, watching as a series of emotions played across Olivia's face. At last the woman raised her eyes and blurted out, "Thelma, do you think only good Christians go to heaven?"

Thelma blinked. "Excuse me?"

"Do you think only good Christians go to heaven?" Olivia repeated.

Thelma's mind raced, trying to sort out exactly what the woman was asking. Was she looking for reassurance that her husband was in the presence of God? Or was she questioning her own life? Death was so . . . final. And funerals did funny things to people—caused them to think about their eternal destiny. This might be a rhetorical question, or it might be a plea for help.

"Hon," Thelma said at last, "I guess it depends on your definition of 'good Christian.' In the strictest sense, you might argue that not a one of us is 'good'—we're all sinners. But on the other hand, we're made in the image of the Creator, and that is very good."

"That is not an answer," Olivia said bluntly.

"No, I suppose not," Thelma hedged. "Just what are you asking?"

Olivia fixed Thelma with a piercing look. "Do you think Robinson went to heaven when he died?"

Thelma leaned back and sighed. "Your husband was a deacon in the church," she said cautiously. "He professed to be a Christian—"

"He *professed* a lot of things," Olivia interrupted with a grunt of disgust. "It's what he did to our daughter that concerns me."

"Ah, yes," Thelma sighed. "The letters."

"Not just the letters," Olivia countered. "Everything! The way he treated Libba—and me. Hiding her letters and letting her think Link Winsom was dead was only the culmination of years of manipulation—the worst evidence of his character . . . or lack of it."

Thelma refilled Olivia's coffee cup and leaned forward. Her eyes flitted around the empty cafe. Madge was in the kitchen making biscuits. Little Mickey was in the apartment with his daddy. The morning coffee crowd wouldn't be coming in for a while. They weren't likely to be interrupted. "Tell me about it," she said.

"I'm just so confused about all this," Olivia sighed. "Sometimes I hope—really hope—that there was some glimmer of goodness in Robinson, something God might see that the rest of us missed. Something that would justify getting him into heaven." She held up a hand to keep Thelma from interrupting. "Oh, I know it's based on faith. But isn't faith supposed to result in some kind of outward change in a person? Isn't it supposed to be demonstrated in life, in character, in the way a person treats others? No matter what Robinson claimed to believe, no matter how good a front he put up, I have a hard time seeing any real faith in God in that man's life. When I think about the way he lived his life, keeping Libba—and me—ground under his heel, I get so angry! I—" She stopped suddenly and lowered her eyes, her hands trembling around her cup.

"It's OK," Thelma soothed. "Whatever you're feeling, the good Lord already knows all about it. And you can be sure that anything you tell me won't go any farther than these old ears."

Olivia smiled weakly. "Robinson could be so mean," she whispered. "Oh, he never beat me, never laid a hand on me—he didn't have to. His temper was enough to keep me in line. All he had to do was look at me, and I cringed like a whipped dog."

"And—," Thelma prompted.

"There were times, when he was being so unreasonable with me or with Libba, that I wanted to just pack up and leave. But I couldn't. I had a daughter to raise. But sometimes, Thelma . . . sometimes I hated him— truly I did. Sometimes—" She heaved a mighty sigh. "Sometimes I wished he were dead." She put a hand over her mouth and shook her head. "And now he *is* dead. . . ."

"And you feel responsible?" Thelma narrowed her eyes and watched Olivia's face closely.

The woman's head snapped up. "I feel *relieved!*" she hissed. "And I feel guilty about feeling that way. And—" Her pale green eyes turned hard. "There have been times in the past few days that I've hoped he burns in hell!"

Thelma sat back against her chair, stunned by the force of this last statement. It was obviously the first time Olivia Coltrain had uttered the words aloud; her face registered as much shock as Thelma felt.

"You must think I'm terrible," Olivia murmured.

"I don't think anything of the sort," Thelma countered with more emphasis than she intended. "I think you're going through some perfectly normal feelings, given your situation."

The woman raised her eyes in a pleading look. "You do?"

"I do," Thelma said firmly. "This has all been a terrible shock to your system, Olivia—being hit with your husband's death *and* his deception all in one blow. Of course you would have conflicting feelings about it." A brief flash of memory ran through Thelma's mind—a resurrection of the pain and anger she had felt when Robert Raintree abandoned her without warning, breaking all his promises and leaving her alone with her shattered dreams. "You're not the first person to feel this way."

A glimmer of hope ignited in Olivia's face. "I don't really want him to go to hell," she said quietly. "I just want him to know—to feel—the pain he has caused Libba and me. I want him to suffer a little. Is that an awful thing for a woman to think about her husband?"

"No, it's not awful," Thelma said, giving a slight shrug. "Maybe it's just human." She paused and looked into Olivia's eyes. "I guess the important thing is to leave Robinson's eternal destiny in the hands of God. God is the only one who knows what was in the man's heart. And—" She paused, framing her words carefully. "If people really do 'know as they are known' in the next life, I'm pretty sure Robinson understands what he did to you and Libba. Either way, I expect he wishes he had done things differently."

Olivia nodded. "Thanks, Thelma. I feel a little better now."

"Have you told Libba how you feel?" Thelma asked, knowing the answer.

"Not really." Olivia shook her head. "She knows I had some mixed feelings about her father's death, but she doesn't know why."

"It might help her if she knew. I expect she's going through some of the same things and doesn't want to tell you."

"I suppose you're right," Olivia conceded. "But she has a lot on her mind right now. In Memphis, she'll have Aunt Mag to talk to. And once Link arrives, she won't be thinking about her father—or me."

Thelma leaned forward and took Olivia's pale, soft fingers in her own reddened, work-roughened hand. "Don't count on it," she said. "A girl needs her mother's support."

Tears filled Olivia's eyes, and for a minute Thelma wondered if she had said the wrong thing. Then the woman smiled and said in a strangled voice, "You think Libba still needs me? She felt so close to you, I know, and . . ."

Understanding dawned slowly in Thelma's mind. "Libba confided in me, it's true. But I'm not her mother. Your daughter loves you, Olivia. Nobody can take your place in her life. Not me. Not your Aunt Mag. And now that Robinson's gone—"

★ ★ ★

Now that Robinson's gone . . .

The words echoed in Olivia's heart like a promise. Robinson *was* gone—not just out of sight, a temporary reprieve from his demands and control, but permanently, utterly gone.

Your daughter loves you. . . .

But Libba was still here. Still within reach. Perhaps they could still be a family—a real family, where people loved and supported one another instead of tearing each other's dreams and hopes to shreds.

Her daughter was a grown woman, of course. Olivia couldn't go back and make up for what the girl had lost as a child. But she could start now being the kind of mother she had always wanted to be. She could be available for Libba, talk with her, confide in her. She could—

But Libba was in Memphis. With Aunt Mag. For an indefinite period of time.

A sense of loss overwhelmed Olivia like a dark wave—an awareness of opportunities missed, time squandered, desires wasted. Then, in the midst of the darkness, an idea.

Perhaps it was not too late. There was nothing to keep her in Eden, after all.

She collected her purse and stood abruptly, jarring the table and sloshing coffee into her saucer. "I've got to go, Thelma."

Thelma looked up with a frown. "Is something wrong?"

A surge of wonder and hope rose up from Olivia's heart and spread in a smile across her face. "Pray for me, Thelma. Pray it's not too late."

Thelma got up. "Where are you off to in such a rush?"

"To pack my bags," she answered. "I'm leaving on the first bus tomorrow morning."

As Olivia reached for the door, Thelma took her arm and wheeled her around. "Are you sure you're all right, hon?"

Olivia leaned over and gave Thelma an impulsive kiss on the cheek. "More right than I've ever been in my life. I'll bring you a present from Memphis."

Then, leaving Thelma in the doorway with a puzzled look on her face, Olivia turned and started for home.

4

★ ★ ★

Conviction

Stork Simpson lay on the bed with little Mickey on his stomach, bouncing the giggling baby up and down. Except for Mickey's laughter, the apartment was empty and quiet. Madge had left an hour ago to work in the cafe, and Stork was thoroughly enjoying Daddy Duty.

He had better enjoy it while he had the chance. In three days he had to report back to the base, to Major Mansfield. It was a stroke of sheer luck—or God, or something—that his request to be reassigned at Camp McCrane had been honored. Maybe Mansfield liked him, after all. Maybe somebody up there was looking out for him.

Stork sighed and cuddled Mickey against his side. The boy's eyes fluttered and drooped, and within a minute or two his breathing grew shallow and regular with sleep.

In the stillness of the morning, Stork's mind drifted, filling with images of his life. The warmth of his infant son snuggled against him . . . the face of his wife smiling up at him with wonder and joy at his return. He was one lucky man, Stork mused. He had everything—life, love, a family, a future.

And he didn't deserve any of it. Or so his mother kept reminding him.

Stork retrieved her last letter from the nightstand beside the bed and read it again. A cold chill crept down his spine as he scanned the vicious words of accusation for the tenth time, but he couldn't keep from doing it. Like a man with a rotten tooth, something compelled him to probe at it again, returning to the pain.

You had no business going back to Mississippi, Mother said, *to that loose man chaser and her illegitimate child. You should come home, where you belong. You*

23

don't owe that woman anything. She manipulated you into marriage by getting pregnant, and she deserves to be left alone in the world to deal with the consequences of her sin. That would teach her a lesson she wouldn't soon forget.

Stork sighed and ran a hand through his hair. It didn't make a bit of difference to his mother that they were legally married, that Madge was his wife and Mickey was his legitimate son. All that mattered to her was the circumstance of the baby's creation. He was, in her words, *conceived in shame and degradation, a product of sinful lust.*

Stork had to admit that his mother was right, in a way. He had coerced Madge into making love with him, resulting in pregnancy and a hurry-up wedding.

He could only imagine what kind of treatment Madge had faced when he left her to live with his parents while he went off to fight the war. They had no choice, of course—Madge could no longer work, and she had no family of her own to turn to. The nation was filled with war brides living with their parents or in-laws, and Stork convinced Madge—and himself—that it would be all right, that his mother would come to her senses and accept his wife and child.

Apparently he had been wrong. Madge had said nothing, other than a few ambiguous phrases about that time being "difficult" for them. But Stork knew his mother, and if she was still this angry and vitriolic about his wife, how had she treated Madge when she was under the Simpson roof? The very fact that Madge had taken Mickey, left Missouri, and traveled alone to Mississippi—without a job, a place to live, or friends to support her—spoke volumes about how awful living with Mother had been.

Still, he couldn't help wondering whether there was some truth in what his mother wrote in her letter. Madge hadn't manipulated him, of course—it had been the other way around. He was to blame; it was his fault, his sin.

Stork shifted Mickey's sleeping form a little and raised the letter to the light. He read a bit further, prodding at the exposed nerve, raw and vulnerable. *You may think everything is fine now that you're back,* Mother wrote, *but mark my words—this woman's sin will not go unpunished. I don't want to see you hurt, Son, but I feel it is my duty as a mother to warn you. If you continue with this disgraceful liaison, with this sham of a marriage, you will pay the price. . . .*

★ ★ ★

Madge looked up from her biscuits and saw Thelma gazing at her through the service window. A strange expression filled the older woman's face—a wistful, faraway look.

"Is something wrong, Thelma?"

Thelma smiled. "No, honey, nothing's wrong at all. I was just thinking."

"About what?"

"About you and Mickey and Stork—ah, Michael. About how wonderful it is for me to have you here."

Madge reached a flour-covered hand across the pass-through counter and patted Thelma's arm. "It's been a blessing for us, too. You're wonderful with little Mickey—just the kind of grandmother he needs."

Thelma blushed to the roots of her henna-dyed hair. "Do you think he'll see me that way when he gets older—as a grandmother, I mean?"

"If I have anything to do with it, he will," Madge said firmly. "You're family to us, Thelma—surely you know that by now. Heaven knows he won't get any grandmothering out of Michael's mother."

Thelma lifted an eyebrow. "Trouble?"

Madge sighed and shrugged her shoulders. "Another letter from Mother Simpson. A pretty nasty one, if Michael's censored reading is any indication. He wouldn't let me look at it. And out of four pages, he would only read a paragraph or two out loud. But I can guess fairly accurately what it said. I certainly heard enough of it while I was living there."

"She's been pretty hard on you, hasn't she?"

Madge shrugged. "Basically, she blames me for deliberately getting pregnant to trap Michael into marriage. I thought she would soften once the baby came, but it just made her worse—a visible reminder, I guess, of my sin. A scarlet letter emblazoned on my chest for all the world to see."

"But you're married, for heaven's sake!"

"Not in her eyes. To Mother Simpson, the marriage, however legal, isn't morally binding. It's a mockery of God and society. All the time I was there, she kept harping on the fact that judgment was just around the corner. I think she was a little disappointed that Mickey wasn't born deformed or retarded. It would have proved her point."

Thelma came around the doorway into the kitchen and stood beside Madge, putting an arm around her shoulder. The touch was comforting, and Madge found herself leaning in to Thelma's side. "Surely you don't believe all that?" Thelma asked softly.

"Of course not." Madge shook her head. "I was forgiven a long time ago for the circumstances of Mickey's conception. I love my husband, and I love my son. No one can convince me that our family isn't blessed by God. But—"

"But what?"

"Well, I'm a little concerned about Michael."

Thelma frowned. "Do you think he believes what his mother is telling him?"

"I don't know. She *is* his mother, and she does have influence with him. But even more than that, I know he feels guilty for putting me in this position. He blames himself for what happened, and for the personal questioning I went through because of it. I've tried to reassure him, but . . . well, Michael doesn't understand forgiveness very well. Thanks to his mother—at least partially—he thinks he somehow has to pay to make up for what he did wrong."

"If we have to pay for sin ourselves, then we're all in trouble." Thelma sighed and squeezed Madge's shoulder.

"That's what I told Michael," Madge said. "But he won't really understand it until he experiences it."

"Then we'll just have to pray," Thelma murmured, "that he discovers the truth for himself."

Madge nodded. "And soon," she added. "Before his mother's condemnation gets the best of him."

5

★ ★ ★

Magnolia

Memphis, Tennessee

Suitcase in hand, Libba Coltrain stood at the gate and peered up the brick walkway. This had to be the right place; the faded letters on the mailbox read *Magnolia Cooley.* But it wasn't at all what she had expected.

The ramshackle white two-story stood out like an open sore against the row of neatly painted little cottages and compact brick homes that lined the street. A huge, ancient mimosa tree spread its branches across the roof and littered the sagging porch with soggy brown blossoms. Scraggly clusters of yellow grass fought with headless dandelions for control of the yard, and a moth-eaten tomcat peered out from under the forsythia bush at the edge of the steps.

Mama said Aunt Mag needed someone to help around the place, Libba thought morosely. *She just didn't say how much help the place needed.*

With a resolute sigh, Libba shifted her suitcase to the other hand, took a deep breath, and made her way up the cracked bricks of the sidewalk. The tomcat flattened its ears, yowled at her, then skittered away with a flourish of white-tipped tail.

A scent of mildew and rotten flowers assailed Libba's nostrils as she stepped onto the porch. Poor Aunt Mag. What an isolated, desperate life she must live here all alone. Libba retrieved a damp newspaper from the mat and pushed the doorbell. No response. She pushed again. Obviously the doorbell was in the same condition as the rest of the house.

Libba set her suitcase on the porch and knocked—softly at first, then with more force.

"Magnolia? Aunt Mag, it's me—Libba Coltrain. Are you in there?"

Maybe something had happened to the old woman. She was in her eighties, after all, and according to Mama, not in the best of health. Had she fallen, broken a hip? Was she lying upstairs, alone and in pain, with no one to help her?

An image flitted through Libba's mind—her frail, gray-haired great-aunt unconscious on the bathroom floor with water overflowing the bathtub and creeping down the stairs. Her stomach knotted with apprehension, Libba twisted the knob, and the door groaned inward on its hinges.

Inside, a dimly lit, musty entryway led to a long, narrow staircase, shrouded in shadows at the upper landing. Libba set her suitcase in the corner and was just about to ascend the stairs when she heard something— an odd, chattering sound, like a gathering of ducks on the bank of a lake. She turned and drew closer to the closed double doors on her left. Sure enough, the noise was coming from inside. Libba put her ear to the heavy wood, straining to hear, but just as she leaned against it, the door swung open. She lost her balance and nearly fell, and when she stepped back, she found herself facing a tall, regal-looking old woman in a flowing purple dress.

"Well, well, what have we here?" The woman's eyes crinkled with merriment, and her broad lips stretched in a smile, revealing two rows of crowded, uneven teeth. Gold earrings dangled nearly to her shoulders, and she placed a hand adorned with four massive diamond rings on Libba's arm.

"I—I—," Libba stammered.

"Spit it out, child!" the woman boomed with a laugh. "What can I do for you?"

Now that the door was open, raucous noise from the other room filtered into the entry hall. Libba craned her neck and looked past the woman into a brightly lit, flamboyantly decorated parlor. Several groups of old women clustered around card tables, chattering like starlings, with an occasional high-pitched laugh piercing the air.

"What—what is this?"

The woman cocked her head and released Libba's arm to adjust a curl on her upswept silver hair. "Why, this is our Monday pinochle group," she said with a chuckle. "A bit rowdy, aren't they?" She fixed Libba with an intense look. "And who, might I ask, are you?"

"Oh!" Libba answered, flustered. "Of course. I'm—I'm Libba Coltrain. I'm here to visit my Great-Aunt Mag . . . Magnolia Cooley. I must have the wrong house." She paused, puzzled. "But the mailbox said—"

"You're in the right place, dearie, never fear."

"But I—is Aunt Mag here? Mother said she was—"

"Ancient, decrepit, and sorely in need of help and comfort?" The broad mouth smiled again. "Indeed she is, my dear. Welcome." The woman reached out and enfolded Libba in a bosomy hug. She smelled of lilacs and baby powder, and some remnant of memory stirred in Libba's mind. "It has been a long time."

Libba drew back in disbelief. "You're Aunt Mag?"

"In the flesh."

"But you're so . . . so—"

"Alive?" Aunt Mag threw back her head and laughed heartily. "Yes, much to everyone's dismay, I am still able to sit up and take nourishment. People keep trying to consign me to a wheelchair, but so far I've fought it quite effectively."

Mag took Libba's hand and steered her through a set of French doors on the other side of the entry hall. There, a formal dining room furnished in mahogany gave way to a large kitchen with tall oak cabinets and a spotless white tile floor.

"Here," Mag said, thrusting a huge crystal punch bowl into Libba's hands. "You can help me make another round of punch for the girls, and we can have us a little chat. Then I'll introduce you." She bustled around the kitchen, pulling orange juice and ice-cube trays out of the humming modern refrigerator. "Equal parts of juice and ginger ale," she instructed as she clattered the ice trays into the kitchen sink. "And there—just above your head in that cabinet—you'll find some red food coloring."

"Food coloring?" Libba repeated, searching through the jumbled shelf until she came up with a tiny vial of red.

Aunt Mag dumped the ice into the punch bowl and gave Libba a conspiratorial wink. "Makes the girls think they're getting something special." She waved a hand derisively. "Posey Matthews raves about my cranberry surprise. The surprise is, it's not cranberry at all." Magnolia chuckled. "Most of them can't taste a thing anyway, so it doesn't matter."

Libba watched in wonder as her great-aunt, the invalid she had come to help care for, whisked around the kitchen like a purple dynamo. "There are tea cakes in the pantry," Mag said, stretching to reach a clear glass platter on the top shelf of the cabinet.

"Here, let me get it," Libba protested. "You'll hurt yourself."

"Posh," Aunt Mag snorted. "I'm taller than you are. Just get the cookies—they're in a blue tin."

When the punch was mixed and the tea cakes arranged on the platter, Mag refilled the ice trays and popped them back in the fridge. "You take the punch bowl," she ordered. "My arthritis is acting up."

Libba raised an eyebrow. *Arthritis?*

As if she had read Libba's mind, Aunt Mag turned and shrugged. "I *am* eighty-three years old," she declared. "At my age, there has to be something wrong with me. It's the law."

Libba followed dutifully with the punch bowl as Aunt Mag swept back through the dining room and into the front parlor. When the cookies and punch were settled on the sideboard, Mag cleared her throat for attention, and the chattering subsided.

"Ah, here's our dummy now!" cackled a gray-haired woman with a face like a road map.

"Don't be insulting, Posey," Aunt Mag retorted, "or you won't get any of my cranberry surprise."

"I was referring to your *hand,*" Posey explained contritely. She pointed to the position opposite her own, where a group of cards lay faceup on the table—obviously Aunt Mag's place, Libba thought.

"You were not," Mag countered with a grin. "You were making derogatory remarks about my intelligence." She leaned close and gave Posey a one-armed hug around the shoulders. "Anyone who plays partners with you has to be a dummy."

Posey feigned offense, and everybody laughed good-naturedly. Then someone asked, "Who's your young friend, Mag? Posey's replacement?"

"This," Mag said regally, raising up and drawing Libba close to her side, "is my grandniece, Libba Coltrain. Olivia's girl, from Mississippi. She's here to help out for a while."

"That's very sweet, dear," Posey Matthews said, smiling so broadly that her wrinkled face folded like an accordion. "Heaven knows, Mag can use all the help she can get. She's totally inept, you know."

"So I see." Libba gave her aunt a sidelong glance.

"Just one word of warning, honey," Posey went on. "Whatever you do, keep your distance from that tomcat of hers."

"The cat I saw outside? The one with the white tip on his tail? He didn't seem very friendly."

Posey lifted a finger. "He's the meanest, most vicious old beast God ever created. He'll scratch your eyes out if you give him half a chance. Don't turn your back on that one—not for a minute."

"Does he have a name?" Libba turned toward Aunt Mag, but Posey answered instead.

"Name's Robinson. Odd name for a creature, if you ask me."

Libba smiled to herself. An eighty-three-year-old woman who wore purple and hosted a pinochle club. Red food coloring in the cranberry surprise. And a nasty-tempered cat named Robinson.

She and Great-Aunt Magnolia were going to get along just fine.

6

☆ ☆ ☆

Family Reunion

Libba leaned back in the mahogany Duncan Phyfe chair and looked across the table at her great-aunt. Magnolia Cooley was nothing short of astounding—eighty-three years old, with enough energy to run circles around people half her age. Libba saw no evidence of the arthritis that supposedly debilitated the old lady. In fact, except for a chronic habit of rubbing her hands together and a little stiffness after she had been sitting a while, Aunt Mag seemed in amazingly good health.

After the pinochle crowd had been fed and shooed off to their respective homes, Mag had tidied up the parlor, settled Libba in her room, and claimed that she would like to lie down for a bit. But within thirty minutes, Libba heard her banging around in the kitchen. When she went down to investigate, she found the old woman at the sink, picking pin feathers from a fresh chicken. An hour and a half later, with only minimal help from Libba, Mag had spread a dinner of chicken and dumplings, biscuits, and fresh green beans on the dining-room table. It was a meal to rival Thelma Breckinridge's best. . . .

Suddenly Libba realized that Aunt Mag was staring at her with a curious expression, an intense, no-nonsense look. Libba pushed the last of her dumplings around on her plate and tried to avoid those piercing pale green eyes, eyes so like her mother's—and her own. Involuntarily, her hand went to the nape of her neck and began twisting the curl behind her ear.

"Don't just sit there, child. Talk to me."

Libba jumped at the gravelly voice and forced herself to meet her great-aunt's gaze. "About what, Aunt Mag?"

The old face relaxed in a smile, and deep laugh lines fanned out from Mag's eyes. "About yourself, of course. About your life, your dreams. About what brings you to me."

Libba frowned, puzzled. "I—I thought I was here because you needed help. Because you were having trouble with—" she paused and glanced up—"with your *arthritis*. That is what you told Mother, isn't it?"

Magnolia threw up her hands and laughed. "All right, I fudged a little. But it was only a slight prevarication. The fact is, I do need you."

"To do what?" Libba countered. "In just one afternoon you've gotten more accomplished than most women half your age do in a week. Why, you—" In a flash of insight, Libba saw the truth. She was not here to help Aunt Mag; she was here so that Aunt Mag could help her. Mama had set it up so that she would have her chance to find Link and make things right.

"Mama told you about my . . . my situation," Libba murmured.

"A little."

"And you offered to let me stay here with you."

"I did. It was entirely my own idea, I assure you."

Libba didn't believe her, but she didn't dare contradict her great-aunt to her face. Still, the very idea shamed her. She would never have come here if she'd known she was Aunt Mag's charity case, some kind of benevolent cause. Coltrains had always paid their own way. They were never beholden to anyone, and Libba wasn't about to start now.

"Look at me, child."

The words drilled into Libba's consciousness, an inescapable command. Reluctantly she raised her eyes.

Magnolia was frowning at her. "You feel as if you've been tricked, and your pride is hurt. Don't bother to deny it. I can see it written all over your face."

Libba's stomach knotted. She didn't appreciate being put on the spot, but she couldn't think of a thing to say.

"Well, let me tell you a thing or two about pride," Aunt Mag went on. "I've seen a good deal of it in my eighty-three years, both outside my own soul and within. And I'll tell you, it's not a pretty picture. Pride makes people do stupid things, child. Things like cutting themselves off from their families. Like throwing away their best hope for happiness and fulfillment, just to live up to the expectations of people who don't matter anyway."

"You're talking about Mama," Libba said quietly. Of course she was. Aunt Magnolia knew all about Mama and Daddy—probably more than Libba knew herself. Just how Mag knew, Libba wasn't quite certain, but she knew. She had named that vicious cat Robinson, hadn't she?

"About your mother, yes. And about myself. I married—the first time—for security. Mother thought Talbot Hardesty was a good match. Father thought I would be well cared for. I was secure, all right—secure but unhappy, and bored nearly to an early death. After Talbot died, I determined not to make that mistake a second time. I met Arthur Cooley and fell in love. My family hated him. He worked for the government, for heaven's sake. He was always traveling off hither and yon—not the ideal life for a cultured southern lady like myself."

"That's why we didn't see you for years," Libba interjected.

"That's not the only reason," Aunt Mag went on. "I was determined to marry Arthur, but I wasn't strong enough to take on my family's disapproval. Instead of standing up to them, I caved in."

"But you did marry him."

"I did. But I didn't have the gumption to defend him, to insist that they get to know him and accept him. We spent one Christmas with my family after we were married. They were horrible to him, and I just couldn't take it. So, against his wishes, we escaped. We went away, just the two of us, and never came back."

Libba's mind conjured up images of her father's deception, of the terrible way he had treated her and her mother. Anger at her father mingled with relief that he was gone, and she felt instinctively that she could understand—at least in part—what her great-aunt had experienced.

"But you were happy . . . with Arthur, I mean?" she asked quietly.

Mag nodded. "Very happy—for a long time. We had a rich, full life together. It wasn't until he died that I realized how much I had missed." She dropped her eyes, and her deep voice grew softer. "My only sister—your grandmother—was barely seventeen when I left. I never got to know her, never saw her grow up, get married. Never knew if she was happy or not. I only saw her once after that, the time I met you. Do you remember? You were so small—"

"Mama says I was five. I don't remember it very well."

Aunt Mag closed her eyes and sighed. "I suppose not. Shortly after that, I went to Africa—"

"*Africa?*" Libba's jaw dropped open. "You were in Africa, Aunt Mag? How? Why?"

Magnolia waved a diamond-covered hand in a dismissive gesture. "Baroness Blixen—Isak Dinesen—invited me to come. We met at a party at the Danish Embassy. She was over twenty years younger than myself, of course, but we had a lot in common, and she seemed to enjoy my company."

Libba shook her head, trying to follow the meanderings of her aunt's conversation. Maybe the old woman *did* need help. She certainly didn't seem lucid at the moment. "Africa, Aunt Mag?" Libba repeated incredulously. "Are you sure?"

"Quite certain," Mag snapped. "I'm old, child, not demented. You see, despite my family's misgivings, Arthur distinguished himself after all. Became an ambassador. The irony of it is that they would have been very proud of him in the long run. Perhaps not for the right reasons, but proud nevertheless."

Aunt Mag's eyes took on a faraway expression, and she leaned her face in her hand. "As I was saying, when I was in Africa I encountered something quite fascinating. Did you know, child, that certain tiny birds live out their whole lives on the backs of rhinoceroses?"

Libba's mind reeled. "Ah, no, Aunt Mag, I never knew that."

"These little birds travel with the rhino herd, sitting on their backs. The rhinos never hurt them, never seem to be bothered by their presence. The birds pick parasites off the rhinoceros's hide. The rhino provides food and protection from predators, and in turn the bird keeps the rhinoceros free from insects. A perfectly harmonized, symbiotic relationship."

Libba pushed her plate aside and leaned across the dining-room table. "What are you trying to say, Aunt Mag?"

Magnolia leaned back and smiled broadly, showing her crooked teeth. "I'm saying, my dear, that what we have here is a similar relationship. You need a place to stay, a chance to find your young man and make a decision that will affect the rest of your life. I need—" pausing, she reached across the table and took Libba's hand in her own—"I need my family back again." She stroked Libba's fingers absently, and Libba felt herself relaxing under the calming influence of her aunt's touch. "I suspect that we're two of a kind, you and I," the old woman said in a throaty voice. "Both willful, independent, and not a little proud." She crooked an eyebrow in Libba's direction. "We just need not to let pride get in the way of more important things. Do you understand, child?"

"I think so," Libba said. "I just need to know one thing."

Aunt Mag withdrew her hand and turned her palm upward. "Ask."

"Are you the rhinoceros or the bird?"

Magnolia threw back her head and laughed so heartily that her earrings did a rhythmic little dance against her wrinkled neck. "You tell me, child."

"The rhinoceros," Libba answered immediately. "Without a doubt, the rhinoceros."

★ ★ ★

By the time Libba went to bed a little after midnight, she had told Aunt Mag everything. How Daddy had belittled her and tried to control her life. How she had almost married Freddy Sturgis just to get away from her father. How she had met and fallen in love with Link Winsom, only to endure incomprehensible pain when she thought he was dead. How Daddy had cruelly kept the truth from her and died with the evidence practically in his hands. How she had to leave Mother right after the funeral because Link was on his way to the hospital in Memphis.

Aunt Mag had said little, only nodding sagely and murmuring quiet encouragements for Libba to continue. She listened solemnly while Libba described her friendships with Willie and Mabel Rae, Madge Simpson, Thelma, and even Freddy, and related how all of them had changed and grown up because of the war.

Libba didn't bother to gloss over her own faults; somehow with Great-Aunt Mag it didn't seem necessary. She admitted that she had been selfish and spoiled, and that even now she had to work hard at not putting her own needs first. When she was finished, she felt as if a heavy burden had been lifted from her shoulders. Aunt Mag applauded her courage and determination, but Libba went to bed feeling as if something had been left unsaid.

All night she tossed fitfully, waking periodically to fuzzy dreams about jungle creatures and tiny birds, seeing visions in her sleep of her father with his menacing stare and her mother in the background, cowering.

She awoke, angry and chilled, just after dawn and couldn't go back to sleep. For a long time she lay under the covers in the unheated bedroom and thought about her dream. It was a familiar scene, dredged up out of her memory from a thousand such experiences—Daddy laying down the law, Mama giving in to him. Leaving Libba alone to fend for herself.

Libba had been mad at Daddy for a long time. Now, suddenly, she realized that she was angry—perhaps even angrier—at her mother as well. Mama should have stopped him, should have done something. At the very least, she should have stood up to him. Instead, she had abdicated, run away. Not physically, perhaps, but she had left Libba alone all the same.

A yowling screech brought Libba upright in bed. She pulled the blanket around her shoulders, went to the window, and looked down into the yard. Aunt Mag's tomcat was tearing into an undersized opponent who had unwittingly crossed over into his territory. The poor kitten, no more than six months old, was getting the worst of the fight, but every time it tried to escape, the tom attacked again. Finally tired of the game, the cat let go and turned his back on his prey and, with a warning hiss over his shoulder, sat down on the back stoop and began to groom himself as if nothing had happened.

"Robinson, you are a vicious creature," Libba muttered to herself. "Why don't you pick on somebody your own size?"

With a start she realized the significance of her own words. Her father had done the same thing to her mother all these years—exerted his dominance over someone who hadn't a prayer of fighting back. Olivia Coltrain hadn't stood a chance against her husband. All she could hope for was to survive.

Libba's anger began to dissipate, and pity welled up within her. Like the kitten out in the yard, Mama had endured the worst of Robinson Coltrain's temper and domination—more than Libba could even guess at, she was certain. Yet Mama had survived. And she had done the best she could, Libba supposed, given the circumstances.

But just what *were* the circumstances? Mama had started to tell her, the day of the funeral, how life had really been with Daddy. It was the first time she had ever even begun to be honest with Libba about her relationship with Daddy. Always before, Mama had just made excuses for him, saying, *That's just the way your father is, dear.* Libba had come so close to getting to the truth, and then the lid had slammed shut. Would she ever learn the truth—the whole truth—about her father?

With a sigh Libba glanced back out the window. Robinson the cat had disappeared, and a weak October sunrise was struggling over the horizon. She returned to bed and bundled under the covers, watching the sun climb higher and the shadows shift against the walls and ceiling. She recalled Aunt Mag's words about pride and family, and a knot formed in her throat. She might be twenty years old, a grown woman on a quest to find the man she loved, but part of her was still a little girl who needed her mother . . . who needed not to be left alone.

A single tear tracked down her cheek as she buried her face in the pillow.

★ ★ ★

Libba jolted awake, aware of movement below her in the house. Sunlight streamed through the streaked windowpane. How late had she slept?

With a grimace she shoved her feet into her slippers, threw on her bathrobe, and ran a brush through her tangled hair. Some rhinoceros bird she was turning out to be—sleeping half the day away while Aunt Mag did all the work. She'd have to do better than this if she was going to earn her keep.

She dashed down the hall to the stairs, then skidded to a stop on the landing. Aunt Mag was up, all right—decked out to the nines in a turquoise dress so bright it made Libba's head hurt. But she wasn't alone. At the bottom of the stairs, in the entry hall, she stood gesturing wildly, arms flailing, in animated conversation with another woman.

Libba ran her hands frantically through her hair. She couldn't be seen like this; she'd have to take time to bathe and dress before going down. But just as she turned back toward her room, a thought stopped her.

There was something familiar about the figure who stood with her back to the stairs—the narrow shoulders, the camel-hair coat, the faded auburn hair. No, it couldn't be. It was impossible. . . .

Then a voice drifted up the stairs toward Libba: "Aunt Mag, it is so good to see you after all these years!"

"Mama!"

Libba raced down the stairs and threw her arms around her mother, nearly knocking Aunt Mag into the hall tree with her exuberance.

"Mama, what are you doing here?" Libba gasped.

Her mother stepped back and put her hands on Libba's shoulders. "Catch your breath, honey. I'll explain later." She looked Libba up and down. "Working hard to help your Aunt Mag, I see. I don't suppose you're aware it's after ten."

"Oh, posh," Mag said, casting a broad wink in Libba's direction. "The child has to get her beauty sleep." She took Libba and her mother firmly by the arm and ushered them into the dining room. "Sit," she commanded. "I've got cinnamon biscuits in the oven, and if they burn, heads will roll."

With a flourish of turquoise, Mag pushed through the swinging door into the kitchen. "Coffee is almost ready," she called over her shoulder. "You two can catch up while I finish making breakfast."

"What does she mean, 'catch up'?" Mother asked. "You've only been gone since yesterday."

Libba gazed into the familiar pale green eyes and smiled. "One day?" she said, leaning over to kiss her mother's cheek. "It seems like years."

"Do you have a fever, Libba?" Mama asked suddenly, putting her wrist to Libba's forehead. "You're behaving quite strangely. Is everything all right?"

"Everything's fine, Mama—now." She sank down into a chair and sighed deeply. "But don't you think it's a bit odd for you to show up on Aunt Mag's doorstep unannounced? *That's* behaving strangely, if you ask me."

"Well then, we're agreed," Aunt Mag chuckled as she reentered the dining room with a tray full of scrambled eggs, cinnamon biscuits, and hot coffee. "We're all strange."

"But we're family," Libba murmured. "So we'll all be strange together."

7

★ ★ ★

On the Rue de Laporte

French Quarter
New Orleans, Louisiana

Mabel Rae Coltrain held on tightly to Andrew Laporte's arm as he steered her through narrow streets flanked by rows of iron-ornamented houses. She might as well be in Paris, she thought. She didn't belong here, didn't fit in, and yet it was exciting and intimidating all at once. The foreign flavor of this infamous city—the unfamiliar smells, the strange, caramel-colored people with their wide smiles and unintelligible language, the raucous music pouring out of open doors on every block—all of it made her head throb and her pulse pound. At the moment, she felt much more like Mabel, the country hick, than Rae, adored fiancée of Lieutenant Andrew Laporte.

Rae looked up at Drew, and he squeezed her hand as if to reassure her. "Isn't New Orleans beautiful?" he said, pronouncing the city's name as if it were one word, *Nawarlens*. "I know you're going to love it as much as I do."

She managed a weak smile. "It is beautiful, Drew. So . . . so different from everything I've ever known. And, I must admit, a bit overwhelming at first."

"Did you enjoy the French Market?" He linked his arm into hers and guided her across the street to a small park bordered with late-blooming flowers and a tall wrought-iron fence.

Rae nodded. The truth was, she much preferred Thelma's coffee to the strong, rich brew mixed with hot milk served at the outdoor cafe in the middle of the French Quarter. But the little square doughnuts—*beignets,*

Drew called them—were absolutely luscious, puffed high in the middle and powdered with sugar.

As they strolled through the park arm in arm, Rae looked around. He was right; this was a beautiful place. A bright blue sky shone overhead, and the air was crisp and clean—fallish, but not too cool. A fountain at the center of the park bubbled cheerfully, and a few old people perched on benches, feeding the birds. Around the perimeter of the park, a number of artists sat with their easels, finished canvases propped carelessly against the fence.

"Bon jour, bon jour!" one of the artists called as they approached to look at his paintings. "Does monsieur wish to buy a landscape—a background, perhaps, for his lovely lady?" He touched paint-stained fingers to his worn wool beret and smiled into Rae's eyes. She felt her cheeks flush, and Drew chuckled.

"Perhaps another day," he said. "Your work is quite nice."

"Merci," the artist responded. "I am here every day except when it rains. You will return with your beautiful companion?"

"If my beautiful companion wishes it." Drew laughed again and took Rae's arm. They left the park and began walking past a row of shops. "You see, darling, everyone thinks you're beautiful."

"He was just trying to get you to buy something."

"Maybe. But you *are* beautiful . . . and his artistic technique is rather good."

"He has the *technique* of an artist, all right," Rae snorted. "A con artist."

"Getting a little cynical, are we?"

Rae sighed. "I'm sorry, Drew. No, not cynical. Just scared."

Drew smiled into her eyes with a look of love that melted all her apprehensions. "I wanted us to have the day together," he said, "so you could enjoy the city before we face the lions in their den."

"Don't say it like that, Drew!"

"I'm only teasing, sweetheart. Mother and Father are perfectly harmless, I assure you. There's nothing to be afraid of."

Rae stopped and turned him so that they were facing a shop window. "Look," she insisted, pointing to their reflections in the glass.

"The little crystal angel on the bottom shelf? It's very nice, darling, but—"

"Not that, silly. Look at us."

"Hmmm," he mused. "You do have a little sprig of hair standing up right here—" He smoothed her hair on top and grinned.

"You know what I'm talking about, Andrew Laporte. You're handsome, cultured, and cosmopolitan. I'm short, dumpy, ordinary—and the daughter of a dirt farmer from Mississippi. If you saw this couple walking down the street, what would you think?"

"I would think that soldier was the luckiest man on earth. And I think there is only one effective way to keep you quiet about this subject." He drew her into his arms and kissed her—a long, lingering, passionate kiss that left her breathless and weak in the knees.

"Drew! We're on the street—in broad daylight!"

"Everyone in New Orleans kisses on the street in broad daylight," he murmured into her hair. "I think it's a local ordinance or something."

She pushed away from him. "You are impossible!"

"Of course I am. That's why you love me."

"Maybe I love you in spite of your impossibility."

He wrapped his arms around her and looked down into her eyes. "No," he whispered intently, "you love me for myself. Just as I love you for who you are. There are thousands of flashy, attractive, available women in this city, Rae Coltrain. But the woman I love has to be more than a pretty ornament, some kind of decoration to make people turn and look as we walk by. To tell the truth, I don't care what anyone else thinks. You are the woman I have waited for all my life. I knew it from the first letter you wrote to me. And when we're both eighty years old and wrinkled beyond recognition, you'll look back on this conversation and laugh—I guarantee it."

Rae closed her eyes and sighed. All her life she had heard about grace—about God's undeserved gifts of love. But until Andrew Laporte had come into her life, she had never applied that word beyond its narrow religious meaning. Now she knew better. God had done this; it was no accident that she had gotten Drew's name when she volunteered to be a pen pal for a serviceman. In the process of writing to him, she had discovered herself, discovered her dreams. And discovered that she was both capable of loving and worthy of being loved. Drew was a gift of grace. And she would always be thankful beyond imagination for him.

She opened her eyes to find him smiling down at her. "All right. If you're sure your parents won't be scared out of their wits by the mere sight of me, let's go. I'm as ready as I'll ever be."

"That's my girl," Drew chuckled. And there, in broad daylight in the middle of the French Quarter, he kissed her again.

★ ★ ★

Mabel Rae fought to keep her mouth closed. She had felt enough like a country bumpkin among the ornate houses and shops of the Quarter. This was just too much.

The taxi ride from the station, where they had left their luggage, was enough to take anyone's breath away. The road wound along the river, with live oak trees arching overhead, trailing lacy gray Spanish moss nearly to the ground. But when they came to the turnoff marked "Rue de Laporte," she found herself approaching an enormous antebellum estate, a white-columned wonder that glittered in the sun like marble.

"Drew, please tell me your parents live in the servants' quarters out back."

He laughed and put his arm around her shoulders. "Just hold on, sweetheart. It's not as bad as it looks."

As the cab approached the house, a gray-haired man in a dark suit stepped onto the front veranda and stood by the door, waiting.

"Is that your father?" Rae pointed.

Drew shook his head sheepishly. "No, that's Daniel, the—"

"Of course. The butler."

"Well, sort of. Daniel runs the house, really. Keeps Father's personal books, oversees the maintenance—that kind of thing. More like a personal assistant."

"And just how did you say your father made his money?"

"Investments. Real estate, mostly. Contrary to appearances, Father is a middle-class working man."

"Middle class," Rae repeated. "Well, your class system in Louisiana must be different from ours in Mississippi."

"Mother brought a rather large inheritance into the marriage, but as far as Father's side goes, the house itself was all that was left. It's been in the family for over a hundred years. It was used as a hospital during the War Between the States, and that probably saved it from being destroyed. Like a lot of other southern families, when the war was over, the Laportes were left with no cash assets—nothing but a house and land. Most of the land has been sold, but we still have a little over a hundred acres in cotton and soybeans."

"Tended by slaves who sing spirituals in the fields as they work, I suppose."

Drew chuckled. "Sharecroppers, mostly, although some of them are actually descendants of the original slaves who worked the plantation. A few of them still bear the Laporte name."

"That must thrill your father."

Drew raised a finger in warning. "I've told you that my father and I don't see eye to eye on the issue of rights for Negroes. He knows my position, and he's not too happy about it. But for the time being, it might be better to avoid discussing controversial subjects."

"Believe you me," Rae said emphatically, "I doubt I'll be able to utter an intelligent word about any subject at all."

"Just be yourself, sweetheart. They'll love you—I promise."

Daniel took their luggage and ushered them into the parlor where, despite the warmth of the autumn afternoon, a small fire burned in a marble fireplace. "Your parents will join you shortly, sir," he said formally. "Addie is bringing tea. I'll see that your luggage is delivered to your rooms." With that, he turned on his heel and disappeared.

Rae skirted the perimeter of the spacious room cautiously, taking note of the heavy rose-colored satin draperies, the high crown moldings, and the elaborate needlepoint settee. "This is incredible," she breathed, fingering a fringed pillow from one of the armchairs. "The design in the rug matches the upholstery."

"The original carpet was pretty much destroyed by the troops housed here," Drew said matter-of-factly. "Mother found one scrap lodged under that sideboard." He pointed to a heavy walnut piece topped by a beveled mirror that reached to the ceiling. "She sent off to France to have a new one loomed especially for this room."

An image flitted through Rae's mind—the dilapidated old Coltrain farmhouse with its sagging front porch and creaking swing. She saw her father in his rust-stained overalls, her mother in a faded cotton housedress, and Willie in the kitchen with her hair going wild and her hands covered with biscuit dough.

She fought against the comparison. Her family might not be rich, but they were good, honest, God-fearing people. Her parents had raised her right, given her love and integrity and strong values. She had nothing to be ashamed of. Nothing.

"So, the wanderer has returned!" a voice thundered through the open doorway.

Rae turned. A tall, broad-shouldered man with graying hair and just the hint of a paunch was pumping Drew's hand. A tiny, birdlike woman with blond hair done up in a French twist stood beside them, one hand on Drew's arm. She stood on tiptoe to kiss his cheek, then wiped off the lipstick with a manicured finger. "Welcome home, Son."

Drew extricated himself from his parents' embrace and came to put an arm around Rae. "This," he said proudly, leaning over to plant a kiss on the top of her head, "is Rae Coltrain. My future wife. Darling, my mother and father—Beatrice and Beauregard Laporte."

Rae watched as an expression passed over their faces, like the shock of glimpsing someone who was severely disfigured. They recovered quickly, but not before she saw.

"Well, my dear," Drew's mother said, rushing over to give Rae a perfunctory peck on the cheek, "we are delighted to meet you. Our Andrew has written volumes about you."

Obviously not enough, Rae thought to herself. Aloud, she said, "Thank you, Mrs. Laporte. It's so nice to finally meet—"

She stopped midsentence. Drew's mother had drawn back and was regarding her with a curious expression. Her mouth still smiled, but her pale blue eyes were brittle and icy. "You must call me Beatrice, dear. Once you're settled and ready to venture out, we'll take in all the finest shops and get you some proper clothes—an entire trousseau, perhaps. New Orleans has some delightful little French-import boutiques that the tourists never find. It will be lovely. I'm sure we will be great friends."

Of course we will, Rae thought. *After all, we have so much in common.*

"So," Drew's father boomed, "this is Andrew's little lady." He gave her an awkward one-armed hug and laughed heartily—a little too heartily, Rae thought. His eyes traveled up and down as if appraising her market value, hesitating for a split second on her hips. "Built for childbearing, I see." He winked conspiratorially at Drew and punched him on the arm.

"Colrane," Beatrice Laporte was saying absently. "Our family had business connections with some Colranes in Natchez, I believe. Solid southern family, generations old. Owned a big Delta estate called Riverbluff."

"It's Col*train,* Mrs. Laporte—ah, Beatrice," Rae stammered. "No relation, I'm sure."

"I suppose not," she sighed. "Well, tell me about your family."

Rae hesitated. "My brother, Charlie, was killed in the war. I have one sister, Willie—a schoolteacher. Daddy farms—cotton, mostly. Some soybeans for feed, and a few peanuts."

"How quaint." The brittle smile returned, and Rae shivered. "It seems that Addie never got here with the tea," Beatrice sighed, looking around helplessly. "Good help is so hard to come by, don't you think?"

"It's the bane of my existence." Rae cocked an eyebrow at Drew, who caught her eye and moved in for the rescue.

"Would you like to rest for a while before dinner, sweetheart?"

"That might be nice. It's been a long day."

"Yes, yes," Beatrice interjected, as if glad to have Rae off her hands for a while. She turned to Drew. "We've put your young lady in the President

Davis suite," she instructed. "You're right next door in the Nathan Bedford Forrest room."

"You didn't tell them, did you?" Rae muttered under her breath as they ascended the wide, curving staircase to the second floor.

"Tell them what?"

In the upstairs hall, Rae turned around to face him. "That I was fat and homely and poor, not at all the kind of girl they'd expect you to bring home."

"Of course I didn't tell them such a thing. Why should I?"

"Because they were expecting Carole Lombard and got Ethel Merman instead."

Drew grinned. "Carole Lombard died two years ago. They truly would have been shocked if I had brought her home. Besides, you never told me you could sing."

"Stop it!" Rae demanded, smiling in spite of herself. "You know what I mean."

"I don't know. What *are* you talking about?"

"I'm talking about the look on their faces when they first saw me. Just what did you tell them about me?"

"The truth. That you are bright and creative and witty and wonderful, and that I love you to distraction." He leaned forward to kiss her, but she pulled back.

"Just a minute, Lieutenant Andrew Laporte—"

"Andrew *Jackson* Laporte, if you please." He grimaced. "I never told you my middle name, did I?"

"Named after the president?"

He shook his head. "Andrew for my grandfather. Jackson for—"

"Let me guess. Stonewall Jackson, hero of the Confederacy. I should have known."

"See? You are bright and witty."

"Don't forget wonderful."

Drew reached a hand to her face and pulled her forward for a kiss. "I could never forget wonderful." He kissed her a second time, then ushered her into her room. "The presidential suite, mademoiselle. Get some rest. I'm going down to talk to my father. I'll come back for you at seven."

He turned to go, then looked back over his shoulder. "You might want to change for dinner."

Rae scowled at him. "I've only got two hours. In that time, I doubt I'd be able to change enough to suit them."

8

✭ ✭ ✭

Beauregard's Battle

Drew found his father in the library, his boots propped on the desk, with a huge Havana Royale between his teeth.

"Come in, Son, come in!" He dropped his feet to the floor, rummaged in the top right-hand drawer, and extended a second cigar. "Have a smoke."

Drew waved a hand at the noxious fumes that filled the room. "No thanks. Rae is resting for a while. I thought maybe we could talk."

For a minute or two Drew's father busied himself with removing his white coat and hanging it on the back of the leather chair. As he watched, Drew wondered for the hundredth time why his father persisted in maintaining the "Southern Colonel" image—white linen suit, black string tie, shiny black boots. His clients liked it, Drew supposed. It gave them a sense of continuity with the past, a feeling of solidarity with their roots. Beauregard T. Laporte might look like a walking anachronism left over from the plantation days, but the facade served him well.

"Andrew," his father said, rising from the desk to stride across the room, "tell me about your young lady."

"What do you mean?" Drew said, a bit taken aback. "I wrote all about her in my letters."

"You actually intend to marry this girl?"

"Of course I do. I love her. She loves me."

"She is, however, quite . . . well, different from what we anticipated."

Drew felt his temper begin to rise, and he fought to maintain control. "Different how?"

"Let's just say she doesn't present the kind of image your mother and I expected."

"Meaning she isn't a Delta beauty queen with a tiara on her head and empty space between her ears."

His father chuckled. "You always were one to swim against the tide, weren't you, boy? Always the rebel, with highfalutin ideas about the way things ought to be."

"Maybe the tide is going in the wrong direction," Drew answered evenly. "Maybe things ought to be different."

"Look, Son," his father said, taking a seat and motioning him toward the opposite end of the sofa, "I don't want to fight with you. You've managed to get through this war and get back in one piece, and for that I am very, very thankful. I just don't want to see you go making a mistake you'll have to live with for the rest of your life."

"Marrying Rae is no mistake," Drew said firmly. "I know what I'm doing. We *are* going to be married—as soon as possible."

Drew's father lifted one eyebrow, and a light of understanding dawned in his eyes. "Ah. I see. When is she due?"

Drew couldn't believe what he was hearing. "Pardon me?"

His father slapped one hand to his knee and leaned forward. "Let's be honest, Andrew—man to man. She's not attractive. She's not a society girl, although your mother will no doubt try to pass her off as one. She's got no money, no status. She's white trash. There's only one way a girl like that can get herself engaged to a handsome, eligible young lawyer like you."

Drew jumped to his feet. "Father, listen to me, and listen good. Rae Coltrain is not carrying my baby—or anyone else's. She is *not* white trash, and she is *not* after my money. I am not marrying her out of obligation or some kind of distorted sense of nobility. I love her—do you understand? *I love her.*"

"All right, all right," his father laughed, shaking his head. "I believe you. And if you care so much about this girl, she must be something pretty special."

Drew leaned back and surveyed his father warily. He had never won an argument with the old man so easily. Beau Laporte did not readily capitulate. "What do you want from me, Father?" he asked.

His father chewed on his cigar and narrowed his eyes. "What makes you think I want anything?"

"Because you're not trying to talk me out of this. Not very seriously, anyway."

"Son, Son," Drew's father soothed, "we—your mother and I—would never try to talk you out of anything that would make you happy. Didn't we encourage you when you decided to go to law school? Didn't we pay the bills and support you at Tulane?" He paused. "When you decided to enlist, didn't we—"

"Ah," Drew interrupted, "I've got you there. You did everything you could to keep me from going."

His father nodded. "You were our only son, Andrew. It nearly killed your mother to think of you in danger over there. And given my connections, I could have pulled some strings with the Selective Service Board—"

"But don't you see, Father, I didn't *want* to have strings pulled on my behalf. I wanted to do my part, like everyone else. I only gave in and agreed to Officers' Candidate School because you insisted."

"A Laporte as an enlisted man?" his father flared. "Impossible."

Drew shook his head. "Never mind, Father. I could talk all day, and I still don't think you'd understand."

"Maybe not," his father answered. "But that's all done and past. Now that you're home, safe and sound, we have to think about your future."

"What about my future? I'm going to do what I went to law school to do. Set up a practice. Help people."

His father smiled, and Drew thought he saw just a hint of condescension in his eyes, a smug, knowing look. Then the expression faded, and he grew serious.

"I have a proposition for you, Andrew. I'd like you to stay in New Orleans and work with me in my business. You're bright and sharp, a real go-getter. We could use your talents."

"Business law?" Drew mused. "I never really thought about it. But no, I don't think so, Father. I want to be down where the people are, where folks really need my help."

"But don't you see—you could do that, too. We'd finance the whole operation. You'd see to our contracts, close all the loopholes, make sure everything's legal and aboveboard, and then you could afford to do your charity work—"

"We don't call it charity, Father. It sounds so snobbish."

The older man waved his cigar. "Well, whatever you call it, you can't make a living giving free legal advice to people who can't pay. And don't forget, you're going to have a family to support. A wife, children—you can't simply ignore their needs."

Drew sighed. Much as he hated to admit it, his father was right—about that much, at least. Helping people who couldn't help themselves was a noble idea, but it didn't pay the bills. If he had only himself to consider, he could well imagine living in meager surroundings, devoting his life to people less fortunate than himself. But now he had Rae to think about. She deserved better than a scratched-out existence living on red beans and rice, or crawfish his clients would offer in lieu of payment. Eventually, of course, he would inherit the family fortune. But he couldn't expect it now, and he wasn't about to take it even if his parents offered. One way or another, he would have to generate some cash income. Put a down payment on a house, buy a car. Establish a real home for the woman he was about to marry. The responsibility of it all settled on him like a heavy weight, and suddenly he felt overwhelmed.

"I'll think about it," he said reluctantly. "Rae and I will have to discuss it."

His father looked at him intently. "In my day," he said, "husbands and wives didn't 'discuss' such things. The man made the decisions, and the woman accepted them."

"Rae and I don't operate that way," Drew responded. "We've agreed to make our decisions together."

"Young people," his father muttered. "Where do they get such ideas?" He chewed on his cigar for a minute or two, then said suddenly, "Your mother's not well, Son."

"Not well?" Drew faltered, and a knot formed in his stomach. "What do you mean, not well?"

"You've got to promise not to let on. Bea would be furious with me for telling you, and she'll pretend she's fine. But you have a right to know. She's been going downhill ever since you shipped out, and the doctors can't determine the cause. They only know that she—well, that her time may be limited." He paused for a moment. "She needs you, Andrew."

"What can I do?"

His father looked at him intently. "Stay close. Give her the one thing she wants more than anything in the world."

"What's that?"

"A chance to plan her only son's wedding. If you're determined to marry this girl, let your mother have the joy of seeing it happen. It doesn't have to be a big affair—just let her do it. Here, in this house. And soon."

"Have the wedding here?" Drew hesitated. "But what about Rae's family? They can't afford a trip like that. And they're expecting—"

"I'm sure you can arrange a little ceremony with them later," his father answered. "Do this for your mother," he urged. "She may never have a chance to see her first grandchild. Give her this one happiness, at least, before . . ." His words trailed off, and he turned his head away.

Drew's mind reeled. This was not what he had planned. How could he ask Rae to have a wedding without her family present? She would be devastated. But if his father was right about Mother's condition, she could never make the trip to Mississippi. Besides, he could just imagine what it would do to his frail little mother to be thrown in among Rae's relatives. A reception, complete with meat loaf sandwiches, at the Paradise Garden Cafe, with Thelma Breckinridge presiding? It would be a disaster.

When he had fallen in love with Rae, Drew had never expected things to get so complicated. Sure, they came from different worlds. But wasn't love supposed to bridge the gap? Was it supposed to be this hard?

"Talk to her," his father was saying. "If she really loves you, she'll accept it."

Drew closed his eyes and took a deep breath. "All right, Father," he breathed. "I'll try."

★　★　★

Rae couldn't believe she was hearing right. "Have the wedding here? Without my family? You can't be serious."

So this was what Drew had on his mind that kept him so preoccupied during dinner. Despite the opulence of the dining room, with its crystal chandelier and fine linens, the elaborate meal of Cornish game hen and stuffing had been a tense and unhappy affair—not exactly the welcome-home celebration Rae had expected. Mrs. Laporte had picked at her food, eating barely enough to justify her sitting there for an hour. Mr. Laporte had carried on a monologue about investments and property values. Drew had been silent, casting glances back and forth between her and his mother, as if trying to make up his mind about something.

Now she knew what it was, and she didn't like it one bit.

"You cannot expect me to allow your mother to plan my wedding—or to have it here, without my family involved."

"I know, sweetheart, I know," Drew murmured, trying to put his arms around her.

She pushed him away. "None of that, Andrew Laporte. You are not going to kiss me into agreeing to this."

"All right," he said, raising his hands. "No hugging. No kissing. Let's talk."

"That's better." She sank onto the bed and stared at him as he walked over to the settee. "So, you had a discussion with your father."

Drew nodded. "Rae, I am their only child. Mother took it very hard when I enlisted. Father says her health has been going downhill ever since and that she may not have much time left."

"She seems perfectly all right to me—except for the fact that she doesn't eat enough to keep a baby bird alive."

"It may be a symptom of her . . . her condition." He frowned. "You don't seem very compassionate about all this. It's not like you to be so cold, Rae."

Tears sprang to Rae's eyes, and she blinked them back. "I'm sorry, Drew. I just—I don't know, I had counted so much on having our wedding at our little country church outside Eden, with everyone there. Willie will be so disappointed."

"I know, darling. I was counting on it, too. I love your family and friends—you know I do. They're wonderful people, the salt of the earth. But—"

"But *your* parents are too high and mighty for the likes of the Coltrains." The tears came in earnest now, despite her attempts to choke them down.

"Rae, that's not fair. My parents don't even know your family."

"And they're not likely to, are they?" she sobbed.

Rae felt the bed shift as Drew came over and sat beside her. "Sweetheart, I'm sorry. I truly am. But what can we do?"

She sniffled and sat up straighter, swiping at her eyes. When she looked into his face, Rae saw an expression of pain and longing that stabbed at her heart. "Oh, Drew, forgive me. I can see how this is tearing you up, and I didn't mean to be so selfish. I just had my heart set on having our wedding in Eden."

Drew smiled and opened his arms, and she moved closer to him. "If Mother weren't ill, it would be different," he murmured. "But with things as they are, well . . ." He paused. "It'll be all right, Rae. I'll have a practice that supports us and gives me time to do the kind of work I want to do. We'll have a house of our own. You'll see. It'll be all right."

Rae pushed her bitter disappointment aside, fighting against the emotions that threatened to overwhelm her. What difference did it make in the long run? She probably should just be grateful the Laportes hadn't opposed the wedding entirely. She and Drew would be married. How much did it really matter where they were, as long as they were together? Besides, she couldn't ask Drew to deny his mother this one simple request. He was her only child, after all.

Yes, she could do this. She could make this one sacrifice. For Drew. For their marriage. For their future.

Rae ran a hand through her hair and managed a smile.

"Just give me a little time," she whispered. "I'll talk to your mother tomorrow."

9

★ ★ ★

Kennedy General

Memphis, Tennessee

Libba fidgeted in front of the mirror while Aunt Magnolia stepped back to make sure her slip wasn't showing. "I am so nervous," Libba breathed. "Do I look all right?"

"You look lovely, child. Now stand still—and quit playing with your hair. You'll have it in a knot before you set foot out of this house." The old woman leaned over and gave a tug on one side of Libba's skirt.

Libba stopped twisting at her hair and turned to give her great-aunt a hug. "I don't know what I'd do without you, Aunt Mag, but—" She fought back the tears that lodged in her throat. "I still wish Mama could be here."

Mag returned the hug, then pushed her back at arm's length. "You knew your mama wouldn't stay but a couple of days," she said matter-of-factly. "She needs to be home, in familiar surroundings, to do her grieving and get her life back on track." Aunt Mag fixed Libba with an intense look. "Just as you need to be here." She paused. "But . . . I gather things are better between you and your mother after her visit, aren't they?"

Libba smiled and sat down on the bed, taking her aunt's gnarled hands and drawing the old woman down beside her. "So much better," she said. "I was so angry at Mama for not standing up for me. I felt so . . . alone. Abandoned. I felt like she was defending all the mean and horrible things Daddy had done over the years. But when she told me the truth about her and Daddy, I understood a little more. She was afraid of him—can you imagine? Afraid of her own husband."

Magnolia smiled sadly. "It happens more than you know, child."

Libba nodded. "I guess so. It's just that—well, you always want to believe that your family is normal, that your parents love each other. I've known for a long time that Daddy didn't really love anybody except himself, but I never expected to hear Mama admit it."

"Your mama admitted a lot of things, didn't she?"

"Yes." Libba lowered her eyes. "You knew, didn't you? That Daddy only married Mama because he thought she was going to have a baby . . . that she had lied to him, and then all those years went on living that lie. She says they had a few good times in the beginning, but it seems like such a waste."

The age-spotted hand, soft as flannel, reached out to stroke Libba's cheek. "Not a waste, child. We have you."

Libba smiled into the pale green eyes. "Thank you, Aunt Mag. I can't tell you how much it means to me to be here with you."

"After all these years . . ." Magnolia mused with a faraway look on her face. "You are a gift to me, child."

Libba sat up straighter. "You didn't answer my question."

"What question?"

"You knew, didn't you? About Mama and Daddy."

"Why do you think I named that nasty old tomcat Robinson?"

Libba threw back her head and laughed. "From the moment I heard that cat's name, I knew we were going to be great friends." She sobered suddenly. "Aunt Mag, promise you won't let me make that kind of mistake."

"Whatever do you mean, child?"

"I can't imagine being married for years to a man like Daddy—a man I didn't love and couldn't respect. A man I . . . feared. It's a horrible thought."

Mag stood up and cocked an eyebrow at Libba, fingering one earring in thought. "Any man you marry," she said deliberately, "will have to pass the Magnolia Cooley Character Test. And it's no picnic, let me tell you. When you find your young man, you'd better give him fair warning."

"I'll tell him." Libba slid off the bed and took another look in the mirror. "I guess I'd better go," she said, exhaling heavily. "I've put it off as long as I can."

Aunt Mag leaned over and gave Libba a kiss on the cheek. "You may not find him today, Libba. Or tomorrow. But don't lose hope."

"I just hope that when I do find him, I'll be ready for what I find."

Mag patted her hand. "You'll be ready," she chuckled. "You've got a lot of your old Aunt Mag in your veins."

★ ★ ★

Standing on the sidewalk in front of the massive doors of Kennedy General Hospital, Libba wondered if she had enough of Aunt Mag in her to get her through this. Her knees shook, and her breath came in short, shallow gasps. If she didn't get herself under control, they'd be carrying her in on a stretcher.

Libba didn't know what she was most afraid of—not finding Link, or finding him. A dark cloud of uncertainty settled over her, and the formidable brick facade of the hospital building did nothing to allay her fears. At last, conjuring up a mental image of Aunt Mag for emotional support, she took a deep breath and swung the door open.

Inside, one glimpse of the drab walls and linoleum floors made her spirits sink. The whole place had the bitter smell of antiseptic and medicine—that "hospital scent" that Libba had experienced only once or twice in her entire life. Somewhere down the hall she heard a man moaning in pain. She fought the urge to turn and run. Then the thought arrested her: *What if that were Link?* She craned her neck, trying to peer down the hallway, but all she could see were more halls intersecting the main corridor, and two or three official-looking people with clipboards going about their business.

A high counter loomed just ahead and to her right, staffed by a hatchet-faced nurse who scowled down at her. "State your business, missy," the woman growled. "This is a hospital, not a peep show."

"I—I'm looking for someone," Libba stammered.

"You and every other girl this side of the Mississippi." The nurse picked up a sheaf of papers and flipped through them. "Name?"

"Link Winsom. Ah, James Lincoln Winsom. Staff Sergeant—or at least he was when he shipped out. He would be coming in from New York."

The nurse lifted one eyebrow and sneered at Libba. "Yes. Every soldier shipped home, living or dead, comes through New York," she said with exaggerated deliberation. "Company? Division? Anything?"

Libba's mind went blank under the relentless stare of those coal black eyes. "Uh . . . I don't remember."

The nurse closed her eyes as if praying for patience, and the thought fleetingly occurred to Libba that if this woman prayed at all, she would be more likely to order the Almighty around than to request a favor. "Couldn't you just look?" Libba asked in a small voice.

The eyes snapped open, and with a martyred sigh, the nurse began to flip through the pages toward the back. "Warren, Washington, Weatherby, Wilson, Winston. Maybe this is it—Winston."

"Not Winston," Libba corrected. "Winsom. W-I-N-S-O-M."

"Odd name," the nurse muttered. "Nope. No Winsoms. Sorry, missy."

The woman didn't sound sorry, Libba thought; she sounded relieved. Here she was, alone in an unfamiliar city, trying to find a wounded soldier in an army hospital, and this nurse was treating her like an annoying child rather than a full-grown woman looking for vital information about the man she loved.

Defeated, Libba turned to go. Then, suddenly, in her mind's eye she saw Great-Aunt Magnolia, splendid in a flowing purple dress, standing up to Nurse Nasty and withering her with a single glance from those flashing green eyes. Magnolia Cooley wouldn't let one encounter with an ill-tempered nurse keep her from fulfilling her mission . . . and neither would Libba Coltrain.

Resolutely she turned on her heel and strode back to the information desk. "Excuse me," she said firmly. The nurse did not look up. "I said, excuse me!"

Slowly the woman raised her head, her black eyes glittering with the look of a rattlesnake about to strike its prey. "Now what?"

Libba raised herself as high as her five-foot-four frame would allow and met the nurse's gaze with an unwavering stare. "My name," she said with a firm quietness, "is Elizabeth Coltrain. I received word a few days ago that my fiancé was being transferred to this hospital. I am aware that keeping up with all of them must be a difficult task—*especially* for you—but I see no reason that I should be treated as an interloper because I've come to inquire about him. I would like to speak to your supervisor—immediately." With a toss of her head, Libba stripped off her gloves and planted both feet firmly on the linoleum floor.

Like a storm front rolling across the Delta, a shocked look passed over the nurse's face. And then, to Libba's amazement, another expression replaced it—an attitude of respect, and a tiny smile of amusement.

"That won't be necessary, missy—ah, Miss Coltrain." The woman gave an apologetic shrug. "To tell the truth, they don't always get the paperwork on new patients to me right away. Your sergeant may not have arrived yet, but you are welcome to look for yourself. Straight down this hallway until it ends, then take a right."

"Thank you." Libba gathered her gloves and bag and turned her back on the nurse.

"Miss Coltrain?"

Libba looked back. "Yes?"

"Some of those boys are in pretty bad shape. I hope you're prepared for what you might see."

Libba could almost hear her great-aunt's encouragement: *You'll be ready. You've got a lot of your old Aunt Mag in your veins.* She nodded to the nurse and squared her shoulders. "Thanks for the warning. But I'm as prepared as I'm going to get. I'll be fine."

"I'm sure you will," the nurse replied. "I just thought I should warn you."

★ ★ ★

As Libba left the halls of Kennedy General Hospital and began the four-block walk down Getwell Avenue to Aunt Mag's house, she found herself chilled to the marrow, and not just because of the damp November wind that knifed through the fabric of her coat. Maybe she had been too confident that Aunt Mag's blood flowed in her veins. Maybe she had spoken too soon. Perhaps she wasn't ready at all for the sight of beardless boys with missing limbs and broken bodies, for the unutterable loneliness in their eyes, for the way they had grasped for her—and anyone else who came near—with a longing that bordered on desperation.

And when they had reached out, Libba shrank back. She couldn't help it. She didn't want to be touched—tainted—by the atrocities that confronted her. All along the wards, bed after bed held spectral visions out of her worst nightmares. She had expected a cast here and there on broken arms and legs, or a man in traction, or a fellow with a patch over one eye. What she saw went far beyond anything she was prepared for.

On the first ward she was greeted by a skeletal figure with sunken eyes and cheeks, slowly pushing himself toward her in a wheelchair. Libba felt a rush of pity, until her gaze fixed on the two bandaged stubs that protruded from the hem of his hospital gown. Her stomach rose into her throat, and she thought she was going to be sick, right there on the linoleum floor. She lowered her eyes, swallowed down the bitter taste of her own bile, and rushed on.

She wanted to run, to get away, to be anywhere except this terrible place. She had to hurry, to find Link and get out. In her haste she careened into the foot of a bed and looked up. There lay a young boy, an innocent-looking lad with a shock of red hair and freckles across his nose. He reminded her of Bobby Hollowell, one of her high school students back in Eden. The class clown, whose antics kept senior English in chaos. She almost smiled.

Then the boy turned his head.

The other side of his face—or what had been his face—was a mass of raw flesh, burned beyond recognition. It didn't look human at all. When he lifted a twisted, mangled hand toward her and tried to smile, only the good side of his face moved, and the result was a ghoulish grimace.

Panic rose up in Libba, constricting her lungs and cutting off her breath. Her only thought was escape—to leave this bad dream behind and awaken to the world she knew. She jerked her gaze away, gripping the bed in terror, and the boy sank back to his pillow.

Libba closed her eyes and fought for control. There was a reason she was here—to find Link. No matter how revolted she might be by what she saw, she had to try. For his sake. And for her own.

Her mind flashed to the early days, when she had first met Link at the USO dance and fallen in love. Life had seemed so simple then, so clean and pure and carefree. She couldn't imagine, back then, that anything would change their love or alter their plans for the future. They would live happily ever after.

But that had been a different world, and she had been a different person. And, now that she thought about it, she hadn't much liked the person she had been back then. She had been selfish and a little spoiled, always wanting her own way, rarely thinking about other people's feelings. Time and anxiety and grief had changed her, had brought her to a meaningful relationship with God. Her faith had grown . . . her heart had grown. How could she go back now?

Then Libba realized—she already had gone back, at least a little. She hadn't been praying for direction, hadn't looked for evidences of God's presence in her life. Even her mother had gently confronted her about this on the day of the funeral. She had been so consumed with herself, with realizing her own dreams of finding Link, that she hadn't thought of much else—even prayer.

And now look at her. She wasn't considering these poor young men with their physical wounds and their emotional pain. She was only thinking about herself, about her reaction, her revulsion. About how badly she wanted to get away from here and never come back.

Libba took a deep breath and willed herself to go on, to make her way through the ward without losing her composure. She tried to fix her attention on the faces of the men as she looked for the one face she longed to see, Link's face. Still, her eyes kept wandering to the empty sleeves and the dangling pajama legs, the tubes, the crutches, the wheelchairs. Her pulse pounded, and her stomach rebelled; and despite all her effort, she couldn't rid her memory of the haunting eyes, of the terrible neediness, of the pain.

Link wasn't there. But she saw hundreds of other young men—soldiers who had given more than they bargained for in the service of their country. And for the first time, Libba allowed herself to ask the unthinkable question: What if Link came home like that? What if he revolted her the way these other wounded soldiers had? What if he never walked again? And worse, what if his spirit was broken, his soul ripped to shreds by the horrors of war? Could she accept that—not just the physical maiming, but the emotional damage? Could she live in the presence of that kind of pain and despair? Was her love strong enough?

She wasn't sure. And the uncertainty that shook her own resolve frightened her every bit as much as the monstrous realities she had seen at the hospital.

It would take more than prayer, Libba thought as she turned the final corner off Getwell onto the block where Aunt Mag lived. More than determination. It would take a miracle.

She found her great-aunt in the front parlor, propped in an overstuffed armchair next to a small fire, reading. Libba gravitated to the warmth of the hearth and stood turning in front of the fire, willing herself to stop shaking.

Aunt Mag looked up. "Well, how was it? I assume from the look on your face that you didn't find your young man."

Libba shook her head but avoided meeting her aunt's eyes. "He wasn't there . . . not yet, anyway."

"Sit down and tell me about it."

Libba didn't want to talk about it, didn't want to relive the aversion and terror she had experienced on those wards. She busied herself with removing her coat and gloves, went out into the entryway to hang her things on the hall tree, and returned, pausing just inside the parlor door. "I don't want to interrupt your reading. I'll start dinner."

"Sit down."

It was not a request; it was a command. With a sigh Libba came back into the room and wedged herself onto the arm of Aunt Mag's chair. "What are you reading?"

Mag peered up at her with a suspicious look. *"Gone with the Wind.* It's a bit overblown, but it keeps me off the streets."

Libba managed a weak smile. "I saw the movie at the theater in Grenada. I've never read the book."

"Movies!" Aunt Mag said derisively. "They take a Pulitzer Prize–winning novel and make it into a talkie, and then go and choose an English girl for Scarlett O'Hara. Hah! Better to stay home by the fire and read," she huffed. "Even if it does go on forever."

Libba peered over the old woman's shoulder. "Where are you?"

"The Yankees have just burned Atlanta."

Libba's mind took her back to one heartrending scene in the Academy Award–winning film—an expansive view of row upon row of wounded, dead, and dying soldiers laid out endlessly, side by side. Thousands of them. Like her images of Link on the battlefront in France. Like the wards at Kennedy General Hospital. She shuddered and closed her eyes.

When she opened them again, Aunt Mag had shut the book and was looking up at her expectantly. "Are you going to tell me or not?" she demanded.

Libba slid off the arm of the chair and sank to the rug at her aunt's feet. "I don't know, Aunt Mag. There were so many wounded men there—some of them just boys, younger than I am—who have had their whole lives changed in an instant. Legless boys who will never walk again, or dance with their sweethearts . . . blind ones who will never see their babies' faces. People say they were the lucky ones, the ones who came back alive. But some of them aren't alive at all—not inside. Some of them just lie there, staring at the ceiling. I felt—" Libba paused. She didn't want to admit what she had felt. She was ashamed.

"Disgusted?" Aunt Mag supplied. "Repelled? Frightened?"

Libba nodded miserably. "Yes," she whispered. "And I can't help wondering—"

"Wondering if your young man will come back like that?"

"And wondering if my love is strong enough to handle it if he does."

The old woman riveted her with an expression of challenge. "What do you think love is, child?"

Libba paused. The gauntlet had been thrown. This was a test, and she knew it. "I . . . I used to think that love was being happy with someone. You know, romance and flowers and dances and—" she felt herself beginning to blush—"and kisses."

Aunt Mag cleared her throat. "And now?"

"Now—" Libba frowned in thought. "Well, when I thought Link was dead, I couldn't believe how bad it hurt. For a while I wanted to die. But then I realized that if I never loved anyone again, it was worth the pain of losing Link for the joy I had in loving him and in being loved." She looked intently into the wrinkled face. "During those difficult months, I discovered myself. I found out who I am. I realized that, with God's help, I am stronger than I ever thought I could be—and I don't need another person to make my life complete. I love Link, and I want to share my life with him. But mostly I just want him to be happy and loved." Libba took a deep breath and prayed that what she was about to say was true. "If not with me, with someone who can deserve him more than I do."

A tiny smile crept onto the old woman's face. "That's not a bad answer for a girl who's only—how old are you, child? Nineteen?"

"Twenty."

"Twenty. Ah, yes. I remember twenty—although very dimly, I'll admit. But take a little lesson from someone who has had four times as many years to think about it. Love isn't about *deserving* the other person. It's about grace. It's both a gift and a lifetime occupation. And doing it well is hard work. You have to give yourself completely to love, but you also have to receive graciously." Aunt Mag reached out and cupped Libba's chin in her hand. "Don't try to deserve your young man, child, or to make up for the pain and loss he has suffered. No matter what has happened to him, he is still the same person on the inside—just like all those boys you saw on the ward. You can't take away the agony, but you can treat him with dignity . . . and with love. He will have to do his own healing. You just be there."

Tears sprang to Libba's eyes as she thought about the men she had seen in the hospital. The sight of them had completely overwhelmed her. They frightened her. The very idea of living with such a burden for the rest of her life had seemed an insurmountable demand.

But maybe she didn't have to take on that responsibility. Maybe she could find a way to learn—before Link returned—how to let him do his own healing, how to "just be there."

10

⭐ ⭐ ⭐

Family Matters

Eden, Mississippi
Paradise Garden Cafe

The Paradise Garden was nearly deserted at eight o'clock when Willie Coltrain walked in. It was almost closing time.

Willie had been in the cafe hundreds of times, of course, and often when it was empty. But it never *felt* empty before—not like it did now. Even the linoleum floor appeared more cracked and worn, the lights dimmer, the green countertops more faded. The place seemed sad, somehow. Lonely.

Or perhaps it was Willie who was sad and lonely. Ever since Mabel Rae and Drew had left for New Orleans and Libba had gone off to Memphis to look for Link, she had been isolated out at the farm with only Mama and Daddy for company. And they weren't very good company, at that.

Willie had plenty to keep her occupied, certainly. Being busy wasn't the problem. Her mother wandered around the house like a zombie, and her father's health seemed to be declining by the day. He moved with a painful slowness, and his thin shoulders sagged as if he bore the weight of the world on them. Willie had taken up the slack for both of them, feeding the animals and mucking out the barn, in addition to cooking meals and cleaning the house. She was thankful it was winter—at least there was no field work to do. But if Daddy continued to go downhill at this rate, she would have to hire help for spring planting, or there would be no cotton to sell, no soybeans for feed.

With a sigh Willie sank down at a table next to the window and put her head in her hands. She missed Mabel Rae and Libba. And if truth were told, she desperately missed herself, the way she used to be. Their life together—the three of them living in the apartment in town, teaching school, going to the USO, gathering here at the Paradise Garden—seemed a hundred years behind her. She couldn't remember the last time she had really laughed. Gray hair and wrinkles would be next. She was getting old before her time.

"You look like you could use a friend."

Willie looked up to find Madge Simpson standing beside the table with Mickey on her hip.

"Thelma's not here right now," Madge said with a smile. "Will I do?"

Willie forced herself to respond. "Of course. It's good to see you, Madge. I've missed you . . . and everybody. And this little guy is always welcome." Willie extended her hands to the baby, who giggled at her and reached out his chubby little arms to be held.

"Watch him for a minute, will you?" Madge handed him over. "I'll get us some coffee."

While Madge went behind the counter for the coffeepot and two cups, Willie bounced Mickey on her lap. "He's getting strong," she called over her shoulder. "Look how he grabs my fingers and tries to stand up."

"He already crawls everywhere." Madge returned and sat down with a sigh. "Once he starts walking, heaven only knows what he'll get into." She leaned back and slipped her shoes off. "It's been a long day."

Willie tickled Mickey in the ribs and was rewarded with a charming smile. "He's adorable. I wish I had two or three just like him."

Madge sipped her coffee. "One's enough at his age. I can't imagine keeping up with two—at least not until he's out of diapers and understands what *no* means. You'll find out someday. Don't say I didn't warn you."

"I doubt it." Willie shook her head. "I expect the closest I'll ever get to motherhood is being somebody's Aunt Willie."

"Willie Coltrain, you'd make a wonderful mother, and you know it."

"Maybe," Willie mused. "I know I'd love having a baby. But motherhood is dependent upon fatherhood, or so I've been told. Maternal instinct isn't what I'm lacking at the moment."

Madge sighed. "This is about losing Owen."

"Not just losing Owen. I miss him terribly, of course," Willie answered. "But I've lost more than a fiancé. I feel as if I'm losing myself. Maybe someday I'll be able to think about meeting someone else and falling in love, but right now it just doesn't seem possible."

"Why not, Willie? You're still young. You're attractive—"

"Humph!"

"Don't interrupt. You *are* attractive. You have a wonderful personality—" Madge crooked a grin, and Willie saw a spark of mischief in her blue eyes. "And you make the best biscuits this side of the Mason-Dixon line."

"Ah," Willie chuckled. "Now we're getting to the really important character assets."

"It's good to see you smile," Madge said, sobering. "Things have been pretty tough, haven't they?"

Willie nodded and cradled Mickey in the crook of one arm. She took a sip of coffee and waited for a minute or two, debating whether or not to tell Madge how life had been for her in the past few weeks. She probably shouldn't burden anyone else with her problems, but Madge was right. She did need a friend.

"Ever since Libba and Mabel Rae left, things out at the farm have been . . . well, difficult," Willie admitted at last. "Daddy's health is deteriorating, but he won't go to a doctor. He just keeps saying he'll come around sooner or later. Mama just kind of sits and stares—"

"And you're left with all the work," Madge interjected.

"I don't mind hard work," Willie said. "I'm used to it—I'm a farm girl, remember?" She managed a faint smile and went on. "I just feel so—so isolated, so alone. This is the first time in weeks I've left the place, and I only came into town this evening because the fan belt on the truck was about to break and I had to get a replacement."

"You need to get out more." Madge refilled their coffee cups and leaned across the table to smooth Mickey's hair back. "We're always here—and we'd love for you to visit."

Willie looked down. The child snuggled close to her, a contented smile on his sleepy face. "I'd almost forgotten how good it feels to be with friends. I love my parents, but I miss Mabel Rae and Libba—and you, and Thelma. I'm not the person I used to be, Madge, and I don't particularly like the person I'm becoming."

Madge leaned forward. "What kind of person is that?"

"Old," Willie sighed. "Stuck. I don't have any sense of hope for the future. Oh, I might go back to teaching, if and when Daddy gets well enough to take care of things at home. But even that idea doesn't give me much joy. I see my life stretching out before me, and it looks like those empty cotton fields I see every day of my life. Eternally the same, all the way to the horizon."

"It can't be that bleak," Madge offered lamely. "Something will turn up."

Willie smiled weakly. "I guess so." Madge was only trying to help, to give her something to hang on to. But she couldn't understand, not really. She had Stork and Mickey . . . and Thelma. She had a family, a future. Something to look forward to.

Mabel Rae and Libba had hope, too. Rae had gone off to build a life with her handsome lieutenant. Libba would eventually find Link. And Willie would be right where they left her—on a broken-down farm with two parents who barely acknowledged her presence, and the memory of a brother and a sweetheart who had gone off to battle and never returned.

Maybe she should think more seriously about going back to teaching next fall. That was ten months away—time enough, perhaps, for Daddy to get better and take over responsibilities on the farm. Time enough for her to resign herself to being an old-maid schoolmarm for the rest of her life.

It wasn't a pleasant prospect. But it was better than nothing. Better than emptiness. At least it would give her something to plan for.

★ ★ ★

As she came through the kitchen toward the service window, Thelma heard the bell over the door ring. She peered out into the cafe, but all she could see was Madge, hoisting Mickey on one hip and wiping down tables with her free hand.

"I'm back, hon," Thelma called. "Did I hear someone leaving?"

Madge turned and waved, and Thelma felt a familiar warmth wash over her. This was her little family, the daughter and grandson she never thought she'd have. An equally familiar twinge of anxiety followed, the reminder that they were not her blood kin and probably wouldn't be in Eden forever. But she pushed the apprehension aside. God had given her a great gift in Madge Simpson and her little Mickey, and she refused to taint the blessing with selfishness or ingratitude.

"There's Gramma Thelma's big boy!" she cooed, taking the child from Madge and swinging him around. "Isn't it about your bedtime?"

"I think it's about *my* bedtime," Madge laughed. "If he had his way, he'd stay up until closing time."

Thelma looked at the clock over the counter. "He almost has. It's nearly nine."

"No wonder I'm so tired. His daddy's on duty tonight, so he's been with me the whole time."

Thelma put an arm around the girl and squeezed her shoulders. "Why don't you go on and take him back to bed? I'll finish up in here."

"It's OK. I'm about done. If you've got a few minutes, I'd like to talk to you, anyway."

Thelma sat down at the table nearest the counter and held Mickey in her lap. "Something on your mind, hon?"

Madge nodded. "Willie Coltrain."

"That was Willie, just leaving as I came in?"

"Yes. We had coffee and talked for a bit, but I'm afraid I wasn't much help."

"What's the problem?"

"According to Willie, her life is the problem—or rather, her lack of a life. She's stuck out there on the farm, Thelma, with nobody to talk to. She's doing all the housework and the farm chores and never gets a minute to herself. Why, tonight is the first time she's been in town for almost a month."

As Madge went on telling her about Willie's dilemma, Thelma thought about the Coltrain girls—how they used to come into the cafe, laughing and carefree, without a worry in the world except what dress to wear to a USO dance. That was before Owen and Charlie were killed, before Link was wounded. Before the reality of war changed them all.

Willie seemed the most changed by the grief she had suffered. Gone was the easy laughter, the humor, the brave confidence she once had exhibited. Even the strength of her faith had begun to waver. And all Thelma could do was pray for her. It didn't seem enough, somehow.

"And now she's talking as if she will never meet anyone and get married," Madge was saying. "She says she has no future, nothing to look forward to."

"I can imagine she'd feel that way, given what she's gone through."

"Yes, but it's more than that. It's like she's given up completely."

Thelma shook her head. "It's not like Willie to give up. She's strong."

"The old Willie wouldn't give up. But even Willie says she's not the person she used to be. She said she felt like she was losing herself."

"What did you tell her?"

Madge shrugged. "Not much, I'm afraid. I told her that it couldn't possibly be that bleak and that something would turn up. I wish I could have found a way to encourage her, to let her know that God hasn't abandoned her, that she's not really alone."

"I'm sure she knows that," Thelma said, patting Madge's hand. "She just may not be able to hear it right now."

"She looked so sad," Madge mused. "I could see it in her eyes."

"So did you, hon, the day you walked through that door with this baby in your arms. And look at you now." Thelma smiled into the girl's blue eyes—eyes that held so much compassion and tenderness. "God has a way of working things out."

Madge nodded. "I believe that, Thelma. I've certainly seen it in my own life. But I just wish we could do something for Willie—something to show her that we love her, that she's not alone."

Thelma sat quietly for a minute, thinking. "Stork's not on duty Thursday, is he?" she asked suddenly.

Madge looked up from her own reverie. "Thanksgiving Day? Not unless the major has changed the schedule. We're planning Thanksgiving here with you, remember?"

"How could I forget? That turkey taking up space in my refrigerator reminds me every time I open the door. But if Stork is willing, I think we should take a Thanksgiving Day drive out into the country."

"It's November, Thelma. Not exactly the best season for a scenic jaunt."

Thelma chuckled. "Maybe not for us, hon. But it just might change the scenery for somebody we care about."

11

★ ★ ★

God's Got Ways

Thanksgiving Day, 1944

Willie stirred the pot of soup on the back of the stove, then went and sat at the battered kitchen table. It was time to get up and make the biscuits, but she couldn't bring herself to move. All day long, images of Thanksgivings past had invaded her thoughts: the whole family gathered around the big table in the dining room, with Charlie telling jokes and Mabel Rae trying to sneak an extra serving of corn-bread dressing when nobody was looking. Laughter pervaded those memories, bringing tears to her eyes and a wistful tug to her heart.

She remembered her father's moving prayers of gratitude around that Thanksgiving table, expressing appreciation for the love and warmth of his wife and his children, his thankfulness for a good crop, for being able to pay the bills, for time together. For all the simple blessings of a simple life.

There would be no such prayer offered this day. Her father had taken to his bed with a bad cough, and her mother didn't have the energy to bother with a Thanksgiving dinner for just the three of them. So instead of turkey and dressing and glazed carrots and homemade rolls, the William Coltrain family—what was left of it—would be having soup made from leftovers.

Willie stared out the kitchen window. A drizzling November rain glazed the cracked glass and blurred her view of the brown rolling hills and pastures. But it didn't matter. The dismal day fit with her mood.

If Mabel Rae were here, they would be having a high old time about now, putting the finishing touches on the turkey and taking the last of the pies out of the oven. Mabel always insisted on three kinds of pie—pumpkin, mincemeat, and apple. Plus a mile-high coconut cake so light it could make a grown man weep for sheer delight. Willie hoped Andrew Laporte knew what a treasure he had in his Rae.

Willie had received only two letters from her sister since she and Drew left for New Orleans, and those weren't particularly informative. Willie gathered that Rae wasn't too crazy about her prospective mother-in-law, but they were trying to get along. She didn't say when they'd be back, but surely they'd be home by Christmas. Willie had promised to be her sister's maid of honor, and there were lots of arrangements to make for an April wedding. It was, Willie realized suddenly, the one thing she had to look forward to, to be thankful for. She murmured a quick prayer of gratitude and felt a little less guilty for her lack of thankfulness.

But that brief flash of blessing didn't make up for everything else. It was still Thanksgiving Day, still raining, still dreary. And she still felt terribly alone.

"Willie?"

Willie turned to see her mother standing in the kitchen doorway, looking frail and drawn in an oversized housedress, one bony hand clutching the frame for support.

"What's wrong, Mama? Is Daddy worse?" Willie started toward her mother, anxiety knotting her stomach, but Mama held up a hand to stop her.

"He's all right. I just checked on him. But—"

"What, Mama?"

"Someone's coming." The words came out frightened and childlike, and suddenly it struck Willie just how fragile and vulnerable her mother had become. "I went out to the porch, and . . . someone's coming up the road. A car. A big black car." She shuddered visibly, and Willie wondered if she was thinking about another day when a big black car came up the road, bearing news of her son's death on the battlefields of France.

Willie patted her mother's shoulder. "It's all right, Mama. I'll go see."

It was a big black car, all right, but it wasn't the car Charity Grevis drove when she had special deliveries for the post office. The car pulled right up to the side of the porch, the doors opened, and a henna-dyed red head appeared from the backseat. "Happy Thanksgiving, Willie!" Thelma shouted.

Willie gaped in astonishment. Here came Madge, with Mickey in her arms, and Thelma, carrying a huge roasting pan. Stork followed, bearing two casserole dishes and a paper sack. And just behind Thelma, Ivory

Brownlee, in a white shirt and red bow tie, struggled from the backseat with a pie in each hand.

When the group had assembled on the porch, Thelma leaned over and planted a kiss on Willie's cheek. "Everybody needs family on a day like this," she whispered. "We wanted you to know how thankful we are for you."

★ ★ ★

Willie looked around the dining-room table, and tears filled her eyes for the hundredth time that afternoon. Little Mickey, with drooping eyelids, sat in his daddy's lap, his face smeared with mashed potatoes. Thelma, at the other end of the table, tried to pass around the turkey platter for a fourth helping. Mama, sitting beside Thelma, patted her hand and actually smiled.

A wave of conflicting emotions washed over Willie as she surveyed the scene. She thought about those who were missing this Thanksgiving Day. Dear Charlie, the brother whose wit and easy laughter once warmed them all. Owen, whom she had loved briefly but oh so deeply. Mabel Rae, the sister whose friendship she missed so much. Libba, off in Memphis looking for Link and the happiness she deserved.

Then the bittersweet memory of those who were not there gave way to genuine thankfulness for those who were seated around her table. For Thelma, whose compassion and thoughtfulness had undoubtedly spearheaded this little celebration. For Stork, Madge, and Mickey, so willing to share their family with her. And for Ivory Brownlee, who now sat at the secondhand piano in the parlor, quietly playing hymns in the background.

Yes, Willie had plenty of reasons to be thankful, if she only opened her eyes to see the blessings of her life. She had family and friends who loved her. She had wonderful memories of those who were gone. And when she had most needed it, God had sent a sign of love, a feast of Thanksgiving right to her doorstep, even though she hadn't thought to ask.

★ ★ ★

Thelma sat listening to Ivory's playing, watching the faces of those around the table. This had been a good idea, an inspired idea. Willie had needed the encouragement. The girl seemed more hopeful than she had in a long time, more positive. Thelma hoped that this day would be the beginning of some healing for Willie Coltrain.

She stood up and tapped her glass for attention. "Today is Thanksgiving Day," she said softly. "And I, for one, am very thankful to be here with the people I consider my family." Thelma cast a loving glance at Madge . . . at Mickey, now asleep in his father's arms. "We all have a lot to be grateful for.

But we all have needs, too, and could use each other's support. Do you think we could take a little time to pray together, to thank God for all our blessings, and to ask for God's help in our difficulties?"

Bess Coltrain shifted in her seat, then excused herself, saying she ought to check on William. Thelma caught Willie's eye. "I hope I didn't offend her."

Willie shook her head. "Mama's not too comfortable with public prayer— unless she's in church," she said. "But don't worry, it's OK. I, for one, think I need some prayer support right now."

"Ivory," Thelma called, "come join us."

Ivory got up from the piano bench and ambled back to the table. He sat down next to Stork and smoothed little Mickey's hair in a tender gesture.

"Ivory told me something yesterday that concerns both of us deeply. Ivory, do you mind if I tell them so we can all pray about it?"

Thelma watched as Ivory's rheumy eyes flitted back and forth across the table. For a minute she wondered if she had made a mistake by putting him on the spot. People might call him "Crazy Ivory," but Thelma knew him better than anyone else. He could be childlike, but he was always loving and gentle. And he was such a private man, and a proud one.

He fiddled with his bow tie for a minute, running his bony finger around the collar of his shirt. Then he said bluntly, "No. I don't want you to tell."

Thelma closed her eyes and sighed. "All right, Ivory. I'm sorry. I didn't mean to—"

"I'll tell it," he interrupted. He looked at Thelma, and she saw a light of pride shining in his eyes. "We're all . . . fam'ly. I'll tell."

He straightened up and took a drink of iced tea. "I got a notice from the gov'ment," he began. "Says I owe a thousand dollars in back taxes on my daddy's land. Gotta pay by January fifteenth, or they'll take it away. The big house, my cabin—ever'thing."

"A thousand dollars!" Willie breathed. "Ivory, that's a small fortune. If any of us had it, we'd help you in a minute, but nobody we know's got that kind of money. What are you going to do?"

He gave Willie a wide grin, showing the dark gaps of his missing teeth. "Pray," he said simply. "That's what Thelma said, ain't it? We're gonna pray."

"Of course we'll pray, Ivory, but—"

He held up a gnarled hand. "We're gonna pray," he repeated. "God's got ways." He looked around the table triumphantly. "I told," he declared. "Who's next?"

Thelma could have kissed him. For the next fifteen minutes, everyone talked honestly and straightforwardly about the challenges they were facing and the blessings they could perceive in the midst of those difficulties. Stork confessed his struggles with his mother's accusations and asked for wisdom in dealing with her—and with his own sense of guilt. Willie admitted her loneliness and hopelessness. And then, amid weeping and laughter, they joined hands and brought their joys and sorrows to the Lord.

When the prayers were ended, Willie got up from her chair and walked to the other end of the table. She put her arms around Thelma, and Thelma could feel her trembling.

"I didn't know what I needed," Willie murmured. "I didn't know how to pray. But it looks as if God knew . . . and sent all of you." She turned and smiled through her tears at the rest of the group. "Ivory's right," she declared. "God's got ways."

12

✫ ✫ ✫

The Eye of the Beholder

As she started down the hallway toward the wards of Kennedy General, Libba waved a greeting to Nurse Pincheon. Amazing, how much her perception of this place had changed in so short a time. After that first experience, Libba had to force herself to come back again—and only the hope of finding Link enabled her to muster the courage. But her own stubbornness and Aunt Mag's encouragement had prevailed. She would not let this get the best of her, not Magnolia Cooley's grandniece.

After a week of daily inquiries, she had been assured by Nurse Pincheon—*Pinky* to her friends—that it wasn't necessary for her to walk the wards every day. Word would be sent to Aunt Mag's the moment Pinky had confirmation of Link's arrival.

Still, Libba found herself returning, day after day. Something else began to draw her—something more than pride. Something more than the appalling idea of disappointing Aunt Mag.

Not that she didn't trust Pinky's promise. The stern-faced matron she had encountered that first day had turned out to be quite friendly, once she and Libba got on equal turf. They had even eaten lunch together a few times in the hospital commissary. Libba found the woman to be a dedicated nurse, if a bit overprotective of "her boys." Libba firmly believed that when Link showed up, she would be the first to know, even if Pinky had to walk all the way to Aunt Mag's in a sleet storm to deliver the news.

But now Libba had other reasons for coming to the wards every day—reasons like Hans Amundson, the handsome, blond Norwegian who would undoubtedly lose his legs to gangrene. And Stevie Sutton, the redheaded lad who at eighteen had half of his boyish face torn off by a mortar blast.

There were so many wounds here—many of them invisible. Once Libba had learned to look beyond the broken bodies to the hearts and souls that needed compassion and care, she found she was able to be there for them, to provide comfort and companionship, and, in Aunt Mag's wise words, "let them do their own healing."

"I never would have thought it possible," Pinky had admitted to Libba yesterday during a coffee break. "Why, when you first came in here, I took you for a weak little jellyfish who'd faint at the first sight of a bedpan. But you surprised me, Lib—you truly did."

Libba smiled at the memory. Pinky had surprised her, too. The old hatchet face had turned out to have a heart of gold, and she was the one who had helped Libba find her place among these wounded soldiers. Pinky had introduced her to Hans and Stevie and countless others and started her on her routine of visiting the wards—writing letters for the men, talking with them, playing cards, and sometimes just sitting with them when they were in pain. At first she had been repulsed by the idea. But she had to try, somehow, to get used to the idea of Link coming home in a body cast, helpless and dependent. Now the crutches and wheelchairs and empty sleeves—even Stevie's ravaged face—didn't bother her so much. She found herself actually looking forward to seeing these men every day, anticipating the light that came into their eyes when she made her appearance on the ward. And she had discovered, much to her surprise, that they were not helpless or dependent at all.

Libba caught sight of Hans Amundson's blond head as she came through the double doors leading to the first ward.

"Libba!" He pushed himself up in bed and adjusted his blankets. "It's about time you got here—I've been waiting all morning."

"Sorry, Hans," she joked. "I had a jitterbug contest to attend. First things first, you know."

He grinned broadly, showing matching dimples in his fair cheeks. "Did you win?"

"Came in second."

Hans feigned an expression of offense. "I'm crushed." He grabbed her hands and moved his shoulders rhythmically. "You should have been dancing with me. We'd have won for sure." His expression sobered. "Has Link arrived?"

Libba sat down on the straight chair beside his bed. "Not yet."

"Well, if he doesn't show up, my proposal still stands."

She punched him playfully on the arm. "Sure, Hans. And we'd move to the tundra and live in an igloo."

"Minnesota's not a tundra," he corrected. "It's the prairie."

"Tundra, prairie—whatever it is, it's too cold for a Mississippi girl."

Hans jerked his head in disdain. "Cold? Nah. This time of year it's only—oh, ten below, with about two feet of snow on the ground. Doesn't get really cold until January."

Libba shivered. "It's cold enough for me right now."

"It's forty-two degrees today," he muttered. "I asked Pinky this morning." He gave an exaggerated sigh and gazed out the window. "Doesn't seem like Thanksgiving without a good blizzard."

Libba patted his hand. "You'll get home soon, Hans. Real soon."

"If the army hadn't misread my papers, I'd be home now. What kind of idiot clerk mistakes Mississippi for Minnesota?"

"The kind who sees a capital *M* and doesn't bother to read the rest." Libba shook her head. "I hope Link isn't on his way to St. Paul."

Hans's blue eyes softened with compassion. "I hope not, too, Libba—for your sake, and for his. If he knows what he's coming back to, he'll get here as fast as he can. You're quite a catch."

"Thanks, Hans. That's a very sweet thing to say. But you have no idea what a terrible catch I really am. My cousin Willie says my biscuits could anchor a riverboat."

"Biscuits aren't that important," Hans declared firmly. "How are you at lutefisk?"

Libba grimaced. "From what you've told me about it, I wouldn't want to get within ten miles of the stuff. Cod soaked in lye? Ugh."

"Ah," he said, raising a forefinger, "but I bet you've eaten chitterlings."

"Down here it's *chitlins.*" She raised an eyebrow at him. "It's—"

"I know what it is," he interrupted. "Uff da! Such parts should stay inside the pig, where they belong. I much prefer lutefisk—wrapped up in lefse, of course."

"Lefse?" Libba frowned.

Hans grinned and shook his head. "Lefse is—well, it's hard to describe. Round and flat, sort of like a thin pancake, but with a different texture. You put butter and brown sugar on it and roll it up—"

"With the lutefisk?"

"No, no—when you eat it with lutefisk, you leave out the sugar."

"Never mind." Libba shuddered. "Maybe when you get home, your girl will make you some."

Hans turned his face away. "My girl won't be waiting for me when I get back."

"Hans, you don't know that. She—"

"I know."

He reached under his pillow and pulled out a sheet of paper. One page. Libba's heart sank.

"Lisa's letter came this morning." His eyes scanned the paper, and he began to blink back tears. "She says that so much has changed in the time I've been gone, and she's not sure we should count on the plans we've made. I can read between the lines." The letter slipped from his fingers and fluttered to the floor. "I never should have told her about my legs."

"You don't know you're going to lose them," Libba protested. "Maybe the doctor—"

"The doctor told me this morning that there's nothing more they can do. My surgery is scheduled for tomorrow at seven."

Libba closed her eyes and fought back her own tears. Blindly she groped for his hand and held on to it. "I'm so sorry, Hans," she managed, anger mingling with sorrow in her choked words. "But if this—this Lisa—can't understand that there's more to you than two strong legs, she isn't worthy of you. She's—"

"She's a normal, healthy, beautiful young woman who wants a normal, healthy man," he whispered. "I can understand that."

"Well, I can't!" Libba's anger flared—at the insensitivity of this girl who was turning her back on a fine young man, at the war, at the senselessness of it all. "I can't understand it for a minute. Link was wounded in the back and legs. From what his friend Stork tells me, he has been in a body cast for months. He may never walk again. But I—"

"Are you telling me that you never, for one instant, considered the fact that it might not work? That your love might not be strong enough?" Hans's eyes bored into hers with a passionate intensity. "Can you honestly say that you have never doubted him . . . or yourself?"

Libba met his gaze. "Of course I have doubted. I have questioned, I have prayed, I have lain awake nights wondering what it would be like, and if I could handle it. But—" she paused and gripped his hand tighter—"I've learned a thing or two in the past few weeks. Thanks to friends like you."

Suddenly Libba realized just how true those words were. These weeks with Hans and Stevie and other patients at Kennedy General had taught her what no amount of self-examination could have accomplished: that a person had worth for what was inside. Not for legs or arms or eyes or physical abilities, but for heart and soul, for compassion and strength, for love and humor and courage.

A warm rush filled her as the truth hit home. God had answered her prayer. She was ready—ready for Link to come home, whatever his home-coming would bring.

"Thank you," Hans was saying as he swiped at his tears with his free hand. "If you can see beyond this—" he motioned to his useless legs, where only empty space would be tomorrow morning—"well then, I guess there's hope for a guy like me. Hope for finding love—real love—and someone to share my life with."

"You're welcome," Libba whispered. But even as she said it, she knew that she was the one who had been given the greater gift.

TWO

Shining Star

CHRISTMAS 1944

13

★ ★ ★

Slaughter's Hero

A German Prison Camp
Early December 1944

Charlie Coltrain flopped into one of the straight-backed chairs and wearily lifted his feet to the battered table in the center of the room. Day after day of forced labor on the roads outside the prison camp was taking its toll, and the daily meals of stale bread and watery soup didn't do much to restore his energy or put meat back on his bones.

He looked across at Owen, who was leaning back with one hand flung over his eyes. Charlie hadn't seen a mirror in months, but if Owen Slaughter was a reflection of his own physical condition, they were both in trouble. The man's cheekbones protruded from a face drawn and thin. His eyes were sunken and darkly circled, his skin ashy and pale. Charlie lifted a gaunt hand and examined his own arm. He could count the bones in his wrist, and except for the fleabites, his skin bore the same pallor that concerned him so much in Owen.

They needed to find a way out of this death trap, and fast. The other men—particularly their ranking officer, Lieutenant Colonel Effington from the RAF, and the Aussie, Tiger Grayson—thought the best course of action was to simply try to stay alive until the Allies made their way into Germany to liberate them. Others had tried to escape, they knew, without success. They had heard the shouts, the barking dogs, the shots in the middle of the night.

Staying put might be the safest course, but Charlie wondered if it was the wisest. There was no telling how long the Allied offensive might take. In the meantime, they were all dying by inches.

Charlie opened one eye and looked across the table at Owen Slaughter. Something about Owen fascinated him, this man who had no memory, no past—only a name and a blood type on his dog tags. How would it feel not to know who you were or where you came from?

From the moment Owen had showed up at the prison camp, Charlie had taken a liking to him. Maybe it was because he knew what it felt like when other people thought you were crazy. Maybe it was the intriguing idea of having all your negative memories erased, of having the opportunity to build yourself, from the ground up, into the kind of man you really wanted to be.

Yes, Charlie felt drawn to Owen, and he'd determined from the beginning to befriend him and help him. But he wouldn't trade places with him. Where would Charlie be—*who* would he be—without his ties to his parents and Willie and Mabel Rae . . . without his history in Eden?

He sat up and stared at Slaughter, who still sat with his hand over his eyes. What did a man with no memory think about? What were his prayers, his hopes? When he fell asleep at night, what images made up his dreams? Was his life before the war hidden away somewhere, back in the dark recesses of his mind, or was it gone forever?

Charlie reached across the table and touched Owen lightly on the elbow. "Hey, pal, you OK?"

Owen moved his arm and opened one eye. "Yeah. Just thinking."

"About what?"

"About Christmas."

"Christmas?" Charlie leaned forward. "You remember Christmas?"

Owen shook his head and smiled a little. "Just vague images. Lights on a tree—right in the living room. Can you imagine that? A tree in the house!"

"Everybody does it, pal."

"Really? Why?"

"It's tradition."

"Tradition." Owen sat up straighter and scratched his head. "Tradition is based on memories, Charlie. Where do I get mine?"

"I guess you have to make your own. What else do you remember?"

"Flannel pajamas. A woman—my mother, I guess—bending over me and tucking me in bed. I'd love to sleep in a real bed again, just once. I don't remember what it's like, but it seems nice."

"It is. Back home, I had this big feather bed in the attic room at the farm. Really private, like a world of my own, where nobody else could intrude."

"A private world of your own is highly overrated." Owen smiled weakly. "Trust me."

"Yeah, but it beats this." Charlie waved a hand at the prison barracks. "One light bulb, a table, and eight chairs—" he pointed toward the sleeping quarters—"torture racks you could loosely call bunks—"

"And an unlimited supply of lice," Owen added. "Do you think we'll ever get out of here?"

"One way or another we'll get out." Charlie shrugged. "I just pray it's not feet first."

★ ★ ★

Owen watched Charlie carefully as he drank his thin soup and choked down the stale crust of hard brown bread. He was worried about Charlie, really worried. Everybody was thin, of course, but Charlie looked the worst of all. His cough had developed a deep rattle in the past few days, brought on, no doubt, by long days of backbreaking work in the chilling cold.

Owen didn't know how much more of this Charlie could take. And he could not—would not—sit idly by waiting for the cavalry to ride in and rescue them while his best friend, his only friend, coughed the life out of his lungs.

In Owen's eyes, Charlie Coltrain was a genuine hero. Charlie had told him about being shell-shocked, about the hospital, about his desire to get back to the front and die with dignity. But he didn't die. Instead, he saved the lives of a whole lot of other people, including three innocent children. Charlie wouldn't have been captured at all if he hadn't tried to fulfill a dying soldier's last request—to find his buddy and make sure he was all right.

In a risk he never should have taken, Charlie had gone deeper into enemy territory and found the soldier's friend—dead from a Kraut bullet in the head. He got there too late, but he tried. And because he tried, he had spent the last six months in a German labor camp.

But Charlie's heroism had more to do with character than with courage. When no one else took the risk to trust Owen, Charlie had befriended him. Charlie had listened, had understood. And by his understanding, Charlie had given Owen hope, and the heart to keep going. If he never regained any of his past, this was one memory Owen was determined to hold on to for the rest of his life—the memory of a selfless man who had, with simple compassion, saved yet another life.

A long time ago, Charlie Coltrain had wanted to die, had prayed to die. Now, when he wanted to live, to get out of this pit and go home to his family, he was in danger of coughing his life away in the frozen wasteland of a

German prison camp. There was no dignity in this, no honor. The man deserved better.

By the time Charlie had finished his soup and gagged down the last of his bread, the common room was deserted. All the other men had drifted back to the sleeping quarters, hoping to get a few hours of rest before they were hauled out to stand in the snow for the next morning's roll call.

Charlie sat staring at his empty bowl. "My sister Willie used to make the best soup," he mused, running his finger around the jagged rim. "And biscuits, slathered with butter and molasses. . . ."

"Tell me about it," Owen urged. "Tell me about Eden."

Charlie leaned back in the rickety chair and linked his hands behind his head. His eyes took on a wistful, faraway look as he began to reminisce about his little Mississippi hometown, his parents, his sisters, the farm, the cafe, and Thelma Breckinridge's apple pie.

To Owen, it sounded like absolute paradise—the kind of place he would want to live, the kind of people he would want as his family. He had heard it all before, but every time Charlie told it, Owen drank it in like a parched traveler at an oasis. He almost felt as if he knew Willie and Mabel Rae, William and Bess Coltrain, Thelma, Ivory, and the prissy, self-centered Cousin Libba. He could see the sunset over the flat Delta cotton fields stretching on forever, the garish neon sign in front of the Paradise Garden Cafe. For a while, as Charlie spun his tales, Owen could believe—almost— that the memories were his.

"I'd love to go there someday," he murmured. "To Eden."

"And you will, too. We—" Charlie leaned forward as a fit of coughing cut his words off in midsentence. "When we get out of here," he went on when he was finally able to catch his breath, "you'll go home with me. Meet everybody. See Eden for yourself."

Owen smiled at his friend. He was a generous man, Charlie Coltrain, willing to share himself, his family, and his memories with someone who had none to give in return. And Owen was determined that Charlie's generosity would not go unrewarded. He would get Charlie out of here and home, no matter what. The man deserved that, at the very least.

That and a medal of honor.

14

★ ★ ★

Royal Wedding

**New Orleans
December 12, 1944**

Rae Coltrain stood in the middle of the Jefferson Davis suite and gazed at her reflection in the huge mirror that spanned one side of the room. Her eyes drifted to the elaborately carved rice bed—so high she had to use a step stool to get into it—with its hand-embroidered ecru spread. Some Louisiana lady, probably Beau Laporte's grandmother or great-grandmother, must have spent years just tying those intricate French knots.

She didn't belong here in this opulent home with its high crown moldings, polished cherry furniture, and hand-loomed carpets. And she didn't belong in this dress, purchased with Laporte money—a lot of it—from a tiny shop off the Quarter where the proprietress spoke French to Drew's mother and treated Rae as if she were nothing more than a dressmaker's dummy.

It was a stunning wedding gown, certainly—yards and yards of flowing off-white satin and velvet, with hand-set pearls in the bodice and a train long enough to slipcover a sofa. Beatrice had been adamant about the styling, insisting that the designer contrive some way to "minimize the girl's hips" and draw attention to her "lovely dark eyes." *Of course,* Rae mused cynically. *We can't have all the socialites in New Orleans discussing under their breath what the bride could possibly be carrying in her saddlebags.*

The dress did make the most of her few assets, Rae admitted reluctantly. And no doubt the ceremony would be lovely, down in the huge gilded ballroom with its crystal chandeliers and leaded windows reflecting the glow of the candlelight.

She just wished. . . .

Rae paused in the midst of the thought and stared morosely into the mirror. What *did* she wish? This was supposed to be the happiest day of a woman's life—the day she had waited for, longed for, but never really believed would happen to her. Yet here she was, dressed for her wedding, looking like a fairy-tale bride, and feeling as if the story had taken a terribly wrong turn.

Marrying Drew was the right thing—of that she was sure, very sure. But this day should have been different. She should have been in the old farmhouse in Eden, surrounded by Mama and Willie and Libba fussing over her. She should have been wearing a dress made by her own two hands with love and anticipation, not by some snooty French seamstress whose only concern was camouflaging her hips. She should have been walking down the aisle of their little country church on her own dear father's arm. . . .

Rae jerked away from the mirror and blinked to hold back her tears. She had to stop this—immediately. The wedding was taking place in less than an hour, in this house, and there was nothing she could do about it. She had promised Drew, and she would go through with it. For his sake, and his mother's.

The problem was, Rae couldn't figure out for the life of her just what was wrong with Drew's mother—if anything. The woman had thrown herself into preparations for the wedding with all the energy and enthusiasm of a twenty-year-old. She had dragged Rae all over the city, looking for just the right shoes to set off her mother-of-the-groom outfit. Beatrice had done the invitations herself, and the "small family wedding" Drew had originally talked Rae into had escalated into a grand affair for two hundred of the Laportes' closest friends, including the governor and his wife. Bea had argued with the baker for days on end about the size of the cake. With only a little help from Addie, she had almost single-handedly rearranged all the furniture in the front parlor and brought in lace-covered tables to display the elegantly wrapped and obviously extravagant wedding gifts.

In short, Beatrice Laporte thrived on the activity and seemed in perfect health for a woman her age; in fact, she seemed in perfect health for a woman half her age. Whatever the mysterious ailment that prevented her from traveling to Mississippi for the wedding, it didn't seem to be slowing her down much.

Rae wasn't normally suspicious, and she did her best to curb any negative attitudes toward her future mother-in-law. When Drew mentioned that his mother seemed to be "doing quite well under the circumstances," she simply nodded in agreement. But she was becoming increasingly convinced that Beatrice Laporte wasn't ill at all, and that someone—perhaps Bea herself, perhaps Drew's father—had conjured up the tale to keep Drew out of the clutches of her family.

Well, it didn't matter now. The wedding was scheduled to begin in—she glanced at the clock on the mantel—exactly seventeen minutes. She would be making her wedding vows in her husband's ancestral home, without the support of her family and friends. They would be married here, and here they would stay. Everything had been decided. Drew had become the legal representative for his father's company, and after their honeymoon they would occupy the west wing of the house until they could find a suitable home of their own.

Rae turned back to the mirror, touched up her lipstick, and tried on a smile. The expression didn't quite reach her eyes, and her heart wasn't in it, but it would have to do. Once she caught a glimpse of Drew, waiting for her as she walked down the aisle, the smile would be genuine enough. In the meantime, she would just make the best of it.

The Coltrains always did.

★ ★ ★

Downstairs, in the small room across the hall from the ballroom, Drew adjusted his tie for the tenth time and exhaled sharply. He had to calm down. Everything was right on schedule. The baker had arrived half an hour ago with a three-tiered cake that took up most of one end of the dining-room table. The rich scent of French-roast coffee drifted out into the hallway from the kitchen, and Addie, dressed to kill in a red velvet dress, had been scurrying about for the last hour, arranging silverware and plates of finger sandwiches.

Drew's stomach growled, and he slipped into the kitchen and wolfed down a handful of chicken-salad tidbits. He hated this kind of society food—little sandwiches cut into fancy shapes, made with cucumbers and cheese paste and other stuff you could barely taste. It took the edge off his hunger, but within five minutes he was sorry he had eaten anything. His insides churned, and he felt as if his heart might lurch right out of his chest.

Wedding-day jitters. That was all. Everybody got them. Once it was all over, he would be able to eat again. And to catch up on the sleep he had missed for the past three nights.

He smiled to himself. Well, maybe sleeping would have to wait awhile.

But as soon as the honeymoon was underway, he intended to find the finest restaurant in Atlanta and order himself the biggest, thickest steak east of the Mississippi.

At the thought of the honeymoon, Drew smiled again. He wasn't much different from most other men, he thought. For his bride's sake he would endure all the pomp and circumstance of the wedding, but he would be glad once it was over and he could get down to the business of living with the woman he loved.

In his and Rae's case, the honeymoon would be especially welcome—two weeks without his parents, two glorious weeks all to themselves, alone. Except for his promise, of course. The last few days of their wedding trip would be spent in Eden with Rae's family. A surprise Christmas visit.

Rae hadn't told them about the wedding. She couldn't justify in a letter, she said, why she was getting married away from home, why there wouldn't be an April wedding with Willie as her maid of honor. They would be disappointed, and they wouldn't understand. Better to tell them face-to-face when there was time for explanations. And for reunions.

Rae hadn't said much, but Drew knew how disappointed she was at the way things had turned out. She was a trouper, that was certain. She had handled everything—the wedding preparations, his mother's domineering ways, his change in career plans—with grace and good humor. The society girls his parents were so stuck on could take a few lessons from Mabel Rae Coltrain, daughter of a Mississippi dirt farmer. Money and prestige didn't hold a candle to dignity. The woman he was going to marry this evening had class. Real class.

Drew's heart swelled as he thought about Rae. She was the kind of girl he had always wanted, though he hadn't had the sense to realize it. But from her very first letter, he knew he had discovered a woman with warmth and charm, creativity, intelligence, and faith. Now he realized, much to his chagrin, that if he had met Rae in the traditional way—seeing her before he got to know her mind and heart and soul—he might not have looked twice in her direction.

Why were people so shallow and stupid, he wondered, to put looks and social standing and money over really important qualities like compassion, faithfulness, and spiritual depth? Drew couldn't imagine living his life with anyone but Rae Coltrain. To him she was the most incredible woman on earth, and he intended to spend the rest of his days convincing her how beautiful she truly was.

★　★　★

Rae stood in the hallway outside the ballroom, shifting nervously from one foot to the other while she listened to the murmur of voices beyond the door. From this angle she couldn't see the center aisle, or the altar that had been set up at the far end, or Drew, waiting for her. She caught a glimpse of candles and festive holiday greenery and several dozen people whose faces she had never seen.

A woman shouldn't get married among strangers, she mused briefly, then banished the thought as quickly as it had come. Drew was not a stranger, and he was the only one who really mattered. Up until this moment, it had been Beatrice's wedding, Beatrice's planning, Beatrice's day. Now it was Rae's turn, and she would let nothing spoil it for her. Not this roomful of strangers, nor the fact that she was two hundred miles from home. Not even Beatrice.

Rae felt a hand at her elbow and turned to find Beauregard Laporte, splendid in tails and a high cravat, standing beside her. "Are you ready?" he whispered.

"Give me a minute." He nodded and stepped back, and as the murmuring quieted and the music of a string quartet began to filter out into the hallway from the ballroom, Mabel Rae Coltrain turned her face toward the wall and closed her eyes.

Dear God, she prayed silently, *I have so many mixed feelings on this day when I thought all I'd feel was sheer happiness. But there's one thing I'm not mixed up about. I love Drew, and I know he is your gift, the person you've chosen especially for me. I don't know why—I'm sure I don't deserve him—but I'm thankful. Help me to enjoy this, in spite of all my apprehensions, and to get through it without making a fool of myself in front of all these people.*

She took a deep breath, opened her eyes, and moved to her place in the doorway. Drew's father came behind her and straightened her train, then offered his arm and waited. As the string quartet finished its prelude and launched into the "Wedding March," they began to move forward.

Rae wasn't prepared for how the grand ballroom had been transformed—obviously Beatrice Laporte had been working overtime. Two enormous Christmas trees, sparkling with white lights, graced the far corners of the room. Evergreen swags tied with white satin ribbons hung over each window, and a thousand candles, it seemed, bathed the room in a warm glow.

On cue, the crowd of strangers surged to their feet and turned toward the center aisle. A few smiled and nodded, while others whispered behind their hands to one another. Rae forced herself to keep her head held high and her eyes straight ahead. Resolutely she planted one foot in front of the other and clung to Beau's arm for support.

Then she saw Drew, stepping out to stand next to the altar, smiling, waiting . . . for her. In his gray tails and starched white shirt that contrasted with his dark hair and tanned features, he looked for all the world like a nobleman—proud and strong and incredibly handsome.

For a fleeting instant, Rae was struck by the irony of the scene. All brides were supposed to be beautiful, she thought wryly; she just hoped she was half as beautiful as he was. She hoped he wouldn't be . . . ashamed.

When she reached the front row, she paused for a moment and withdrew a single white rose from her bouquet. Pressing it into Beatrice's hand, Rae kissed the woman solemnly on the cheek, and her heart wrenched within her. She should have been giving this rose to Mama while Daddy held her arm and beamed with pride. But she couldn't think about that now. She wouldn't.

Rae moved to stand beside Drew and looked up . . . and in that moment, all apprehensions fled. Tears trickled down his handsome cheeks—tears of wonder and joy and love.

She could have been in a castle or a hovel, a country church or a cathedral. The time and place, the circumstances of this ceremony, no longer mattered. The man she loved was here, and the God she trusted.

Whatever the future held, they would face it . . . together.

15

★ ★ ★

Circle of Love

Libba sighed as she pulled open the front door of Kennedy General Hospital and stepped inside. As always, the scent of antiseptic washed over her, and Pinky towered over the lobby from her accustomed place at the high reception desk.

She could hardly believe it had been six weeks since she first set foot in this place. Then, the hospital had been a nightmare of unknown terrors. Now it seemed like an old friend, shabby and worn and a bit gruff, but welcoming in its familiarity nevertheless. These wards were filled with people who cared about her—young men, mostly, who looked forward to her visits with eager anticipation. She had helped a number of them find a way to cope with their wounds and learn to live again. They, in turn, had helped her prepare for the inevitable.

Or she *hoped* it was inevitable. Link should have been here weeks ago, but no one—not even Pinky, who had ingenious ways of getting information—could seem to find out where he was or what had delayed his arrival. Every morning Libba went to the hospital with hope in her heart; every evening she came back to Aunt Mag's disappointed.

"Have patience, child," her great-aunt would say. "He will come in God's own good time."

Theoretically, Libba agreed with Aunt Mag—the Lord did have his own timetable for such things. And good was coming out of the situation. She had spent the time productively, after all, learning to acclimate herself to the hospital, to face the grim reality of the war, to look beyond disabilities to see the person within. But as days stretched into weeks, she began to wonder if maybe the Almighty was taking a little too seriously the principle that "a thousand years to the Lord is like one day." Surely God could speed things up a bit if he had a mind to.

Libba waved a greeting to Pinky and headed for the ward. Hans Amundson's bed was empty, but Stevie Sutton sat up and welcomed her warmly, the good side of his face turning up in a beaming smile.

"Hi, Stevie," Libba said as she reached his bed. "You look like you're doing pretty well this morning. Where's Hans?"

"He's in the commissary getting some breakfast. Then he's going down to have his new legs fitted. Says he can't wait to get out of that wheelchair." Stevie chuckled. "Marlene is with him, of course."

"That's wonderful." Libba's thoughts drifted to Hans, who only a few weeks ago thought his life was over when his girl back home in Minnesota had brushed him off in a letter. But the handsome Norwegian had rallied when Nurse Marlene Henley had been assigned to Kennedy General. Now the two were engaged, and Hans planned to stay in Memphis once he was discharged. Marlene—a strong, steady girl with a good head on her shoulders—hadn't thought twice about falling in love with a man who had no legs. She adored Hans, and her love had given him the confidence he needed to become his old self again.

"Marlene has been good for Hans," Libba mused out loud. "They make a good pair."

"That's true," Stevie agreed. "But don't forget your part in all of this."

Libba looked at him. "What do you mean?"

He shook his head in disbelief. "Surely you know the truth, Libba. You gave Hans something to hang on to—some reason to keep on living after that idiot Lisa dumped him. You gave him hope. Without your encouragement, I don't think he would have been able even to consider a relationship with Marlene. He would have thought she was pitying him. You showed him that a man is more than his legs—" Stevie paused. "Or his face."

Libba allowed her gaze to linger on Stevie's countenance, a study in contrasts. The left side was bright and boyish, with ruddy, freckled skin and a faint dimple in the cheek. The right side was a distorted mass of scars, pulled tight, that crimped his mouth and twisted his eye. Libba knew that on first glance, most people would consider him grotesque. But she no longer felt the horror she had experienced the first time she saw Stevie. He was a wonderful, sweet, compassionate boy who always thought of others before he thought of himself. . . .

"You've helped all of us, Libba," Stevie was saying. "Just by being here, by coming every day to see us, to spend time with us, to write letters for those of us who can't do it for ourselves—" he held up his twisted right hand—"by being our friend."

Libba reached out and grasped the scarred, clawlike fingers. Tears clogged her throat, and words failed her. She hoped—she prayed—that Stevie would find someone, someone who had the sense to see the soul behind the scars. She shut her eyes for a moment, and when she opened them, Stevie was gazing at her with an odd expression.

"You'll have stars in your crown for all you've done, Libba Coltrain." He grinned. "But before that, you may have stars in your eyes. Look."

Libba turned. There, in the doorway, stood Nurse Pincheon, holding a medical file in one hand and a mug of coffee in the other. Libba didn't even have to ask; the look on Pinky's face said it all.

Link Winsom had finally arrived.

★ ★ ★

"What do you mean, I can't see him?" Libba protested as the nurse guided her down the hall toward the commissary. "Pinky, stop that!" She jerked her arm away and wheeled around to confront the stone-faced Pincheon. "I don't want to go to the commissary. I don't want coffee. I don't want to sit down. I have been here every day for six weeks, and if Link is in this hospital, I have a right to see him. I've earned that right."

"Yes, you have," Pinky replied, recapturing Libba's arm and steering her obstinately through the commissary doors. The nurse pushed her into a chair at the first empty table, plunked the coffee down in front of her, and seated herself with a sigh. "But you can't see him. Not right now. First we have to have a little talk."

"Pinky, no offense, but the last thing I want to do right now is talk to you."

"I know, I know." Pinky smiled. She laid a restraining hand on Libba's arm. "Don't try to escape, you little wildcat. Even if you find him, you won't be able to see him . . . yet."

Libba had started to rise, then caught the look on Pinky's face and sat down again. "What happened? Where is he?"

"He's in surgery." The nurse flipped the file open and started to read. "Before they brought him here, they made a little side trip to Baltimore—"

"Give me that!" Libba snatched at the chart, but Pinky was too quick for her.

"You know these files are off-limits to civilians, except for medical personnel."

"I don't care."

"Well, you should care. Link's medical history is in here—information that may make a difference in what happens to him now." She lifted an eyebrow. "I know this is difficult, Lib, but if you'll just calm down and listen, I'll tell you everything you need to know."

Libba crossed her arms and sank back against the chair.

"That's better. Now, as I was saying, Link was released to come home in October—"

Libba nodded. "I know. I got the telegram the last week of October. The same day my father died." *Two pieces of good news,* she thought grimly.

Pinky scanned the file. "Apparently he was scheduled to come directly here, but they thought he might benefit from some of the surgeons in Baltimore. That's why his arrival was delayed so much. According to this, they gave him a thorough round of examinations and X rays, then ultimately decided to send him on to Memphis." She paused. "The trip wasn't good for him. By the time he arrived here last night, he was in a great deal of pain. First thing this morning, the doctors ran some more X rays and discovered that the shrapnel in his back had moved and was pressing against the spine. They had no choice but to operate immediately."

Libba closed her eyes and fought back tears. "And?"

Pinky reached out, covering Libba's hand with her own. "I won't try to lie to you. It could go either way. If the surgery is successful, he'll live. He might not walk, but he'll live. If not . . ." She left the sentence unfinished.

"He could die on the table without ever knowing I was here."

A foreboding silence hung in the air between them, broken only by the clinking of silverware and murmured conversations around them. "Yes," Pinky finally said in a hoarse whisper.

"How long?"

The nurse frowned. "What do you mean?"

"How long?" Libba repeated dully. "How long will the operation take? How long before they know?"

Pinky looked at her watch. "If there are no more complications, the surgeons should be finished by noon. After that, several more hours before he comes to. If he—"

"Go ahead and say it. If he *lives.*"

"If he lives through the surgery, he's got a good chance, although not a hundred percent. It's a very delicate procedure, that close to the spine. They won't know whether he'll have the use of his legs until the swelling goes down, and—"

"I don't care about that," Libba said bluntly. She tried to maintain a calm facade, but her control was rapidly falling apart. "I don't . . . care about his legs. I just . . . want him to . . . live."

She put her head down on the table and gave in to her tears, sobbing out the anguish and fear in her heart. For a long time—she didn't know how long—she sat there, weeping, feeling Pinky's presence. Then, suddenly, when she was almost cried out, she felt something else—a hand, solid and comforting, on her shoulder.

At first Libba thought she had imagined it. Then without lifting her head, she reached up and touched it. A strong hand, lined with prominent veins, its skin as soft as old flannel.

"It'll be all right, child," a deep, resonant voice murmured in her ear. "We'll get through this—together."

Libba sat up. Through her tears, she saw a blurred image sitting next to her—a tall, regal woman with upswept white hair and a flowing blue-green dress. Except for the outrageous earrings, it could have been an angel.

Or maybe it was.

★ ★ ★

"Aunt Mag, you really don't have to stay," Libba protested for the tenth time. It was nearly six in the evening, and her great-aunt had been with her since midmorning. The elderly woman had to be exhausted from the waiting and the tension and the maddening inactivity. Libba certainly was. Her nerves were frayed to the breaking point. She had snapped at everyone in sight—Pinky, the doctor who avoided all her questions, even Aunt Mag.

Magnolia smiled and lifted an eyebrow. "Nurse Pincheon went to all the trouble to send for me," she murmured. "It would be rather ungrateful for me to abandon ship now, wouldn't it?" She strode across the room and looked down at Libba, who was shifting uncomfortably in a straight-backed chair. "Besides, you little rhinoceros bird, you need me. And don't you forget it."

The image made Libba smile—the first smile since this morning, when Pinky had brought the news of Link's situation. Aunt Mag could be stubborn, that was certain. At the moment, though, it was one of the traits Libba loved most in the old woman.

And Mag was right. Libba did need her.

Around one-thirty in the afternoon, nearly four and a half hours ago, the tight-lipped doctor had come by—at Nurse Pincheon's insistence, apparently—to let them know that Link had survived the surgery and was being taken to a recovery ward. That was all. No encouragement, no prognosis for the future. No compassion. The man had insinuated that there was no room for visitors at an army hospital and that they'd just be underfoot. He had suggested—strongly—that they go home and wait for someone to call.

Libba wasn't about to be put out, of course, but she was so emotionally and physically exhausted that she couldn't face standing up to this intimidating little weasel. That's when Aunt Mag had moved in, completely disarming the man with a combination of devastating charm and lethal determination. By the time she was finished with him, he had brought coffee and doughnuts from the commissary, shown them a picture of his wife and children, and was nearly convinced that he should recommend Libba for a commendation in recognition of her contribution to the morale of his wounded soldiers.

Aunt Mag certainly knew how to handle people, Libba mused. The old woman was completely comfortable anywhere she went, and everyone seemed to recognize it. Her presence filled a room—even this drab little room—with life and hope.

And hope was something Libba desperately longed for right now.

"It's been such a long time," she said. She was trying to be strong, to show the kind of courage Aunt Mag obviously expected from her, but she heard the catch in her own voice and couldn't stop it.

"Nonsense, child. It's only been a few hours. He'll be all right—you'll see."

Libba put her arms around her great-aunt and melted into the older woman's embrace. "I wish I had your faith, Aunt Mag."

"When you're eighty-three, you will," Mag answered firmly, stroking Libba's hair. "I've had many, many years and a lot of experience to build on."

"But how can you be so sure? You seem so . . . so certain . . . of everything."

Mag lifted Libba's chin and looked intently into her eyes. "One thing age teaches you, child—there are only a few things in this life you can be certain of."

"And those are—?"

"Love. God's grace. The power of prayer."

Libba nodded miserably. "I've been praying, Aunt Mag—really I have. But I don't feel as if my prayers have much impact right now."

"All prayers have impact, child. Especially when others are praying with you."

Libba gazed into those serene green eyes, eyes that held a world of wisdom and understanding. "Others?"

Mag nodded. "I took the liberty of calling your mother earlier this morning. Everybody's praying, Libba—Olivia, those friends of yours in Eden. Even some woman who runs the cafe—name of Thelma somebody-or-other. Your mother seemed to set great store in the power of her prayers." She smiled down at Libba. "A lot of people love you, child. Including your old Aunt Mag."

Libba pressed her head against Magnolia's shoulder. Tears came again, but this time they weren't the result of anger or frustration or fear. They were tears of relief—calming, cleansing tears. Tears that brought peace to her soul.

With her eyes closed and her head buried in the silky fabric of the old woman's dress, Libba wept and waited. Gradually an image rose to her mind—a vision of her mother in the Paradise Garden Cafe, surrounded by Thelma Breckinridge, Madge and Stork Simpson and baby Mickey, her cousin Willie, and even old Ivory Brownlee. Hands joined, they were praying—for her, for Link, for a miracle.

It was a circle of love.

And somewhere, deep in her spirit, Libba felt God smile.

★　★　★

Link Winsom struggled to open his eyes, but his eyelids wouldn't cooperate. He felt drugged, groggy. His body, somehow disconnected from his mind, wouldn't move. His arms felt like lead, and his legs—well, he couldn't feel his legs at all.

Where was he? He couldn't quite remember. Something about a hospital and an operation. . . .

Memphis. Kennedy General. After innumerable maddening delays and several weeks of being poked and prodded in some military facility in—Baltimore, was it?—he had finally made it . . . or had he?

Bright light surrounded him, piercing through his half-closed eyelids and making his head throb with pain. It wasn't a hospital after all. Everything was white and hazy, like a thick fog with the sun reflecting behind it. Above him, nebulous figures moved about in silence, hovering over him and then flitting away again.

He hadn't anticipated that death would be like this.

He hadn't expected literal streets of gold and angels playing harps, of course, but he had hoped at least for consciousness. A chance to be reunited with his mother, whom he barely remembered, and with Owen Slaughter, whom he remembered like it was yesterday. He had thought that heaven would bring an end to the pain. . . .

But the pain was still with him—a fire in his back, shooting upward through his shoulders and neck into his head. Maybe this wasn't heaven at all. Maybe he had missed something—something important—and now he was in hell, destined to an eternity of agony without being able to move.

TILL WE MEET AGAIN

It *was* hot in here, now that he thought about it. Sweat trickled down his neck, and he shivered with a sudden chill. He licked his cracked lips. "Slaughter?" he whispered hoarsely.

"Water," a voice above him said. "He wants water."

Someone slipped a straw into his mouth, and the monumental effort of sucking was rewarded by a trickle of icy water. If he could get water, it must not be hell.

"Am I dead?" he croaked. "Is this heaven?"

An angel appeared at his side, a vision in creamy white, bending down over him. She took his hand and held it. "I'm here, sweetheart."

Sweetheart?

Link didn't know much about angels, but he doubted one would be calling him sweetheart. He forced his eyelids further open and squinted into the light, trying to focus. It was an angel, all right—a young one, with an older, taller angel standing behind her. A very old angel, in fact, with white hair and a bright blue dress.

Then his eyes grew accustomed to the light, and he blinked. The heavenly vision grasping his hand had auburn hair and eyes the color of weeping-willow branches in the spring. . . .

96

16

★ ★ ★

Divine Intervention

Link Winsom awoke in a different room, a different bed. Weak winter sunlight filtered in through the streaked windows, and the murmur of conversation surrounded him.

Coffee. He smelled coffee.

"Morning, soldier."

A nurse with a face like Mount Rushmore loomed at the foot of his bed. He craned his neck. "Where am I?"

"Kennedy General Hospital, Memphis, Tennessee. Nurse Amanda Pincheon at your service." She came forward and set a tray on the table next to his bed. "Feel like eating?"

Link swallowed. His throat hurt, and he still felt groggy, but the rumbling in his stomach took precedence. "I could eat. What are you offering?"

She lifted the lid and peered at the plate. "Soft scrambled eggs. Grits. Juice. Coffee, if you want it."

"No bacon? No toast? No potatoes? What kind of resort is this, anyway?"

Nurse Pincheon grinned, and the expression softened her craggy countenance. "Good to see you didn't get your sense of humor blown out of you," she quipped. "You'll have to be on a soft diet for a couple of days; then you can have whatever you want."

Link raised his head and looked around. This was just like a hundred other hospital wards in a hundred other army hospitals, but to him it was heaven. Kennedy General. He had finally made it home—or as close to home as he was likely to get for a while.

Suddenly a thought struck him—a vague memory of an angel standing

97

beside his bed, holding his hand. "Last night—," he began. "I thought . . . or maybe I dreamed. . . ."

The nurse smiled and leaned over him, helping him to sit up a little. She handed him a glass of orange juice and a small paper cup with two pills in it. "Take your medicine, soldier." When he obeyed, she plumped the pillow up behind him and sat down in the chair next to his bed. Her eyes misted, and a faraway expression came over her face. "It wasn't a dream, Link Winsom. She was here. She's been here for weeks, waiting for you. I hope you know what a lucky man you are."

In his mind's eye, Link saw the image again—a vision in creamy white, with auburn hair and green eyes, calling him sweetheart, gripping his hand as if she would never let go.

"Libba," he murmured. "I thought I was dead. I thought she was an angel."

The nurse lifted one eyebrow. "She is an angel, if you ask me. Lib Coltrain has done more for the boys on these wards than all the medicine or surgery in the world. And you—hah! She's been coming every day since the first week of November, searching for you, waiting for you. You'd better be worth it."

Link let his head fall back onto the pillow. "She's been here all that time?" he breathed. The very idea amazed him. All those months in the hospital overseas, he had prayed, of course, had asked for direction. He had even, on a few occasions, begged for a miracle. But when he had sent letter after letter with no response, he had finally given up. If Libba didn't want him, he'd go back to Missouri, to his father and family, and try to build a life without her.

Almost immediately, the orders had come transferring him to Memphis, to Kennedy General. Close to Libba. To the memories. To the pain. And after considerable soul-searching, he had determined that maybe God was giving him a chance—if not to reconcile their relationship, at least to resolve it, to see her face-to-face and say good-bye with dignity.

This was more, much more, than he had dreamed of. She must still feel something for him. The nurse said she had been here since the first of November . . . that would have been just after his telegram. Apparently she had come right away, searching for him, waiting through the long weeks of his ordeal in Baltimore. That had to mean she cared for him in some way. Was it pity? Obligation? Or something deeper?

She had called him *sweetheart.* . . .

Link accepted a forkful of scrambled eggs and looked up at the nurse. "Is she here?" he asked, frantically casting his eyes around the ward. "Did she come back?"

"Keep your shirt on, sonny," Nurse Pincheon snapped. "Finish your breakfast."

Link grabbed the woman's hand. "I have to know. Does she—" he felt a flush creep up his neck—"does she . . . still love me?"

The nurse's eyes fixed intently on his face, then drifted upward, toward the doors that led into the ward. "Why don't you ask her for yourself?"

Link turned his head. There, in the doorway, stood Libba Coltrain. Her auburn hair fanned across the shoulders of her coat; her green eyes glistened in the morning light.

And she was smiling. At him.

★   ★   ★

Link gazed in wonder at Libba as she leaned down over him and smoothed the blanket around his shoulders. He hadn't let go of her hand for more than a minute during the past two hours, and when she withdrew it to make him a little more comfortable, he felt as if he were dying a small death.

The pain in his back was like fire, but it was nothing compared to the fire in his heart. He waved away the painkillers offered to him. He didn't want to risk losing a single minute with the woman he loved . . . not even to get relief from the suffering.

She had explained to him how her father had intercepted his letters and kept them from her. Not until the day her father died did she know that Link was alive—alive, and still in love with her. According to Libba, God had surrounded her with friends who supported her and kept her going. Even Freddy Sturgis, whom Robinson Coltrain so despised, had become a significant person in Libba's life and the development of her faith.

Then, reluctantly, she had related the story of how she had almost married Freddy after all, and how God had used Freddy's proposal to help her realize that she was strong enough to live on her own, without anyone to take care of her.

Through her story ran the same theme that had marked his own life in the past year—experiences of trial, of struggle, of growth and loss, of a developing faith that had enabled them both to survive. As she talked, Link found himself offering up silent prayers of gratitude that God had protected her, had kept her safe, had brought him back to her in one piece.

Except that he wasn't in one piece—not really. He had survived the surgery, and the shrapnel that could have ended his life had been removed.

But he still didn't know whether he would ever walk again. And until he knew, he couldn't make any decisions that would affect their future and their life together.

★ ★ ★

Eight months. Libba could hardly believe it had been that long since she had seen him. Now that Link was here with her, the agony of waiting was over, and the memory of the pain faded into the background.

With a sense of wonder, she stroked his thick brown hair and looked into his dark eyes—eyes deep enough to drown in, she had once thought. By a series of events she could only call miracles, God had given him back to her, and she would spend the rest of her life giving thanks for that gift.

He was terribly thin, of course, and obviously in pain. But his eyes, when he looked at her, were full of love, and her heart soared at his touch.

This was what she had waited for . . . what God had saved her for. Link was home—home with her, home in her arms. If she had anything to do with it, they would never be separated again.

Still, something was bothering him—something he wasn't admitting. A shadow crossed his face when she told him about Hans and Stevie and other boys on the wards, about how she had learned from them what was really important in life. Surely he wasn't jealous of her friendship with these broken young men? She would bring Stevie and Hans—and Marlene—to meet him, and then he'd understand.

Libba looked at the clock on the wall. She had been here nearly three hours, and Link was looking increasingly tired. He needed to rest, to heal. One of the nurses had finally convinced him to take medication for the pain, and his eyelids were beginning to droop.

She stood up and leaned over to kiss him. "You need to get some rest, sweetheart," she murmured. "Go on to sleep. I'll be back later."

"Don't . . . leave." He clung to her, his words slurring with drugs and exhaustion.

Libba smiled and squeezed his hand. "I'll be back, darling. Soon—I promise. Now, go to sleep." She withdrew her fingers from his grasp, and by the time she had gathered up her purse and gloves, he was snoring softly.

★ ★ ★

He was on the beach—Omaha Beach, he thought. The sand was littered with shell casings and debris, with hulks of burned-out jeeps and charred trucks, with abandoned equipment and personal effects of soldiers who had moved on . . . or been transported, without warning, to another life.

The toe of his boot caught on something buried in the sand, and instinctively he covered his head and threw himself facedown into a shallow foxhole. But nothing happened. No explosion. Just silence, and the continuous rhythmic sounds of waves lapping onto the shore.

He dragged himself from the foxhole and dug at the sand with his foot. It was a Bible—a small New Testament, soggy with seawater and encrusted with mud. Or was it blood? Had some poor GI been reading, searching desperately to make his peace with God, even as the Krauts rained mortar fire down on him?

Link held the tiny book in his hands, and its pages fell open. A small dried rosebud, pressed flat, marked the place. "I am the resurrection, and the life. . . . He that believeth in me, though he were dead, yet shall he live: And whosoever liveth and believeth in me shall never die. . . ."

The dead soldier's legacy of a small Bible had given him hope. The words had brought him to faith in God. . . .

With a start Link jerked awake. Why had he dreamed about finding the dead soldier's Bible and the dried rosebud that marked Christ's words about resurrection and life? With agonizing slowness, he groped on the table beside his bed and found it, just where he had left it. He held the pocket-sized Testament in his hands, stroking the worn leather, tracing with one finger the faded lettering on the front cover. He let the pages fall open, lifted out the rose, and twirled it between his thumb and forefinger.

How long ago it seemed, that day he had unearthed the Testament on that beach back in Normandy, coming face-to-face with his own need to believe. So much had happened since then. Losing Owen Slaughter in the raid on that French château filled with German ammunition. Lying in a mine crater with Randy Coker as the boy's life ebbed away. Feeling the flame shoot through his legs and back as the Kraut patrol opened fire on the road.

Through it all, these verses from the dead soldier's Bible had stayed with him, echoing in his mind and heart. The God he had started to believe in that day on Omaha Beach had not let him down—had, in fact, brought him home, back to the woman he loved. Link had overcome so many obstacles along the way. But this last hurdle seemed the most impossible of all.

Yes, he was alive, snatched back into this world—more than once—by the God who specialized in raising the dead. And while the Lord had been working in his life, God had apparently been active in Libba's as well—bringing her to a depth of faith that had sustained her through months of emotional agony and uncertainty. Now they were together again, and that was its own kind of resurrection. For all this, he would ever be grateful.

But Libba obviously expected them to pick up where they left off—to plan a future together. A wedding. Children. A life.

He wanted that too, but how could he ask a healthy, vital, loving woman like Libba Coltrain to marry him when he didn't know whether or not he would ever walk again? She would be saddled with an invalid. When he thought about life with her, he imagined being on his feet, providing for his family, playing baseball in the backyard with his children. He could not imagine having Libba push him everywhere he wanted to go or taking his babies for wheelchair rides.

Link closed the Bible and slid it under his pillow. It was simply too much to ask. Perhaps he should let her down easy, make his peace with her, and let her go on to a normal life . . . to a normal man. Maybe he should—

"Link Winsom, right?"

Link looked up to see a tall, blond Viking with broad shoulders and startling blue eyes smiling down at him. Awkwardly the man shifted his right crutch up under his arm and offered his hand, then sank into the chair next to the bed with both legs stiffly out in front of him.

"I'm Hans Amundson," the Viking said amiably. "Libba told me you had finally arrived."

Link's mind scrambled. Hans . . . ah, yes, the soldier who got sent to Memphis because some illiterate clerk couldn't tell the difference between Minnesota and Mississippi.

Hans grinned and thumped on one leg with his knuckles. The gesture made a *thunking* sound, like a knock on a solid oak door. "Just got my new legs," he said proudly. "I'm having a little trouble getting used to them, but I'm coming along. Marlene says I'll be chasing her all over the ward before too long." The young man blushed and shrugged his shoulders. "She doesn't run too fast, though."

"Marlene?" Link repeated.

"Nurse Marlene Henley. Actually, she's both my nurse and my fiancée." Hans beamed. "We're getting married as soon as my discharge comes through."

For an instant Link wondered if God—or Libba—had set him up. Here was a man who had lost both his legs, yet he seemed comfortable with himself and apparently anticipated the joys of married life. Was somebody trying to tell him something?

But no, it couldn't be. Link had nothing in common with this Minnesota farm boy. Nothing at all.

"How did it happen?" Link asked, taking refuge in the kind of small talk common to recuperating soldiers.

"German mortar shell," Hans answered matter-of-factly. "On Omaha Beach, a couple of days after D day. Only saw one day of action and—*boom*—I end up like this."

Link raised his head and looked intently into the blue eyes. "You were at Normandy?"

"Wasn't everybody?" The Viking's eyes flared. "Seemed like it. Thousands and thousands of us, swarming the beaches. You wouldn't think the army had troops anywhere else."

"I was at Omaha too," Link said quietly. "A couple of weeks later. Lost one of my best friends in an ammo raid. Watched a kid—just a boy—bleed to death in a mine crater. It was horrible."

"I was lucky," Hans said firmly. "Only it wasn't luck, not really."

Link narrowed his eyes. "What was it?"

The young man ducked his head and gave a sheepish grin. "I don't want to sound like some kind of fanatic," he began, "but I think God protected me."

"What makes you think that?" Link said, more sharply than he had intended. "You lost your legs."

"Yeah, but I'm alive. Besides—this is going to sound crazy—the night before we took the beach, I was on board ship, reading. You know those little New Testaments the army issues?"

Link nodded, feeling his stomach beginning to quiver.

"I read in there—in John, I think—about Christ raising that fellow Lazarus from the dead. We're all Lutherans back home, and I hadn't really heard people talk about the Bible as if it's supposed to mean much to individual people's situations. But that night I read these words—I'll never forget them: 'He that believeth in me, though he were dead, yet shall he live.' And right there on that ship, I felt like God was saying that was going to happen to me: that I was going to be dead—or at least should have been dead—and would be brought back to life again."

"And it happened," Link whispered. It wasn't a question.

"It happened twice, actually. Once with my legs—" Hans thumped his wooden leg again—"and once in here." He prodded a forefinger at his heart.

Link nodded at him to continue, and Hans took a deep breath. "I guess Libba told you I got sent here by mistake—or at least I thought it was a mistake. When my girl back home found out about my amputations and dumped me, I kind of went dead inside. But I came back to life again, just like the words in the Bible said—and partly because of your Libba."

"Libba?" Link swallowed. "What did Libba have to do with it?"

"She accepted me like I was—no legs, no heart, no hope. She helped me see that a person's worth doesn't depend upon having two good legs, but on having one good soul." He looked at Link with an expression that shook him to the core. "Take it from me, buddy, not many women have what it takes to accept this—" He waved a hand at his artificial limbs. "Libba saw beyond all that. She's a strong woman, Link, a wonderful woman. You're a fortunate man."

"Yes," Link breathed. "I'm beginning to see how fortunate."

Hans struggled to his feet and propped his crutches under him. "I wish I still had that New Testament," he said wistfully. "I put a rosebud in it—one I carried in my pack, from the girl who dumped me—to mark that place, those words about resurrection." He smiled. "I don't care about the rose anymore, but I'd have kept that Bible forever."

Link's heart hammered in his chest, and his mind spun. "You—you lost it?" he choked out.

"Yeah. When I was hit, I guess. Probably got washed out to sea."

Link took a deep breath and reached under his pillow, his hand closing over the battered Testament. He extended it toward Hans, and his fingers trembled. "It didn't get washed away," he said hoarsely. "It saved me, too." He paused. "The rosebud's still there, marking the place."

A look of utter disbelief swept across Hans Amundson's face, and he sank back down into the chair. Shakily he took the Testament from Link and opened it, fingering the pages lovingly. His eyes misted over. "I—I don't understand."

"It was no accident, no mistake," Link said through his own tears. "It was a miracle."

And quietly, overcome by his own sense of wonder, Link told him the story that bound them together forever as brothers.

17

★ ★ ★

Home Where We Belong

In the living room of the tiny apartment behind the Paradise Garden Cafe, Stork Simpson sat on the couch with his son on his knee and his wife cuddled up to his side. Thelma was taking the dinner shift, and Stork was enjoying the time alone with his little family.

"He's getting a lot of hair, isn't he?" Stork tousled the blond head playfully, and Mickey responded with a giggle.

"Uh-huh," Madge answered. "He's almost nine months old." She sat up and took the baby's hand in her own, stroking it tenderly. "Nine months—can you imagine? The time has gone so quickly. When I was carrying him, when you were gone, nine months seemed like an eternity." She gave Stork a look that melted his heart. "He looks like you."

"Boy, I hope not," Stork said, holding Mickey at arm's length and surveying him critically. "He's got my coloring, but that's all. He has your features, and your beautiful smile." He settled the child back in his lap and leaned over to kiss Madge. "I'd hate to think I brought another Stork into the world."

Madge pulled away a little. "Michael, I wish you wouldn't use that name. Every time I hear it, I'm reminded. . . ." She let the sentence hang unfinished between them.

"It's just a nickname, honey. Because I'm so tall and thin. It doesn't mean anything—not anymore. Nobody even thinks about the name being related to—" He paused, feeling awkward. "To the circumstances of Mickey's conception."

Stork tried to keep his voice light and his tone casual, but the truth was, at least one person did think about it—all the time. Stork himself. He loved his wife and adored his son, but sometimes when he looked at them, a wrenching in his gut reminded him that because of his own selfish desires, he had done something terrible, something for which he could never be forgiven. He had let his passion overcome his good sense and had caused Madge no end of pain. He had coerced her into making love with him, and in the process had created Mickey. He had shamed her. Their hurry-up wedding and present respectability could never make up for what he had taken from her.

The guilt plagued him, haunted him like a specter. He had gone to the front, been wounded, and returned to a loving wife and a beautiful baby. Others, like Link Winsom and Owen Slaughter—much better, nobler men than he was—had not been so lucky. Somehow he had escaped the judgment he deserved. But his reprieve gave him no peace.

It wasn't that Stork was unhappy—quite the opposite, in fact. Most days, the awareness of his good fortune nearly overwhelmed him with gratitude. When he came home from duty on the base, his heart swelled with anticipation of seeing his wife and son. He had no greater joy than spending time with them. He loved those times when Madge was working in the cafe and he had Mickey all to himself. And he looked forward to quiet hours with Madge, walking down by the river or taking Mickey to play in the sandbox at the elementary school. He was unbelievably happy.

Happier than he deserved to be.

Whenever Stork thought about how wonderful his life was, an insidious cloud of doubt crept in to hide the sun. His mother had warned him—more than once—that judgment was just around the corner. Their sin—in his mother's eyes, *Madge's* sin—would not go unpunished. The other shoe was bound to drop sooner or later. Some kind of punishment was inevitable. Sometimes he just wished he could go ahead and get it over with.

Thelma Breckinridge had talked to him about it once, privately, while Madge was in the apartment nursing Mickey. She told him that what had happened eighteen months ago was water under the bridge . . . or over the dam, he couldn't remember which. She said that God looks at the heart and that Mickey was no mistake, no matter what the circumstances of his conception. She talked about forgiveness and love and grace—and the need to put the past behind him and rejoice in his blessings.

Stork liked Thelma a lot, and he respected her relationship with God. And she had been so good to his family—a mother figure to Madge, a grandmother to Mickey. He tried to listen to what she said and heed her advice, but how could Thelma understand? The only sin she probably had to deal with was gossiping about somebody or having unkind thoughts. She couldn't possibly comprehend the depth of his guilt, the need to exonerate himself with some kind of penance.

Thelma meant well, of course, but Stork came away from their little discussion feeling more alone than ever. He had read in the Bible about David, whose sin with Bathsheba was punished by the death of his firstborn. The story terrified him, but he kept it to himself. He couldn't talk to anybody about this—not even Madge. This was his burden to bear, and he would bear it until he could figure out what to do to absolve himself. He just hoped that when the judgment came it fell on him, rather than on his wife or his innocent son.

He was determined, of course, to do right by Madge and Mickey—not out of obligation, but because he truly loved them. He had already bought a life-insurance policy that would take care of them if anything ever happened to him. He would be a devoted husband, an attentive father. He would provide for them, give them the best life he could possibly manage.

Starting now.

Stork turned to Madge. "I have a surprise for you."

"A surprise? How sweet, Michael. What is it?"

He grinned. "I'm not telling. That's why it's called a surprise."

She raised one eyebrow. "Do I get it now or later?"

"In a little while." Stork looked at his watch. "In about twenty minutes, to be exact."

"Tell me what it is."

"No."

Madge turned a menacing look on him. "Are you going to tell me, Michael Simpson, or do I have to drag it out of you by force?"

"What can you do to me?" he baited.

"I can do . . . this!" She began to tickle him unmercifully, poking at his ribs until tears of laughter streamed down his face. Mickey squealed with delight, and Madge tickled him, too.

At last Stork regained his composure, gasping for breath. "All right, all right, you win. Get Mickey's coat, and your own. We're going for a walk." He leaned over and kissed her, and she clung to him, sending a fire shooting through his veins. "Unless you want to postpone the surprise for a little while," he added huskily.

Madge drew back and looked at him, the smoldering passion in her eyes matching his own. "I do not," she said deliberately, then smiled. "Well, actually I do, but I won't. The surprise, Michael—come on, tell me!"

"This isn't a telling surprise," he answered mysteriously. "This is a showing surprise."

★ ★ ★

Madge watched her husband out of the corner of her eye as they walked through the crisp night air. Michael hoisted Mickey onto his shoulders and carried him piggyback down the sidewalk, past the schoolyard, and onto a tree-lined street. Above them, between the bare branches, stars glittered like diamonds against an inky black sky. The moon seemed close enough to touch. Madge held back a little, walking slightly behind them, savoring the quiet peacefulness of the little town she had grown to love.

"We're here, sweetheart." Michael's voice in her ear drew her out of her contented reverie.

"We're where?"

He put his arm around her and drew her close, then inclined his head. "We're home. Maybe. If you like it."

Madge's eyes followed his gaze. A narrow stone walkway led up to a neat little white cottage, its front door and shutters painted blue. A waist-high picket fence partially enclosed the yard, and to one side, toward the back, she could see a huge pecan tree with a tire swing drifting gently in the night breeze.

Her heart pounded in her chest as his words sank in. But she couldn't let herself hope, not until she was sure. "What do you mean, home?" The words came out hoarse and unsteady.

He shifted Mickey from his shoulders to one arm, then took her hand. "I mean," he said in a strangled voice, "that it's ours. Our home. Yours and mine and Mickey's. If you approve, that is." His eyes searched hers. "What do you think?"

She threw her arms around his neck, squeezing the baby between them. "I think you're the most wonderful man in the whole world, Michael Simpson." Tears lodged in her throat, and for a minute she couldn't speak. "When can we see it?"

Michael extricated himself from her embrace and fished in his jacket pocket. After a moment he triumphantly held up a key and grinned like a mischievous schoolboy. "Right now, of course. Unless you want to wait until tomorrow. . . ."

"Wait?" Madge laughed through her tears and closed her fingers around the key. "I don't want to wait another minute." She ran down the walk with Michael and Mickey in tow. "How did you find it?" she asked over her shoulder. "Tell me everything."

"It belonged to old Miss Ivy Stennis, who's lived in Eden since the Ice Age. Apparently she just got too far gone to live by herself any longer." He tapped a forefinger against his skull. "Senile, I guess. Anyway, after she got the idea she was still a teacher at the school and showed up in the first-grade class in her nightgown, something had to be done. Some relatives from Sardis took her up there to live with them and left their lawyer to dispose of the house." He gave her a conspiratorial look. "This information came from Charity Grevis at the post office."

"Of course. Who else?" Madge giggled. "So Charity passed on the word to you. What's her concern in all of this?"

"Some 'floozy divorcée from Jackson'—her words, not mine—apparently had her eye on the place to buy it and turn it into a beauty shop. I got the impression Mrs. Grevis didn't approve of her."

"And she approves of us—a couple of Yankee so-and-so's from north of the Mason-Dixon line?"

Michael shrugged. "At least people here know us. Know what they're getting, so to speak. I suppose it's a case of the lesser of two evils."

"That's been my lifelong goal," Madge quipped. "To be the lesser evil. Well, I suppose—"

The rest of her sentence caught in her throat as she opened the front door and switched on the light. Miss Ivy might have been senile, but her house was perfection. Hardwood floors gleamed with a fresh coat of wax, and ivory Cape Cod curtains adorned the windows. The only indication that anyone had ever lived in the house were the few hooks on the walls where the old lady's pictures had hung.

The living room, though not large, was spacious enough, with a cozy fireplace at one end. Through an archway to the right was a small dining room with a built-in china cabinet of burnished cherry. Madge moved through the empty rooms methodically, trying to keep her rising anticipation under control. But she could just envision a blue hooked rug on the hardwood floor, a delicate rose pattern of china to go with the wallpaper in the dining room. There was one fairly large bedroom and two small ones, all with adequate closets, and off the hall a gleaming white-tile bathroom with a claw-foot tub.

The kitchen, much to her delight, had plenty of cabinet space, a nice gas range, a nearly new electric refrigerator, and even a bay-window alcove where a kitchen table could overlook the backyard. The back door from the kitchen opened onto a small stone patio and a private yard lined with trees.

Madge could contain her enthusiasm no longer. Moving into a house—a real home of their own—meant that, at least for now, they would be staying in Eden. "Oh, Michael, it's—it's perfect!" She clutched his arm. "How much is the rent? Can we afford it?"

He shook his head, and his eyes sparkled. "No, honey. We can't afford to rent it." Madge's spirits began to sink, but before she could say anything, he went on. "We can only afford to buy it."

He was smiling at her with so much love and pride that she thought her heart might burst. "Really? You mean it, Michael?"

He set Mickey down on the floor and took her into his arms. "I've been thinking," he murmured against her hair, "that Eden would be a wonderful place to raise our son. It's a good family town. A peaceful place."

"So, when you're discharged—?"

He squeezed her tighter. "We'll be staying right here. Where we belong."

18

★ ★ ★

Invasion on the Home Front

December 18, 1944

Stork awoke slowly, with a peaceful kind of drowsiness that made him smile. It was his day off. Madge had taken Mickey with her to the cafe and left him to sleep a while longer, and the enticing scent of the coffee she had made for him wafted into the small bedroom. He pulled the covers up around his shoulders and sank back into the warmth of the bed, utterly content.

For a minute or two, at least.

Then he began to rouse a bit more, and the old familiar premonition of foreboding crept into his consciousness. His ancient Irish grandmother, a confirmed pessimist, always said, "If things are going too well, watch out." The warning must have taken root years ago, lodged in some remote corner of his mind. In recent days it had come back to haunt him, coupled with that pervasive sense of impending judgment he could not shake. He was happy, and it made him very nervous.

Madge was delighted with the house they were buying, of course. Their savings from his combat pay, combined with the more-than-generous salary Thelma paid Madge—without ever taking a dime for rent on their share of the apartment—enabled them to put a large down payment on the house, buy furniture, and still have some savings put away for a rainy day. Later today, in fact, when Madge got off work, they planned to drive into Grenada and pick out a couch, bedroom furniture for their room, and a new crib for the baby. They should be moved and settled in time to celebrate Mickey's first New Year's Eve in their own home.

Stork got up and went to the kitchen to pour himself a cup of coffee. On the counter he found a note: *Biscuits still warm in the oven. Come over when you're dressed. I love you.*

He fingered the note and smiled. He had expected to make his own breakfast or go into the cafe for a plate of eggs. But Madge was so thoughtful, so considerate of him, always surprising him with little gestures like this.

He took out the biscuits and sat down at the table with his coffee. The newspaper, the Memphis *Commercial Appeal,* was folded neatly at his place. He flipped it over and shoved it aside. No war news this morning. He didn't want anything to spoil this day.

He buttered a biscuit and spread on a generous layer of Thelma's homemade peach preserves. But as he took the first bite, his eye caught the headline of a small personal-interest article at the bottom of page 1: *MISSISSIPPI GIRL BRINGS HOPE TO SOLDIERS.*

Stork pulled the paper closer and squinted at the grainy picture. The caption read, *Elizabeth Coltrain with PFC Steve Sutton.* It was Libba, all right, standing next to the bedside of a young soldier with a terribly scarred face, holding his hand and smiling. He scanned the article.

> Elizabeth Coltrain, a former schoolteacher from Eden, Mississippi, is doing her part for the war effort in a most unusual way. Entirely on her own initiative, Miss Coltrain has spent the better part of two months on the wards of Kennedy General Hospital, bringing hope and encouragement to the brave men who have been wounded in our fight for freedom. . . .

Amazed, Stork went on to read how Libba had come to the hospital every day and spent time with the wounded men. In glowing testimonies, the soldiers who were interviewed told how Libba had literally "saved their lives," giving them a reason to hope. "She is the light of this ward," one soldier named Amundson said. "Because of her, we've got a future. We're going on with our lives."

The quotes from Libba were uncharacteristically self-effacing—at least for the old Libba Stork knew. She spoke of how she had learned more than she had taught, received more than she had given—how her own life had been enriched by knowing these men and spending time with them.

Intrigued, Stork turned to the back of the paper for the completion of the article and read:

> And Miss Coltrain has discovered that kindness does not go unre- warded. After months of separation, she has been reunited with her

own fiancé, Second Lieutenant Lincoln Winsom, in the very hospital ward where she has done so much good for others. Her compassion and generosity are an example to us all.

Stork smiled at the last paragraph. Link was going to be all right. He just knew it. He grabbed the paper and headed for the bedroom, tearing off his pajama shirt as he went. Madge would be so thrilled to see this—everyone would.

This was going to be a Christmas they would never forget.

★ ★ ★

Madge was clearing dishes and wiping down the tables by the window when the bell over the door jingled. She looked around. Thelma was nowhere in sight, and Mickey was safely captured on Ivory Brownlee's lap, happily banging at the keys as Ivory played a Glenn Miller tune. She squinted toward the front of the cafe. Morning sunlight was pouring in, making a dark silhouette of the figure standing in the doorway. But it was plainly a woman. A short, square woman with her feet planted in an attitude of hostility.

A familiar figure, almost like . . .

No, it couldn't be. Not after all these months of relative peace and contentment.

The woman let the door shut behind her and took three deliberate strides into the center of the room. As she moved out of the sunlight, her face came into focus, and Madge braced her hands on the table. Mother Simpson.

"I don't suppose I should expect the courtesy of a greeting," the woman said, her eyes glinting challenge.

Madge sighed. "Forgive me, Mother Simpson," she responded meekly. "I was just, well . . . I never expected to see you here." She moved forward and placed a perfunctory kiss on her mother-in-law's cheek. "This is such a surprise." Despite her best attempt to infuse her voice with a pleasant tone, panic constricted her throat, and the words came out as a high-pitched squeak.

"I'm sure it is," the woman said, lifting one eyebrow. "No doubt you thought you were rid of me forever."

"I thought no such thing!" Madge flared, then fought to control herself. "I . . . I just didn't think you would—"

"Track you down?" A sneer crept over Lorna Simpson's pale, flabby face, and her beady eyes narrowed. "Do you think I have no right to see my son and his child?"

His child. The emphasis, obviously for her benefit, did not escape Madge. Her eyes darted to Mickey, still pounding away at the piano, and a sudden rush of protectiveness swept over her, like the rage of a mother wolf guarding her cub.

Mother Simpson's eyes followed the direction of her gaze, lighting on the child. An expression of utter distaste came over her countenance when she caught sight of Ivory. "That's him, I presume. Can't you make him stop that terrible racket? My head is already pounding."

Madge went to the piano and lifted Mickey from Ivory's lap. The boy squealed and wriggled in her arms, reaching down toward the keyboard insistently. "Not now, sweetheart," Madge soothed. "You can play some more later." She carried him over to Lorna Simpson, still standing in the center of the room. "Your grandson, Michael James Simpson," she said, feeling suddenly as if she were offering up her firstborn in sacrifice to Baal. It was a wild, unreasonable thought, and yet she held forth the child reluctantly. "He's certainly grown since the last time you saw him, hasn't he?"

Mickey, accustomed to winning over strangers with a single smile, giggled and reached out his chubby arms. But his wiles didn't work on his grandmother. The woman took a step back, as if he were a snake about to strike. "Michael James," she murmured. "I had forgotten. At least you had the gratitude to give him my maiden name."

Madge's mind raced. She hadn't recalled that Lorna Simpson's maiden name was James. In Michael's absence, she had chosen Link Winsom's first name as a middle name for their child. The idea had pleased Michael to no end. Neither of them had ever once entertained the thought of bringing Michael's intractable mother into the picture.

An involuntary shudder ran through Madge. Should she tell the woman the truth? No, let her think that if she wanted to. Maybe it would make a difference in her attitude.

It didn't. As Madge stood there holding Mickey out to his grandmother, she watched a variety of emotions parade across the woman's face. Disgust, followed by critical scrutiny, then a cool aloofness. No trace of softening, no response to the child at all. Here was a woman who, truly, had no maternal instincts.

"Aren't you going to offer me a seat?" she said abruptly, looking around with disdain at the shabby furnishings of the Paradise Garden Cafe.

"Of course—forgive me." Madge shifted Mickey to her hip and scurried to clear away the dishes. When she turned back, Lorna Simpson had fished a white linen handkerchief out of her purse and was carefully wiping off the seat of one of the chairs. She sat down primly, settling her bulk on the chair with a small grunt and holding her purse in both hands. Her eyes darted this way and that, as if debating whether it was safe to touch anything.

"Would you like coffee?" Madge asked, hating the solicitous tone in her own voice.

"That would be acceptable. If it's fresh, of course." She placed her bag on the table in front of her.

"If you'll just watch Mickey for a minute." Before her mother-in-law could protest, Madge plunked the baby down in her lap and headed for the kitchen.

As Madge raced through the door into the kitchen, Thelma stuck her head out of the storage room. "Where's the fire, hon? If you're not busy, I sure could use help with this inventory—"

Madge had never seen a more welcome sight than the beautiful craggy face of Thelma Breckinridge. She grabbed the inventory notebook out of Thelma's hands, threw her arms around her neck, and held on tight.

"What's wrong, honey?" Thelma pried her arms loose and stepped back to look at her face. "You look like you've seen a ghost."

"More like a witch," Madge gasped. "Pray for me, Thelma. My mother-in-law just showed up."

"Uh-oh." Thelma squeezed her hand. "It'll be all right, hon."

"You didn't see the look on her face."

"She's wearing war paint?"

"Just about. I'm going back with coffee. Give me five minutes, and then come rescue me."

Thelma nodded, and Madge rushed out the door with a plate of fresh doughnuts. With shaking hands she carried a tray to the table, poured coffee, and set the doughnuts out, all the time avoiding Mother Simpson's gaze. At last, when she had run out of evasive maneuvers, she sat down opposite her mother-in-law and pasted on a smile.

"How's the coffee, Mother Simpson?" she babbled, hiding behind small talk. "Do have a doughnut—Thelma made them this morning."

"You know I never eat sweets," the woman answered curtly. "Or you would know, if you had ever paid attention all the months you lived under my roof."

Madge's head snapped up. Lorna Simpson was still holding Mickey, stiffly, at arm's length, with the child perched on the edge of her meaty thighs. Mickey looked distinctly uncomfortable.

Suddenly the woman jerked him up and looked down at her lap. An oval stain was spreading across the fabric of her dress. Gingerly, as if disposing of some dead prey the cat had dragged in, she handed him across the table.

She said not a word, but her expression clearly communicated her opinion that if Madge had really been a good mother, her nine-month-old child would have been better disciplined than to soak his diaper without warning.

Madge opened her mouth to apologize; then suddenly her she-wolf instincts kicked in. Without a word she snatched Mickey up, carried him back to the kitchen, and gave him to Thelma, then stalked back to the table. "His Gramma Thelma is changing him," she said with emphasis. "She'll bring him back out in a few minutes. She's really been looking forward to meeting you."

"Someone else changes his diapers?" Mother Simpson craned her neck and looked over her shoulder to the kitchen door, where Thelma stood holding Mickey, tickling him, making him laugh. Her right eye twitched. "It figures."

Madge felt her temper begin to rise. "What figures, Mother Simpson?

"That you would abdicate the care of him to that—that hussy. And—" she waved a hand in the direction of the piano, where Ivory was still playing softly—"that derelict."

Something in Madge snapped. She had groveled too long, and she was going to put an end to it, here and now. "Thelma Breckinridge," she said in a low voice, "is the most loving, most caring, most godly woman on God's green earth. And she has been the only grandmother Mickey has ever known."

Lorna Simpson pursed her thin lips. "And whose fault is that? You're the one who disappeared, if you recall, without a word of gratitude or a by-your-leave. I had no idea where to find you."

The blatant lie galled Madge, and she met her mother-in-law's stare without wavering. "Dad Simpson knew where I was all the time. He even cared enough to send a letter now and then. Besides, where else would I be? I had no family except Michael, and even though he had shipped out, Eden seemed the logical place to come." She exhaled sharply. "And I see you had no trouble finding me now, did you? Or were you just on a scenic tour of the South and decided to stop in for breakfast?"

"Michael wrote to us when he got back," Mother Simpson said defensively. "I cannot understand for the life of me why he would choose this place instead of coming home—"

"This is his home," Madge interrupted. "With me and our son."

"So you may think," the woman answered in clipped tones. "But we'll see. Blood is thicker than water, you know. Family ties are stronger than some shotgun marriage." A malevolent look came into her eyes. "My son belongs with you about as much as the pope belongs in a brothel."

The vicious words cut deep, and in spite of her best intentions, Madge felt tears run down her cheeks. Blindly she groped for the table edge, seeking support, then shot to her feet and dashed toward the kitchen.

★ ★ ★

Stork came through the back door of the cafe just in time to see it all. He couldn't hear the words, but he recognized all too well the expression on his mother's face. Stunned, he stood rooted to the spot, watching through the service window with disbelief as his mother launched a volley of words at his wife. When Madge came through the door crying, he tried to put his arms around her. But she brushed past him, took Mickey from Thelma, and ran for the sanctuary of the tiny apartment.

For a minute or two Stork waited, clenching his fist around the newspaper he held in his hand. He took one last look at the back door, squared his shoulders, and marched forward to meet the dragon.

He had never seen such an instantaneous metamorphosis. As soon as he came through the swinging door into the cafe, his mother caught sight of him. Her expression changed to a look of magnanimous concern, and she rose and moved toward him like a benevolent monarch granting audience to the crown prince.

"Sweetheart!" she gushed. "Oh, Michael, it's so good to see you after all this time." She took his face in both hands and kissed him on the cheek. "Your father and I have been so worried about you."

"I wrote to you," he said guardedly. "I wrote all about our life here, and about Mickey. You never responded."

Tears filled her eyes, and she shook her head sadly. "I wrote, didn't I? You know I did. But I couldn't bring myself to approve of this—this situation. This whole horrible thing has taken so much out of me."

"What 'horrible thing'?" he challenged. "My marriage? My happiness? My beautiful son?"

"How can you speak to your mother like that?" Her shoulders slumped. "I've been so—" she paused and looked into his eyes—"I've been so afraid for you," she finished in a whisper.

"Mother, sit down." Stork took her arm and led her back to the table. "We need to talk."

Meekly she took a seat. "Yes, we do," she said quietly. "We do indeed."

"Look, Mother," he began with resolution. "I am very happy with my life here. Madge and I love each other. We're doing quite well."

"I'm sure you believe that's true," she answered, her eyes averted. "But you must believe me, Michael. Sooner or later, something is going to happen—something disastrous. Why don't you come home, Michael? You can build a new life there, away from all this. You can leave your past behind you—"

"Madge and Mickey are not 'my past,'" Stork interrupted. "They're my present, and my future."

"Present, perhaps," his mother said. "But future . . . who knows?"

"What do you mean by that?" Stork felt a churning in his stomach, a sense of impending doom. "What are you going to do?"

"I'm not going to *do* anything, sweetheart," his mother said soothingly. "You know I'd never do anything to hurt my only son." She smiled at him warmly. "But—well, you read my letters, didn't you? I didn't write all those things to hurt you, but to try to protect you from being hurt. This thing with that girl began badly, and it's bound to end up that way. You can't continue on a wrong road and expect to come out in the right place."

"And what do you define as the right place?"

"A place of respectability, of course. A life—a future—you don't have to be ashamed of."

"I'm not ashamed of Madge and Mickey," Stork protested.

"Of course not, dear. Did I say you were? But the fact remains, in a situation like this a person will eventually reap what she has sown. You were young, Michael—you didn't know what you were getting into. Anyone can make a mistake. But you're older now, and wiser. Surely you can see that continuing in this charade will only bring you heartbreak—or worse. I can't sit idly by and watch that happen."

"So you came here to torture my wife?"

His mother's face fell. "Torture? Oh, Michael, really. I came to see you, to try to talk some sense into you. I don't know what happened with that girl just now. We were conversing, and I was very calm and gracious, and suddenly she just got up and walked out on me. I won't hold it against her, of course, but she was very rude."

Suddenly it occurred to Stork that his mother had not said one word about her only grandson. "And what about Mickey?"

"Mickey?" She looked at him blankly.

"My son. Your grandson. Remember? He was here not five minutes ago."

Stork's mother brushed absently at the stain on her skirt. "Oh, yes. The child."

"Not *the* child, Mother. My child. *Our* child—mine and Madge's."

"The child of sin," she murmured.

Stork's heart pounded in his chest, and his throat clogged so that he could barely get his words out. "What do you mean by that, Mother?"

"I have tried to tell you gently, lovingly," she said, "but you would not hear. Now I must tell you directly, no matter how it might hurt me to do it. I have a responsibility—to you, and to your future." She raised her eyes and looked into his with an intensity that shook him to the core. "I have seen it," she whispered ominously. "God will not be mocked. Judgment is coming and will not be denied."

Within Stork's spirit, in the silence that stretched between them, the words tolled like a death knell.

19

★ ★ ★

Best Friends

December 20, 1944

"You can't be serious!" Libba stared at Link and felt a strange feeling wash over her—the sense that she had never seen this man before in her life. As if from a great distance she studied him. His broad, high forehead furrowed in a frown, and his dark eyes gleamed with intensity. The muscles in his square jaw, now set in an expression of determination, jumped as he clenched his teeth.

"Can't you understand?" he said slowly, emphasizing each word. "I've thought about it a lot. I don't know if I'll ever walk again, Libba, and until I know—well, I can't make any decisions about the future. In the meantime—" he lifted his shoulders in a resigned shrug—"I won't hold you to any promises about marrying me."

The cruel words stabbed at her soul. No, she couldn't understand. This wasn't like Link—not like him at all. Everything had been going so well. Link had developed a close friendship with Hans Amundson; the two men talked several times a day. Surely the example of Hans, who had accepted his limitations and was eagerly looking forward to getting married and setting up housekeeping with Marlene, should have had some impact on Link. The body cast was off; he was getting stronger. Even if he never walked, they could have a good life together. It just didn't make sense.

Maybe it was her fault. Maybe she had put too much stock in her hope that everything would work out, waiting for him, loving him. But she was a different person now than she had been when he shipped out. She could handle this—if he gave her half a chance. It wasn't fair.

Tears sprang to Libba's eyes, and she turned away for a moment. When she had regained her composure, she wheeled around and glared at him. "Can't *you* understand that it doesn't make any difference to me whether you walk or not? And since when are *you* the one who makes all the decisions about *our* future?" Her temper was beginning to rise, and Libba fought to remain calm. She didn't want to say something in the heat of the moment that she might regret later. "Tell me one thing, Link Winsom," she challenged. "Do you or do you not love me?"

A wild collage of expressions ran across his face—pain, fear, and finally, dismay. Then his countenance went blank. He closed his eyes and waited for a moment. At last he whispered, "I don't know," and turned his face to the wall.

Pain and panic surged within her into a monumental wave, knocking all her supports out from under her. Her knees went weak, and her breath came in shallow gasps. The tears would not be pushed back any longer. "All right, then," she choked out. "Have it your way."

Sobbing, she turned and fled the ward, pushing blindly past a soldier at the door. Just as she reached the doorway, she heard her name.

"Libba?"

She didn't turn around. She couldn't. She wouldn't give him the satisfaction. She had to get out—now, before she made a complete and utter fool of herself.

★   ★   ★

Link flung a hand over his eyes and leaned back against the pillow. He could hardly breathe, and his pulse pounded hard in his ears. His lie had hurt her, he knew, but what choice did he have? If he had told the truth, Libba wouldn't have let it go. She would have insisted on going forward, planning the wedding, committing themselves to a lifetime together.

And he couldn't do it.

He couldn't do it to her.

She was different than she had been when he left, that was certain. Stronger. More capable. A lot more compassionate. What she had done for the soldiers here was nothing short of a miracle. The *Commercial Appeal* had even run an article about her, praising her efforts with the wounded at Kennedy General. Hans and Stevie had told him things about Libba that he might never have known, and he was very proud of her.

But he also had a responsibility to protect her. To make sure she didn't do something stupid—like marrying a cripple—out of obligation. It might be fine for Hans and Marlene, but Marlene was a nurse, and she was trained to deal with such situations. Libba was—well, was Libba.

He didn't want to lead her on, to hurt her more in the long run. And so he had lied. He had told her he wasn't sure he loved her.

But he was sure. He was very sure. He loved her more than his own happiness. And because he loved her, he had to push her away.

Maybe, if things came out all right, if he did walk again, he could patch things up with her, explain it to her so she'd understand. If he ever got a second chance, that is.

"Link?"

His eyes still closed, Link waved a hand in dismissal. "Go away."

"Link, it's me."

"I said, go—" The voice registered, and Link's eyes snapped open. There at the foot of his bed stood Stork Simpson, flashing a crooked grin at him. Instinctively Link tried to sit up, but the bolt of fire that shot through his back reminded him of his recent surgery, and he sank back to the pillows in pain.

"Take it easy there, buddy," Stork said. "I don't think you're ready to be doing calisthenics. Of course, I doubt you'd care if you never saw another exercise drill in your life." He sobered and came around to the side of the bed. "What happened here, Link? I just saw Libba tear out of here crying. She brushed right past me and didn't even notice. You two have a fight?"

Link tried to put on a smile. "Last time I saw you, Stork, you were trying to interfere in my life. Haven't changed much, have you?"

Stork reached down and gave him a one-armed hug, then settled into the chair next to the bed.

"How did you get here?" Link asked. "How's Madge—and the baby? How are things at home—uh, I mean, in Eden? Is Madge still working at the cafe?"

"Hold it, hold it!" Stork protested, holding up his hands. "One at a time. The major loaned me his car, and Madge and I came up to look for furniture and . . . uh, get away for a while."

"Get away?"

Stork shrugged. "Mother showed up a couple of days ago. She's been . . . well, stirring up trouble, to say the least. I'll tell you about it later." He looked at his watch. "I don't have a lot of time—I left Madge and Mickey at the furniture store downtown. But once I knew you were here, I couldn't come to Memphis without seeing you."

"How did you know?"

"Libba's aunt Mag called. Then, like all the other peons in the world, I read the story in the newspaper. The article about Libba."

Link grimaced. "I should have contacted you directly, I know, but things have been so—"

"Yeah, I saw how things were, written all over Libba's face." Stork patted Link's arm. "It's OK, pal. Don't worry about it."

Link sighed and leaned back, looking into Stork's hawkish face. His presence brought back some painful memories, but it was a bittersweet pain. It felt good to be with his old friend again—his best friend, the one who had seen him through the best and worst times of his life.

"Tell me everything."

"Oh, no," Stork said. "You first. What happened with Libba?"

Link shook his head. A memory flashed through his mind, a discussion he and Stork once had at the army hospital in Birmingham, England, when Link was determined to let Libba think he was dead. If he recalled correctly, Stork had told him in no uncertain terms that he had no right to make decisions on Libba's behalf—that she deserved to be told the truth. The challenge Stork had issued had brought Link back to the States—and thus to Kennedy General—for his recovery, and to a reunion with the woman he loved. Now he had lied to Libba and left her with the impression that he didn't love her, and he was pretty sure Stork wouldn't approve.

"We—ah, we had a disagreement."

"About what?" Stork pressed.

"About marriage."

Stork grinned. "She's putting you off, is she? Smart girl."

"Not exactly," Link admitted. "She wants to get married, just like we planned."

"So what's the problem?"

Link took a deep breath. "I told her I couldn't make any decisions about the future until I knew whether I would be able to walk. I told her—" he paused—"that I wasn't sure I loved her."

Stork stared at him blankly.

"Stork? Buddy? Did you hear what I said?"

"I heard." Stork exhaled a heavy sigh. "Link Winsom, you have to be the stupidest man on the face of the earth."

Link felt his hackles rise. "What do you mean, stupid?"

"I mean stupid," Stork repeated. "Idiotic. Certifiably insane. Completely—"

"All right, all right!" Link stopped him. "I get your point."

"Why on earth would you say such a thing? You didn't mean it, did you—about not loving Libba?"

"Of course not."

"You lied to her? Good grief, Link. I've heard of fellows lying to a girl and telling her they loved her when they didn't, but I've never heard of a guy saying he didn't love a girl when he did."

"You wouldn't understand. It's kind of complicated."

"Oh, is it? It sounds pretty simple to me. You told Libba you didn't want to marry her, lied about not loving her, and sent her out of here in tears. What's not to understand?"

"This!" Link snapped, pointing to his useless legs. "You came back whole, Stork. You can carry your baby piggyback and make love to your wife. You can hold down a job and walk in the park with your family. I could well end up in one of those for the rest of my life—" he pointed across the ward to an empty wheelchair in the corner—"an invalid. Do you get it, Stork? A dependent invalid."

"So you're feeling sorry for yourself, and you took it out on Libba."

"I did not," Link answered, feeling defensive. "I did the right thing. I . . . I prayed about it." It wasn't the truth, and it sounded incredibly feeble when he said it, but he didn't take it back.

"And God told you to break Libba's heart? I don't think so."

Link sighed and leaned back. "I don't want to have this discussion."

"All right. We won't."

Link narrowed his eyes at his friend. "Really? I thought you'd fight me on this. You did once before."

Stork raised one eyebrow. "So you *do* remember. And do you remember what you concluded?"

"That I needed to tell Libba the truth and let her decide for herself whether or not she wanted to be with me," Link answered hesitantly.

"That's right." Stork paused and looked at Link intently. "Maybe you've already got your mind made up, but think about this. Madge and I were with Libba when she found out you were alive after all. We saw her reaction. And she wasn't worried in the least about whether or not you would walk again. She just thanked God you weren't dead. Maybe you should do the same."

"Maybe so," Link said, feeling utterly miserable. "I'll think about it."

★ ★ ★

When Aunt Mag entered the bedroom, Libba was storming around, flinging clothes into a suitcase, her emotions vacillating between raw pain and a finely honed fury.

"What's happened, child? What are you doing?"

"I'm going home," Libba snapped. "Where I belong."

Magnolia went over to the bed and began removing items from the suitcase. "They'll wrinkle less if you fold them, dear." She smoothed each one neatly and replaced it, bringing order to Libba's chaos. Just her presence in the room seemed to bring calm and comfort, and at last Libba quit packing and sat down on the bed.

"Can you tell me what happened?" Aunt Mag's deep voice was incredibly gentle and filled with compassion, and her words broke through the last of Libba's anger. She lay across the bed and began sobbing uncontrollably. For a while Aunt Mag just held her and let her cry, then finally drew her to a sitting position and handed her a tissue.

"I—I don't understand," Libba sniffed. "He—he said he couldn't make any decisions about the future until he knew if he was going to walk. He said—" The tears came again, and she drew in a shuddering breath. "He said he wasn't sure if he loved me."

Aunt Mag closed her eyes and pulled Libba against her shoulder. "Why is God doing this?" Libba mumbled against the fabric of the woman's dress. "I tried so hard. I faced my fears and learned so much. What did I do wrong?"

Mag pushed her back and looked into her eyes. "What makes you think," she asked deliberately, "that God is responsible for Link Wineom's stupidity? What makes you think you've done anything wrong?"

"Well," Libba stammered, "Link said he had prayed about it."

"I've heard that Hitler and his cohorts are claiming God's direction in the abominable things they're doing to innocent people in Germany, too," Mag snorted. "Just saying so doesn't make it true."

"I guess not," Libba conceded. "It makes me so mad, Aunt Mag! He's acting like he's the only one involved in this, like he has a right to make decisions for me, too. It's so—so—"

"Demeaning?" Mag supplied. "Condescending?"

"Yes," Libba whispered. "And it hurts."

"Is it possible he thinks he's doing the right thing?"

"It's possible, I suppose," Libba said reluctantly. "But when I asked if he loved me, he said he wasn't sure. That doesn't sound too promising." She sighed and resumed packing. "I feel so empty, Aunt Mag, so exhausted. I just want to go home."

Mag caught Libba's hand and turned her around. "Perhaps it *would* be best if you went home for a while, child. Your mother would love having you home, I know. And you need to spend Christmas with your family. But—"

She paused, and tears filled her pale green eyes. "It will be terribly lonely around here without you. I'll miss you."

Libba flung herself into her great-aunt's arms and held on. "I'll miss you too, Aunt Mag. I love you so much, and you've been such a help to me." A sudden thought struck her, and she smiled. "Come to Eden for Christmas, Aunt Mag, please! I know Mama would love it, and we've got plenty of room." She leaned back and looked into the dear, ancient face. "You need to spend Christmas with your family, too."

Aunt Mag reached up a hand and patted Libba's cheek gently. "All right, child, I'll come."

"That's wonderful! I'll help you pack, and we can take the bus together. It'll be a wonderful surprise."

But Aunt Mag shook her head. "You go on, child. Take the afternoon bus, and tell your mother I'll come along in a day or so. I have some business to attend to first."

The tone of her voice—secretive and not a little threatening—piqued Libba's curiosity. "What kind of business?"

"Personal business." Aunt Mag smiled. "About pinochle."

"Pinochle?"

"Just someone who needs a bit of coaching," she said mysteriously, "not to renege when he's holding a perfect hand."

20

★ ★ ★

Jesus in Our Mist

Paradise Garden Cafe

A haunting, dissonant tune drifted in through the service window of the Paradise Garden Cafe. Thelma stuck her head out of the kitchen to see Ivory Brownlee, his head down over the piano keys, deep in improvisation.

She went to him and touched his shoulder gently. "I've never heard you play the blues, Ivory. It's nice. Different, but nice."

He lifted his head and gave her a soulful look. "I spent me some time on Beale Street," he said quietly. "A tune like this, it gives a fellow a chance to 'spress what he's feeling. Lets the pain out, you know?"

Thelma sat down in a chair next to the piano. "Play some more," she urged. "And tell me what you're feeling."

His gnarled hands rippled across the keys. "This," he said, reaching for a minor bass chord, "is the uneasiness in my soul. This—" his right hand slammed down in a discordant clash—"this is the folks who want to take my land away." He played on for a moment, ending in a soul-wrenching arpeggio, and turned to face her. "I don't know what I'm gonna do, Thelma. It's almost Christmas. January's just around the corner, and I ain't no closer to having the tax money than I was at Thanksgiving." His thin shoulders lifted in a gesture of helplessness. "What's that expression? You can't squeeze blood outta a turnip? Well, this old turnip is dry, I'll tell you. All I got left is my daddy's house and land, and once that's gone—" He swallowed hard, the round knot of his Adam's apple quivering in his wrinkled neck.

Thelma patted his arm. "I know, Ivory. I've been praying about it, but I don't know what to do, either."

"I told ever'body that God's got ways. And I believe it, too. But maybe I just don't believe it enough. Maybe I just ain't got the faith it takes for a genuine miracle."

Thelma smiled and looked into his watery blue eyes. "I don't think God's miracles are dependent upon how much faith we have. A miracle is something completely unexpected, totally out of the ordinary—God making a way where we only see a dead end."

Ivory nodded. "That's prob'ly true. But I sure wish there was something we could do to help the miracle along a little."

"We can pray."

"I been praying, Thelma. It don't seem to be getting me nowhere."

"Then maybe we all need to be praying together."

Ivory's sagging face brightened. "You mean like, 'Where two or three are gathered, Jesus is in the mist of them'?"

When he said, "in the mist," Thelma smiled. That was exactly where they were—in the mist, with a fog around them they couldn't see through. "Yes, just like that," she murmured. "I'll tell you what, Ivory. Once every day, when the cafe is empty, you and I will get together and pray for that miracle. How does that sound?"

"That makes two," Ivory mused. "Sounds like enough for God." He paused. "There's just one thing—"

"What?"

"Well, it don't seem quite fitting that you should be praying for my troubles when I don't have anything to pray for on your account." He leaned forward intently. "You got anything you want us to pray about, Thelma?"

Tears sprang to Thelma's eyes. People who called Harlan Brownlee crazy had no idea what he was really like. He had endured the terrors of war, the disorientation of shell shock, the loss of his family's wealth. Yet he had come through it all as an uncomplicated, compassionate soul, a truly selfless person. Surely God must honor the faith of a man like Ivory, who had lived through all manner of suffering and yet believed with simple, childlike trust.

"Yes, Ivory, I do have something I want us to pray about. You know that Stork Simpson's mother is in town, staying over at Larkins' boarding-house?"

Ivory made a face. "Uh-huh, I seen her. She called me a—a derelict. I'm not too sure what that means, but I'm pretty sure it wasn't nice. And she didn't want me touching little Mickey." He stared down at his hands. "Is something wrong with me, Thelma?"

Thelma shook her head. "No, Ivory, nothing is wrong with you. But something is very wrong with her."

Ivory's head shot up. "Is she sick? Do we need to pray for her?"

"She's not sick—not in the way you mean. But yes, we do need to pray for her. And for Stork and Madge."

"They're not very happy about her being here, are they?" Ivory asked. "Madge is real nervous all the time, and Stork looks like he's playing the blues in his head. Even the baby seems cranky these days, and he's usually real cheerful."

"Mrs. Simpson doesn't think her son should be here with Madge and the baby," Thelma explained, searching for words that Ivory would understand. "She thinks Stork should leave them and go back to Missouri with her."

Ivory's eyes widened. "But they're married. They belong together. They love each other. And they're getting ready to move into that nice little house." He shook his head miserably. "I don't want him to leave, Thelma. He's nice to me. And Madge would be so sad."

"We'd all be sad, Ivory." Thelma choked back her own tears. "But it's pretty complicated. It has to do with something about Mickey—" She paused, trying to find a delicate way to explain Lorna Simpson's perception of the Simpson baby as a child of sin.

"You mean because he was born too early?" Ivory raised his eyebrows. "I know all about it. I know about sex and about how sometimes people make babies before they get married. I had shell shock, but I'm not stupid." He raised his chin defiantly.

"I know you're not stupid, Ivory," Thelma soothed. "It's just that—well, people don't talk about this kind of thing very openly. Mrs. Simpson believes that Mickey is bad, somehow, because he was conceived before Stork and Madge were married. She thinks Madge is to blame, and that something terrible is going to happen if her son doesn't leave them if he doesn't repent, in her words, and put his sin behind him."

"And people say I'm crazy," Ivory muttered. "I may not be too smart, but I'm smart enough to know that baby isn't evil. And neither is Madge. She's one of the kindest, sweetest ladies I ever met. And her little boy is an angel." He narrowed his eyes. "Seems to me like what Miz Simpson is doing don't have nothin' to do with God. Seems to me like she just wants to keep her boy in her clutches, where she can control him."

Thelma chuckled. "You missed your calling, Ivory. You should have been a psychiatrist."

"A head doctor?" He grinned. "I sure seen enough of them in my time, that's the truth. And most of it's just plain common sense."

"You're probably right. The problem is, Stork is pretty influenced by his mother. She's got him believing that some kind of judgment is going to fall on him—and on Madge and the baby—if he doesn't repent of his sin."

"Seems like she's holdin' on to sin a whole lot longer than Jesus would," Ivory declared firmly. "They made a mistake a long time ago, and it's been done and forgiven. It don't affect what they got now."

"Maybe not. But if Stork listens to his mother, it may mean the end of what they've got now."

"So what do we pray for?"

Thelma studied him. "What do you think we should pray for?"

Ivory thought about that for a minute, furrowing his brow. "I think," he declared at last, "we pray that ever'body in this mess will see the truth." He leaned forward, fixed his gaze on Thelma's face, and rested one hand on her arm. "And we pray you don't lose the little family you waited so long for."

Tears gathered in Thelma's throat, and she couldn't speak. So he did understand, after all, how much she loved them, how much they had come to mean to her. He could see, in his simple way, how all this turmoil was tearing at her soul.

"Thank you, Ivory," she finally managed, covering his hand with her own. "You're a good friend."

"You're a good friend too," he repeated solemnly. "We're two very good friends. And Jesus is in the mist of us."

21

⭐ ⭐ ⭐

A Gift of Hope

With a heavy heart, Libba set the table in the dining room with the good china and arranged a rose-colored linen napkin at each of the three place settings. This evening the task, usually a mindless, routine chore, brought back so many memories. Wistful memories, like the time Link sat here, next to her, and told her father that his intention was to marry Libba and make her the happiest woman on earth. Agonizing memories of all the arguments and confrontations that had taken place around this table.

But her father would not be sitting at this table tonight. Nor would Link Winsom.

Her father's absence brought only relief. But the thought of Link brought heartache, a painful stirring of the emotions she had felt when she left the hospital for the last time.

Mama had been wonderful, of course—now that she didn't have to defend Daddy for his irrational attitudes. She listened carefully as Libba told her what Link had said about not making any decisions, about not being sure he loved her. And Mama had concurred with Aunt Mag's advice—that all Libba could do was step back and wait, ask God for direction, and then go on in the way God showed her.

"I trust you, honey," her mother had said, and her tone of respect had amazed Libba. "You'll make the right decision."

Libba hadn't been home twenty-four hours before Freddy Sturgis had telephoned from Oxford, saying he had a Christmas present for her and wanted to come to Eden to see her. She was surprised at how pleased she felt to hear his voice, and suddenly she was overcome with an awareness of how much she had missed him—and Willie and Mabel Rae and Thelma—and everybody. Strange, that she'd have to come home before she felt the homesickness.

But then, she was alone now. Alone, and no longer caught up in the excitement of being with Link, of seeing the progress of the fellows on the wards, of hearing Hans and Marlene's wedding plans. All her reasons for getting up in the morning had been pulled out from under her, and she felt deflated, empty. All that was left now was the pain of Link's rejection.

"That looks very nice, dear," her mother's voice murmured in her ear. "What time will your young man be here?"

Libba turned and gave her mother a cynical smile. "He's not my young man, and you know it."

"Ah, but it did make you smile, didn't it?"

Libba chose to ignore the jibe. "Freddy said he'd be here at six-thirty. What time is it?"

"Almost that now. Iris has fixed an absolutely beautiful baked hen with stuffing."

"Sounds wonderful." Libba turned her head toward the kitchen. "And it smells pretty good too."

"Iris has been a lifesaver. Since your father died and she moved into the back bedroom, she has not only been a big help around the house, but she's been good company, too. I couldn't have done everything—getting the business squared away with Richard and all—if she hadn't been here to help."

Libba put an arm around her mother's shoulders. "I don't know if I've said this to you directly, Mama, but I want you to know how proud I am of you. Taking over the store like that. Everyone just expected you to sell it, you know."

"Well, I still don't know much about pipe fittings and electrical circuits, but Richard, your daddy's old assistant, takes care of the sales and ordering. You have to remember, Libba, that I helped your father build that business from the ground up. I kept the books, paid the bills, and maintained order in the office. It was only after you were born that your daddy decided not to let me work anymore." She grimaced. "Not *let* me. Funny how that idea grates on my nerves now. I'm not sure how it happened, really—abdicating control of my life to him. Little by little, I just found myself taken over. And then it seemed easier to keep the peace, not to protest."

"I know, Mama." Libba squeezed her shoulder. She didn't want to talk about her father, to resurrect the old pain. "It's all water under the bridge now. Can we let it rest?"

"Of course, honey. I'm sorry I brought it up. We'll just have a nice dinner, and then I'll leave you and Freddy to yourselves so you can catch up. He is a sweet boy, isn't he?"

Libba smiled. "He's a very sweet boy, Mama, but you will find him quite different from the meek little soul I brought to dinner so long ago."

"I remember your father called him a 'pansy artist' and all but threw him out of the house. It made you furious."

"He's an artist, all right—a good one," Libba countered with a laugh. "But he's no pansy. He's found himself, Mama, discovered where he fits, what he was created to do. He's still a gentle soul, but he knows his own mind. Did you know he was commissioned by the Pilgrimage Association—they put on the tour in Oxford every year—to do pen-and-ink sketches for their brochure? The originals will be displayed in the museum, and he's bound to get more work because of the publicity. He'll probably be famous some-day."

"I only know he helped you a lot when you were struggling, believing Link was dead. For that I will always be grateful."

Just then the doorbell rang, and Libba went to answer it. Freddy stood on the porch with a huge package in one hand—a package that looked suspi-ciously like a framed painting, covered with bright paper and secured with a big red ribbon.

"Merry Christmas, Libba!" He kissed her on the cheek and handed her the package. "For you."

"Thank you, Freddy. Come on in."

As he removed his coat and hung it on the hall tree, Libba surveyed him. He had filled out a bit since she last saw him. His shoulders had grown broader, and his blond hair curled in ringlets around his ears. His skin, whipped by the chill December air, had lost its pallor and taken on a ruddy, healthy tone. And something else was different too—he carried himself straighter, with more dignity and confidence. In dark slacks and a slate blue sweater, he looked almost . . . handsome.

"Mrs. Coltrain," Freddy was saying as he shook her hand warmly. "It is so good to see you again." He flashed a smile at Libba, then turned back to her mother. "I was so sorry to hear of your loss."

"My loss?" Mama faltered. "Oh, yes—Robinson's death. Thank you, Freddy. I received your nice note and appreciated it so much."

"It was the least I could do." Freddy wandered toward the archway leading to the dining room. "What is that delicious smell? Surely you didn't cook this wonderful dinner, Libba?"

Libba punched him playfully on the arm. "No, I didn't. But I'll have you know I do cook now—at least a little. My biscuits are almost as good as Willie's."

"I wouldn't bet on it." He turned to her and swept her into a spontaneous hug. "I've missed you."

She held on for a moment. "I've missed you, too, Freddy. There've been so many times I've wanted to talk to you."

"Then you should have called." He stepped back and looked her over. "After dinner, we'll sit down and have a long, long talk. And then you will promise me that if you ever need me, you'll get on the telephone. Immediately. Agreed?"

"Agreed," Libba answered. She took his arm and steered him into the dining room, feeling, for the first time in days, as if she wasn't really alone after all.

★ ★ ★

"He said *what?*" Freddy sat up straight in his chair and stared at Libba incredulously. After dinner they had moved to the living room and built a small fire, and Libba had proceeded to tell him all about her time at Kennedy General, her work with the wounded soldiers, and her reunion with Link.

"He said that he couldn't make a decision about our future until he knew if he would walk again, and—" Libba swallowed against the pain in her throat—"that he wasn't sure he loved me anymore."

Freddy shook his blond head, and his shoulders sagged. "And he didn't take into account the fact that you've spent the past how many weeks on that ward, helping those wounded soldiers? Or that maybe—just maybe—God had been preparing you to deal with a husband in a wheelchair? I can't believe it! Why, that's worse than disrespectful, Libba—it's downright arrogant!"

Libba smiled a little. Somehow Freddy's anger on her behalf helped her feel better. At least, hearing his response, she could believe that her own emotions weren't completely unreasonable. And he was so sweet, coming to her defense like a medieval knight rescuing a damsel in distress.

"Let me ask you a question," Freddy ventured. "Do you love Link Winsom?"

"Of course I do," Libba responded instantly. "More than I ever thought it was possible to love anyone." She paused. "Oh, Freddy, I'm sorry—I didn't mean it to come out like that."

He waved her concern aside. "Never mind about that, Libba. My feelings aren't hurt because you were never really in love with me. To tell the truth,

I love you as a friend, but I wasn't really in love with you, either." He grinned. "Maybe we were just using each other—you to get away from your daddy's control, me to bolster my faltering self-image. But just in case you're wondering, Libba, you *did* do a lot for my ego. You were—are—quite a catch." His eyebrows knitted in thought. "Link Winsom is a fool."

A moment of silence stretched between them. Then Freddy leaned forward. "You love Link. Do you think Link loves you—in spite of what he said?"

Libba thought about this for a minute. "Yes."

"So why would he lie to you? Why would he say such a thing, knowing it would hurt you?"

A variety of answers ran through Libba's mind, at last settling on one that seemed most reasonable. "He's trying to protect me?"

Freddy leaned back. "I think so. At least partly."

"But what is he protecting me from? Myself? The 'burden,' as he sees it, of having to be saddled with an invalid? I'm not stupid, Freddy, and my time at Kennedy General has taught me a thing or two about dealing with wounded soldiers. When Hans lost his legs—" She paused. A tiny pinpoint of light was beginning to break through in the recesses of her mind . . . a light of understanding.

"Tell me about Hans," Freddy urged.

"Well, when Hans lost his legs, he lost his hope, too. His girl in Minnesota deserted him. He felt like . . . like he wasn't a real man anymore."

"Bingo."

"What are you saying, Freddy? That Link thinks he's protecting me, when he's actually protecting himself? He wouldn't do that—put his own feelings above mine."

"Maybe not consciously. But you can rationalize doing something until it seems like the right thing to do, and for very noble reasons. Link's probably not aware that he's protecting himself; he probably genuinely thinks he's sacrificing himself for you. He's a man, Libba, and a man has a certain image to protect—"

"Wait a minute," Libba interrupted. "You're a man, and you seem pretty honest and straightforward about your own feelings. What does being a man have to do with it?"

Freddy smiled and scratched his head. "I may be a man, Libba, but I'm—well, maybe being an artist has enabled me to be more aware of—and honest about—my own feelings. But most men I know have a tough time admitting their own weaknesses or emotions, and they have no concept of marriage as a partnership. They hold very rigid ideas about what they're supposed to do, the roles they're supposed to fulfill. Being the breadwinner, the protector, the head of the household—that kind of thing. Sort of an 'I hunt, you nest' mentality. The idea that a woman might have to help and support them—either financially or in other ways—is completely unthinkable."

"You're saying it doesn't matter that we love each other and want to be together—if the man can't be in control, the deal is off?" Libba shuddered. "Sounds like my father."

"It's not quite that bad," Freddy laughed. "Your father was an extreme case. You know, people talk about how complicated women are, how impossible to understand. But men are pretty hard to figure out too. It seems fairly simple to you: You and Link love each other, and you'll do whatever is necessary for the two of you to be together. For him, it's a different story. I suspect his whole concept of what it means to be a man is tied up in whether or not he will walk again, whether he will be able to be the kind of husband you deserve."

"So he's willing to throw everything away to save his precious pride?" Libba snapped. "That's the stupidest thing I've ever heard."

"Oh, I've heard a few things that are more stupid," Freddy quipped. "But I'd be willing to bet that's how Link sees it, and he thinks he's being very noble and self-sacrificing about it. The problem is, he's sacrificing more than himself and his own chance for happiness. He's sacrificing you in the process."

Libba closed her eyes. "What do I do, Freddy? I can't force him to marry me—and I wouldn't want to. Even if I believe he truly loves me, I don't want him to marry me out of some distorted sense of duty."

"And he doesn't want you to marry him out of obligation, either," Freddy said softly.

"So we're at a stalemate."

"Until Link sees the light, yes. That's where prayer comes in."

Prayer? Libba flinched. Oh, she had prayed about it, all right—she had raged at God about the injustice of it all, had pleaded that the Lord would change Link's mind, had begged that he would walk again so that everything would be all right. But she had never, until this moment, considered that Link might have inward struggles and heartbreak that needed to be addressed. She had asked God to change Link's attitude, but she had not yet prayed that the Lord would heal his soul.

Give him space to heal. Just be there. Aunt Mag's words pierced their way into Libba's consciousness. She had expected—foolishly, perhaps—that once she and Link were reunited, everything would go back to normal, that they would pick up right where they left off when he shipped out. His life had been spared, and he had been returned to her. But he wasn't whole. Even if the feeling returned in his legs and he did walk again, there were no doubt hidden wounds, far below the surface, that needed to be mended. And no matter how much she loved him, her love could only do so much. God would have to do the rest.

"You haven't opened your Christmas present," Freddy was saying. "I hope you'll still want it once you see it."

Libba forced her thoughts back to the present and smiled at him. "Of course I'll want it, Freddy." She gave an apologetic shrug. "I'm afraid I don't have anything for you. I've been so busy at the hospital—"

"Don't worry about it," he said lightly. "Just make me some biscuits sometime—I'm dying to see if they're really as good as Willie's."

Libba took the package from him and laid it on the sofa next to her. "Speaking of Willie, I drove out to the farm yesterday afternoon for a while," she said as she carefully removed the ribbon. "Uncle William and Aunt Bess aren't doing very well. But Willie is determined to join us for Christmas Eve dinner at the cafe. She's awfully lonely, I think. I know if I were stuck out there, I'd miss everybody terribly. And it doesn't help having Mabel Rae so far away."

"How is Mabel?"

"What can I say? She's in love. She doesn't write very often. But we're still planning for an April wedding." Libba sighed. "If Uncle William lasts that long."

"Is it that bad?"

"Charlie's death seems to have taken all the life out of him. He's taken to his bed, and the doctor doesn't know quite what's wrong with him. It's like he's just run out of steam. Willie doesn't know what to do. She's working herself to death, but she says it keeps her mind off other things."

"Like Owen Slaughter?"

"Probably. I don't think she'll ever meet anyone who lives up to Owen's memory. And if she stays out on the farm, she'll never meet anyone at all."

"Maybe getting together with everyone for Christmas Eve will help," Freddy offered.

"I hope so." Libba carefully lifted the paper from the edges of the package. "You're welcome to come too, Freddy, if you don't have other plans. We'd love to—"

She broke off in midsentence as she pulled aside the last of the wrapping paper. "Oh, Freddy, it's—it's beautiful!"

It was a framed picture, all right, but not at all what Libba had expected.

It was a portrait of her and Link, both gazing into the distance, with him standing slightly behind her with his hands on her shoulders. Freddy had captured their expressions perfectly—Libba with a look of wonder and love in her eyes, and Link, in his uniform, wearing an expression of pride and protectiveness. Beyond them, in the background, was a shadowed scene of battle, and from above, like a heavenly blessing, light filtering down through the clouds.

"You like it, then?"

Libba's eyes filled with tears, and she nodded. "I don't know how you did it. It's perfect." And it was. It reflected all her desires for the future, all her dreams, all her love. Everything she had hoped for, counted on. Everything that, at this moment, hung in the balance. "You are really good, Freddy. A true artist."

As she fought to regain her composure, she peered at the signature in the lower right-hand corner. *F. Gardner Sturgis.*

"What's this—F. Gardner?"

He ducked his head and grinned sheepishly. "With the Pilgrimage job and all, I figured—at least I hoped—that my name would get out, that people would start to know who I was. And 'Freddy' seemed—well, not the right name for an artist. I've changed so much since I discovered what I was really meant to do, Libba. It just seemed fitting to start my new career with a new name." His eyes darted away. "What do you think?"

"I think it's perfect, Freddy. Very professional, very dignified." She smiled. "Do you want me to start calling you 'Gardner'?"

"No . . . I guess to you, I'll always be Freddy."

Libba held up the picture and shook her head in wonder. "When you're famous, I'll be able to say I had one of the first original paintings by F. Gardner Sturgis. I'm very touched."

"I wanted to do something . . . special. Just for you, Libba. Something that would last, something you could show to—" he hesitated—"to your children and grandchildren, I guess. I hope I wasn't being presumptuous."

"No . . . of course not," Libba answered absently. Something he had said, something about children and grandchildren, struck a chord in her. Gradually, like a photograph emerging in a developing tray, a scene appeared in her mind . . . not an actual vision, perhaps, but more like a waking dream. She saw herself as an old woman in the midst of a celebration, standing with Link and gazing at Freddy's portrait, reminiscing. A powerful sense of nostalgia washed over her, as if she had been transported fifty years into the future and was looking back over this day as a fond and cherished memory.

A deep peace filled her spirit, and she smiled. "It's a wonderful gift, Freddy," she murmured. A gift of friendship. A gift of love. And more important, a gift of hope.

Hope for the future.

22

★ ★ ★

Magnolia's Last Stand

It had been two days since Stork's visit, and Link still couldn't get their conversation out of his mind. What was it about the man that enabled him to say anything—anything at all—to Link, and Link would take it? Maybe it was the depth of their friendship, the fact that Link could count on Stork to be honest with him—even if it hurt.

In this case, it hurt a lot.

But Link wasn't angry. In fact, even in the midst of his pain and confusion, he appreciated the fact that Stork had been so blunt with him. Not many fellows had friends like that, friends who would tell them the truth even when they didn't want to hear it. *Especially* when they didn't want to hear it.

As Link lay in his bed, alone and missing Libba, he thought about what Stork had said to him. He had done it again—making decisions for Libba without even consulting her. Trying to protect her when he was really protecting himself. He was a selfish idiot, and he didn't deserve her, but he wanted her more than ever. And he didn't know what in the world to do about it.

He wished Stork would show up again, to talk him through this and help him sort it out. But the guy had his own problems to deal with. That mother of his was a real case, undermining Stork's happiness with her prophecies of doom. Once Link had gotten out of himself long enough to listen, he had tried to reason with his friend, to assure him that the old bag was just blowing smoke and trying to control him. But Stork was buying it, hook, line, and sinker . . . almost as if he *wanted* to be punished.

A shadow fell across his bed, and Link looked up. There, towering over him, stood the most formidable female he had ever seen—or at least a close second to Nurse Pincheon. The woman was tall and regal-looking, like an ancient Amazon queen, with upswept white hair and a flowing dress the color of American Beauty roses. For a brief moment Link felt as if he had been set down in the presence of royalty and should kiss one of her diamond rings.

Then he was struck by a sense of déjà vu. He had seen this woman before, but where? Then he remembered . . . that first night, coming out of the anesthesia, standing behind Libba . . . the matriarchal angel, hovering over him.

Libba's Great-Aunt Magnolia.

He had not formally met the woman yet, but he had heard enough about her to be apprehensive. Libba adored her, but Link knew that she was a no-nonsense type and that, according to Libba, he would have to pass the Magnolia Cooley Character Test before he would be approved as a prospective spouse.

The look on her face indicated he was well on his way to failing the test already, and she hadn't even spoken with him.

"I am Magnolia Cooley," she said in a subdued voice. "I presume you have heard of me?"

"Oh, y-yes, ma'am," Link stammered. "Libba's told me all about you. I—I've been looking forward to meeting you."

"I'm sure you have," she murmured. "May I sit?"

"Of course. Forgive me." Link waved a hand at the bedside chair, and the elderly woman took it, her back straight as a ramrod.

"I'll come right to the point," she said. "You are—or were—engaged to my grandniece?"

The way she said *grandniece* made Link's stomach quiver. He felt, irrationally, as if somehow he had offended a reigning monarch by refusing to marry the crown princess.

"Yes."

"You are—or have been—in love with her?"

"Yes."

"And now you have changed your mind."

"No—no, it's not like that," Link stammered, withering under her unwavering stare.

"It is exactly like that, young man," she corrected. "You asked her to marry you, did you not?"

"Uh-huh . . . I mean, yes, ma'am."

"And now you're not going to marry her."

"Yes, ma'am. I mean, no, ma'am. I mean . . . oh, I don't know."

"I apologize, young man. I was wrong about you. You haven't changed your mind. You *have* no mind." Her icy gaze swept over him. "Do forgive me—I had no idea you had been wounded in the head."

She was an angel, all right, Link thought—an avenging angel, coming to do battle for her beloved Libba. He could almost see the fiery aura surrounding her.

He heaved a deep sigh. "Aunt Mag—is it all right if I call you that?"

She raised one eyebrow. "It depends."

"You have to give me a chance to explain—"

"I have grave doubts, young man, that I am the one you should be explaining to."

"You're probably right."

"Of course I am." A brief smile flitted across the wrinkled face and sparked in her pale green eyes.

"Yes, of course," he conceded. "But you're here, and Libba's not, so would you please hear me out?"

She waved one hand in a gesture of permission. "By all means."

"I—I thought I was doing the right thing," Link began hesitantly. "I don't know what the future will bring for me, and I didn't want to subject Libba to a life of—"

"Hogwash!" Mag interrupted. "Don't try that double-talk with me, young man. It won't work. I didn't just fall off the hay wagon, in case you haven't noticed. I know fear when I smell it, and you, Link Winsom, are afraid. The question is, are you afraid of hurting Libba, or is that just a smoke screen because you're afraid for yourself and won't admit it?"

Link winced inwardly. Magnolia Cooley intimidated him no end, yet he found himself liking her. And somehow her forthright manner led him to believe if he ever got on her good side, he'd have an advocate for life. But this might be the only chance he ever got to win her over, and he didn't want to blow it.

He took a deep breath and met her gaze without blinking. "I am afraid, Aunt Mag—partly for myself, and partly for Libba. I thought—foolishly, perhaps—that if I dealt with my problem alone, without bringing Libba into it, it would be easier on both of us in the long run. Once I have the use of my legs back and can walk again, I'll—"

"And what if you never get your legs back?" She said the words quietly, without malice, but with a directness that unnerved him. He had been trying to avoid thinking about that possibility. "Perhaps it's time you faced reality head-on, young man. The question is not what you will do *when* you walk again, but what you'll do, what kind of man you'll be, if you find you have to spend the rest of your life in a wheelchair."

Link fell silent, considering her words. She was right, as much as he hated to admit it. He had to prepare for the worst and hope for the best.

"Let me tell you something about your Libba," Aunt Mag was saying, a soft light of love now filling her countenance. "She is strong—much stronger than you give her credit for. She is quite capable of handling whatever life may throw at her. And she deserves not only your love but your respect." The old woman cast a meaningful glance at Link. "Furthermore, I intend to see to it that she never settles for less than she deserves. Do we understand one another?"

Link smiled, and a feeling of relief washed over him. "We understand one another perfectly, Aunt Mag. I've been a fool."

The ancient face creased into a broad smile. "Ah, we do agree on something."

"My best friend, Stork Simpson, was here a couple of days ago," Link mused. "He told me almost exactly the same thing."

"A wise man. I'd like to meet him sometime."

"And I suppose, if I'm going to be honest about it, I'd have to admit that God was telling me the same thing, too."

"Another wise counselor," Aunt Mag murmured. "You should listen more often." She pointed a crooked finger at him. "And you should be careful—very careful—about calling upon the Almighty to justify your own conclusions. The next time you claim to have prayed your way to an answer, make sure you have done so."

Link grinned sheepishly. "I stand corrected." He looked down at his lifeless legs, stuck straight out under the blanket. "Figuratively speaking, of course."

Magnolia Cooley stood and adjusted her gloves, then bent down to give Link a kiss on the forehead. "Make this right, young man, before it's too late," she whispered, patting his shoulder.

"I will, Aunt Mag." He reached up and squeezed her hand. "Thank you for coming."

"We'll see each other again, I'm sure." She moved toward the doors of the ward, then turned back to face him. "By the way, Link Winsom," she called from the doorway, "you pass."

Pass? What did she mean? Then he remembered what Libba had told him about Aunt Mag's Character Test. He waved a hand in salute. "Thanks."

"Not exactly with flying colors," she quipped, "but enough to merit a rematch."

Before he could come back with an answer, she was gone.

★ ★ ★

Throughout the afternoon, Link dozed and woke and dozed again, with Libba Coltrain floating in and out of his dreams. In one scene she was dressed all in white, waiting for him at the end of a long, dark corridor—a gauntlet flanked with thousands of eyes watching and hands waiting to grab him. In another she appeared as an old woman in a brightly colored flowing dress and dangling earrings, pointing a gnarled finger at him. From this second dream he awoke with a bizarre sense that he was seeing into the future . . . and that the woman he loved had turned out a lot like her Great-Aunt Mag.

Then, just as the last slanting rays of sunlight receded from the ward, he jerked to consciousness with the distinct feeling that he was being watched. A figure, shrouded in shadow, stood at his bedside.

"What? Who's there?" Link blinked, trying to adjust his eyes to the waning light. When at last his gaze focused, he could have sworn he was still dreaming.

"Hello, Son," a deep rumbling voice said. "How are you feeling?"

"Dad?" Link squinted and ran a hand over his face. "Dad? Is that really you?"

A hand reached for the lamp on the bedside table and snapped it on. In the warm yellow pool of light, Link recognized his father's face smiling down at him. A bit more gray mixed with the dark hair that swept back from his temples, and the crow's feet around his eyes seemed deeper than Link remembered. But he had never seen a more welcome sight.

He struggled to sit up a little, and his father reached behind him to prop the pillows under his back. "What are you doing here, Dad?"

"I came to see you, of course."

"But—what about—what about your clients? Your law practice?"

"My clients can take care of themselves for a while. I would have been here sooner, but I had some loose ends to wrap up." His father slung his overcoat over the foot of the bed and took a seat in the chair. "To tell the truth, Son, I don't have much of a practice left. I never cultivated the high-paying clients from St. Joe—business contracts and the like. Maybe it was a mistake, but I felt other people needed me more—the folks who couldn't help themselves, who couldn't afford an attorney. The problem is, even the people who once paid in chickens and beans don't have any chickens and beans left. There's just not much call anymore for a small-potatoes lawyer like me."

Link smiled as he drank in the sight of his father's face. "You're not small potatoes, Dad. You never have been. You just have different values."

"That's a nice way to put it. Most of my colleagues would say I'm a fool because I didn't take advantage of my 'earning potential.' I think that's legal terminology for making a fast buck any way you can." He smiled. "But it doesn't matter. The house is paid off, and I put enough away to make sure your sister has a little nest egg in case of emergency. RuthAnn's taken a teaching position, driving into St. Joe every day and coming back at night. She's making enough to support herself and then some—which is more than I ever did, I guess."

"Don't put yourself down, Dad," Link protested. "You did what you believed was right. You were a good father, a good man. We never went hungry, did we? And look how many lives you affected—"

His father held up a hand to silence him. "I know, Son, I know. And I appreciate your saying it. But I didn't come here to talk about me. Tell me about you."

"I'm doing pretty well, I guess, all things considered. The shrapnel in my back—I wrote to you about it from England—they did surgery on me the first night I arrived, to remove it." Link grinned. "And as you can see, I'm still here." Then he sobered. "They don't know if I'll walk again, Dad. So far I haven't gotten any feeling back in my legs—from the hip joints down, they're just dead."

Tears filled his father's dark eyes, and he swiped them away with the back of one hand.

"It's all right, Dad. Honest it is," Link said, swallowing against a lump in his throat. "A very wise woman told me just this morning that it was time for me to face reality, to decide what kind of man I was going to be, even if I did end up in a wheelchair." He smiled at the memory. "She accused me of not having a mind, but on that count she was wrong. I do, and I can still use it."

His father smiled and gripped his hand. "So what do you intend to do now, Son?"

"The first thing I intend to do," Link said resolutely, "is try my best to clean up a big mess I've made."

As his father listened, Link told him about Libba, about his ill-conceived plan to protect her from marrying him, about his foolishness, about his eye-opening confrontation with Libba's Great-Aunt Magnolia.

"Sounds like my kind of woman," Link's father said when he was finished. "A woman of substance . . . and spunk."

"She's that, all right." Link grinned wryly. "But just a tad too old for you, Dad."

"I wasn't talking about *marrying* her," his father returned. "But she'd be a great addition to the family."

"She won't ever be part of this family," Link said, "unless I can convince Libba to give me one more chance."

A strange expression passed over his father's face—a look of exhilaration, as if he had just taken on the most challenging case in his entire legal career. "A lawyer," he mused, "speaks for those who cannot speak for themselves." He peered at Link. "Do you have a quarter?"

Puzzled, Link fished in the drawer of the bedside table and came up with two dimes and a nickel. "Here." He tossed the coins into his dad's outstretched hand. "What's it for?"

"A retainer," his father said triumphantly. "Consider yourself represented."

23

⋆ ⋆ ⋆

The Bethlehem Factor

Christmas Eve
Paradise Garden Cafe

Bennett Winsom had no trouble finding the place. It was, as Link had told him, a squat clapboard building right on the main road, with a garish neon sign proclaiming its identity as both the cafe and the bus stop. He pulled his car into the gravel parking lot and sat for a moment, considering his next move.

His ultimate aim, of course, was to find Libba Coltrain and have a talk with her about his son—to pave the way, he hoped, and help her understand why Link had done what he did. Stork Simpson had told Link they would all be gathering for Christmas Eve dinner at the cafe, and Link felt it might be wise to meet Libba on neutral ground.

Bennett gazed at the flashing sign, augmented by multicolored Christmas lights strung around the roof and sides of the building. The cafe looked like what his wife, Catherine, used to call a roadhouse, and a none-too-respectable roadhouse at that. Still, Link said it was the central gathering place for the folks of Eden, Mississippi, and, thus, the place where Bennett Winsom's quest would begin.

It was still early—only about five-thirty—but already the sky was beginning to darken. Low on the eastern horizon, a single bright star appeared. Bennett knew it was Venus making her nightly appearance just after sundown. But the Christmas lights and the holiday music drifting faintly from the cafe tugged at his heart, and he pretended—just for a moment—that it was the Bethlehem star, the miraculous sign that led the wise men to the infant Son of God. A sense of wonder and nostalgia washed over him, bathing him in the glory of that presence. Immanuel. God with us.

And God *was* with him. He didn't know quite how, or why, but Bennett felt that he had been led to this place. Not just for his son's sake, to be with him in his convalescence, but for some other reason, some reason he did not yet understand. Maybe he was, like the wise men, following a star of his own, leaving everything behind to respond to the call.

The problem was, Bennett Winsom didn't feel wise, no matter how much he felt called. He had no idea what he was doing here, what God's ultimate purpose was in sending him to Eden. Was it just to support his son? To help reconcile the relationship between Link and his girl? Or was there something else? Something only God knew and hadn't told him about yet?

Well, he certainly wouldn't find out sitting in a cold, dark Packard waiting for revelation. The lights from the cafe beckoned to him, inviting him inside, to warmth and human companionship. His stomach rumbled, and he reached on the seat next to him for his fedora, buttoned his overcoat, and stepped out of the car.

Maybe with a little luck, they'd invite him to stay for dinner.

★ ★ ★

Thelma Breckinridge was in the kitchen putting the finishing touches on the turkey when the bell over the cafe door jingled. She glanced at the clock—they couldn't be here already! The church service started at five, and it wasn't even six yet. With all the singing and the children's pageant and the well-wishing afterward, they were bound to be there until at least six-thirty.

She peered through the service window toward the door, but all she could see was the dark shadow of a male figure, standing just inside the cafe and looking utterly lost.

"I'm sorry," Thelma said as she pushed through the swinging door from the kitchen. "We're not open to the public tonight. As you can see, we're set up for a private dinner." She waved a hand at the line of cafe tables, pushed together and covered with lace tablecloths.

"The door was open," a deep, rumbling baritone said, and the man took a step forward.

"Yes, but—" Thelma stopped suddenly, and for the first time looked at the man. Really looked.

He was of medium height, with broad shoulders emphasized by a woolen topcoat. A soft gray scarf hung open around his neck, drawing her eyes upward to his face. And what a face! Thelma's heart leaped against her rib cage, and she fought against the temptation to stare. He had dark, smiling eyes, crinkling at the corners with most becoming crow's feet. A dazzling smile, with even white teeth and just a hint of a dimple on the right side. And a full head of dark brown hair, nearly black, with a distinguished sweep of gray at the temples. Handsome. Very handsome, in a mature, distinguished way.

And he looked somehow . . . familiar. As if she had seen him before—in a dream, perhaps?

Nervously she wiped her hands on her apron and pushed back an errant strand of hair. She had to stop this. Here she was, a middle-aged businesswoman, behaving like a silly schoolgirl. But try as she might, she couldn't stop the fluttering in her chest. She hadn't felt this way for years. Not since . . .

Since Robert Raintree.

The memory of the fiancé who had abandoned her without warning jerked her back to reality, and Thelma found her voice.

"Good evenin', sir," she said shakily. "I'm Thelma Breckinridge, owner and manager of the Paradise Garden."

He nodded graciously, removed one glove, and took her hand. "I'm pleased to meet you, Mrs. Breckinridge."

"Miss—ah, Thelma," she stammered, flustered again by the warmth and gentleness of his touch. "Call me Thelma."

"All right, Thelma." The voice was as smooth as old satin. "And you must call me Bennett."

Bennett. The name fit him. Sophisticated, distinguished. Class. Real class.

"Mr. —ah, Bennett. I apologize if you've come expecting the cafe to be open. But we're having a private gathering tonight, a family dinner, so to speak." She looked up at him and found herself caught by the expression in his eyes—amusement coupled with anticipation.

"Turkey and dressing? It smells wonderful. And mincemeat pie, unless my nose deceives me."

"Yes, but—" Thelma stuck her hands in her apron pockets. "I'm sorry to disappoint you, but my guests will be here in half an hour. I really can't—"

He smiled warmly. "I understand, of course. I won't take up any more of your time. Actually, I came here for information, not for dinner."

"Information?" Thelma frowned at him. "What sort of information?" Her mind raced. Maybe he was a public official of some sort, or a lawyer. He certainly looked the part. Maybe this had something to do with Ivory and the back taxes he owed. Well, nobody was going to push Ivory around, not if Thelma had anything to do with it. Nobody was going to spoil the poor man's Christmas. She'd see to that. She'd send this slick city fellow packing—

"Yes, about Libba Coltrain."

Thelma narrowed her eyes at him. "What do you want with Libba?"

"I just want to talk with her." A confused expression passed across the man's face, as if he hadn't the faintest idea why Thelma had suddenly turned on him. Oh, he was slick all right—very slick. He could charm the stripes off a tiger, this one could.

"I was told that Libba would probably be here tonight for dinner," the man went on. "That's why I've come—to see her."

Before Thelma could ask him just exactly what he wanted to see Libba about, the door opened and a gust of cold air rushed into the room. Thelma looked past his shoulder to see Libba, followed by her mother and Aunt Mag, entering the cafe.

"Merry Christmas, Thelma!" Libba called merrily. "We came straight from church—thought you might need some help setting out the food."

The man turned and took two steps in Libba's direction. He stopped in front of her and looked her up and down, smiling faintly. Then he gave a brief nod and said, "Libba Coltrain, I presume? And this must be your mother . . . and your Great-Aunt Magnolia, the avenging angel."

Libba stared at him for a moment, and Thelma watched her face take on an expression of tentative recognition. "Are you—are you who I think you are?" she whispered.

"Bennett Winsom at your service, my dear. My son has told me all about you, and he did not exaggerate your attributes."

Thelma felt her jaw drop. Link Winsom's father? This charming, handsome man with the dazzling smile and a voice that could melt butter? Of course. She could see it now—in his eyes, in the high forehead and thick dark brows. What she had recognized in him was Link Winsom, thirty years from now.

Bennett Winsom had taken Libba's arm and was steering her toward the back booth. "If you'll give me a few moments of your time," he was saying, "I think we can clear up a serious misunderstanding."

★ ★ ★

Libba felt her knees shaking as she sat down across the table from Link's father. She couldn't keep her eyes off his face; every time he laughed or smiled or cocked his head in a certain way, all she could see was Link. Link's charm. His wit. His enthusiasm for life. Characteristics she hadn't

150

seen in a long, long time. A bittersweet pain assaulted her—the memory of how things once were between her and the man she loved. And a nagging doubt that they would ever be that way again.

"Just for the record," Link's father was saying, "my son is not deliberately playing games with your heart. He thought—erroneously, perhaps—that it would be easier on you if you didn't have to live with the uncertainty of his condition. Once he knew whether or not he would walk again, he intended—"

"He intended to make *his* decision about what *he* was going to do with *his* future," Libba snapped. "And whether or not he would condescend to let me share in it." She leaned forward. "Doesn't that seem just a little self-centered, Mr. Winsom? Doesn't it seem a bit disrespectful of me?"

"Indeed it does, Libba," Bennett Winsom answered. "And Link realizes that. Your great-aunt made it very clear to him that—"

"My great-aunt?" Libba blinked. "Aunt Mag went to see Link?"

"Yes, of course—I assumed you knew that."

"I had no idea." Libba smiled and looked across the room to where Aunt Mag was helping Thelma arrange the turkey in the center of the table. So that's what she meant by teaching someone the principles of pinochle—not to renege when you had a good hand.

Bennett Winsom followed the direction of her gaze. "She's apparently quite a woman, your Aunt Mag."

"I suppose Link thought she was being a meddling busybody."

"Quite the contrary, as a matter of fact. She scared him to death, I think, but he liked her. Called her an 'avenging angel.' She set him straight, that's for sure."

Libba turned back to him. "And what was your response?"

Link's father winked at her—a gesture that stabbed at her heart. "I told Link I thought she'd make a wonderful addition to the family."

Libba averted her eyes. "That may not be possible now."

"I know."

The words were simple and sincere, obviously full of compassion for her and heartbreak for his son. She reached out and touched his hand, and his warm strong fingers closed over hers.

"Link asked me to tell you that he's sorry—sorry he pushed you away, sorry he lied to you. He knows you're strong enough to handle this, Libba. He just wasn't certain he was." He paused, and an expression of sorrow filled his face. "Link knows it may be too late for reconciliation, but at the very least he's asking for your forgiveness."

Libba looked at Bennett Winsom intently. "How did he lie to me?" She knew the answer, but she wanted to hear what Link's father would say.

"He told you he wasn't sure he loved you. He thought that was the only way to convince you to go away. But he did—he does—love you. He always has."

Libba fought against a wild desire to beg Link's father to take her to Memphis—now, tonight—to see Link and tell him all was forgiven. But deep inside she knew she couldn't shortcut the process. As much as she wanted Link back, she had to take it one step at a time.

"Why didn't Link tell me these things himself?" she asked. "Why didn't he just send word for me to come?"

Link's father shook his head. "He wasn't sure you would. You did come the last time he asked for you, and he sent you away. He didn't have any right to expect you to just jump up and run to him after what he did."

"And what if—" Libba took a deep breath. "What if he doesn't regain the use of his legs? What if he never walks again? How do I know he won't push me away a second time?"

"You can't know for sure," Bennett Winsom said honestly. "I guess you just have to trust. But you can know this—my son sees you differently now from the way he did before. He no longer thinks of you as a helpless girl who needs to be protected. He's willing to try to build a life with you as equal partners. He wants to face whatever you'll have to face . . . together."

"This is a pretty quick turnaround," Libba muttered.

"It seems your Aunt Magnolia tends to have that effect on people." Link's father shook his head in amusement. "Apparently she has a way of making people see the light—and putting the fear of God into them."

The tight coil of anxiety deep in Libba's chest released, and she found herself able to smile. "Aunt Mag is a wonderful woman. I just hope I can become half the person she is."

Bennett Winsom squeezed Libba's hand and held it for a moment. "From what I can see," he said with emotion, "you're well on your way."

★ ★ ★

By seven-fifteen, the Paradise Garden Cafe buzzed with conversation and happy laughter. From her place at the head of the long table, Thelma looked down the row of friends and loved ones—people who, through good times and bad, had become family to one another.

To her right sat Madge and Stork Simpson, with baby Mickey in a high chair between them. His eyes were bright with excitement, and his flushed round face was smeared with sweet potato. On the other side of Stork was the one dour face in the gathering—Mother Simpson, picking at her food and sending hostile glances at Thelma every chance she got.

To Thelma's left were Ivory Brownlee and Willie Coltrain. Ivory was smiling broadly, showing every gap in his teeth, and carrying on an animated conversation with Willie, who had the look of a prisoner just released from solitary confinement. Next to Willie was Libba, then Aunt Mag, and across from them, Olivia Coltrain and Bennett Winsom.

Thelma was too far away to talk to Bennett, but she knew from the little Libba had told her that there was a chance things could be patched up with Link. What a wonderful Christmas present for Libba . . . for them all. And Bennett and Olivia seemed to be getting along fine. As Thelma watched them laughing and talking, she felt a stab of—what was it? Some emotion she couldn't readily identify. She only knew she was glad when Stork leaned across his mother to engage Bennett in discussion about Link.

After second helpings had been passed around and the turkey carcass was beginning to look like a mere shadow of its former self, a lull in the conversation gave Thelma the chance she had been waiting for. She tapped her water glass for attention, and everybody looked up.

"I just want to take this opportunity to thank you all for coming—and for all the wonderful goodies you contributed to our Christmas dinner. We'll have pie and coffee in a little bit, and maybe—if Ivory will do the honors on the piano—sing a few carols. But right now I'd like to welcome Stork's mother, Lorna Simpson—" Mrs. Simpson glared at her and whispered something in her son's ear that made him frown. "And Magnolia Cooley, Olivia's aunt from Memphis—" Mag waved her hand and gave a rich, full laugh. "And last but not least, Bennett Winsom, Link's father, who sort of appeared out of nowhere tonight, just in time to share this celebration with us." Bennett nodded and smiled, and when he caught Thelma's gaze and winked at her, she could feel herself blushing to the roots of her hair.

Thelma was about to say more when Madge got up from the table and took Mickey out of his high chair. "Sorry, everybody," she said. "I'll be back in a few minutes. I'm going to go put Mickey to bed. I think he's got a bit of a fever."

"He does look a mite flushed," Thelma said, leaning over to place a hand on his cheek.

"See," Mrs. Simpson declared, loud enough for all to hear. "The child is sick. I told you something like this would happen."

"It's nothing, Mother." Stork left his place and went to his wife and son. "It's probably just all the excitement."

"He'll be fine," Madge added. "Babies do this all the time." She headed for the kitchen door with Stork on her heels. "Save us some pie. We'll be back as soon as we get him settled."

"The hand of the Lord," Mrs. Simpson murmured.

Thelma gave the woman a hush-your-mouth glance and turned back to the other guests. "I want you all to know how thankful I am God has put you in my life. You are, truly, my family, and I am more grateful for you than I can say."

Bennett Winsom stood to his feet and saluted Thelma with his water glass. "Except for Stork, I've never met any of you before tonight," he said. "But I feel that God led me here, and I want to thank you for making me so welcome." He turned and smiled down at Libba. "And on this night when we celebrate the birth of our Savior, I want to express my thanks to God for sparing my son's life . . . and for giving me a chance to meet the lovely young woman who—I hope—will soon become my own daughter." His gaze moved to Aunt Mag and then to Olivia. "And for these two gracious women, as well, whom I would be proud to have as part of our family."

Thelma forced a smile, but when Bennett leaned down and kissed Olivia's hand, she shut her eyes and fought against the emotion that she now recognized all too clearly. She was jealous! She had met this man not three hours ago, and she was jealous of the attention he was showing someone else! It was outrageous . . . and not at all characteristic of her. The emotion made her feel cheap and catty, and she didn't like it one bit.

When Ivory got to his feet and cleared his throat, Thelma shifted her attention to him with relief.

"Some of you was there when we brought the Thanksgiving to Willie's house," he began, "and I told you how the tax people was going to take my house and land if I didn't pay a thousand dollars by January fifteenth. Well, me and Thelma, we been praying about it most every day." He held up a sheet of cream-colored paper and smiled. "At Thanksgiving, I said that God's got ways. But I didn't know for the life of me how God was gonna solve this one. Here's the answer, and thank y'all for praying."

"What is it, Ivory?" Thelma took the paper from him and looked at it. "It's a proposal from somebody called the Southern Historical Preservation Society. They're offering Ivory ten thousand dollars for his land, and they say he can keep the house and cabin and two surrounding acres." She turned to him. "How much land do you have left, Ivory?"

"Round a hunnert acres, more or less. My granddaddy had near a thousand, but it got sold off gradual-like when my daddy got sick. That's a good price, ain't it?"

"Sounds like a lot of money to me," Willie said.

"Sounds like a miracle," Libba added.

"Maybe. Maybe not." Bennett Winsom rose from his chair and came to Thelma's side to peer over her shoulder. She caught a whiff of the fresh scent of aftershave and had all she could do not to lean against him. She had to get hold of her reactions, or she was going to make a fool of herself.

He took the paper from her, and his hand brushed against hers.

"It says here there is a contract enclosed. Where is it?"

"I signed it, Mr. Bennett. Signed it and sent it back before they could change their mind." Ivory grinned. "I'll have me a check for ten thousand dollars in time to pay the gov'ment for my taxes."

Bennett frowned, and a sick feeling rose up in Thelma's stomach. "Do you have a copy of the contract?" he asked Ivory.

"Sure do. Back at my cabin. It came with—what's that word? A black piece of paper you put in between?"

"A carbon," Bennett muttered.

"That's it. Why are you asking about the contract, Mr. Bennett?"

"Mr. Winsom is a lawyer, Ivory," Thelma explained. "It's his business to know about contracts—whether they're legal or not, whether people are being treated right."

Ivory's face fell. "Did I do wrong to sign it, Mr. Bennett? It sure seemed like a godsend."

"It's probably fine, Ivory. Don't worry. But if you're willing to let me look at it, I'd be glad to check it out for you." He handed the letter to Ivory and went back to his seat. "Now, let's all sit down and finish this wonderful dinner."

Bennett Winsom smiled, but Thelma had the distinct feeling he was just trying to make Ivory feel better. Before she could think about it much longer, however, the bell jingled, and the door opened to reveal two people, bundled in heavy coats, their faces all but obscured by a stack of brightly wrapped Christmas presents.

For most of the dinner, Willie Coltrain had been relatively quiet, listening to Ivory on one side and Libba on the other. From what Thelma could make out of the conversations, they were mostly about Ivory's land and Libba's problems with Link. Willie said little about herself, about how she was holding up out there at the farm with a sick father and a helpless mother. Thelma figured she just wanted to enjoy her evening out without reliving her own troubles. But Thelma had never seen Willie so lifeless. No laughter, no joking—not even a fraction of the animation that had always characterized her. Even at this joyful Christmas Eve celebration, she had seemed . . . empty.

Now, suddenly, her face lit up, and she smiled in a way Thelma hadn't seen for months—since before the boys shipped out, since before Charlie and Owen were killed. "No!" Willie gasped, lunging to her feet so quickly that she toppled her chair over. "Can't be!"

Laughing and choking back tears at the same time, she made a beeline for the door and swept one of the figures up in an exuberant hug. Packages scattered everywhere, and at last Thelma saw it—the round, beaming face of Mabel Rae Coltrain.

★ ★ ★

"I just can't believe it!" Willie said for the tenth time. She reached out and took her sister's hand and squeezed it to reassure herself that she wasn't dreaming. She had known that she missed Mabel Rae, of course. Until Rae had gone to New Orleans with her handsome lieutenant, the two sisters had never been separated. But until this moment, with Rae sitting within arm's reach, she hadn't realized how much of her own life was tied up with her sister's. Willie hadn't just felt alone; she had felt like half a person.

Her eyes lingered on the round, moonlike face, so familiar, and yet completely new. It wasn't just Rae's absence, either—she really had changed. She seemed so confident, so radiant, so . . . loved.

Willie's heart constricted with an old torment. It would be Rae's wedding, not her own, that they would celebrate in April. Rae's children, not her own, who would fill the old farmhouse with rambunctious activity and childish laughter. But for Rae's sake she would be happy. Despite her own loss and sorrow, Willie would find a way to triumph in her sister's good fortune. She would not let herself miss this. She would walk the aisle as maid of honor and stand proudly with her sister as she said her vows. She might not be able to experience that kind of love for herself, but she had put those dreams behind her now. She would share in Rae's happiness, and—

Against her will her eyes drifted to Drew's hands on Rae's shoulders, stroking gently, intimately.

He was wearing a wedding band.

24

★ ★ ★

Stalag Christmas

Snow swirled down in huge flakes as Charlie Coltrain and the rest of the prisoners stood for morning roll call. If it hadn't been so blasted cold, Charlie would have enjoyed this. He had never seen a white Christmas before—never seen more than an inch or two of snow on the ground, not even enough to make a snowman.

As kids, of course, they had tried to take full advantage of whatever meager snow came to Mississippi. Sliding down the gentle slopes of the cow pasture on burlap seed bags, they usually ended up with their dungarees coated with mud and manure, and Mom scolded them and made them wash their own clothes. But it was worth it.

Charlie had always longed to see the kind of postcard scene depicted on Christmas cards—gentle lights from window lamps washing over a white wonderland, a horse-drawn sleigh carrying a laughing, gift-laden family to Grandma's front door. Like most southerners, he loved snow and was fascinated with its purity, its intricacy, its ability to soften and transform the ugliest scene into a beautiful illusion.

Having to stand ankle-deep in the stuff for two hours at five in the morning, however, took a little of the romance out of it. His feet were numb, and his chest ached from breathing in the icy air. Surely it wouldn't be too much longer. Even working on road repairs, shoveling rocks and dirt and filling potholes, was preferable to an extended roll call. At least the activity kept them a little warmer.

But this morning the camp had a special guest, so they weren't likely to be dismissed anytime soon. A strutting officer in the feared black uniform and high jackboots of the SS stood before them, speaking arrogantly in broken English.

"You may haff heard," he bellowed, "that the Allies haff overtaken the armies of the Reich and are pushing them out of France." A sneer crossed his handsome Aryan face. "Not true. In fact—" he slapped his swagger stick against his thigh—"the superior forces of the Fatherland is at this moment launching an attack that will give Deutschland the victory. Heil Hitler!" He raised a hand in salute. "To the gory of der Führer!"

Charlie had been imprisoned for nearly six months, and he had heard this kind of propaganda dozens of times before. It didn't mean anything, except that their captors were attempting to break their spirits in addition to their bodies. They endured the verbal assault and went on. But when the self-important Kraut spoke so glowingly of "the *gory* of der Führer," Charlie couldn't help himself. He laughed.

Immediately he knew he had made a mistake—maybe even a fatal one. In three strides the SS officer reached him and slashed him viciously across the face with his swagger stick. Charlie fell facedown, his blood staining the snow. He lay there for a moment, panting, then raised up on his knees and looked at the officer.

"Something funny?" the man snarled.

Charlie shook his head and lowered his eyes.

"Get up. Schnell!"

Slowly Charlie began to struggle to his feet, but a fit of coughing assailed him, and he sank down again, gagging. The officer motioned to one of the guards, who jerked Charlie up by the elbow and pinned his arms behind him. Just as the SS officer raised his stick to strike again, Charlie saw movement out of the corner of his eye.

"NO!" With a great lunge, Owen Slaughter abandoned his place in line and flung himself toward the Nazi. He grabbed the officer's wrist and held the stick suspended in midair. But he wasn't strong enough to hold on. With a mighty effort, the officer wrenched free and sent Owen reeling to the ground, then whipped out his pistol and pointed it directly at Owen's head.

No one moved. For an eternity, it seemed, the Nazi officer stood with Owen in his sights, his eyes flitting back and forth between Charlie and Owen. At last he fixed his gaze on Charlie and gave a malevolent smile. "Good friend," he said with an evil chuckle. "Stupid friend."

He turned back to Owen and fired.

Charlie shut his eyes and shuddered. A tear seeped from his closed eyelids, and then he heard the SS officer begin to laugh—a diabolical sound that chilled Charlie more than the frigid morning air.

Charlie's eyes flew open, and he saw Owen, still very much alive, crouched on the ground. Not two inches from his head snow and dirt were ripped up where the Nazi's bullet had landed. The man continued to laugh, his head thrown back and his weapon dangling from his fingers. At last he sobered, looked at Charlie, and pointed a forefinger at him. "Good joke," he said. "Now you laugh." He leaned forward until his nose was just inches from Charlie's. "If you live," he whispered savagely, "you tell. Tell how good the soldiers of the Reich treat prisoners. Tell how your stupid friend's life is spared. How do you say? A Christmas present."

The Nazi spun on his heel and saluted the guard. "Heil Hitler!" Then he stalked away, into the darkness and falling snow.

★ ★ ★

Much to everyone's surprise, there was no work detail on Christmas Day. Owen attributed it less to the Krauts' humanity than to their selfishness. There seemed to be a smaller contingent of guards about the camp, and surely they didn't want to go out and stand in the snow to watch the prisoners work.

Owen was relieved. They all needed the rest, especially Charlie. The cut on his face, though not deep, could easily get infected in a rat hole like this, and Owen wanted to make sure his friend got treated with whatever meager supplies they could round up.

Shortly before noon, a baby-faced guard brought an extra ration of coal, and by the time he got back with food and fresh water, the common room was warmer than it had been since September.

"Lookee here, mates!" Tiger Grayson exclaimed when he saw the provisions the boy had brought. "Real meat. Fresh bread—and butter. This is fair dinkum, I'll tell you."

The men crowded around while Tiger divided up the meat and bread, then sat down at the table.

"I don't get it," Grayson mumbled around a mouthful of food. "After what happened this morning—" he cast a baleful glare in Owen's direction—"I'd think they'd be givin' us worse than usual."

"I'll say," one of the Brits chimed in. "That was a right stupid move, if you ask me, Slaughter. You could have got us all killed."

Owen felt his temper begin to flare. "And what did you expect me to do? Just stand there while some swaggering Nazi beat up on Charlie for no reason?"

"This is a prison camp, Slaughter. War, remember? How do you expect prisoners to be treated? Besides, what do you think our boys are doing to the Germans we've captured?"

"Well, I certainly don't think they're torturing them for the fun of it."

Tiger Grayson gave a cynical laugh. "You are the innocent, aren't you, boy?"

Owen jumped to his feet, fists clenched, but Charlie reached up and drew him back down to his seat again.

"I've heard," Tiger was saying, "that conditions in the Allied camps are even worse than they are here. We're all barbarians, and that's the truth."

Effington, the senior officer, raised a hand for silence. "This is exactly what they want from us," he said quietly. "To believe their propaganda, to start fighting among ourselves. They're counting on it." He turned toward Tiger. "Don't believe anything you hear—it's all carefully orchestrated to get a response out of us."

"Like what?" Grayson countered.

"Like that load of manure the SS officer piled on this morning," Effington answered. "It was designed to dishearten us, to make us lose hope. As for this food and the coal—they will do anything to keep us off guard. Even shoot us—" he glanced at Owen—"or spare us. Whatever suits their purposes at the time."

The Aussie raised a chunk of bread. "If this is propaganda, I'll swallow it."

Everyone laughed. "We'll take what we can get to survive," Effington muttered. "But don't let yourself forget who the enemy is and what they're after."

"Yeah." Charlie touched his wounded cheek. "The gory of the Fatherland."

★ ★ ★

When everyone else had turned in for the night, Charlie and Owen still sat huddled around the iron stove with their moth-eaten wool blankets, taking advantage of the last of the coal.

"It's nice not to be cold for a change," Charlie sighed.

"Yeah," Owen agreed. "I can't remember when I've felt this warm."

Charlie grinned. "You can't remember a lot of things, remember?" A startled look passed over Owen's face, and for a minute Charlie thought he might have hurt his friend's feelings. Then Owen smiled in return, and Charlie relaxed. Good. If he could joke about it—even just a little—there was hope.

"I still can't believe what you did for me this morning." Charlie shook his head.

"What are friends for?"

Charlie held out his hands toward the stove and rubbed them together. "Good friend. Stupid friend," he chuckled. "I thought you were a goner."

"So did I. My ears are still ringing, that bullet passed so close."

"It could have lodged in your brain, pal."

"Then it wouldn't have damaged any vital parts," Owen returned. "I guess it wasn't a real smart move."

"There's a fine line between courage and craziness. But it was a pretty brave thing to do, anyway."

"You'd have done it for me."

Charlie thought about that for a minute. Yes, he probably would have done it, had Owen been in danger. For all the friends he had known in his life, all the people he shared a common heritage and common experiences with, he had never had a friend like Owen Slaughter. This man without a past, without memory, without a life beyond the fences of this prison compound, had become closer to him than anyone he had ever known.

People said that war makes strange bedfellows, that the circumstances and dangers of battle forge bonds between men who would never, under ordinary circumstances, have any common ground. And yet, instinctively, Charlie knew that Owen Slaughter was the type of man he would choose for a friend no matter what his situation. Ironically, here in this terrible place, where he had ended up because he had wanted to die, Charlie had found the brother he'd always longed for.

Charlie looked up and found Owen staring at him. "What?"

"I'm worried about you," Owen said. "You look terrible."

"You don't look so pretty yourself, if you want to know the truth."

"You know what I mean. Your cough is getting worse."

"It's just winter." Charlie waved off his friend's concern. "When it warms up a little, I'll be fine." He pulled the thin blanket around his shoulders. "I always wanted to see a white Christmas," he mused. "We never got much snow down south, and never in December. Now—" he shrugged—"I expect I'll be glad to see the last of it."

They sat for a while in silence as the coal fire waned and the room grew chilly. At last Charlie reached into the inside pocket of his jacket and drew out a battered photograph. He handed Owen the photo, a picture of the entire Coltrain clan on the front porch of the farmhouse. "This is Mom and Pop," he said, pointing. "And this is Willie, the biscuit queen. Next to her is Mabel Rae. And that, of course, is yours truly."

"You look a lot different." Owen handed the photo back to him. "Nice family."

"Yeah." Charlie closed his eyes. "It's Christmas. At Christmas a guy ought to be with his family."

"I guess so. Problem is, I don't have a family—at least not one I know of." Charlie pressed the photograph back into Owen's hand. "Yes, you do. I want you to keep this. It's a Christmas present, from me to you. You'll always have a family in Eden."

Owen shook his head and turned his face away. When he looked back, Charlie thought he saw tears in those dark-rimmed, sunken eyes. "You can't give this to me," Owen protested. "It's all you've got."

"So what are friends for? Merry Christmas, pal."

"Merry Christmas," Owen murmured. "Good friend. Stupid friend."

THREE

Winter Chill

JANUARY 1945

25

⭐ ⭐ ⭐

Storm over Paradise

Paradise Garden Cafe
January 2, 1945

Libba sat at a table next to the wall and stared glumly at her half-empty coffee cup. For the past four days, everything north of Greenwood—up past Memphis as far as Blytheville, Arkansas—had been held in the grip of a vicious ice storm. So far the power lines had held, but all the telephones were out, no buses were running, and the only sane means of transportation was walking—very slowly and very carefully.

Bennett Winsom had gone back to Memphis on Christmas Eve night so he could spend Christmas Day with his son. But Aunt Mag had stayed one day too long, and Mabel Rae and her lieutenant had also gotten stuck, out on the farm with Willie and their parents. Stork and Madge, who were supposed to have moved into their new house yesterday, still occupied the apartment in back of the cafe.

Nothing was moving. Nothing. The whole town was eerily quiet. Most folks were just staying put until it was over and life could get back to normal.

Libba loved her mother, and she adored Aunt Mag, but after three days of pinochle lessons, cabin fever had set in, and she had to get out. It had taken her nearly an hour to make her way to the cafe, going the long way around to avoid the hill just below the schoolhouse. She had to walk like a duck, putting each foot down flat and holding on to tree trunks and branches along the way.

The cafe was deserted, of course, but Thelma was there and had a pot of

165

fresh coffee going. She offered to make Libba a sandwich or get her a slice of pie, but Libba declined. All she wanted was coffee, and even that was optional. What she really needed was peace of mind.

"Honey, it just can't be helped," Thelma said, patting her hand. "I'm sure Link understands that you can't get to Memphis just now. I'm sure Bennett—" she paused abruptly, and a strange half smile flitted across her face—"I'm sure Link's father has told him about your conversation."

"Yes, but I need to hear it from him," Libba protested.

"I know you do—and you will." Thelma sighed. "Just not today, I'm afraid."

"How long is this supposed to last?"

Thelma shook her head. "That weather fella on the radio said it'll be Thursday or Friday before the temperature warms up enough to melt this. Till then, I guess, we just pray that the power lines stay put."

"Maybe the telephones will be back in use soon," Libba said hopefully.

"I wouldn't count on it. I don't think the phone crews can get out in this weather either." Thelma gave Libba a soulful look. "I think we'll just have to wait it out."

"It sure is quiet around here," Libba murmured. "Ivory is stuck in his cabin, I presume?"

"Believe it or not, he did get into town," Thelma chuckled. "Two days ago. Walked all the way. He said he couldn't stand being out there on the place by himself like that." She smiled. "He's been sleeping on my sofa the past two nights."

"That little apartment of yours must be getting pretty crowded."

"Yeah, but we're having a good time. Trying to make the best of it." She laughed. "Mickey loves all the attention. I don't know what that child's going to do when his mama and daddy move him to that house."

"Madge will bring him here when she comes to work, of course," Libba said. "And he'll charm everybody, just like he always has." She drank the last of her coffee, and Thelma poured another cup for each of them. "How is the little guy feeling, by the way? Is he still under the weather?"

"He's been a bit puny," Thelma answered slowly. "A little on the fussy side, which is unusual for him. I think he's getting a cold."

The door swung open, and Ivory ambled in, stomping off his shoes and rubbing his arms. "I ain't never seen it so cold. Must be twenty degrees out there."

"Hans Amundson, the soldier from Minnesota, would call this a heat wave," Libba laughed. "Where he lives, it gets down to thirty below. He says southerners are too soft—we couldn't take it."

"Don't want to take it," Ivory mumbled. "Druther give it back."

"Did you get to the post office, Ivory?" Thelma asked.

"I got there." Ivory shook his head. "Didn't do me no good."

"Charity Grevis wasn't there?"

"She was there, all right. That woman wouldn't take the chance of missing any gossip less'n she was dead. And even then she'd prob'ly come to her own funeral just to hear what folks was saying about her." He chuckled. "But she's talking to herself today. Ain't nobody out. And there ain't been no mail coming, either."

"Since when are you so interested in the mail, Ivory?" Libba asked. "You got a girlfriend in Little Rock?"

Ivory grinned. "Naw, Miss Libba—now don't you go on like that. You'll embarrass me. Fact is, I'm expecting my check from the folks who's buying my daddy's land."

"Already? I didn't think the deal was going to be finalized until later in the spring."

"That's true enough. But they're sending me what they call *earning money*—part of it up front, so's to make the deal legal."

"Earnest money, you mean?" Thelma smiled.

"That's it. Fifteen hunnert dollars. More'n enough to pay my taxes. I get the rest when we sign the papers." His face fell. "But there ain't no mail coming today."

"You've got plenty of time," Thelma said. "It's still almost two weeks before your taxes are due."

"I guess so. God provided, so I don't s'pose I should worry about whether it gets here early or not." Ivory grinned. "You shoulda seen that postmistress's face when that official letter came for me. I ain't got no mail to speak of in prob'ly ten years. Then here comes this highfalutin fancy packet addressed to Mr. Harlan Brownlee, Esquire. That Miz Grevis was fit to be tied, wanting to know what was in that letter." He gave a high-pitched laugh. "I didn't tell her." A frown crossed Ivory's face, and he stopped suddenly. "What's an esquire, Thelma?"

She glanced at Libba and smiled. "An esquire is a country gentleman, Ivory. A landowner."

"That's me." Ivory puffed his chest out. "Only pretty soon I'm gonna be a much smaller esquire—only about two acres worth." A cloud passed over his features. "Am I doing the right thing, Thelma?"

"I'd say you're doing the only thing you can do to keep your home."

"I guess. Sometimes it seems like a miracle, and sometimes . . . sometimes I wonder."

"I know. But Mr. Winsom has promised to look over your contract and make sure everything is legal and aboveboard."

"Yeah, but when's he coming back? I gotta pay those taxes by January fifteenth."

"I don't know," Thelma murmured absently. "Soon . . . I hope."

Caught by the wistful tone in Thelma's voice, Libba stared intently into the older woman's face. She had a faraway expression, a look of—what was it? Longing?

Libba took a sip of her coffee, trying to hide a smile. Unless she missed her guess, Thelma Breckinridge was dangerously close to developing a serious crush on one Bennett Winsom, attorney-at-law. And she didn't even know it.

★ ★ ★

Bennett sat at his son's bedside, watching. Asleep, Link could have been a boy again, the muscles of his face relaxed, his skin smooth, his mouth slightly ajar.

Love welled up in his heart, and Bennett could barely restrain himself from stroking an errant hair back from the broad forehead. His boy—his youngest, the child of his heart—had grown into a fine young man. A good-hearted man. Even the mistakes he made, like trying to push Libba Coltrain away, came out of a sense of nobility, distorted though it might be. He had some growing up to do yet, some spiritual maturing, particularly. But he was well on his way, and Bennett was immensely proud of him.

Link sighed in his sleep and turned his head, and Bennett held his breath and watched. How many times had he sat like this at Catherine's bedside in the last months of her illness, watching her sleep, praying for her, asking God to spare her life? He needed her so, and when she died, a part of him went with her.

Bennett had tried to cope with his mourning by throwing himself into his work. The other children—particularly RuthAnn, the oldest at nineteen—were mature enough to understand and to help out. But Link, the baby, was only five. Too young to comprehend why his mommy had gone away. Too young to grasp the depth of his father's grief.

RuthAnn had taken up the slack and raised Link as if he were her own child. RuthAnn taught him to count and tell time and tie his shoes. RuthAnn sent him off to his first day of school, conferred with his teachers about his progress, helped him learn to keep his eye on a fastball, and knotted his tie for his first date.

RuthAnn had stayed home. And for the first time in his life, Bennett realized how much his eldest daughter had sacrificed for the sake of his youngest son. Link was the man he was, not because of Bennett's influence, but because of RuthAnn's.

Now, after nearly twenty years of grieving and escaping in his work, Bennett Winsom was coming out of his fog. He looked down at Link and began to weep—tears of regret for the years he had lost, tears of commitment that he would not lose this second chance at fatherhood.

He picked up a book that was lying on the bedside table—one of two last-minute Christmas presents he had purchased for Link. One was Ernie Pyle's *Brave Men,* a collection of the reporter's columns from the front. The other was Robert Frost's Pulitzer Prize–winning poetry book, *A Witness Tree.* Bennett fingered the volume lovingly. He had always responded with deep emotion to Frost's poetry, and he realized with chagrin that he had bought it because he loved it, not because he had any idea that Link would like it. He flipped through the pages, and his eye caught on a brief poem that made his heart stand still:

A voice said, Look me in the stars
And tell me truly, men of earth,
If all the soul-and-body scars
Were not too much to pay for birth.

Bennett read the poem over and over, his eyes flitting back and forth between the page and Link's face. His son had endured more than his share of soul-and-body scars, and Bennett himself bore a few that still troubled him. Was Frost right—was it too high a price to pay? Was life too difficult to justify human existence?

Bennett shook his head. No. All the soul-and-body scars in the world would never convince him that life wasn't worth living. For all the pain, he would never have missed the love he had known with his Catherine. The kind of love that Link and Libba, despite their difficulties, were discovering. The kind of love that maybe, with the right person and at the right time, Bennett himself might find again. . . .

The unexpected thought startled him, and he shut the book. What was he thinking of? He was nearly sixty years old—he had been thirty-five when Link was born, forty when Catherine had died. He had already had his one great love, and lost her almost twenty years ago.

Still, he was in good health, a robust man who got his share of subtle and not-so-subtle offers from women ten and fifteen years younger than he. But he had never been interested. He had always assumed he would never fall in love again, never find a woman with the kind of fire and spark and passion—and spiritual depth—that characterized his Catherine.

Most of the women he had met over the past years had been simpering homebodies who made a point of letting him know how pliable and submissive they were. Maybe they thought that's what a man wanted—a woman who had no original thoughts, a woman who hung on a man's every word as if he spoke some kind of universal truth, a woman who never argued, always obeyed, and had dinner on the table at six o'clock sharp.

Bennett shuddered. The very idea of such a woman bored him beyond belief. He had been at least half serious when he told Link that Libba's Aunt Mag was "his kind of woman," a woman who knew her own mind and refused to grovel to anyone. Apparently Libba was cut from the same cloth, which was one reason Bennett liked her so much. In some ways she reminded him of Catherine. She would be good for his son, he thought. Very good.

But what about me? he thought. Was it possible that he could let himself love another woman? Now that the thought was out—the thought that he had never once, in nineteen years, seriously considered—he turned it over in his mind. If he were to fall in love again, it would have to be someone very special. Magnolia was available, but she was twenty years too old.

Bennett smiled to himself at the idea of courting Magnolia Cooley. Now, there was a turn of events that would set Eden, Mississippi, on its ear! It was out of the question, of course, but it was rather amusing to think about. If he ever were to marry again, what he needed was a younger version of Aunt Mag. Someone more like . . .

He shook his head. It didn't pay to speculate, to let his mind go in those directions. God had sent him here for other purposes—for Link, and for Libba. Perhaps to help Ivory Brownlee. Not to let his imagination run wild about finding the second great love of his life.

A man only got one chance like that. The Lord had given him twenty years with Catherine—years of love and laughter, years that produced seven beautiful children. And now God had given him one more gift—his son's life, and the opportunity to see him through his recuperation. It was more than any man had a right to expect. It was enough.

Link stirred and opened his eyes. "Dad?" he said groggily. "You're still here?"

"I'm here, Son," Bennett said. "And I'll be here as long as you need me."

26

$$\star \quad \star \quad \star$$

Sisters

Rae watched her sister's back as Willie busied herself with cutting vegetables for the pot of stew. Drew was off somewhere feeding the livestock or surveying damage from the storm. They should have been back in New Orleans by now, but the ice storm had locked up travel in three states, and it might be a couple of days yet before they would even get back into town, much less to Grenada to catch the Crescent City Special

"Don't you want any help, Willie?" she offered. "I could—"

"I can handle it," Willie snapped. "I've *been* handling it for quite some time now."

"Willie, please. Don't shut me out like this."

Her sister turned and fixed her with a withering glare. "I'm shutting *you* out? That's a funny one." She gave a dry, humorless laugh and turned back to her potatoes and onions.

Rae sighed and scraped a fingernail over a clot of dried syrup on the kitchen table. Willie was angry—justifiably so—but Rae didn't know how to reach her, how to make her understand. In the tense silence that stretched between them, she heard Willie sniff once, then a second time.

Rae got to her feet and went to stand behind her sister. "If you cut those under running water, they won't make you cry so much," she offered gently. Then she looked over Willie's shoulder. The onions lay untouched on the counter.

Taking her by the shoulders, Rae turned Willie around and looked into her eyes. Tears streamed down Willie's face, and her eyes were beginning to go puffy.

"I am so sorry," Rae whispered, reaching one hand up to wipe the tears from Willie's cheeks. "You know I would never deliberately hurt you."

"I know," Willie sniffed, swallowing hard. "I just—well, it seems so cruel, you getting married in New Orleans without any of us there—without even letting us know." She gulped. "We said we would plan it together, that I would be your—your maid of—"

Willie dissolved into tears, and Rae drew her into a firm embrace. When Willie had calmed down a little, Rae led her over to the table and lowered her into a chair. She sat down at right angles to Willie and grasped her hands tightly. "It isn't just the wedding, is it?" Rae asked quietly. "There's more—a lot more."

Willie nodded miserably.

"Can you tell me about it?"

Willie shook her head and rubbed a hand over her face.

"Come on. It's me. Mabel Rae. Remember? The one you tell everything to."

Willie looked up and gave her a cynical half smile. "Used to," she corrected. "You haven't been here for me to tell." She took a ragged breath. "Besides, you're not Mabel Rae Coltrain anymore. You're Rae Laporte, New Orleans socialite."

In spite of herself, Rae began to laugh—quietly at first, then with more force, and soon Willie was laughing right along with her.

"That is utter nonsense!" Rae panted when she got control of the giggles. "I'm still the same person, Willie—I just have a different name."

"And a huge diamond ring," Willie quipped. "Not to mention an elegant French wardrobe."

"Hah," Rae snorted. "And a mother-in-law who would make Attila the Hun look like a nun." She shook her head. "You wouldn't believe this woman, Willie." Rae looked around to make sure the kitchen door was closed and lowered her voice. "She has to control everything—she battled for days with the designer of my wedding dress to make sure my 'ample hips' were suitably camouflaged."

"I wish I could have been there," Willie sighed. "I bet you looked gorgeous."

"Well, at least my hips looked good." Rae chuckled. "It was downright embarrassing," she went on. "Usually people comment about how beautiful the bride looks. The talk of this wedding was how beautiful the groom was."

Willie laughed and dried the last of her tears. "Well, he is."

"I know. And believe me, it's a mixed blessing."

"I'm sorry I got so upset," Willie sighed. "I was just looking forward to this wedding so much. I'm afraid I was counting on it too much."

"That's all right. I understand." Rae patted her hand. "And if I could have done it the way we had planned, I would have enjoyed it so much more. But Drew's mother—"

"Yes, tell me about Drew's mother," Willie prompted. "You say she's sick? What's her problem?"

Rae shrugged. "She's got a problem, all right—maybe more than one." She lowered her voice. "I hate to say this, Willie, but I have my doubts that there's anything wrong with her—anything physical, that is. She's supposed to be so frail, and yet she ran circles around me getting ready for the wedding."

"Is she faking it? You know, so she can have her own way, keep her precious son from leaving home?"

"I don't know. If she's faking, I would think she'd act a little more sickly. I'm not sure she even knows she's supposed to be sick. I suspect that Beau—Drew's father is named Beauregard, can you imagine it?—has cooked up this 'your mother isn't well' stuff for his son's benefit."

"The father? What does he get out of it?" Willie asked.

"He gets Drew to agree to stay in New Orleans and jump through legal loopholes for his real-estate companies. Beau has promised him plenty of time for his own work with people who can't afford his services. Drew won't admit it, but I think he's feeling pressured to do it so that we can have what he thinks of as a 'real life.' You know, a nice house, a new car—"

Willie looked around the shabby farmhouse kitchen and lifted one eyebrow. "Sure. He wants to support you in the manner to which you've become accustomed."

Rae laughed curtly. "I see your point. He obviously isn't thinking about the fact that I've lived—ah, shall we say, quite a simple life."

"I don't mean to be indelicate," Willie said, "but I thought Drew's family had money. Why does he have to work for his father to buy time to help people? Why does he need to work at all?"

"He'll have a sizable inheritance someday, that's true," Rae mused. "But right now it's tied up in land and trusts and other stuff I don't quite understand. And Drew wouldn't ask for it, even if he could get to it. He's too proud."

"But not proud enough to refuse to work for his daddy."

"I don't think that's quite fair," Rae protested. "I've got my suspicions, it's true, but Drew really believes his mother is dying. He is her only child, after all. I don't think he would even consider it if she were in good health."

Willie narrowed her eyes. "You're relating this as if Drew has made all these decisions for the two of you, Sister. What happened to that equal partnership you raved about?"

The barb struck home, and Rae winced inwardly. She had thought about it, too—how their plan to make all their decisions mutually had somehow gotten lost in the muddle of wedding plans and Beatrice Laporte's mysterious illness. "I agreed to it," she whispered. "The wedding, the work arrangements—all of it."

"You gave in," Willie corrected.

"I felt I had no choice, Willie. Drew was so devastated about his mother's condition, so worried about her. Believe me, walking down that aisle in the middle of all those strangers was the most difficult thing I've ever done in my life. It broke my heart not having you and Mama and Daddy there—not to mention Thelma and all our friends."

"I believe you," Willie said quietly. "But I also believe that there would have been a huge class distinction between us and the Laportes' society friends."

"You think I'm ashamed of you and Mama and Daddy and our friends?"

"No." Willie sighed. "I think Drew's parents conned him—and you—into not having to face that possibility."

Tears sprang to Rae's eyes, and she fought to hold them back. "Drew and I agreed that once he gets settled in his job, we can come back here and have a second ceremony to celebrate with all the people we love in Eden."

"That would be nice," Willie hedged. "But it wouldn't be the same, would it?"

No, Rae thought. *It wouldn't.* And she was terribly afraid nothing would ever be the same again.

27

⋆ ⋆ ⋆

Judgment Day

At last, Madge thought. *The day I've waited for all my life.*

She stood on the sidewalk in front of the neat little house on Acorn Street and watched as Michael and a couple of friends from the base unloaded their meager belongings from the back of an army truck. Most of the furniture, purchased new from stores in Memphis and Grenada, had already been delivered. The precious blue hooked rug was in place on the living-room floor, covered by an old sheet so the men wouldn't track it up as they went in and out.

"Be careful with that one," she called to a baby-faced private as he leaned into the truck to retrieve a large carton. "That's my new china."

Madge couldn't wait until they were finished and gone. She longed to get into the kitchen and organize, to unpack the delicate china with its tiny pink rosebuds and gold trim and arrange it in the cherry cabinet.

Her first home. *Their* first home. In her mind's eye she could see Michael wrestling with Mickey on the rug in front of the fireplace. She could imagine their first fine dinner around the magnificent oval dining-room table Thelma had given them for a housewarming present. Even now, in midwinter, she could almost smell the scents of spring, the fresh breeze blowing through the kitchen windows, could hear Mickey's laughter as he ran and picked flowers in the backyard.

It was perfect. Absolutely perfect. A place of love and peace and contentment, where nothing bad could possibly ever happen.

Michael came down the walk, swept her up in an embrace, and kissed her. "Happy?"

"Ooh, you're all sweaty," she laughed, hugging him hard. "But I don't care. Yes, my darling, I am happy. Deliriously, incredibly happy."

"We're all done." He put an arm around her and stood back to look at the house admiringly. "The fellows are ready to take the truck back to the base."

"Did you tell them they're invited for dinner next week?"

"I did." Michael grinned. "Although I don't know how proper it is for an officer to be fraternizing with lowly enlisted men."

Madge punched him playfully on the arm. "It's not fraternizing. It's payment for all their hard work." She smiled and waved as the two privates came out of the house and got into the truck. "Fried chicken," she called after them. "And homemade apple pie. Don't forget!"

"No, ma'am!" the baby-faced private answered. "We'll be here."

The truck roared to life and pulled out into the street, and Madge stood waving until they had rounded the corner and were out of sight. She felt Michael's lips nuzzling at her neck, and she turned in his arms to receive a kiss. "Where's the baby?" she murmured.

"Sound asleep in his crib. He must have been exhausted."

"He's had a busy day—and so have we." Madge brushed a strand of hair out of her eyes. "What time is it?"

Michael looked at his watch. "Almost four-thirty."

"No! Michael, your mother is coming in less than two hours, and I've still got to organize the kitchen and get things straightened up."

"I'll help. I can put the clothes away and—" He raised one eyebrow. "Make up the bed."

Madge wrinkled her nose at him. "I think your first job should be to get a bath. Then you can make the bed." She winked at him. "But don't expect to be using it anytime soon."

"Killjoy." He laughed and took her arm. "Your castle awaits, milady." He took her hand and led her to the front door, then threw it open and scooped her up in his arms.

"Michael! What do you think you're doing?"

"Carrying you across the threshold, of course."

"This isn't our honeymoon," she protested. "In case you've forgotten, we got married a long time ago."

"It is our honeymoon," he insisted huskily. "Our new beginning." He carried her across the doorstep and set her down gently in the entryway. "Have I told you recently how much I love you?"

"Yes," she whispered. "Every time I come into this house, I'm reminded of your love. Thank you, Michael. Thank you for loving me, for being such a wonderful husband, for . . . for everything." Madge looked deep into her husband's dear, familiar face—the warm hazel eyes, the unruly shock of blond hair at his forehead, the hawkish nose, the angular planes of his cheeks. He wasn't, by any objective standards, a man the world would consider handsome, and yet the light of love that shone from his eyes was the most beautiful sight on earth. She stroked his stubbled cheek. "You need a shave, sweetheart."

"Ah, you women!" he joked. "Won't kiss a man unless he's clean-shaven."

"I didn't say that." Madge melted into his arms and kissed him—a long, lingering kiss.

"Keep that up and we sure won't be ready when Mother arrives." He leaned down and kissed her again.

"All right." She pulled away and looked up into his face. "You get a bath. I'll get the kitchen in shape and put the chicken in the oven. When you're done, I'll clean up."

"We could . . . save water." He gave her a crooked grin.

"No, we couldn't." She turned him around and nudged him in the direction of the bathroom. "Check on Mickey, will you? And don't use all the hot water."

★ ★ ★

At six-thirty, Madge stood in the dining room, surveying the table with satisfaction. She had been right—the china with the tiny rosebuds set off the wallpaper to perfection. An arrangement of soft pink carnations would have been ideal, but fresh flowers were far too expensive this time of year. The antique-footed bowl, with its subdued pink-and-green tones, would have to do.

She went to the china cabinet and brought it out, caressing its satiny finish with her fingers. It had belonged to her grandmother and was the only thing she had left from her mother. When the fire had destroyed everything—her family, her home, her life—Madge had been just a child. But her Aunt Sylvia had found the bowl among her own things, borrowed from Madge's mother for a family gathering, and when Madge was old enough to appreciate it, she had given it to the girl. Madge had carried it with her everywhere, and now it held a place of honor in the cherry cabinet.

She set the bowl in the center of the table and nodded. It was fitting, bringing this one piece of her long-dead past into the present, into her new home. Everything was coming together. She had a family of her own now, and a place of stability to raise her son. And somehow, even though Madge couldn't remember her face, she sensed that her mother would be pleased.

"I hope you can see this, Mother," Madge whispered wistfully. "I hope you're proud of your daughter . . . and your grandson."

"I'm sure she is, hon," a voice murmured in her ear as an arm slipped around her shoulders. "I know I am."

"Thelma!" Madge whirled around. "I didn't hear you come in."

"Door was open." Thelma shrugged. "I knocked, but—"

"The door is always open to you." Madge hugged her warmly. "What is this?"

Thelma held out a covered dish and a paper-wrapped parcel. "A little housewarming present. I know Lorna Simpson will be here any minute, and I don't intend to stick around. I just wanted you to have these. And this—" she leaned over and kissed Madge on the cheek—"the dish is just a little bread pudding I whipped up this afternoon. Open the package."

Madge complied, and gasped with delight. Inside the brown paper were a dozen pastel pink carnations.

"I thought they'd look nice with your new china, maybe cut and arranged in your mother's—" Thelma stopped as her eyes went to the table—"Ah. Great minds think alike I see."

"They're wonderful, Thelma. Just what I was wishing for." Madge gave her another hug. "And you're wonderful."

"Wasn't nothing," Thelma said sheepishly. "Just a token."

"A token," Madge repeated. "Like the token of this beautiful dining-room table and chairs?"

Thelma grinned. "You needed it. I wasn't using it. Made sense to me." She ran a hand over the rubbed finish of the wood. "Looks nice in here. In fact, the whole place looks absolutely beautiful. Just like a little dollhouse."

Madge nodded. "It is, isn't it? I'm exhausted, Thelma, but I'm too excited to rest. I can't stop thinking about all the things I'd like to do—new curtains, pictures I'd like to get for the walls. Don't you think a beveled mirror would look good over the fireplace?"

"I do," Thelma agreed. "But don't go wearing yourself out the first week. It'll keep. Besides, it's adorable just like it is." She glanced into the kitchen. "Something smells mighty good."

"Baked chicken," Madge said, "with vegetables. I didn't have time for anything elaborate."

"I'm surprised you had time for anything at all," Thelma muttered. "Don't make sense to me that woman wanting to come for dinner your first night here. Selfish, that's all it is. She should be fixing for you."

"She's been staying at the boardinghouse, Thelma, you know that. Judith Larkins doesn't allow anybody in her kitchen."

"Still, she could have taken y'all out for a nice dinner in Grenada. Or you could have come over to the cafe."

"Mother Simpson says she's tired of restaurant food."

"You mean she's too high and mighty for the Paradise Garden—and for me." Thelma frowned. "How long do you reckon she's going to stay, anyway?"

Madge shrugged. "I don't know. I thought she'd be long gone by now. But then, she thought she'd be taking Michael back home with her—or at least getting him away from me. I wish Dad Simpson was here with her—at least he might temper her comments. But he's probably just glad to have a little peace and quiet, for once. I swear, Thelma, if I hear one more word about God's judgment on the unrighteous, I think I'll scream."

Thelma patted her hand. "Hang in there, honey. It can't last forever."

"Thelma, I don't know what I'd do without you."

"You'd be fine, that's what you'd do. You're strong, and you know your own mind." Thelma grinned. "But I hope you don't have to find out what you'd do without me."

"I hope not, too." Madge looked around and smiled. "And now that we've got our own place, I expect we'll all be together for a long, long time."

Thelma smoothed Madge's hair over her ear affectionately. "I'd best go before you-know-who arrives."

"All right. Pray for me. I'll see you at the cafe in the morning."

"Give that precious baby a kiss for me. And get some rest." Thelma thrust the bread pudding into Madge's outstretched hands and headed for the door.

★ ★ ★

"So, what do you think?" Madge held her breath as she watched Mother Simpson surveying the little house with a critical eye. Surely the woman would see how perfect the place was for them, how neat and tidy, with homey touches everywhere. Madge had worked oo hard making sure everything was perfect, doing in one day what might have taken a week under normal circumstances. There were a few unpacked cartons here and there, pushed into corners and covered with tablecloths and throw rugs. But surely even Lorna Simpson could overlook that, considering the fact that they had just finished moving in that afternoon.

"I suppose," Mother Simpson said with an exaggerated sigh, "that you've done the best you can with what you had to work with."

Madge's spirits deflated like a balloon. This was her mother-in-law's idea of encouragement? But what did she expect? Lorna Simpson had never yet been pleased with anything Madge had done—why should it be any different now?

"But don't you—don't you think it's nice?" Madge prompted. "It's just perfect for us. Mickey has his own little room. We've even got a guest room. Once we get furniture in there, you could—" Madge stopped suddenly. The last thing she wanted was for this woman to come and stay with them, under the same roof. Having her in the boardinghouse on the other side of town had been bad enough.

"It's not quite—" Mother Simpson paused and cleared her throat—"not quite what my son has been brought up to expect. But I suppose it's better than a dismal little apartment in the back of a greasy-spoon diner. At least that woman won't be nosing around all the time."

That woman. Madge had never yet heard Lorna Simpson use Thelma Breckinridge's proper name; she was always "that woman" or "that floozy" or "that hussy." Her temper began to flare.

"Mother Simpson," she said through gritted teeth, "that woman, as you call her, is my closest friend in the world. Her cafe is not a greasy-spoon diner, and I felt more welcome in her crowded little apartment than I ever did in—" She took a deep breath. "What I mean is, I'd appreciate it if you'd show her a little more respect. She is part of this family, whether or not she is related by blood."

"Family," Lorna muttered. "I can see what you're doing to my boy. You're brainwashing him, making him believe that these—these yokels—care about his welfare. Well, there's only one person who truly cares about him, who wants the best for him—and it's not you, Miss High-and-Mighty. It's—"

"Mother, that's enough." Michael's voice was low and subdued, but carried a definite hint of anger. "We're going to have a nice dinner and behave like civilized people."

Lorna turned, but not before Madge saw the open expression of malice in her eyes. "Of course we are, dear boy!" the woman gushed, going to Michael and taking his face in both her hands. "I was just telling your girl here how clever she was to make this house such a charming little place." She kissed his cheek. "Even if it is temporary."

"We just finished moving in today," Michael said pointedly. "We don't consider it temporary."

"Of course not, sweetheart. Whatever makes you feel good about it."

Michael glanced over his mother's head and cast a helpless look at Madge. "Is dinner about ready?"

Madge nodded. "Thelma brought the flowers and a bread pudding," she told him, placing undue emphasis on Thelma's name. "As a housewarming gift, and to help me out since I've been too busy to cook much." She lifted one eyebrow at Michael's mother. "The dining-room table and chairs are also a gift from Thelma."

Lorna slanted a glance in Madge's direction. "Oh, my. I suppose I was expected to bring a housewarming gift as well. I just didn't think—"

"It's all right, Mother," Michael soothed. "You're here, and that's what matters."

"Yes," Madge added, rolling her eyes, "the place just wouldn't be the same without your presence."

★ ★ ★

"I can't believe Mickey has slept this long," Stork commented over dessert. Dinner had been a tense and uncomfortable affair, and Stork felt as if he had been at the center of a tug-of-war between his mother and his wife. Madge was trying so hard to please Mother, but as usual it just wasn't working. He kept hoping his mother would get tired of trying to influence him and just go home. Heaven knows, he was tired of her.

She had been in Eden for nearly three weeks, staying at the Larkins's boardinghouse and generally making life miserable and inconvenient for everyone. On the days he was on duty at the base, she would hang around the cafe, driving business away with her condescending attitude toward what she called "the natives," and deliberately making Madge's life unbearable. When he had time off, she would spend the entire day harping at him about the Lord's impending judgment.

At this point he was thankful they hadn't had the money to furnish the guest room right away. They had planned to clear out the boxes and use part of next month's paycheck for a bed and dresser, and perhaps a nice chair for the corner. But maybe they would postpone those plans—at least until Mother was safely on the bus back to Missouri.

The one overriding emotion Stork felt in his mother's presence was guilt—guilt over the sin she talked about incessantly, guilt for putting Madge through the ordeal of Mother's constant bickering, guilt for letting Mother ruin their Christmas and spoil his wife's joy in her new home.

It had to end—and soon. But Stork couldn't bring himself to stand up to her, to tell her to go home where she belonged. She was his mother, after all. And something inside him kept nagging at him, arguing that she might just be right about the judgment he deserved. Madge and Thelma disagreed, of course, and tried to get him to think about God's forgiveness instead. But the guilt just wouldn't go away.

Stork looked at his wife, then at his mother, then back again to Madge.

Mother had eaten almost nothing, pushing her chicken and vegetables around on her plate and muttering every now and then about not liking food that was cooked all together like that. Madge hadn't eaten much either, and Stork could see the look of abject misery on her face. Now that he thought about it, his own stomach was churning.

"I think I'll go get Mickey up," he said, rising from his place. He took his plate and Madge's, stacked them, and reached for his mother's. "If he sleeps any longer he'll be awake all night." He gave Madge a kiss on the top of the head as he passed by. "You stay put, sweetheart. I'll take care of the dishes, and when I get back with Mickey I'll serve up the dessert." He forced a smile in his mother's direction. "Thelma's bread pudding is legendary."

"None for me," his mother said curtly.

"Coffee, then?" Stork kept the smile pasted on.

"It's on the back of the stove, honey, all ready to go," Madge murmured. "Just turn on the gas."

"I suppose I could have a cup of coffee." His mother lifted her chin. "But I'm sure you don't want me to stay too long."

Stork bit his tongue to keep a sarcastic remark from coming out. "Don't be ridiculous, Mother. You're always welcome in our home."

By the time Stork got Mickey up and changed, however, he had forgotten all about the dessert and coffee. He came back into the dining room with the boy in his arms, and one look at Madge told him that his concern registered on his face.

"What's wrong?" she snapped, her voice unnaturally high and tight.

"Maybe nothing," Stork hedged. "I think he's got a little bit of a fever. He seems really sluggish, and his eyes look funny."

Madge jumped up from the table and placed her forearm across Mickey's face. "He is hot. Did you take his temperature?"

"Not yet. I couldn't find the thermometer."

"Couldn't find it? Or didn't want to use it?"

Stork hesitated. "He just hates it so much."

"And you hate doing it, too."

"Yes, but I guess we have no choice." He bounced the baby against his chest. "Sorry, sport."

Madge went to him and held out her arms. "You find the thermometer. I'll do the dirty work. But if he grows up hating his mother, don't blame me."

Relieved, Stork gave her a kiss on the cheek and handed the baby over. "He adores his mother, and you know it. What's not to love?"

He returned from the bathroom with the thermometer and a wet washrag, and they went into Mickey's bedroom with Stork's mother right behind them. "He looks bad," she said in the doomsday voice Stork now recognized so well. "Very bad."

"He'll be fine, Mother," Stork said. "He's been nursing a cold for the past few days, but it's nothing serious."

Madge peered at the thermometer. "A little over a hundred, that's all." She took the washrag from Stork, wiped Mickey's face down with it, then folded it and laid it across his forehead. "There's some apple juice in the icebox, Michael. Will you get it for him? Half water and half juice." She smoothed back the baby's damp hair.

"You're just going to let him lie there like that, under that thin blanket?" Stork's mother demanded. "There's only one way to get a child's fever down. Bundle him up, and he'll sweat it out."

Madge looked at Stork uncertainly. "I—I don't know," she stammered. "I thought you were supposed to try to keep him cooled off."

Stork watched as his mother fixed his wife with a what-kind-of-mother-are-you-anyway? look. "It's a well-known fact," his mother said. "My mother did it, and my grandmother before her. When you had the chicken pox, Michael, what did I do? Do you remember?"

"Yes," he answered. "You put me under about a hundred blankets and kept me there until the fever broke." He shrugged. "I was pretty miserable, as I recall, but I guess it worked."

"Sounds like an old wives' tale to me," Madge interjected. "I was always told—"

"And just how many children have you raised, may I ask?" The older woman's double chin went up, and her eyes blazed. "Three generations of the James women have doctored a total of fourteen children and never lost a one. And you're going to stand there and argue while your baby burns up with fever?"

Madge turned to Stork, but all he could do was shake his head helplessly. He had never been a father before, never had to deal with this sort of thing. What did he know? And this was Madge's only experience with mother-hood. For all her maternal instincts, she didn't know much more than he did. Perhaps his mother was right, that sweating out the fever was the best remedy.

"Maybe we should try it her way," he told Madge, avoiding her eyes. "If he's still running a fever in the morning, we'll go for the doctor." He patted his wife's shoulder awkwardly. "I'll get the juice."

Stork headed for the kitchen with his mother hot on his heels. "I told you," she hissed. "Something bad was bound to come out of this sooner or later. If you had listened to me, this might not have happened."

He busied himself with the bottle, carefully fitting a sterilized nipple around the lip of the glass.

"God's hand will not be stayed," she intoned. "God's judgment will not be mocked."

"You mean that if I had left my wife and child like you wanted me to, Mickey wouldn't be in his crib with a fever right now? That's absurd."

But even as he said the words, a knot of fear formed in the pit of his stomach. Fear for his baby son. Fear that his mother just might be right after all.

28

★ ★ ★

Render unto Caesar

When Bennett Winsom entered the Paradise Garden Cafe, he felt an unexpected sense of anticipation, as if he were returning to an old and cherished friend. His eyes roamed around the room, taking in the cracked linoleum floor, the scarred green countertops, the battered piano in the corner. It was all quite garish and shabby, and yet there was something special about this place, something . . familiar.

Yes, he mused, *familiar* in the archaic sense of the word—pertaining to the family. He felt comfortable here, as if he belonged. Strange how that happened. He had only set foot in the place one other time—a week and a half ago, on Christmas Eve. But he had been welcomed with a warmth and love that few people ever experience.

He felt like he had come home, and a sense of well-being washed over him as he took a seat. And for some reason he didn't begin to understand, his heart leaped at the sight of Thelma Breckinridge coming through the door from the kitchen. Her henna dyed hair encircled her head like a halo, and a light shone from her eyes as she approached him.

"Well, Mr. Winsom, welcome back," she said in a throaty voice as she leaned over him to pour coffee into a cup. "I take it you got Libba back to Memphis all right."

"News travels fast in Eden, doesn't it?" Bennett smiled. "Once the roads had cleared, I decided to drive down here and take her up myself. I'm afraid my son couldn't wait another twelve hours for the bus to bring her."

Thelma laughed, and Bennett found himself enjoying the sound immensely. "I suppose that means the two of them are going to figure things out after all," she said. "Mind if I sit for a spell?"

"Please, do join me." Bennett rose from his seat and pulled out a chair for her. Obviously she wasn't accustomed to such gentility, for the gesture flustered her, and they bumped into one another as she sat down. He smiled into her eyes and saw there the most amazing combination of self-confidence and humility—a peace that, despite the momentary confusion, infused her whole being.

She chuckled at her own clumsiness. "Forgive me, Mr. Winsom. We don't get gentlemen around here too often."

Warmed by her honesty, he shook his head. "That's their loss, I'd say. And my gain. If there were other gentlemen in the vicinity, I doubt if I'd have you all to myself for very long. And I thought we had gotten past the *Mr.* on Christmas Eve."

Thelma averted her eyes for a moment. "That's a very sweet thing to say, Mr. —ah, Bennett. You do know how to turn an old girl's head." She paused. "Lawyers are known for their smooth talk, if I recall."

A sudden desire to let her know that it wasn't just empty flattery stirred within him. Thelma Breckinridge was a woman who, by all accounts, lived in faithfulness and integrity, serving others without any thought of what she'd get in return. His son had praised the woman to the skies, and Libba, on the trip to Memphis, had confirmed Link's evaluation. From everything he had been told, Thelma was a rock, a spiritual hub of the community, a pillar of faith. Call it curiosity or personal interest, but Bennett was determined to find out what made her tick.

"Forgive me if that sounded hollow, Thelma. I certainly didn't mean it that way. I just—" He paused, not knowing quite how to continue. "I guess I'm too accustomed to having to make a case for myself—sell myself, if you know what I mean."

"I'm not sure I do," Thelma said. "Tell me about it."

"Part of a lawyer's gift—or curse, depending upon your perspective—is the ability to seem believable, to make people think that no matter what you say, it is the absolute truth. In court, or in private negotiations, that's an important part of winning your client's case. In personal interactions, however, it sometimes comes across as false, so that even when you are telling the truth, people don't quite believe you."

"Ah," she said. "So you can be perfectly sincere, and yet people think you're putting on the dog. Like me, accusing you of flattery."

"That's right."

"And were you—sincere, I mean—when you said what you did about other gentlemen?"

"Absolutely. Both my son and Libba have told me about you, Thelma Breckinridge. And everything they've told me makes me believe you'd be a good person to have as a friend."

"Thank you," she said. "I love Libba, and I respect Link a great deal, so their regard means a lot."

Bennett looked at Thelma's unaffected countenance, and he was awed by the simplicity with which she accepted his compliment. No false modesty. No pretension. Just a guileless "thank you."

"I've always thought," Thelma was saying, "that being a lawyer would give a person some wonderful opportunities to help people." She leaned forward. "What kind of legal work do you enjoy most, Bennett?"

Incredible, how naturally this woman made him feel the center of attention, as if what he had to say was the most important thing in the world. He watched as her hands moved, pouring coffee, wiping up a tiny drip from the tabletop, holding her cup with a familiar gentleness, as if she were cradling an egg. Then, suddenly, he realized he had lost track of the conversation. "I'm sorry. You asked me a question?"

Her eyes twinkled. "What kind of legal work do you do?"

"Not very profitable cases, I'm afraid. Mostly work I do for a worthy cause but don't get paid for. In my little town in Missouri they think I'm crazy. I'm the lawyer who gets paid in chickens and beans, and occasionally rabbits and squirrels."

Thelma chuckled. "I've got a great recipe for squirrel stew."

He nodded. "Maybe you'll make it for me sometime. I'll provide the meat." He paused for a minute, then went on. "I'm afraid that over the years my practice hasn't done much more than put food on the table—quite literally—for my family. My colleagues drive fancy cars and own big new houses, and a few of them are judges now. Most of them have huge investments to leave as an inheritance for their kids. My children, I fear, will be left with far less."

"Or far more."

Bennett looked up and saw in her eyes an expression he could only define as admiration. "I beg your pardon?"

Thelma smiled at him, and the corners of her brown eyes crinkled in merriment. "People talk about you behind your back, too, Bennett Winsom. Libba told me what Link said about you in his letters—about how he had come to appreciate you so much more since he discovered faith in God for himself. From what I hear, you're a man who puts God first and your family second, and whose life has been a testimony of service to people who can't do for themselves. In my book, that's quite a legacy to pass on to your young'uns."

Bennett stared at her for a minute. How did a simple woman like this come by such depth of wisdom? He felt reprimanded and encouraged all at the same time—chastised for putting too much stock in financial stability, and affirmed for the faith in God he had modeled for his children. But he had made mistakes, and if he was going to be honest with her, she would have to know those, too. Otherwise, their relationship would be based on something less than complete integrity.

Their relationship? The idea stunned Bennett, and for a moment he couldn't speak. Then he pushed the idea aside. Thelma was a friend of Libba's and Link's—a good friend, like part of the family. That was all.

"I—I'm afraid you have rather a one-sided view of me," he stammered, trying to regain his composure. "You've heard some complimentary things, it seems, but—"

"So why don't you tell me about the other side?" she asked smoothly.

That rich, low voice distracted him for a few seconds. Then he said, "Well, you see, I—I don't know how to explain it."

"Straight out is usually the best way."

"I see your point. I'll try," he said. "Yes, I tried to instill in my children a hunger for faith, a desire to discover God's best for themselves. But I'm afraid I didn't always live it to the fullest extent myself. Link was only five when my wife died." The memories washed over him, and his eyes misted. "For years, Thelma, I was caught up in my own pain, in my grieving. I threw myself into work and let Link's older sister RuthAnn take over responsibilities at home. He was too young to make any strong connections with most of his brothers and sisters. But RuthAnn raised Link, so any positive influences in his life must have come from her." He averted his eyes, not wanting to see the disapproval on her face. "I missed so much, Thelma—too much. Oh, I made sure the physical needs of my children were met—food and shelter and education. But I wasn't able—not for a long time—to be a real father to them. I failed them, I'm afraid—and I failed God."

He paused and exhaled a ragged sigh, then finally lifted his head to look at her. But what he saw on her face was not condemnation or disappointment, but compassion and understanding. He shrugged. "So . . . now you know the truth about me."

"I suppose I do at that."

Bennett frowned at her. "What do you mean?"

"I know you're a man capable of making mistakes. That means you're human. But you're also a man capable of listening to God and admitting when you've been wrong. That makes you pretty special, as far as I'm concerned. Most folks are too concerned with keeping up their image to open the gate and let God work. Humility's a rare commodity, Bennett Winsom—harder to come by than a pot roast without a ration card. Your children are blessed, and I hope they know it."

Bennett started to protest, then recalled her example of simple acceptance. "Thank you," he said quietly. He leaned over the table and looked intently into her eyes. "You're a wise woman, Thelma. Do you have any advice for me, now that my son is back and I have another chance at fatherhood?"

Thelma pursed her lips and thought for a moment. "Seems to me you can't go back and make up for the time you've lost. But you can go forward."

"Such as?"

She smiled at him. "Look at God's example of parenthood. What do you see?"

Bennett narrowed his eyes at her. What was she getting at? "Well," he began hesitantly, "I see a lot of love and a lot of sacrifice." She nodded, and he went on. "In terms of my own relationship with God, I see a father who gives me principles to live by and then trusts me to put them into action. A God who forgives me and offers grace without measure. A God who, despite my sin and shortcomings, accepts me as I am. A God who enables me to become more than I thought I could be."

"Roots and wings," Thelma murmured.

"Excuse me?"

"Roots and wings," she repeated. "God gives us roots so we'll be strong and stable, and wings so we can fly free. It appears to me that God isn't much interested in telling us every little thing to do, or when and how to do it. Like a parent, God teaches us what we need to know and then lets us choose how we're going to live—what we're going to do with the character that's been built into us."

Bennett smiled broadly. *A waitress with the soul of a prophet and the heart of a poet,* he thought.

"So you're saying that I need to be there for Link, to love him and stand by him, but to let him make his own decisions—even his own mistakes, if he has to."

"And not just Link," Thelma added. "There's someone else in the picture now, somebody who needs a father more than you can know."

"Libba."

Thelma nodded solemnly. "That girl has been hurt badly, and she's made some mistakes; but she's also grown a lot, and she's an honest, trusting soul. She'll need to be shown she can count on you, too."

Bennett thought about this for a minute. Already he adored Libba—loved her fiery spirit and her independence. She would be a good match for his son. A woman who would bring out the best in Link the way Catherine had brought out the best in him.

"Libba told me a little about her father and what he had done with Link's letters," Bennett mused. "I'll do my best not to let her down."

"I know you will."

★ ★ ★

Thelma got up, refilled their coffee cups, and went behind the counter to fix a platter of apple turnovers. The whole time she was moving around, she watched Bennett Winsom out of the corner of her eye. She couldn't help herself. He was a handsome one, and that was the truth; but her reaction to him was based on far more than his distinguished graying hair, his lively brown eyes, and the aura of dignity that surrounded him. It was his spirit. A person could fake charm, and ride on his personality, but there was no pretending the kind of humility of spirit she discerned in him. Here was a man as committed to God as anyone she had ever met, but there was no trace of self-righteousness in him, no hint of falsehood. He was a university-educated lawyer, and yet he had asked the advice of an unschooled waitress—and accepted it with grace.

Thelma fought against the rising tide of her feelings. This was no time to be letting her imagination run wild with her. There was no way—absolutely none—that there could ever be anything but friendship between them, a friendship based on her relationship with his son and prospective daughter-in-law. So what if he represented everything she had ever wanted in a man—all the things she tried so long ago to pretend that Robert Raintree had? She was nearly fifty, for heaven's sake. She could enjoy Bennett Winsom's company and cultivate his friendship, but that was all. Period.

Thelma went back to the table and set the turnovers in front of him. "Made them fresh this morning. Help yourself."

He bit into one, obviously savoring the flavor of tart apples spiced with cinnamon and brown sugar. "Mmm, this is wonderful. Is there anything you can't do, Thelma?"

You bet there is, she thought. *I can't tell you what I'm really thinking.* Aloud, she said, "Sewing. I was never worth beans with a needle and thread. My mother tried to teach me, but I was totally worthless at it. All thumbs, I guess."

"I'd pick a woman who cooks over one who sews any day." He laughed. Then a fleeting look of panic filled his eyes, and he stopped suddenly. "My wife was a wonderful cook. And my daughter RuthAnn, too."

Without thinking, Thelma reached a hand out to brush a crumb of pastry off his cheek. When her hand grazed his skin, she realized what she was doing and snatched it back as if she had been snakebit. Her heart pounded, and her mind grappled for something to say. "So, you never remarried?" she blurted out.

What in the name of all that was holy had ever made her ask such an idiotic question? Now he'd probably think she was after him, and he'd hightail it out of here and never look back. Thelma felt a hot flush creeping up her neck, and she bit her lip. "I—I'm sorry. I didn't mean to pry. It was a stupid thing to say."

"Not at all." His baritone voice was warm and rich, and she raised her head to meet his eyes. He was smiling. "For a long time, as I told you before, I immersed myself in work too much to think about anything else—even my own pain at losing Catherine."

Catherine. An elegant name. A lady's name. Thelma could see such a woman in her mind's eye—tall and graceful and self-contained, at ease among judges and ambassadors. Long dark hair, probably, swept up like royalty, with a diamond tiara and—

"After a while the pain subsided," Bennett was saying, "and some of my friends—couples, mostly, that Catherine and I had socialized with—tried to set me up with single women they knew. But they were all so—I don't know, so elegant and brainless that I had nothing in common with them. Not like you."

"You don't consider me elegant?" Thelma gave a self-deprecating laugh and fluffed at her hair. "I'm disappointed."

He joined in the laughter, then fixed her with an intent look. "I don't consider you brainless," he corrected. "You're a woman of great wisdom and intelligence, Thelma, not to mention spiritual depth. I don't find that very often—at least not among the women I've been introduced to." He smiled wanly. "In fact, you remind me a lot of Catherine."

Thelma frowned and shook her head. "Not me. I'm—"

"You do. Really. Not in looks, of course—Catherine was shorter and had kind of honey blond hair. But she had the same wonderful smile that made her eyes crinkle at the corners when she laughed." His expression grew thoughtful. "She never finished college—gave it up to marry me, I'm afraid. But she was bright and quick and never let me get away with any kind of rationalization. She challenged me, made me think. And she was so far ahead of me spiritually that she constantly urged me to a deeper relationship with God." Bennett raised one eyebrow. "I've missed that."

"She sounds like a remarkable person."

"She was. And I never thought I'd meet anyone with half her qualities, until—"

The bell over the cafe door rang, and Thelma let out a frustrated sigh. *Until what?* her mind demanded.

But she never got an answer.

★ ★ ★

Ivory Brownlee stood in the doorway, dressed in a new double-breasted, chalk-striped suit and shiny black-and-white shoes. Holding a sheaf of papers under one arm, he rushed over to the table and shook Bennett's hand.

"Howdy, Mr. Bennett. I was hoping you'd be here. Got my contracts all right here for you to look over." He pulled out a chair and plopped his wiry frame into the seat next to Thelma, grinning so broadly that you could have driven an army truck through the space left by his missing teeth. "Like my new duds, Thelma? They're the cat's pajamas, don'tcha think?"

Since most cats she had known were striped, Thelma could nod an affirmative without too much guilt. Actually, he looked like an underfed Chicago mobster badly in need of dental work, but she didn't say so. Instead, she rose from the table and excused herself. "I'll leave you gentlemen to your business."

"Hear that, Mr. Bennett? She called me a gennelman. An es-quire, that's me." Ivory gave a high-pitched, cackling laugh.

Bennett flashed her an apologetic glance, and Thelma patted Ivory on the shoulder. "Want some coffee, Ivory?"

"Yes'm, if you please." He reached into his pocket and drew out a wad of bills. "I can pay, just like a reg'lar customer."

"Put your money away, Ivory," Thelma sighed. "I'll get the coffee." She went behind the counter and brought the pot and a clean cup to the table. "Have a turnover, Ivory."

He reached for the plate and jostled her arm, and the coffee sloshed onto the table, dripping over the edge onto his new pants.

Thelma dashed for the counter and grabbed a towel, but by the time she got back his pant legs were soaked. "I'm so sorry, Ivory—and on your new suit."

Ivory looked despairingly at his lap and blotted at the stain, then brightened. "It's all right, Thelma. I can buy another one just like it." He gazed into her eyes with an expression of wonder. "People treat you so different when you got money, Thelma. The fella who sold me this suit acted like I was some kind of royalty. Called me 'Mr. Brownlee' and ever'thing."

Thelma bit her tongue to keep from asking how much the horrible suit had set him back. She turned to go, but Bennett caught her arm. "If you have time, Thelma, I think it might be a good idea for you to join us. If Mr. Brownlee doesn't mind, that is." He turned and smiled gently in Ivory's direction. "It might be helpful to have someone you trust knowing what we say here, Ivory. In case you ever need any advice when I'm not around."

"Sure," Ivory agreed. "I trust Thelma."

Thelma resumed her seat and folded her hands on the table.

"First, let's make it clear that everything that is said among us is strictly confidential. It's called attorney-client privilege." He fixed his gaze on Ivory. "Can you pay me a dollar, Ivory?"

Ivory dug in his pocket and came back up with the cash. "Sure. I can pay you—I don't know, how much do I have here?"

"Enough." Bennett withdrew a dollar bill from the roll and pushed the rest back into Ivory's hand. "This is my retainer. It makes everything legal—makes me officially your lawyer."

Ivory grinned. "I ain't never had a lawyer before."

"Well, you do now. Would you let me see the contract?"

Ivory handed it over and sat fiddling with his money while Bennett read. Thelma watched Bennett's face. His eyebrows lifted, and then his forehead knitted into a frown.

"Something wrong?" Ivory leaned forward and tried to peer at the document sideways.

"You said you paid your taxes on the property, Ivory. Did you go to the courthouse?"

"No, sir." He pointed a clawlike finger at the document. "Says right here that when I sign the contract, I get fifteen hunnert dollars. Then I'm s'posed to pay their legal repre—representative a thousand dollars to take care of the back taxes. When they—what's it called—take possession? When they take possession, they pay me the rest of the ten thousand." He gave Bennett a puzzled look. "I done paid the taxes, just like I was s'posed to. Fella met me out at the place a couple of days ago. And I still got most of the extra five hunnert left—minus what I paid for the suit."

"Did he misread the contract?" Thelma asked.

Bennett sighed. "No, he read it right. He gets fifteen hundred dollars in earnest money for the deed to his land—except for the house and cabin and two surrounding acres. But instead of paying the taxes directly, as he would under normal circumstances, which would still give him control of the property, he has agreed to funnel the tax money through the buyer's representative."

"Does it matter, as long as the taxes get paid?"

"It matters a lot. The fine print says that the buyer will pay 'additional remuneration up to ten thousand dollars,' depending upon the appraised value of the property. And the document specifies that the appraisal will be done by an appraiser of the buyer's choosing."

"Yeah," Ivory put in. "So when we finish the paperwork, I get the rest of the ten thousand."

"Not necessarily," Bennett countered. "I've seen this kind of scam before. Technically, it's legal. The buyer pays you a percentage up front for the property, but doesn't pay off the taxes you owe. When the taxes are one day past due, the purchasing company can come in and buy the property for the back taxes. Depending upon the appraised value, he may or may not pay the rest of the ten thousand. He brings in his own appraiser, who devalues the property and says it's only worth fifteen hundred dollars. So you end up with a new suit and the rest of the five hundred dollars, and he gets your land."

"But what about the rest of my money? The way I figure it, I get ten thousand, minus the thousand for back taxes."

"You would," Bennett agreed, "if he paid the whole price. But according to this contract, he doesn't have to. Fifteen hundred dollars has changed hands, and your signature is on this document. Any other payment you might get is strictly up to the purchaser."

"Wait a minute," Ivory protested. "They promised me ten thousand."

"I'm afraid not. They promised you a *maximum* of ten thousand." He shuffled through the papers. "Here's the original letter, Ivory, summarizing the deal. It says, 'an initial payment of one thousand, five hundred dollars upon receipt of the signed contract, *up to* but not exceeding a total of ten thousand dollars.' That's why I wanted to see the contract before you signed it."

Ivory put his head in his hands. "You mean because it says 'up to,' they can get away with buying my daddy's land—the land my granddaddy built into the Brownlee plantation—for fifteen hunnert dollars—and out of that I end up with four hunnert dollars and a fancy suit?"

Bennett patted Ivory's scrawny arm. "Maybe not."

"But what can we do?" Thelma asked. "He signed the contract. You said yourself it was legal."

"They won't pay the taxes until after the due date. When are they due, Ivory?"

"January fifteenth," Ivory said miserably.

"All right. That gives us nearly ten days. The first thing we'll do is file a request for an extension on the taxes. If we get it, the purchasing company—this Southern Historical Preservation Society—can't touch the land until the extension runs out. That will give us time to track down the source of this scam, pay off the taxes, and get our own appraisal done. If we round up the right information, we can break the contract, I'm sure of it. But it's going to take some time."

"How much time, Mr. Bennett?"

"Three or four months, at least. I'll request an extension on the taxes until June fifteenth. And I'll have to ask for a temporary license to practice in Mississippi. Then we'll get started."

"What can *we* do?" Thelma asked. A feeling of vulnerability had flooded over her during Bennett's discussion with Ivory, a hopelessness she had rarely experienced in her life as a Christian. Almost always, God had given her the ability to see the greater good that could come out of dark times and difficult struggles. But Harlan Brownlee was an innocent, a man of gentleness and compassion. He didn't deserve this. Where was God in the midst of this kind of senseless deception?

"For starters, you can pray," Bennett said bluntly. "And Ivory, don't spend any more of that money. You're going to need every dime you can get your hands on. We'll still have to pay the back taxes eventually, plus filing fees and—if it gets that far—court costs."

"I'll get my suit cleaned and take it back," Ivory offered.

Thelma gazed at him and saw, to her amazement, a look of hope on his face—hope and absolute trust. He obviously had no doubt that Bennett Winsom, with God's help, could work this miracle. No doubt at all.

"I'll find a way to pay you," Ivory was saying. "If it takes the rest of my life." He lowered his eyes and shrugged. "I'm sorry, Mr. Bennett, for causing all this trouble. I'm sorry I signed the paper. But it just seemed—well, too good to be true."

"If something seems too good to be true, Ivory, it probably is." Bennett gripped the man's thin shoulder. "But try not to worry, Ivory. I'll do my best. And—" he held up the dollar bill he had taken from Ivory's bankroll— "you've already paid me, so don't worry about that, either."

As Thelma watched the two of them, the knot in her stomach gradually released. Bennett Winsom was a good man, a godly man; he would listen to the Spirit's direction, that much was certain. And whether she understood it or not, she had to believe that somehow this situation was under control, that God knew what the outcome was going to be. She had to trust that either indirectly through Bennett or directly through divine intervention, the Lord would protect Ivory Brownlee from losing everything.

"Mr. Bennett," Ivory asked hesitantly, "you're not going to leave anytime soon, are you?"

"Leave? What do you mean, leave?"

"I mean, go back home." The pleading tone in his voice caught at Thelma's heart. "I reckon God sent you here, Mr. Bennett. Maybe for other reasons too, or maybe just for me. Maybe you're an angel in a lawyer's suit. But whatever you are, I need you. I just wanted you to know."

Thelma's heart stood still as Bennett Winsom caught her gaze and smiled deep into her eyes.

"I'm no angel, Ivory," he said softly, still looking at Thelma. "I'm just a man who tries to do what God calls him to do." He shrugged. "And apparently God wants to keep me around—maybe for a long, long time."

Thelma drew in a breath and held it. And deep in her spirit, a light began to dawn, illuminating and warming her soul. In the midst of poor Ivory's misery, she shouldn't feel this wonderful, but she couldn't help herself.

Bennett Winsom was staying in Eden.

29

☆ ☆ ☆

King David's Lament

January 6, 1945

Scarlet fever.

Stork sat in the living room with his head in his hands, waiting for the doctor to come out. Madge had gone in there hours ago, it seemed, although the clock on the mantel said it had been only a few minutes. What was taking them so long?

He got to his feet and paced into the dining room. He should go in there. He should. But he couldn't bring himself to do it. He couldn't face her, couldn't look at the baby, flushed with fever. The boy's cries through the night still rang in his ears, even though the nursery was now ominously quiet.

Madge had said little, going about her business with deadly calm, giving Mickey hourly sponge baths with alcohol or cool water. Her face, the few times she looked at him, had been expressionless. But he knew she was angry, and she had a right to be.

Mother had been wrong. Bundling up the child had been the worst thing they could have done, the doctor told them. A lot of old grandmothers still believed that a fever needed to be sweated out, but it just drove a baby's temperature up and didn't remedy the situation at all. Mickey's fever was now dangerously high, and they could do nothing but try to cool him down and hope for the best.

Hope for the best. What a stupid thing to say, Stork thought. Meaningless nonsense. The *best* would have been for Mickey not to come down with the fever. The *best* would have been for him to have been born two years later, after Madge and Stork had been married for a while and had a chance to adjust to their new life. The *best* would have been if Stork had shown the sense to keep his hormones under control that humid Fourth of July night in his buddy's borrowed car.

No, there was no hoping for the best any longer. All they could hope for—pray for, beg for—was that their child would live.

Stork forced himself to sit down again. He tried to pray, but his mind wouldn't focus. His hands shook and his breath came in ragged, shallow gasps. All he could think to say was *God, God, God.* . . .

He was to blame—he knew that much. He had read the Bible story over and over again, like a man obsessed, torturing himself, tormenting his soul with accusation, trying to get relief from the guilt. But it wouldn't go away. The memories, the images, haunted him by day and invaded his dreams by night: King David at the bedside of his dying son.

Like David, Stork had given in to his lust. He had let his own desire run roughshod over Madge's principles. David had looked at Bathsheba and wanted her. He took her, and when she became pregnant, he had her husband killed to try to cover his own sin. Stork hadn't killed anybody—unless you could count the deathblow to Madge's purity—but the rest applied all too well. Like David, he had been greedy for what he should not have had. Like David, he had taken what he wanted. Like David, he had sinned. And now he was paying for it with the life of his firstborn.

But why, he raged, should an innocent child have to suffer for what he had done? Why should someone else pay the price for his sin?

His mother would say that judgment always came sooner or later, that eventually you reap what you sow. But she always talked about it in terms of Madge's sin, as if his wife were some kind of remorseless hussy doomed to wear a scarlet *A* for the rest of her life.

It wasn't Madge's fault, Stork knew. He was to blame. And he couldn't get past the guilt and the shame. It sucked at him like quicksand, pulling him downward into a bottomless pit of self-loathing.

Maybe it would have been better if he had died on the front. But he hadn't, and there was nothing he could do about it.

Or was there?

A jolt went through him like an electrical current, and his hands stopped shaking. Wait a minute. This wasn't like him. Considering suicide? The very idea shocked him back to reality. Whatever had happened in the past, Madge loved him, and he loved her. His family needed him. Right this minute, his wife was in the nursery with a very sick little boy, a baby who might not live until tomorrow morning. And if Mickey was suffering because of Stork's guilt, it was time to deal with it, here and now.

Stork got up and stalked out onto the front stoop. The cold January air cleared his head, and he stood leaning against the porch post. After a moment or two he walked around to the backyard, cleared his throat, and muttered, "All right, God, we're going to have it out and be done with this."

There was no response, but Stork wasn't really expecting any. He just had to get this off his chest, and God was going to listen whether he wanted to or not, whether it made any difference or not.

"If you're punishing me for the things I've done wrong, OK," he began hesitantly. "But don't take it out on my son. Strike me with lightning, if you want to. Take my life. But don't expect me to do it for you. And leave my baby alone!" The last words reverberated off the blank pewter sky, and Stork found himself shaking his fist at the clouds.

Feeling sheepish, he lowered his hand and fixed his eyes on the ground. A cold wind sliced through his sweater and rattled the leafless tree limbs. Somewhere, in the back of his mind, Stork felt an urging: *Tell it all.*

"I know I've sinned, and people like Madge and Thelma keep telling me that all I have to do is reach out, to ask for forgiveness, and I'll be free. They keep saying what a loving, gracious God you are. But to tell the truth, all I feel is guilt, like a dark tunnel with no light and no air. And I sure don't see any love or mercy in a little baby getting scarlet fever because his daddy brought him into the world the wrong way. If you have to punish somebody, God, deal with me directly, not with my baby boy. Mother keeps talking about justice. Well, answer me: What justice is there in the innocent dying for the guilty?"

Stork waited, shivering in the cold, with his arms wrapped around him. The wind in the trees seemed to mock him, whispering, *Innocent . . . innocent . . . innocent . . . .*

He closed his eyes, and when he opened them, he saw something, far in the distance, that he had never noticed before. A line of trees ran across the back property boundary, and beyond them, an open field, now stubbled with the remains of cotton plants. Out in the field, almost to the horizon, stood a lone tree, its trunk reaching upward to the sky and two branches, high up, stretching to the east and west.

He rubbed his eyes and looked again. It was still there, looking for all the world like . . .

Like a cross.

Stork couldn't catch his breath. His heart rammed against the side of his rib cage, and his knees went weak. And then an idea appeared, fully formed, inside his mind—what some people might call a revelation.

The Innocent has already died for the guilty. No other sacrifice is required.
It wasn't a new concept to Stork, of course. He had heard it all his life. Hadn't Thelma Breckinridge told him almost the same thing? Hadn't his wife said it too?

But now it struck him with the force of a physical blow. He would have willingly given up his own life to save his child. And that was exactly what God had done. Only Jesus hadn't done anything to deserve punishment. Stork had.

And suddenly he realized how arrogant he had been. He had tried to pay for his own sin, to carry his own guilt, rather than accept what Christ had already done on his behalf. It was a slap in the face to God, not accepting the forgiveness offered to him. It was like saying that Christ's sacrifice wasn't good enough.

In a daze, Stork wandered toward the back door and sat down on the low retaining wall that bordered the patio. He had done everything, he thought. He had confessed, begged, pleaded, demanded, and finally given himself over to the guilt and shame. He had done everything except receive.

"I get it, God," he whispered. "I finally get it. You just want me to accept what you've already done."

Innocent . . . innocent . . . the wind whispered in the trees.

"And you want me to let go of the past. All right, I accept. I let go. I can't change the past, and I can't control the future. But I can do something about here and now, with your help. So I accept your forgiveness, and I promise—"

Stork never got to his promise. As if a dam had burst somewhere inside, a wave of warmth rolled through him. Tears filled his eyes, and words failed him. He just sat there crying in the cold January afternoon, and all he could say was, "Thank you. Thank you."

After a while he became aware of a sound. Someone was knocking on the window behind him. He turned to see Madge, standing at the breakfast nook in the kitchen.

He saw her mouth the words *Are you all right?* How he loved this woman, his wife, the mother of his child! Stork swiped at his tears and nodded, then got to his feet and went to the back door. With his hand on the doorknob, he paused.

I know now, Lord, that Mickey's illness didn't come because of my sin—or his, he thought. *Whatever happens, he's in your hands. Just give me the strength to deal with it.*

Then he pushed the door open and went into the house, where his wife and infant son waited for him.

30

✯ ✯ ✯

Reunited . . . Again

Libba watched as Link was wheeled through the doors and out into the hall, then gathered up her purse and gloves and headed for the commissary. Pinky would be waiting, just as she had for the past four days. The nurse always took a break when Link was scheduled for physical therapy so that she and Libba could spend a little time together.

How odd it was, Libba thought as she threaded her way through the hospital corridors, that Nurse Amanda Pincheon, who had been so intimidating on Libba's first visit to Kennedy General, had become such a good friend. Under normal circumstances, the two would probably never have met, much less had anything in common. But wartime, even here at home, far from the fighting, had proven to be anything but normal.

As Libba came through the doors of the commissary, she caught a glimpse of Pinky at a table next to the wall, and she waved. The nurse's craggy face broke into a wide smile—a transformation that still amazed Libba, given the woman's ordinarily stony countenance. Daddy would have said Amanda Pincheon was "homely as a mud fence," but there were times, like now, when she seemed almost beautiful.

Libba slid into the chair across the table from Pinky and plopped her purse into her lap. "Sorry you had to wait. Link just left for therapy."

Pinky shook her head. "No problem. How's it going?"

"Pretty well, I think. It seems like we've spent the last four days doing nothing but talking about all the *what ifs*. What if Link doesn't walk again, what if he does, what if he can't get into law school, what if he can and we can't afford it . . . you know."

Pinky settled back into her chair and gave a broad grin. "Seems to me like I remember you doing something besides talking—at least once."

Libba felt heat rise into her face. "All right, Pinky. You caught us kissing. You're never going to let me live it down, are you?"

"Of course not!" Pinky laughed. "It was the highlight of my day—maybe my whole week. Quite a show."

"And just how long were you standing there, may I ask?"

"A good fifteen or twenty minutes, at least."

"You were not!" Libba protested. "It was—it was—"

Pinky leaned over and patted her hand. "Don't get your undies in a twist, Lib. So you kissed the man." She gave a sly wink. "Rather passionately, I might add."

"Oh, you—"

"There's nothing wrong with that. I suspect you rather enjoyed it." She grinned. "I know I did."

"Let's just forget about it, OK?"

"Not likely," Pinky chuckled. "Until I've got a man of my own who will pucker up like that, I expect I'll remember it for a long, long time."

Libba said nothing, and after a minute or two Pinky leaned across the table and asked conspiratorially, "How was it?"

"It was fine, Pinky. Just fine."

"Fine? That's all?"

"It was wonderful. Incredible. Romantic." Libba kept her voice flat, emotionless. "It was . . . like fireworks. Like being transported to another world, where music was playing and angels were singing. Satisfied? Now drop it, will you?"

"You're no fun." Pinky cleared her throat. "Link seems to be getting stronger all the time."

Relieved to move on to a less embarrassing topic of conversation, Libba nodded. "He does, doesn't he? We're—well, cautiously hopeful."

"That's probably wise. You two got your problems straightened out?"

"I think so. Link's father was a big help, I'll have to admit. After what happened, I would have been too stubborn—and too hurt—to come back on my own. And Link was too ashamed to ask me to come. But now that we've talked things out, Link understands my perspective a lot better. And I believe I can understand why he was trying to protect me. In a distorted way, he did it out of love. Bennett helped me see that."

"Link's father is some kind of man, isn't he?" Pinky said wistfully.

"Amanda Pincheon! Is it possible that you're attracted to my future father-in-law?"

The nurse smiled sheepishly. "Not seriously. But he's a fine specimen, I'll say that for him."

"Yes, he is. Sometimes I look at him and feel like I'm looking at Link thirty years from now. And he is every bit as handsome on the inside. He's a remarkable person, Pinky. A gentle, considerate, compassionate man. And a wise one. He treats me like a daughter, you know?"

"I know, Lib. And I'd venture a guess that you regard him like the father you never had."

A wave of bittersweet longing rose up in Libba, and she nodded. "The kind of person I always wished Daddy had been," she agreed. "Is it disloyal, do you think, for me to look at Bennett as a father? I mean, Daddy's only been gone a few months—"

Pinky shook her head. "From what you've told me, your daddy has been gone for years—as a real father anyway."

"Bennett helped Link see me as I really am," Libba said. "Not the selfish, spoiled brat I used to be."

"I doubt that Link ever saw you that way, or else he would never have fallen in love with you."

"Maybe not. But when Link and I met, I didn't have much more on my mind than myself. Creating the right image, having people cater to me, playing the Southern Lady."

"It's hard to imagine." Pinky furrowed her brow. "You're not like that now."

Libba smiled. "Thanks. I did a lot of growing up, I guess, while Link was away. I faced myself—and God. And despite the struggles, a lot of good things came out of that dark time." She sighed. "It has just been more difficult than I anticipated for Link to make the transition. Until the past few days, he still thought of me as fragile and sheltered, the kind of girl who needs to be protected from the real world—and from the possible burden of his disability."

Pinky let out a laugh. "You sure he's not thinking about some other girl?"

"In a way, he was. This war has changed everybody, Pinky. We've all had to grow up. Link's changed too. Fortunately for us, most of the changes have been positive ones—at least in the long run. I guess situations like this either bring out the best in people or the worst."

A warm smile softened Pinky's granite features. "In your case, Lib, it's definitely brought out the best."

"I appreciate that. But I've had some good examples to follow."

"You mean your Aunt Magnolia?" Pinky chuckled. "She's a formidable woman, that one. A tough old bird. If Link wants to see what *you'll* be like in fifty years, all he has to do is take a long look at Magnolia Cooley."

"That's probably the nicest compliment I've ever received, Amanda Pincheon. I could do a lot worse in life than becoming like Aunt Mag."

"You love her a lot, don't you?"

"Yes. She gives me something I never had before—unconditional acceptance. And yet she challenges me to grow, to become more than I thought I could be. It's largely because of her that I had the courage to come to the hospital and spend time with people like Hans and Stevie."

"I think a lot of that was you, Lib. The inner strength that was always inside you, just waiting for an opportunity to come out. But I have no doubt your Aunt Mag played a part in it. She adores you, I know that much."

"She has been a gift to me, that's for sure. She's—I don't know—strong and self-confident, yet tender and understanding. Like a rock covered in velvet. The kind of person I'd like to become someday."

Pinky smiled. "I'd say you're well on your way, Libba Coltrain. Well on your way."

★ ★ ★

Back in the ward, Link waited for Libba, keeping his eyes fixed on the door. His physical-therapy sessions always exhausted him, but just the sight of her made him feel better. She always wanted to know what kind of exercises they had done and whether or not his muscles seemed stronger—almost as if she were preparing for a time in the not-too-distant future when she would be responsible for helping him. The very idea had shamed him at first, made him feel helpless. But his father had set him straight. Now he was beginning to realize that the woman he loved had remarkable strength of character, and that whether he ever walked again or not, their love would carry them through.

Amazing, how their relationship had changed in the past few days. After confessing his idiotic attempt to shield Libba from being hurt, Link had found himself able to tell her other things—about his own fear, for example, of being confined to a wheelchair. His guilt over losing Owen Slaughter in the raid on the château, his anger as he held young Randy Coker in his arms and watched him die in the mine crater.

For the first time in their relationship—maybe the first time in his life—Link had taken the risk of being really candid about himself, his fears for the future, his hopes and dreams. And to his surprise, Libba didn't seem to love or respect him any less because of it. In fact, she seemed to be more in love with him than ever. As a result, he felt free. He didn't have to be so careful about covering up his feelings anymore, about protecting her from knowing the truth.

It was very liberating, this new honesty between them. Why hadn't anyone ever told him that a man didn't always have to be strong, or that the relationship between a man and a woman could be a partnership, on equal ground? Didn't anybody else know this?

Obviously his father did. Dad had encouraged him to give up the charade, to let Libba in on what he was really feeling, to give her a chance to support him. And although his father never talked much about his relationship with Link's mother, he had said enough about the kind of woman he *didn't* find attractive to let Link know there had been something different and very special about his parents' relationship. Once, in jest, his dad had said that if Libba's Aunt Mag were twenty-five years younger, he'd be making some courting calls of his own. And more seriously, Dad had indicated that Libba had a lot of Magnolia Cooley in her soul.

Link smiled as he thought about Aunt Mag. Flamboyant, determined, and a little dangerous, the woman intrigued him. And intimidated him, he had to admit. But she was a good soul, and she loved her grandniece with the fierce loyalty of a lioness. If Libba aged as gracefully and with as much dignity as Aunt Mag, he had a very interesting life to look forward to. One thing he was sure of: He would never be bored.

At last the doors to the ward swung open, and Libba came toward his bed. Her pale green eyes focused on him as if she saw nothing else in the world. His heart leaped, and his arms reached out for her. She came into his embrace willingly, leaning down to kiss him. But when he tried to prolong the kiss, she backed away.

"Is something wrong?" He frowned at her. "That wasn't a very enthusiastic kiss for a man who's been pushed around by physical therapists half the morning."

Libba sat in the chair at his bedside and fixed her eyes on the linoleum floor. "I'm sorry. It's nothing, really. Pinky has just been giving me a hard time about kissing you the other day."

"She was offended?"

Libba chuckled. "Quite the contrary, actually. She enjoyed it immensely. A vicarious thrill, I suppose."

"But you're embarrassed."

"Well, yes. I guess I shouldn't be. We *are* practically engaged, after all."

"Not practically," Link corrected. "Definitely. I just haven't been able to get the ring yet."

"Still, it made me feel funny. It's not easy, making all these adjustments.

Girls—especially southern girls—are carefully taught what kind of behavior is appropriate for a young lady. You spend your growing-up years saying no to boys who want you to be free with your affections. Then suddenly you're in love and engaged, and the rules change. Practically overnight. It can be very confusing."

"It's not simple for guys, either," Link agreed. "I've been thinking about it a lot. Most of us are taught that we have to put up a strong front, to protect the fair damsel from distress." He laughed as she rolled her eyes. "But then once you find the person you want to spend your life with, you have to learn everything all over again. You have to start being honest about your weaknesses, too." He reached out and took her hand, stroking it gently. "Especially if you have the kinds of challenges we're likely to face."

"We'll face them, sweetheart," Libba said softly.

"I know." Link smiled into her eyes. "Come here."

She raised one eyebrow. "I'm here."

"No, over here." He patted a hand on the side of the bed. "I believe you owe me a kiss—a real one this time."

Libba moved to sit on the side of the bed and put her arms around him. The warmth of her nearness enticed him, and he drew her head down to his shoulder. "I love you, Libba Coltrain," he whispered, almost strangling on the depth of his emotion. "I am so sorry I hurt you."

"Shhh." She laid a finger on his lips and shook her head. "It's all over and forgiven, remember?" Then she pulled back and scowled. "Just don't try it again, OK? You'll have to do more than that to get rid of me."

"Oh, don't worry. I learned my lesson. And I never want to get rid of you, Libba. Never." He pulled her back into his arms, and their lips met. This time she returned his kiss, deeply, passionately, a kiss that promised a lifetime of love.

"So, you're at it again, are you? I declare!"

Libba jerked back, and Link looked up to see Nurse Pincheon standing at the foot of the bed, her hands on her hips and a Cheshire-cat grin pasted on her craggy face. "I can't leave the two of you alone for a minute."

"Pinky!" Libba's exasperated sigh cut through the nurse's laughter. "What are you doing, sneaking up on us like that?"

"Sneaking? Who's sneaking?" She pointed at her rubber-soled white shoes. "Even an old barge like me doesn't make much noise wearing these. But I wasn't sneaking. No. Absolutely not. Amanda Pincheon never sneaks."

"What do you want?" Libba snapped.

The nurse seemed totally unaffected by Libba's impatient tone of voice. Her grin never wavered. "You have a visitor. If you're not too busy, that is."

Libba got off the bed and straightened her skirt. "I'll be going, then. I have to—"

"Not him," Pinky corrected. "You."

"I can't have a visitor," Libba countered. "I *am* a visitor."

"You're a fixture, that's what you are. And you do have a visitor."

The nurse pointed toward the door. There, tall and splendid in a vibrant yellow dress, stood Aunt Mag.

"Just a minute," Libba said. "I'll be right back." She hurried toward the hallway, leaving Link to deal with Nurse Pincheon on his own.

"Feeling better I see." The nurse gave him a pointed look.

"I was until you came along," Link grumbled.

"Physical therapy appears to be doing wonders for you." The woman's eyes fixed on Libba as she stood just outside the door, talking in hushed tones to her great-aunt.

"Cut it out, Pincheon." Link glared at her. "You've embarrassed Libba enough as it is."

The nurse grinned at him. "All right. I was just having a little fun. You two lovebirds are so sweet, though. I just couldn't resist."

"Force yourself." He shook his head. "Or find somebody else to torment. Hans and Marlene would probably do. Better yet, try kissing somebody yourself. You'd be amazed at how much better it is in person."

"Good idea," Nurse Pincheon said evenly. "Is that handsome father of yours around?"

Link rolled his eyes and was just about to respond when Libba came back to the bedside. Her face was blotchy, and her eyes were rimmed with tears.

"Honey, what's wrong?" Link reached a hand toward her, and she gripped his fingers so tightly his knuckles went white.

"I'm afraid I'm going to have to go home for a few days," she said in a hoarse whisper. "Thelma called Aunt Mag's house a little while ago. Little Mickey has come down with scarlet fever. Thelma asked if I could help out in the cafe, but I think she really wants me there for moral support. Stork and Madge have their hands full already dealing with Stork's mother. They're going to need a friend or two." She looked into Link's eyes with an expression of utter misery and helplessness. "I don't know what to do."

"You'll have to go, of course. I'll be fine."

"I know. I just don't know if I will be. Sweetheart, what will we do if that precious baby doesn't make it?"

Link pulled her into his arms and stroked her hair. "Don't think about that. Just go. Be there for Madge and Stork. And pray like crazy." He pulled back and looked at her. "What time does the bus leave?"

"Three-thirty. Time enough for me to throw some clothes into a suitcase."

"Give me a minute or two. I want to write a note to Stork."

Libba nodded and sat down weakly in the chair. While Link scribbled his note, Pinky stood beside Libba with one hand on her shoulder. "It'll be all right," she murmured. "Babies survive scarlet fever all the time."

Link fought to compose his thoughts, to say something encouraging to his best friend. But a lump had settled in his stomach, and the best he could do was, *I'm praying for you, buddy—and for Madge and the baby. Don't lose hope. We've survived a lot worse, and we'll get through this, too. Sorry I can't be there, but I would if I could.* After a moment's hesitation, he added, *God's there, and he won't let you down.* He folded the note and wrote his friend's name on the outside, then handed it to Libba.

"I'll leave you two alone," Pinky said softly. "Don't worry, Lib. I'll take good care of him while you're gone." Link watched as the two hugged each other, and then Nurse Pincheon was gone.

Link could hardly stand to think of Libba's leaving again, but at least this time it was for a good reason, and he knew she'd be back. Still, he held on for a long time, not wanting to let her go. He kissed her repeatedly, tasting the tang of salty tears on her face. When at last she picked up her coat and purse and prepared to leave, he thought his heart would break.

"Good-bye, sweetheart," she choked out, standing at the foot of his bed. "I'll be back as soon as I can. And I'll let you know what's happening."

She reached out and squeezed his foot under the blanket, then ran for the door.

For a long time after she left, Link lay against his pillows, his breath coming in shallow gasps. His heart pounded, and his hands were shaking.

He had felt her touch against his toes.

31

★ ★ ★

One Blow for Liberty

New Orleans, Louisiana

"I'm sorry, sweetheart, there's nothing I can do about it!"

Rae blinked and took a step back. She had never heard this tone of voice from Drew before, and she didn't think she liked it very much.

She tried again. "Honey, I know you promised your father. But don't you understand? I'm miserable here, and I'm worried. Daddy is so sick, and Willie really needs help with him and Mama and the farm. Couldn't we go back—just for a little while?"

A cloud passed over Drew's handsome features, and he frowned. "Come on, Rae, we've talked about this. You know we can't. Not now. My father needs me, and Mother—"

"There's not a thing wrong with your mother," Rae snapped. "She's healthier than I am." As soon as the words were out of her mouth, she knew she had made a mistake, and a big one. The cloud on Drew's countenance escalated into a full-scale thunderstorm. His jaw clenched, and his lips narrowed to a thin line.

"Listen," he grated, "you can leave my mother out of this. You have no idea what you're talking about."

"Drew, be reasonable. You said yourself that she doesn't seem very sick. And you told me you had some concerns about what your father is asking you to do."

"So now I'm being unreasonable?" He shook his head. "I'll deal with it, Rae. With my mother, with Father's business. Just don't meddle in it, OK?"

"Don't meddle?" Rae fought to keep a lid on her temper. "When we got engaged, Andrew Laporte, you promised me that this marriage would be an equal partnership. That we would make decisions together. And now I'm just supposed to stay out of it, to go off shopping with your mother like nothing's wrong, to be a nice little decoration to your career? What's happened to all that equality?" She paused. "Drew, what's happened to *you?*"

His eyes flashed, and he ran a hand through his hair. "I've got to get to work," he muttered, glancing at his watch. "I'm late as it is."

"You're going to leave? Just walk out and go to work as if nothing's wrong? Drew!"

"I don't have any choice," he sighed. "I've got a job, remember? Responsibilities."

"And what about your responsibility to me? To our marriage?"

"Look," he said with his hand on the doorknob, "I can't deal with this right now. We'll talk about it later."

"And what about me?" Rae challenged. "What do I do in the meantime?"

He opened the door, then turned to face her again. "You're living in the lap of luxury, without a worry to your name. I'd think you'd appreciate what you've got." He glared at her. "You want to be a writer, don't you? Well, you can start this morning. I ordered a typewriter and some paper for you— Daniel brought it up a few minutes ago. You can use the sitting room next door."

Rae narrowed her eyes but said nothing. She felt reprimanded, as if she were a small child being given a box of crayons to keep her out of trouble. But she didn't say so. Obviously Drew was upset, even angry, but she suspected that his concerns centered, at least in part, on problems that weren't directly related to her.

"Are you going to talk with your father about the business dealings that are worrying you?" She looked him in the eye. "Are you going to talk with *me* about it?"

He shrugged. "I said I'd deal with it." He stalked back across the room and gave her a perfunctory kiss on the cheek, then turned on his heel and was gone.

★ ★ ★

As a weak winter sun slanted through the lace curtains, Rae leaned against the head of the bed in the huge Jefferson Davis suite and stared up at the carved medallion that encircled the light fixture. She had been lying here for an hour stewing about her argument with Drew, getting nowhere. Her eyes fixed on something—what was it?—that cast a faint shadow between the brass of the lamp and the white plaster of the medallion.

She squinted, trying to focus, then smiled grimly. There, among the opulence of carved plaster and polished brass, hung a spiderweb. And at its center, still faintly struggling for its freedom, a common housefly.

For several moments she watched the insect fight against the translucent threads that held it fast. But it couldn't escape. The web simply captured it more tightly, and every movement made the housefly's bondage more certain.

A surge of pity welled up in her heart, bringing a rush of tears, and she puzzled over the feeling. Why on earth was she crying over the plight of a housefly? Back at the farm, she would spend the entire summer carrying a flyswatter everywhere she went. She hated the pesky little creatures. But . . .

In a flash of insight she understood. The web that trapped her was luxurious, to be sure, but just as deadly. She could thrash all she wanted, but she couldn't break free. And it would be the death of her—if not physically, at least spiritually and emotionally.

Then Rae saw a fleeting movement from the corner of the ceiling—a streak of black, darting toward the light fixture in a zigzag pattern.

"No you don't!" she shouted impulsively, jumping to her feet in the center of the bed. She reached for the web, but it was too high above her. For a second or two the spider froze, then resumed its movement toward the fly.

Rae leaped from the bed and grabbed a long-handled poker from the fireplace. Now she could reach it . . . just barely. She swiped at the spiderweb once and missed, grazing a long black char mark across the white ceiling. The second time she caught the edge of the web, but on its way down the poker slipped and banged against the plaster ceiling medallion, gouging a chunk out of one side and covering her with a shower of white powder.

When the web gave way, the housefly managed to break free. It banged against the window, reeled, then zoomed out the bedroom door without so much as a thank-you.

Panting, Rae leaned back against the pillows and surveyed the damage. The comforter was covered with broken plaster, and surely someone would confront her about the black swipe on the ceiling and the chipped medallion. But it didn't matter.

The fly was free. The spider would go without breakfast this morning. And Mabel Rae Coltrain Laporte had struck the first blow for her own liberty.

★ ★ ★

By eleven-thirty, Rae had been in the sitting room for nearly two hours, pounding away at the big black Underwood. She had been trying to write a story about war brides, about the struggles and difficulties of sustaining a marriage during the uncertainties of wartime. But everything she wrote came out in a whiny poor-me voice, and she hated it. All she had to show for her effort was a pile of crumpled papers—a few of them in the waste can, even more scattered on the floor at her feet.

She sighed and leaned her head against the typewriter. "This isn't working," she murmured to herself. "I just can't concentrate."

She rolled a fresh sheet of paper into the typewriter and stared at the blank white space. Maybe she was going about this all wrong. Maybe what she needed to do, instead of trying to be objective, was to write to herself, to get all her feelings out on paper where she could analyze them and where they wouldn't clutter up her mind.

Rae closed her eyes and breathed a quick prayer, then began to type. Within a few minutes she had written several pages—honest, gut-wrenching pages about the housefly in the spider's web, about how much she hated being here, how trapped she felt, how frustrated she was with Drew, and how she didn't trust his parents and didn't understand how Drew couldn't see the truth. Then, gradually, the tone of her writing changed, and she began to pray—not aloud, but on paper—asking God to help her see things from her husband's perspective, to understand his point of view. Her anger subsided, and she began to experience a bittersweet longing for the way things used to be with her and Drew in the early days of their relationship, when he valued her thoughts and feelings, when he wanted to know what was on her mind.

I am convinced, she wrote, *that there is nothing—at least physically— wrong with Beatrice Laporte, that this mysterious "illness" of hers is just a ploy to keep Drew in New Orleans where his parents can control him. Maybe it's not Beatrice at all; maybe Drew's father has conjured up this sham so he can keep Drew under his thumb. But something is wrong, very wrong, with what Beau expects from his son. And I'm worried about Drew. He's not the same person I fell in love with. He used to be so full of life, so excited about what he could accomplish by helping people who couldn't help themselves. He used to be so caring, so considerate. I don't want to be selfish, but I do want him back, the way he used to be—*

The sound of a footstep at the door startled Rae, and she looked up. Drew was standing there, leaning on the doorjamb. He looked at his watch. "It's almost time for lunch," he said in a quiet voice. "Can you take a break?"

She snatched the paper out of the typewriter and laid it facedown on the stack. "Of course," she stammered. "I was just getting to a stopping place."

"I see you've been writing." He leaned down and gathered up several of the crumpled pages, tossing them into the wastebasket. "Is it going well?"

Rae shook her head. "Not really. Mostly I've been thinking on paper, trying to sort things out."

"What kind of things?"

She took a deep breath. "You. Me. Us. Our . . . situation."

Drew bit his lip. "Yeah. Me too. I didn't get much work done this morning." He came to stand beside her, took her hand, and began stroking it. "I think we need to talk."

Rae got up and followed him over to the sofa. The sitting room was chilly, and when she shivered, he drew her down next to him and wrapped his arms around her. "I'm sorry about this morning, sweetheart," he murmured into her ear. "I'm an idiot."

"You're not an idiot," she corrected. "But something is bothering you, and I think I deserve to know what it is."

He took a deep breath, and when he looked into her eyes, she saw an expression of utter confusion and pain. "I love you, Rae—more than you can possibly know. You're the best thing that ever happened to me, the best gift God ever gave me."

"But?" she prompted.

"But I feel . . . I don't know, torn. I love my parents, too, and I feel some responsibility toward them. I know you don't think there's anything wrong with Mother but that something is very wrong with my father. And on that point I'm beginning to agree with you. The further I get into his business dealings, the more I see that I don't like. I can't put my finger on it quite yet, but there's something shady going on. Everything looks legal on the surface, but "

"You think he's involved in some kind of illegal dealings?"

"Not illegal, probably, but most certainly unethical. Still, I can't make any accusations—or any decisions about what I'm going to do—until I know the full story."

"Why didn't you tell me this before?"

Drew stroked Rae's cheek and shrugged. "I didn't have any evidence— not much, anyway. He's very careful about what he lets me see. But I'm not stupid. And what he's *not* telling me is pretty revealing." He swallowed hard. "He puts on a good show, you know, but he's hiding something. I suspect it's only a matter of time before he lets me in on it, but by then I'll be so involved that I'll be stuck . . . or so he thinks."

"What are you going to do?"

Drew's eyes crinkled in a smile. "I'll do what an attorney of my stature does best, sweetheart—dig for the truth. Father is a cunning businessman, but he's no lawyer. If he is involved in underhanded or unethical dealings, I'll find it. And I'll find it before he's got me involved in doing something that will compromise my integrity."

Rae held her breath for a moment. "And then what?"

"Then you and I will decide—together—what to do about it." He pulled her into his embrace, and his warmth radiated into her. For the first time since they had left Eden, she felt safe.

"Can you be patient with me for a little longer?"

She drew back and looked into his eyes. "What do you mean?"

"I mean," he said slowly, "that if you can just give me a little more time, we'll get to the truth and then get on with our lives."

"Are you saying we might leave New Orleans, Drew?" Rae's heart leaped, but she tried to contain her anticipation, afraid to hope for too much.

"I realized this morning that I couldn't keep on pretending everything was all right," he admitted. "It was hurting you, and it was hurting us. Our relationship was suffering." He took a deep breath. "I know you're miserable here, darling, and I'm discovering that it's possible I don't fit either—especially if what I suspect about my father is true. I can't work in a situation like that, not and hold my head up."

"And what about your mother?" Rae hated to bring up the subject, but the question had to be asked.

A shadow passed over Drew's face. "I guess we'll have to cross that bridge when we come to it. In the meantime—" He paused.

"Yes?"

"Try to trust me, OK?"

Rae fought back tears as she buried her head against her husband's shoulder. How could she ever have doubted him, this wonderful, honorable man God had given her? A wave of remorse washed over her, and her tears dampened the sleeve of his coat.

"There's something else we need to discuss."

She sat up and blinked. "All right."

"If what I suspect proves to be true and I have to withdraw from my father's business—"

"Yes?"

"We . . . well, we won't have much to live on." He waved a hand at the elegant sitting room. "It won't be like this. We'll be—"

"Poor?" she supplied.

He ducked his head and grinned sheepishly. "At the very least, struggling."

"I've spent most of my life poor," she answered immediately. "You've seen my family's farm. I can make do."

"Yes, but I wanted to give you so much more—"

Rae wrapped her arms around Drew's neck and pulled him down for a long, lingering kiss. "You give me everything a woman could possibly want," she murmured against his cheek. "As long as we are together— really together—that's all that matters."

A light of love filled his eyes, and he hugged her close. "I love you, Rae Coltrain Laporte."

She pulled away a bit and looked him in the eye. "There is, however, one luxury I must insist upon."

He leaned back. "What's that?"

She grinned at him. "Can I keep the typewriter?"

"Forever," he laughed. "I charged it to my father's business."

32

★ ★ ★

Confrontations

January 12, 1945

Madge watched her husband pace back and forth over the blue hooked rug in the living room as they waited for the doctor to emerge from Mickey's room. Lorna Simpson sat stone-faced on the sofa, her arms crossed in an attitude of defiance.

"I told you that something like this was bound to happen," she muttered for the hundredth time. "It's the judgment of the Almighty, that's what it is."

Madge seethed inwardly, but she made no attempt at a response. She could only take so much more of this before she exploded. All she had heard from this woman for the past week was how her infant son's battle with scarlet fever was her fault—God's righteous retribution for her sin in conceiving him out of wedlock.

Tears sprang to her eyes, and she turned toward the kitchen. "I'll get some coffee," she stammered, hating the strangled, high-pitched sound of her own voice.

"Wait!" The single commanding word from Michael brought her to a stop halfway through the dining room. "Come back in here, Madge. I've got something to say, and I think you should hear it."

Madge hovered at the edge of the dining room and watched in wonder as her husband turned to face his mother.

"All right, Mother," he began, "it's time for you to do some listening." His voice quivered slightly, but his deep-set hazel eyes held a look of astonishing determination, and his fists clenched and unclenched as his lanky frame towered over her.

"I beg your pardon?" Lorna Simpson's question came out as a squeak.

"You've been doing more than your share of talking in the past few weeks," Michael went on, "and particularly in the past eight or nine days. And I've heard about all I intend to hear from you about God's judgment and righteous retribution."

Madge gasped, and Michael's eyes cut to her briefly, then flitted back to his mother. With his gaze firmly fixed on the woman's shocked countenance, he motioned for Madge to join him and wrapped a protective arm around her. "This woman," he said with conviction, "is my wife, and I love her more than I ever thought it possible to love anyone." He smiled at Madge and squeezed her shoulder. "And that child in there is my son. I would give my life for him." He paused. "In fact, I asked God to take my life in exchange for his."

Madge closed her eyes and fought against the rising tide of emotion. But Michael wasn't finished.

"And God made it clear to me," he said forcefully, "that nobody has to die to pay for somebody else's sin. It's already been done, once and for all. So you can just stop all this drivel about God's judgment. Any judgment that might be coming to me—to *me,* Mother, not to Madge—has already been accounted for. My son will not be paying the price for my mistakes. And if you think otherwise, Mother, I suggest you go back and read that precious Bible you're so fond of quoting. Try the New Testament this time—there's a lot in there about love and grace that you might benefit from knowing."

Lorna Simpson's jaw dropped, and her pasty face flushed a violent red. "How dare you speak to me this way? I am still your mother!"

"So you are." Michael nodded. "But unless God's standards have changed, a man is supposed to leave his father and mother and cleave to his wife." He drew Madge even tighter to his side. "This is where my responsibility lies." His eyes shifted toward the doorway of Mickey's room. "And in there." Then he lifted his head and glared at his mother. "There won't be any more of your talk about sin and judgment in this house, and unless you can show my wife and son the respect they deserve—well, the bus goes back the way it came."

All the blood drained from Lorna Simpson's face, and she stood shakily to her feet. She opened her mouth to speak, but no words would come. At last she gathered her purse, retrieved her coat from the arm of the sofa, and headed for the front door.

"I think I need some air," she gasped. "If you need me, I'll be at the boardinghouse."

★ ★ ★

When the door closed behind his mother, Stork flopped onto the sofa and let out an exhausted sigh. Madge was still standing, frozen in place like a statue, staring at him.

"Well, did I do all right?" He grinned.

She sank down beside him, a look of absolute astonishment on her face. "You—you were magnificent!" she breathed. "Where did all that come from?"

"She was about due to hear the truth, don't you think?"

For the first time in weeks, it seemed to Stork, his wife smiled. "I'd say so. If not a little past due."

"About a year and a half late, I'm afraid. Sorry it took me so long."

Madge laughed. "What happened to you, Michael Simpson?"

He shrugged. "A week ago, that first day the doctor came and told us it was scarlet fever, my whole world just collapsed. I really believed that God was punishing me through Mickey—you know, like King David losing his son because of his sin with Bathsheba. I did just what I told Mother, offered my own life in exchange for Mickey's. But then I realized—God told me, I guess, although I'm not quite sure how—" he paused and scratched his head, remembering that moment as if it had just happened—"I didn't hear any voices, you know, but in my heart I knew, really knew, that God didn't operate that way. That Christ's sacrifice on the cross was the only time anybody had been allowed to die for somebody else's sin. Just that one time, for all of us. And he didn't even deserve it. So—" he paused, groping for the right way to say what was on his mind—"I gave up, I guess. Stopped trying to earn anything or be good enough. Accepted the sacrifice for myself."

Tears filled Madge's eyes, but Stork could tell from her expression that they were good tears, happy tears. "Why didn't you tell me about this?"

"I was scared, I think. Scared it wouldn't take. Scared Mickey might die anyway. I decided to wait awhile, give it some time. I wanted to make sure it was real . . . and to be perfectly honest, I guess I didn't want to make a fool of myself if it wasn't. I've done a lot of praying and reading in the past week, and I'm convinced that no matter what happens, God loves us and somehow will bring something good out of all this."

Madge leaned in close to him, and he wrapped his arms around her, savoring her closeness. "I think God's already done that," she murmured.

He chuckled. "Mother wouldn't think so."

"Probably not," she agreed. "But whether she likes it or not, she needed to hear the truth."

"I didn't want to hurt her or offend her. But I was more concerned about the ways she was hurting you."

"What do you think she'll do?" Madge asked suddenly.

"I don't know. I don't really expect her to change overnight, to come back and say, 'Thank you so much, Son, for opening my eyes.' But whether she understands or not, I won't allow her to hurt you or say those things to you any longer. I love you too much to let that happen, and I'm sorry it took me so long to stand up to her."

"It's all right."

"No, it's not all right. I should have done it a long time ago."

"But you've done it now, and that's what counts."

"Lieutenant Simpson?" a voice called from the hallway. "I think you and your wife should come in here."

Stork bolted from the sofa with Madge right behind him. He stopped at the doorway to Mickey's room and grabbed on to the doorjamb for support. The room was dark and quiet, and he could barely make out Mickey's still form in the crib.

"Is he—?" Stork grabbed the doctor's arm.

"He'll be fine." The doctor led them into the room and stood next to the bed. "His fever has broken," he said softly. "He's still a sick little boy, mind you, but he'll make it."

Stork reached a hand down and pushed back the damp strands of hair from his son's forehead. Mickey's skin felt cool to the touch, and Stork's tears fell on the pillow next to the boy's face.

"He'll be all right, then?" Madge asked in a choked voice.

"He'll live. Keep him still and give him lots of fluids. In a few days we'll know if there have been any complications from the fever."

"Complications?" Stork frowned. "What kinds of complications?"

"Let's not worry about that right now," the doctor soothed. "I'll be back in a day or two. In the meantime, try to keep him quiet and comfortable, and call me if you need me."

Stork ushered the doctor to the door, handed him his hat and coat, and shook his hand vigorously. "Thank you," he said over and over again. "Thank you."

"He's a wonderful little boy," the doctor said. "And a very lucky one."

But Stork knew luck had nothing to do with it. When the doctor was gone, he dropped to his knees in the living room and sobbed his relief and gratitude into the sofa cushions. His voice was useless, and his mind could find no words; but somehow he felt sure God understood his tears.

33

★ ★ ★

Shady Business

Drew Laporte paused outside the door of his father's study, listening. He hadn't really meant to eavesdrop, but the angry sound of his mother's voice stopped him cold. He had never in his life heard his mother raise her voice to his father, never heard them argue. She had always passively submitted to her husband's wishes—at least in public. Now her tone indicated not just anger but outrage.

"Beauregard Laporte, how could you! I have never heard of anything so underhanded in my entire life! I should cut you off, honestly I should—and then where would you be without my family's money?"

Drew heard unintelligible murmurs from his father, obviously intended to pacify his mother. It didn't work.

"Don't give me that drivel about wanting what's best for this family. You've deceived your son, and that is unforgivable!"

Deceived his son? Drew leaned forward, straining to hear.

"How could you do something so cruel?" his mother's strident voice continued. "You told him I was *dying?* Just so you could keep him here under your control?"

"Don't make it sound so . . . so premeditated," Drew's father said, his voice rising. "I just—well, it happened so quickly. I needed him to stay, don't you see that?"

"What I see," his mother answered acidly, "is that you cared more about yourself and your precious profits than about your own son. You didn't think he'd want to work with you, to do your legal dirty business, so you concocted this absurd fantasy about me having a terminal illness. And Andrew fell for it? He's more naive than I thought." She paused. "And just what were you intending to do when he finds out I'm *not* dying? Or did you expect me to roll over and expire on command?"

Drew winced and pulled back from the door. Maybe he *was* naive . . . or stupid. Rae had seen through it. She'd tried to tell him. But he hadn't listened to his own wife. His mouth went dry, and he swallowed hard. He should leave—now. He didn't want to hear any more. But his feet remained rooted to the carpet.

"I need a lawyer I can trust," his father was saying in a defensive tone. "Someone who's loyal, who won't betray me."

"And why are you so worried about being betrayed?" she shouted. "If this plan of yours is so lily-white, you wouldn't be concerned about someone finding out the real story."

Drew heard a muttered curse from his father. "It's legal, I tell you—all legal and aboveboard. I wouldn't take the chance—"

"Of getting caught?" His mother's acid tone made Drew shudder. "You would use your own son to protect you from your own unethical dealings?"

"Ethics!" His father spat out. "Ethics are for the weak, Beatrice, for those who don't have the guts to put their necks in the noose out in the real world. The big money is in high-risk ventures like this one. And they're perfectly legal, I assure you. We're doing these people a favor, I tell you—protecting them from the shame of foreclosure, saving their reputations—"

"Don't try to sway me with that nonsense," his mother interrupted. "Save it for your investors—they might believe you. Mark my words, Beau Laporte, the truth will catch up with you one day. And when it does, don't come crawling to me for sympathy."

"The truth, my dear, is that these little people are stupid louts with no vision and even less capital. Somebody is going to make a killing off their mineral rights, and it's not going to be them. So it might as well be me. Besides, they get paid—more money than most of them have ever seen. Everybody's happy."

Drew leaned against the wall and looked at the sheaf of papers he held in his hands—surveyors' reports from Alabama, Oklahoma, Arkansas, Texas—confidential results from unauthorized oil testing for corporations he had never heard of. What he suspected, then, was true. His father and his father's partners, under a variety of corporate names, were buying up land that was in danger of being repossessed for unpaid taxes, land rich in mineral deposits, particularly oil.

His father was right, of course—it was legal, at least technically. These poor people were being paid for their property. But they were no doubt signing contracts they didn't understand, and they certainly had no idea of the potential riches underneath their land.

It was, as his father said, a high-risk venture. Father and his partners could end up owning thousands of acres of worthless prairie grass and cotton fields. But the odds were on their side. They had done their research and, apparently, were buying very selectively.

But why? Father didn't need the money. His parents owned the house outright, and they made a good income just from the sharecropping. Besides, with Mother's inheritance—

Of course. That had to be it. Beauregard T. Laporte had too much vanity to live on his wife's money, even if it landed him in the lap of luxury. He had to make it on his own, to be his own man. Everything Father did, from the white suit and black boots to the self-aggrandizing swagger, was designed to present an image, to project himself as successful.

Pride. A proverb flitted through Drew's mind: *Pride goeth before destruction, and an haughty spirit before a fall.*

He sighed and shook his head. He didn't want to see his own father fall, of course, but he couldn't, with any kind of personal integrity, be involved in a scam like this.

"We'll be rich, Bea," his father was saying in a booming voice. "Richer than we could ever imagine. There's no limit to what we can accomplish."

"We're already rich," Mother answered. "What else do we need? How much is enough?"

"Enough is more than you have right now," Father returned with a laugh. "And you'll see—once that boy gets a taste of the kind of money he can make, he'll put his precious honor on the shelf. Money talks, Beatrice. He'll give up this absurd notion of doing charity work. And if he doesn't, just see if that dowdy little wife of his doesn't convince him. There's nothing more attractive to a woman than financial security, especially if she comes up from a dirt farm the way that girl has."

Drew ducked around the corner as he heard his mother's high heels click across the hardwood floor toward the study door. The doorknob turned and the door opened just a crack, so he heard his mother's parting shot: "Don't count your chickens where Andrew is concerned, Husband. That boy still has the keys to the henhouse."

Drew watched as she marched down the hall, unaware of his presence, and he smiled. His mother had a lot more courage—and a lot more honor—than he had ever given her credit for.

★ ★ ★

Drew found Rae in the upstairs sitting room next to the Jefferson Davis suite, pounding away at the big black Underwood. He waited in the doorway until she looked up.

"Can I interrupt you for a few minutes?"

She reached out a hand to him. "Of course."

Drew went to where she sat and wrapped his arms around her shoulders. She craned her neck for a kiss, and he whispered in her ear, "You may have to postpone your writing for a while."

Rae frowned. "Why? Drew, if this is about going shopping with your mother—"

He shook his head and laughed. "Nope. It's about packing."

She turned in her chair. "Packing? Packing what?"

"Our things—clothes, wedding gifts—everything." Drew nibbled at her earlobe. "Unless you're not interested in going home to Eden."

"Eden!" Rae jumped up, toppling her chair over and pushing him backward onto the rug. "For a visit, you mean?"

He rubbed at his bruised backside and grinned. "No, darling. Not for a visit. To stay. At least for the time being. If I live long enough, that is."

"Oh, honey, I'm sorry!" She knelt on the rug beside him. "Are you hurt?"

He made a face and groaned. "I'm mortally wounded. Here—" he pointed to his forehead, and she leaned over to kiss it—"and here—" She kissed him on the nose. "And here—" He indicated his upper lip, and when she bent toward him, he wrapped his arms around her and pulled her down in a long embrace.

"Sweetheart," she said when she caught her breath, "what happened? Just the other day—"

"Just the other day I was an idiot," he answered. "I guess you might say I've found out what I needed to know. So . . ." He raised his head to look her in the eye. "Did you mean what you said, darling, about not minding being poor?"

"Of course I meant it." Her eyes glowed with love and anticipation. "Why?"

"I heard somewhere," he said, trying to keep his voice light, "that a woman values financial security above everything else, especially if she hasn't had it."

Rae sat up and gave him a puzzled look. "Whoever said that didn't know much about women."

"You're not interested in security?"

"I didn't say that. But for a woman, security doesn't necessarily come from financial stability. It comes from an assurance that she is loved."

Drew breathed a sigh of relief. Now that he had his answer, he was overwhelmed by an awareness of just how blessed he was to have Rae Coltrain Laporte as his wife. "Then you, my darling, will be the richest woman on earth."

Rae leaned into his arms and pressed against him, and their lips met in a kiss that set Drew's nerve endings on fire and clouded his mind. He was only vaguely aware of a knock at the door of the sitting room, and then the distinctive sound of his mother clearing her throat for attention.

"Children, please, not on the antique rug!"

Drew scrambled to his feet and pulled Rae up beside him. He ran a hand through his hair and straightened his tie, all the time aware of his mother's eyes on him and of the hot flush creeping up his neck.

"Sorry, Mother, we were just—"

"I can see what you were doing," she interrupted sternly. "I'm not blind, you know." Then her brittle face broke into a smile. "Young love is wonderful, isn't it?"

She went to the sofa and sat down, obviously expecting them to follow. Drew took Rae's hand, and they sat down beside her.

"Andrew, I need to talk with you about your father. Apparently he has led you to believe something about me that is entirely untrue."

"That you are ill . . . dying," Drew supplied.

Her pale blue eyes widened. "You know?"

Drew nodded. "I went to see Father in his study a little while ago. I couldn't help overhearing."

"I see." She fixed him with an intense look. "I thought I had taught you better than to eavesdrop."

"I wasn't eavesdropping, Mother. I just happened to be there."

"So you heard . . . everything?"

"I think so. Enough, anyway."

"I need to apologize to you for what your father did, Andrew. And to you, Rae. I don't suppose Andrew has had time to fill you in on the details." She cocked an eyebrow at Rae. "You seemed rather . . . ah, busy with other matters when I came in."

"Yes, I, um, well—," Rae stammered.

"Never mind that," Drew's mother said with a dismissive wave of her hand. "Andrew can tell you about the conversation later. Suffice it to say, in Twain's words, that 'reports of my death are greatly exaggerated.' I am not ill, I am not dying—in fact, if I recall, young woman, I could outlast you on our shopping trips to the city." She turned back to Drew. "I assume, then, that you will be leaving?"

The wistful tone in her voice caught Drew by surprise, and he felt a lump rise to his throat. "Yes. I don't see that we have any choice, Mother. I can't go on working for Father and have any self-respect left. Besides, Rae's father is quite ill, and—"

"You don't need to make any excuses, Andrew," she interrupted. "Beau was so certain that your head would be turned by the prospect of wealth."

"So I heard," Drew said. "He was wrong."

"And what about you, Rae?" his mother asked. "Will it be so easy for you to give all this up?"

"This is a lovely home," Rae said, obviously measuring each word carefully, "and I hope you won't take offense, but I'm honestly much more comfortable in, ah . . . simpler surroundings."

"I expected as much." She reached out and patted Rae's hand, then looked at Drew. "Andrew, I have only one word of motherly advice for you. Take care of this girl. If I ever hear of you not treating her right, I'll disinherit you quicker than a cottonmouth can strike."

"I will, Mother." Drew caught Rae's eye and winked at her.

"And speaking of inheritance," his mother went on, "you realize that the bulk of this family's money is—at least for now—under my control." She stood, walked over to the fireplace, and then turned back to them. "With your permission, I'd like to arrange to have a sum sent to you each month—not a fortune, mind you, but a little something to help you get started."

Drew shot a quick glance at Rae for confirmation, then said, "That's very generous, Mother, but we couldn't possibly accept it." He got to his feet, went to her, and kissed her gently on the cheek. "I think it's important to us to make it on our own."

"All right," she sighed. "But I will establish a trust fund for my grandchildren." Drew's mother slanted a look at Rae. "From what I saw just now, I assume I will have grandchildren to dote on."

Rae laughed. "I expect so, Beatrice. We're not quite sure when, but you can count on it."

"If I die first, half my estate will go directly to the two of you. Your father will keep this house, of course, until his demise. But eventually it will all be yours." She put an arm around Drew and looked up into his eyes. "For the first time in generations, this family's estate will be handled by someone who has some sense. I'm proud of you, Son."

Tears stung Drew's eyes as he embraced his mother. She felt so frail and delicate in his arms, like a thin little bird who might be blown away by the first gust of wind. But she wasn't frail. She was strong and generous and loving, and he was very thankful for her.

Rae got up from the sofa and came to join them beside the fireplace. She kissed Drew's mother gently on the cheek. "You will come visit us soon, I hope."

Drew looked into his wife's eyes and knew she meant it. And when he looked at his mother, he was surprised to see a single tear track down the woman's high-boned cheek.

"I'd love to," she murmured, taking Rae's hand. "I'd be honored to meet your family, you know. Drew tells me they're good people—the salt of the earth."

"They're wonderful people," Rae agreed. "Just like your son."

34

✯ ✯ ✯

Final Farewells

Rae snuggled close to Drew in the cold bus on the last leg of the trip home to Eden. "So you didn't tell your father what you found out about his business dealings?"

"I didn't see any point in it. He didn't ask, and I didn't volunteer what I had discovered. Confronting him wouldn't have changed his mind. It would have just made things more difficult between us—and between him and Mother, I expect."

"You told him my father had been sick?"

"Yes, and that I didn't see any way to continue representing him and still do the kind of legal work I feel called to do. He mocked me, of course, and called me a fool, but he didn't try to talk me out of leaving."

Rae looked into her husband's handsome face and felt a rush of pride. "You're no fool, Andrew Laporte."

He slid his arm around her and smiled. "Sometimes I wonder. We're leaving a lot behind, you know."

"Nothing I'll miss, as long as we have each other."

"Have I told you lately what an incredible woman you are?"

"Not in the last five minutes. I was beginning to wonder."

"Well, you are. Incredible, wonderful, and—" he leaned down and breathed in her ear—"unbelievably desirable."

She turned, with her forehead almost touching his, and laughed. "I was wrong. You are a fool."

"You really know how to spoil a moment, don't you?" He sat up and looked out the window, pretending to be miffed.

"Oh, all right." She tapped him playfully on the nose. "I'm desirable. Satisfied?" Rae shook her head. "I can't believe I said that with almost a straight face."

"You are," he protested. "How long will it take before you believe me?"

She snuggled close to him again, relaxing into his warmth. "About a hundred years, give or take a few. How does that sound?"

"Perfect."

They rode in silence for a while, watching headlights pass and listening to the rhythmic thump of the bus tires against the pavement. Rae was almost asleep when Drew spoke again.

"You sent a telegram to Willie?"

"Uh-huh," she answered groggily. "Told her to meet us at the cafe."

"Well, she's not here," he said. "Unless she's traded your father's old pickup in on a brand-new Packard."

"We're home?" Rae sat up and looked out the window. Sure enough, the neon lights of the Paradise Garden Cafe were shining up ahead. But the gravel parking lot was empty except for a black Packard parked to one side.

"She must be running late." Rae looked at her watch. "And the bus is a little early."

"That's a first."

As the bus slowed to a stop, Drew extricated himself from the seat and began gathering up their smaller belongings. Three huge trunks were stowed underneath the bus, along with several boxes of law books and a crate holding Rae's typewriter. It had been a challenge negotiating the switch from the train station in Grenada to the bus that would take them into Eden—two trips in Grenada's only taxi and a generous tip for the cabbie.

In the parking lot, Drew helped the bus driver lug the heavy trunks out of the driveway and set them under the awning outside the cafe door. "For two people who don't have anything, we sure have a lot of stuff," he muttered.

Rae started to reply, then turned as she heard the bell jingle over the door. Thelma rushed out into the cold night air, followed by Bennett Winsom, whom Rae recognized from the Christmas Eve dinner. What was he doing here?

Thelma fell on Rae's neck and hugged her, then ran to Drew and gave him an awkward embrace around the last of the boxes.

"Come inside," she insisted. "You'll catch your death out here."

"Where's Willie?" Rae asked as Thelma poured steaming coffee into four cups. "She was supposed to meet us—I sent her a wire."

The look on Thelma's face made Rae's stomach twist into a knot of apprehension. "Willie's out at the farm," Thelma said quietly. "Bennett's going to take you soon as you warm up a bit."

Rae looked at Thelma, then at Bennett Winsom, whose handsome face bore an expression of sympathy. "What's happened, Thelma? Is Daddy all right?"

Thelma reached across the table and squeezed Rae's hand. "You came just in time, hon. He's bad, real bad. Willie couldn't leave, and the doctor is out there right now. You leave your trunks here—I'll take care of them for you. But you need to go pretty soon."

"Drew?" Tears blinded Rae as she reached for his hand.

"It'll be all right, sweetheart." He turned to Bennett. "Can we leave right away?"

"As soon as you're ready."

"Can I use your bathroom first?" Rae asked Thelma. She swiped at her tears. "I can't have Mama and Daddy seeing me like this."

"'Course, honey, you go on. We'll get the smaller stuff loaded into Bennett's car."

Rae made her way to the bathroom and stared at her reflection in the mirror. The single bare bulb overhead added ten years to her appearance, and she didn't look very good to start with, considering that they had spent all day and half the night traveling. Her eyes were all red and puffy, and her skin looked sallow.

She splashed cold water on her face and patted it dry with a towel, then raced for the door, where Bennett Winsom sat behind the wheel of the Packard, idling the engine.

It didn't matter how she looked. Nobody would care. The important thing was that she get there in time.

★ ★ ★

The farmhouse had a damp, musty smell about it, as if it had been closed up for years. Rae took the stairs two at a time, vowing to herself that no matter how cold it was, she would help Willie air things out in the morning, to get rid of this . . .

This stench of death.

The thought sent an involuntary shudder through her, and she stumbled on the top step. Drew caught her and held her fast. "Are you all right?"

She nodded mutely and led him to her parents' bedroom. She didn't want to see it, didn't want to face what she would find there, but she had no choice.

The room was eerily quiet, lit by a single lamp next to her father's bedside. He lay still under the blanket, his hair, thin and gray, damp against the pillow. Mama sat in the chair next to the window, rocking back and forth slowly, methodically, her eyes fixed on some far point outside. Willie stood at her father's bedside, holding his hand, while the doctor listened for a heartbeat.

When Willie saw Rae, she gently released her grasp on the old man's hand and came to the doorway. "Thank God you've come," she whispered as she hugged Rae.

"Is he—?"

"He's hanging on," Willie said in a choked voice. "But just barely."

Rae looked into her sister's face, haggard and etched with lines. Willie had borne all the burden of their father's illness, and it showed. But now Rae was home, and she vowed silently, with a fierce determination, that she would help Willie shoulder the load.

Willie led Rae to their father's side while Drew hung back near the door. If Rae hadn't known it was Daddy, she would barely have recognized him. "He's gone down so much since we were here at Christmas," she murmured in Willie's ear.

"I know. He was bad then, but in the past two weeks he's—"

"Mabel?" Daddy said in a weak voice. "Mabel Rae?"

"I'm here, Daddy."

"Come into the light and let me see you."

Rae moved so that the lamplight shone on her face and bent down over his bed. She took his bony hand and stroked the protruding veins gently.

"You look good, girl." He attempted a chuckle, but it degenerated into a fit of coughing. When at last he regained his breath, he squinted up at her. "That fancy lawyer boy's treating you right?"

"Yes, Daddy. I'm very happy."

"Good, good." He sighed. "Take care of your mama. And tell Charlie I love him."

Willie leaned forward. "What did he say?"

Rae battled against the tears that threatened to overwhelm her. "He's delirious. Said to tell Charlie he loves him."

"Charlie's gone, Daddy. For a long time now. You'll be seeing him soon," Rae said.

A faraway look filled her father's eyes. "You'll be seeing him soon," he repeated. "Tell him I . . ."

He never finished the sentence. A rattle filled his chest, and his head sagged on the pillow. Rae felt his hand go limp in hers.

"Daddy!" she gasped.

The doctor moved in and laid two fingers on her father's neck, then shook his head. Gently he closed the old man's eyes and started to cover his face with the sheet.

"Not yet," Rae protested. She leaned down and kissed her father on the forehead. "I love you, Daddy."

Willie was kneeling beside their mother's chair, talking to her in low tones. Rae went to them and put a hand on her mother's shoulder. "Mama?" she said. "Daddy's gone."

Her mother did not respond. She never stopped rocking, never looked up. Never said a word. Her eyes, vacant and empty, just stared out over the stubbled cotton fields.

With a sinking feeling Rae knew that her father wasn't the only one who had died tonight.

★　★　★

The funeral for William Coltrain was a small one. A dozen or so people, mostly relatives, huddled together in the chilly country church where Willie and Mabel Rae and Charlie had grown up and been taught that Jesus died for their sins and that God was a loving, compassionate Father.

Willie didn't feel that love and compassion, at least not from God. The people who surrounded their family—or what was left of it—took God's place that day, offering the support and sympathy she so desperately needed. Libba was there, along with her mother and Bennett Winsom. Thelma stood at Willie's elbow at the graveside, and Stork came, although Madge had to stay home with Mickey. Ivory Brownlee played the piano in the church and sang a heartrending "Amazing Grace" into the frigid January air over the cemetery. The pastor spoke about resurrection and life and hope, but all Willie could feel was a helplessness bordering on despair.

How could she, by herself, run the farm and take care of Mama? Her mother hadn't been herself in a long time, and as Daddy had gone downhill, Mama had gotten worse, until finally all she did was sit in that chair and rock. Willie wasn't sure Mama even understood that Daddy had died. She just stood at the burial plot with that same vacant look on her face, staring out into the distance. She didn't speak, didn't acknowledge anyone else's presence. She would only eat if Willie brought the food to her. Otherwise she just sat and rocked. Willie didn't know how she was going to manage it, but what choice did she have?

Then, at the house after the funeral, Mabel Rae drew her aside and told her what, amid the chaos of the visitation, she hadn't had a chance to say earlier—that she and Drew weren't just visiting but had come home to stay.

For the first time in months, a tiny glimmer of hope sparked in Willie's heart. She would not be alone, would not have to bear the load by herself. Her sister would be by her side, helping to shoulder the weight.

The hope came just in time.

Two days after her father's funeral, Willie found Mama dead in the bed she had shared with her husband for thirty-two years. She had just given up, the doctor said. It happened like this sometimes. She had just gone to sleep, never to wake again.

In spite of her grief, Willie found a growing seed of thankfulness sprouting in her heart. Mama had been gone for a long time now, even though she kept on breathing and walking. She and Daddy hadn't been the same since the news had come of Charlie's death. Now the three of them were all together, and Mabel Rae had come back home.

Maybe God did care after all.

35

★ ★ ★

Revelation

German Prison Camp
Mid-January 1945

Charlie Coltrain sat straight up in his bunk, wide awake. It was pitch black, and the prison barracks was silent except for the rumble of snoring here and there.

No one was stirring; it couldn't be time to get up. Charlie's feet were like blocks of ice, but that was nothing new. He had learned to sleep in spite of cold and lice and gnawing hunger in his gut.

But something had awakened him.

Now he remembered: the dream. His father, calling to him, saying, "I love you, Son." His mother, reaching out to embrace him.

Charlie had always known he was loved, of course. But Pop had never used those words, as far as Charlie could remember. His father wasn't a demonstrative man, and he rarely spoke about anything other than crops and livestock and the price of cotton. He never talked about his feelings, if he had any to speak of. And Mom showed her affection with chocolate pies and hand-knitted socks and apple turnovers, not with hugs and kisses.

Why, then, would he dream about Pop saying "I love you" and Mom reaching out to hug him, unless . . .

Suddenly a feeling washed over Charlie that he couldn't explain—a sense of emptiness, a longing for home greater than any he had experienced since he had left the farm for the front. Tears sprang unbidden to his eyes, and he swallowed against a lump in his throat.

Shivering, Charlie got out of his bunk and wrapped his thin wool blanket around his shoulders. As soon as his eyes had adjusted to the darkness, he tiptoed over to where Owen Slaughter lay sleeping. "Slaughter!" he hissed. "Wake up!"

Owen's eyes snapped open, and his face went rigid. Then he saw Charlie and relaxed. "What's the matter?"

"Come out to the other room," Charlie whispered. "Bring your blanket."

Owen rose and followed, draping his blanket around him, and when they were settled at the rough wooden table with a single candle between them, he turned to Charlie. "What's up?"

"Something's happened," Charlie said, realizing how stupid it sounded now that it was out of his mouth. "Something's wrong at home."

To Owen's credit, he didn't ask how Charlie knew this. He simply said, "What is it?"

"I don't know exactly. I woke up all of a sudden and felt . . . I don't know, empty. Alone. I had been dreaming about Pop."

"And you think something's happened to him." It wasn't a question, and there was not a hint of sarcasm in Owen's voice. Silently Charlie blessed Owen for being such a good friend, for trusting him so completely.

"In my dream, Pop was saying, 'I love you, Son,' and Mom was reaching out to me, like she was going to hug me. I woke up crying."

Owen scratched his head. "Was it like a memory of something that happened when you were home?"

"No, that's the strange thing about it. I've told you about my folks. They loved us, and we knew it, but there wasn't much mushy stuff in our family. Mama didn't hug us a lot, and I can't even imagine Pop saying the words *I love you.*"

"So where do you suppose this dream came from?" Owen's tone was completely straightforward, very matter-of-fact, as if he didn't think Charlie was the least bit crazy.

"I think they're dead, Owen." As soon as the words were out of his mouth, Charlie knew they were true. His eyes stung with tears, and he couldn't say any more.

"Were they sick when you left home?"

"No, they were fine. Pop was running the farm, and Mom was always tired, but there was a lot of work to do. Still, I've been gone a long time. A lot can happen."

Owen pursed his lips in thought. "What do you want to do about it?"

Charlie began to cough, and for a minute or two he couldn't catch his breath. He drew the blanket closer around him and waited until the spell subsided. "I want to get out of here."

"I've been thinking about it, too," Owen said. "We can't last much longer. You look like death on two legs as it is."

"Thanks a lot, pal."

"You know what I mean. Your cough has gotten worse since Christmas. How long can we sit on our duffs and wait to be rescued, anyway?"

"Not much longer, the way I see it. But can we convince the others to go with us?"

"I don't know. We'll have to try."

"We'll have to wait until the snow melts."

"I know," Owen said. "But that will give us time to plan." He held his hands to the candle flame to warm them. "Can you hold out for another two months?"

"I'd rather not." Charlie couldn't help thinking about his mother and father, and Willie and Mabel Rae. They needed help—needed him. He had to get out of here and get home as soon as possible. No matter what the risk, he had to try. "But I guess I don't have much choice. If we try it now, we're bound to be caught—or freeze to death. I suppose another two months won't matter so much."

"It'll take that long to get supplies together and decide how and when to do it." Owen frowned. "We'll need matches and candle stubs, and newspapers, if we can get them, to put inside our boots. I suppose stealing a gun is out of the question."

Charlie shook his head. "How do you intend to get a gun without killing a Kraut for it?"

"I don't know—it was just an idea."

"If we're careful, we might be able to get some fragments of iron from the railroad tracks and make a couple of knives."

"Yeah," Owen said, "but if we're caught, we're dead."

"We won't get caught. How's your German?"

"I understand most of what goes on between the guards." Owen grinned wryly and tapped a forefinger against his skull. "I guess when you don't have much memory, there's plenty of room for a new skill."

"Good. Keep your ears open, and find out as much as you can about any changes in schedule or work details that might be coming up."

"Then what?"

"Then," Charlie said evenly, "as soon as the snow melts, we take off."

"It could be dangerous."

"It *will* be dangerous," Charlie corrected, wheezing as another round of coughing overtook him. "But not nearly as dangerous as staying put."

36

★ ★ ★

Small Blessings

January 15, 1945

Madge peeked into the nursery. Mickey was sleeping in his crib, his mouth slightly open and his arm wrapped around his favorite toy, a ratty-looking stuffed bear Thelma had given him shortly after they came to Eden. The bear would have to be burned, of course, along with the sheets and blankets and other things the child had touched that couldn't be disinfected. But it was a small price to pay. Mickey was out of danger.

For the past few days, the baby had slept almost constantly, crying only when he was wet or hungry. The angry red rash had faded, his smile had returned, and the brightness had come back to his eyes again. He was quieter, more subdued than usual, but that was, no doubt, a result of exhaustion.

"He looks so sweet, doesn't he?" Michael's voice came from behind her.

"He's beautiful," she said without turning.

"I can't help thinking what a close call we had with him," Michael went on in a low voice. "If I live to be a hundred, I'll never take him—or you—for granted again."

Madge looked over her shoulder. Michael, in his bathrobe and still rumpled from sleep, stood leaning against the doorframe, a wistful smile on his unshaven face. She went to him and put her arms around his waist. "You have never taken us for granted, Michael Simpson. You're a wonderful husband and a magnificent father."

He dangled a clean diaper in front of her. "Yes, I am. And I'll prove it."

"Do you think you should wake him? He probably needs the extra sleep."

"What he needs is some time with his daddy." He turned toward the crib. "Time to get up, sport," he called. "We're going to get you back on a regular schedule—starting today."

Mickey didn't stir.

"Mickey? Let's go, buddy. Up and at 'em."

Still the child did not move.

Madge cast an apprehensive glance at her husband and started toward the baby bed. Her foot grazed one of the child's toys—a large hollow ball with rattlers and bells inside. It made a terrible racket as it flew across the floor and bounced off the far wall.

But Mickey slept on.

"Michael?" Madge's heart constricted, and a knot formed in the pit of her stomach.

By now Michael was standing over the crib. He reached down and touched Mickey's face, and the boy's eyes fluttered open. "Da-da!" Mickey beamed with delight and raised his arms to be picked up.

"See, he's fine," Michael said, hoisting the baby to his hip.

"Mama!" Mickey reached toward Madge and giggled.

She took him and walked several paces to the doorway. Mickey, engaged in playing with the ribbon at the collar of her nightgown, snuggled against her. "Call him."

"What?" Michael started to come toward them.

"No, stay there. Call him." Madge turned so that Mickey's back was toward his father.

"Mickey?" he called apprehensively. "Son, it's Daddy."

No response.

"Mickey?" he said, a little louder. "Mickey, over here!"

Still no reaction.

Michael stepped up behind the boy and leaned in toward his ear. "Mickey!" he bellowed.

The child kept playing with his mother's collar as if he'd never heard.

Tears filled Madge's eyes, and she pressed Mickey's head against her shoulder. "No," she whispered. "No, it can't be."

★ ★ ★

"I'm sorry," the doctor said for the third time. "It's impossible to predict what—if any—residual problems will result from scarlet fever. Considering the involvement in the ear canal, deafness would be one of the possible outcomes."

"One of those 'complications' you mentioned."

"Unfortunately, yes."

"Unfortunately?" Madge's eyes flashed, and her voice grew tight. "That's all you can say—that it's *unfortunate* our son can't hear?"

"I beg your pardon, Mrs. Simpson, if I sounded overly clinical," the doctor apologized. "Certainly this is a tragedy for your family. He was such a fine little boy."

Stork took him by the arm and led him into the dining room while Madge went back to the nursery. "Doctor, I don't mean to sound brusque, but I'd appreciate it if you wouldn't talk about my son in the past tense. He's not dead. He's deaf."

"Yes, of course," the doctor murmured. "Well, if there's nothing more, I'll be going."

Stork felt his hand clamp the man's arm like a vise, and he forced himself to let up on the pressure. "That's all? Just, 'I'm sorry, your son is deaf'? What are you going to do about it?"

"Do?" The doctor gave a puzzled frown. "There's nothing I *can* do about it, Lieutenant Simpson. I'm a G.P., not a specialist. Perhaps there are physicians in Memphis who specialize in this sort of thing. I'll look into it and send you some information. In the meantime, I'd suggest you reconcile yourself to the reality of the situation and be glad your baby is alive."

When the doctor was gone, Stork slipped back to the nursery and stood in the doorway, watching. Madge sat in the rocking chair next to the window with Mickey on her lap, singing a lullaby to him, rocking. His eyes were wide open, his ear against her chest. As she sang and rocked, his fair head nodded in time with the music.

Was he hearing the sound or merely responding to the vibrations as she sang?

Stork looked at his son's face, and suddenly he realized that it didn't matter. Mickey's eyes were bright and clear, and a soft smile lit his round little face. The fever was gone; he was alive.

Whatever challenges they had to face from here on, they would deal with. God had given their son back to them, and Stork would be grateful. He would.

FOUR

Easter Song

MARCH 1945

37

★ ★ ★

Made for Each Other

March 15, 1945

Link held the hand mirror up and surveyed his appearance one piece at a time. His hair looked neat enough, he supposed, although he could use a trim. The collar of his shirt seemed a bit too large; but his tie was neatly knotted, and his lieutenant's bars gleamed. This was the first time since he was wounded that he had been in dress uniform, and he felt strangely out of place.

The fact that he wasn't wearing pants didn't do much to make him more comfortable, either. An image flitted through his mind—a paper doll, dressed for a party, but only from the waist up. He looked down at the loose-fitting pajama bottoms that covered his legs. He could manage the shirt and tie and uniform jacket, but the dress pants and shiny black shoes would have to wait for a later time. With a self-deprecating shrug, he laid a blanket across his lap and tucked it firmly into the sides of the wheelchair.

"Well, aren't you the handsome one this morning! Got a date, soldier?"

Link looked up to see Libba clicking across the linoleum floor in three-inch heels. She was stunning in a wispy dress of light blue-green, a color that set off her auburn hair and pale green eyes to perfection. She leaned down for a kiss, and he caught a whiff of perfume that sent his mind reeling.

"I do now," he countered, grasping her around the waist and settling her on his lap.

"Link, behave yourself," she said with a light laugh.

He kissed her warmly, then released her. "So," he said, fingering his lapels, "you approve?"

"I do indeed. You look wonderful!"

"Only half of me." Grinning, he pulled the blanket back to reveal the pajama bottoms. "I'll be the first man on record ever to attend a military wedding wearing pajamas."

"During this war?" Libba chuckled. "I doubt it. But you will probably be the first to go half-and-half."

"I always dreamed of making a fashion statement." Link winked at her. "Today, my fondest dream comes true."

"It's almost time. Are you ready?"

He wheeled around toward the bed. "Almost. But first, this." He retrieved a small florist's box from the bedside table. "For you, sweetheart. Because I wish this could be our wedding day."

Libba opened the box. "A corsage! Oh, gardenias!" She held the flowers up for him to smell. "They're my favorite, darling. How did you know?"

"Lucky guess." He paused, admiring the way the creamy whiteness of the flower petals complemented her skin. "Actually, I had a little help from Pinky. I sent her out for them first thing this morning."

She handed the corsage to him and bent down for him to pin it on her dress. He fumbled with the filmy fabric for a moment, then gave up. "It's hopeless," he said. "You'd better do it, or we'll never make it to the wedding."

"A little distracted this morning?" She took the flower and pinned it on her left shoulder.

"You distract me," he murmured, reaching for her. "We could skip the wedding."

"Hans and Marlene would never forgive us."

"They'd understand."

"They probably would, but Pinky would never let me live it down." Libba extracted herself from his embrace and picked up her purse. "Shall we go?"

"I suppose, if we really have to."

"We have to. After all, you have a fashion statement to make."

★ ★ ★

The small hospital chapel was lit with candles and decorated with white satin ribbons. Soft organ music filled the air. As Libba sat at the end of one pew, with Link next to her in the wheelchair, her mind began to wander to the day when she and Link would take their own vows.

She wanted candles, certainly. And lots of flowers. Gardenias, she thought, looking down at the velvety petals of her corsage. They smelled so sweet. She would wear a dress covered in lace and pearls, with a long train. And Link would be so handsome, standing there in his—

Would he be standing? She tried to envision walking down the aisle to take the hand of a man sitting in a wheelchair, as Link was now. It wasn't her girlhood dream of a wedding, that much was certain. Not the stuff of which fairy tales were made. And yet somehow it didn't matter very much, as long as Link was there.

As the prelude began, Libba came out of her reverie and looked around. A number of the soldiers on the ward were there—friends of the groom who had supported him during the worst of his dark times. Pinky, seated at the front, caught Libba's eye and waved to her. It seemed most of the nursing staff had put in an appearance, and Libba wondered briefly who was minding the wards. Stevie Sutton fidgeted nervously at the altar, as if he were getting married himself rather than simply serving as best man. Then Hans Amundson walked stiffly to the front, leaning on his crutches.

Libba reached out and squeezed Link's arm. He gave no response, no indication that he was even aware of her. He simply stared straight ahead with an expressionless countenance. She leaned over to ask if he was all right, but the opening chords of the processional interrupted her.

Libba stood and, with her hand on Link's shoulder, watched as Marlene made her way down the aisle. The nurse looked radiant, Libba thought—but then, all brides were beautiful, weren't they? Not for a second did Marlene even seem to take notice of the crutches or the awkward braces on her fiancé's legs. Her eyes were fixed on Hans's face as he stood waiting, blond, ruddy, and handsome, in his dress uniform. Except for the crutches, he could have been a Viking warrior.

Made for each other, Libba thought, and tears clouded her eyes.

Link sat stiffly, his expression inscrutable, with his arms folded across his chest.

★ ★ ★

I have to keep control, Link thought, gritting his teeth. *If I let go, even a little, I'll embarrass myself—and Libba.*

The truth was, his own tears threatened to overwhelm him, especially when he heard Libba sniff and saw her blotting her eyes with a handkerchief. What was it about weddings that made women go on so?

But he was a man, and despite all his efforts, he was about to break down and cry, too. He couldn't help it. He kept thinking about his own wedding, about Libba, about standing—yes, *standing*—with her to pledge his love to her forever.

And he would stand. No matter what it took.

For weeks now he had kept his secret. Gradually, bit by bit, the feeling was coming back into his legs. Sometimes the pain was excruciating, but he drove himself on, working like a madman with the physical therapist, pushing himself to the breaking point.

He had no intention of getting married in this blasted wheelchair, even if Libba protested—as she did almost daily—that it wouldn't matter. He was going to walk. And not with heavy braces and crutches to support him, either. He knew it now, as surely as he knew that he wanted to spend the rest of his life loving the woman who sat beside him.

"I, Hans Amundson, take thee, Marlene Henley, to be my lawfully wedded wife. To have and to hold . . ."

Link's palms were sweating, and he wiped them on the blanket draped over his lap. He reached out and took Libba's hand, gently stripped off the white glove that separated her skin from his, and stroked her fingers tenderly. She jerked to attention, fixing him with an expression of both surprise and delight.

He gazed into those cool green eyes and smiled. Hans was stammering through his vows, but Link's voice was strong and steady. "As long as we both shall live," he whispered in her ear. "Forever."

38

★ ★ ★

Plans

Germany
April 1945

Owen Slaughter unfolded the strip of cloth he had hidden under his mattress and ran his finger along the edge of the crudely fashioned iron knife. It wasn't anything like the Bowie knife he had owned as a boy, but it would have to do.

A Bowie knife? Where had that sliver of memory come from? He had no idea. He could see it, though, in his mind's eye—its carved deer-horn handle, its bluish steel blade. He could almost feel its weight in his hand, sense its leather scabbard hanging from his belt.

Maybe it wasn't his memory at all. Maybe it was Charlie's—or a fabrication out of Owen's own imagination, based on all the stories Charlie had told him about hunting and fishing with his dad in the woods and streams around the farm. Anymore it was hard to determine where Owen left off and Charlie began.

Owen shrugged and replaced the knife in its hiding place. It had been a miracle that the Krauts hadn't discovered it, but in the past month or so Owen was becoming more accustomed to the idea that, even in this hellhole, God might be watching out for them. Charlie, thank heaven, was still alive, perhaps even a little stronger than he had been at Christmastime. And winter seemed to be breaking early this year. During work detail yesterday the wind had felt a little warmer, and the sun had come out for a few minutes. The snow was almost melted, and he thought he had seen a robin.

Soon it would be time. Very soon. But not if they couldn't convince the others.

"Owen," Charlie called from the main room of the barracks. "Get in here—everybody's waiting."

"Coming." Owen lowered the mattress back onto the wooden slab and went into the adjoining room to find a sullen group of men staring at him.

Tiger Grayson, the Australian, went on the attack immediately. "What's this Charlie's saying about a plan to escape?"

Owen nodded slowly. "That's right. We have to get out of here, fellas. We can't just sit around and wait for the cavalry to ride in."

"You're a bloomin' idiot, Slaughter!" Grayson snarled. "If you and Coltrain escape, they'll kill us all, that's what."

"That's why we all have to go together," Charlie put in. "Once we're outside the wire, we can split up so they can't find us."

"And you think these Krauts are going to just open the blasted gates and let us walk free?"

"Of course not," Owen said. "Charlie and I have it all planned. You see, we'll—"

"What I see," the Aussie interrupted, "is that we got two genuine nut-cases on our hands. Right, mates?"

A murmur of assent went around the circle. Clearly, Tiger Grayson thought he had won. He leaned back, folded his arms, and grinned.

But Grayson wasn't the ranking officer here. Owen turned his back on the man and faced Lieutenant Colonel Marshall Effington. "Marsh, what do you say? Do we go for it or not?"

Silence descended, broken only by the soft wheeze in Charlie's chest, as all eyes turned to Effington. The man's mustache twitched, and his beady eyes flicked back and forth from Owen to Grayson. At last he cleared his throat. "I must say, Slaughter, you present me with a conundrum. Word has it that the Allies have broken through and may be on their way even as we speak."

"Rumors," Owen snapped. "About as reliable as the propaganda we hear every day. According to our captors, der Führer is on the verge of being elected pope."

"Perhaps," Effington hedged. "But I tend toward concurrence with Grayson's evaluation of the situation." Tiger let out a snorting laugh, which Effington silenced with a glance. "The wisest course, it seems to me, is to wait it out. This is bound to sort itself sooner or later. Our boys will get here, and I'd prefer we be alive when they do. If we attempt an escape, they'll likely be liberating our corpses."

Behind him, Owen heard Charlie gasp as he was overtaken by a fit of coughing. Spring might be on its way, but Owen had no assurance the Allies were. And even if the war ended tomorrow, it might take weeks for the troops to get this far into Germany . . . wherever they were.

No, he and Charlie would not stay. Even if they had to go it alone, they would go. But he wasn't about to reveal that to Effington and the others. For months they had been expecting the Allied army to march into camp with bands blaring.

But Owen had no such hope. He had no memories of home and hearth to cling to, no sweetheart waiting for him, no family praying for his release. The only images that filled his mind were of this camp, with its daily terrors and nightly exhaustion. He could stand no more, and he knew in his heart that, spring or no spring, Charlie could not tolerate many more weeks of it either.

He and Charlie Coltrain were on their own.

Owen turned and fixed Charlie with a look, silently begging him to trust, no matter what. Then he nodded to Effington. "All right," he said. "I guess the majority rules. No more talk of escaping."

"That's more like it, man," Marsh congratulated him, slapping him on the shoulder. "One for all and all for one, that's the ticket."

"I still say they're both bonkers," Grayson muttered as he scraped his chair back and rose to his feet. "But there's no place else to send them, now is there? We got the worst loony bin in creation right here at our doorstep."

★ ★ ★

"Thanks for not giving me away," Owen said to Charlie when they were alone.

"I got the message," Charlie said. "But what was all that, anyway? Are you giving up, too?"

Owen shook his head. "How can you even ask that, Charlie?"

"But you said—"

"What I *said* is that there would be no more talk of escaping. And there won't be. We're done talking, for all the good it did us. Now we're just going to do it."

Charlie grinned and tried to speak, but his breath came in shallow gasps. "All right," he said when he caught his breath. "What's the plan?"

"The plan is the same as it's always been," Owen answered. "We go out the back and around to that narrow space between the barracks and the fence. Nobody can see us back there. When we get to the wooded side, we cut under the fence and into the woods." He paused. "It'll be dangerous, Charlie, and difficult. Are you up to it?"

"No," Charlie said, shaking his head. "But what difference does that make?"

"I'll help you." Owen squeezed Charlie's shoulder, feeling the bones under his hand. "We'll make it."

"Even if we don't, I won't be sorry." Charlie gave a wan smile. "I didn't come all this way to die like a dog in a cage."

"Nobody's going to die, Charlie."

"You don't know that."

Owen thought about it. No, he didn't know. They could both die—in fact, the odds were undoubtedly against them. But something in him, some germ of hope or faith, firmly believed that they had a chance. Not a good chance, but a chance. And it was the only chance they had.

"When do we go?" Charlie looked at him, and Owen saw a clear light in those familiar eyes—the look of a man ready to do battle, ready to face his destiny.

"Let's give it a week or two. We don't want Grayson and the others breathing down our necks. By then the rest of the snow will be gone—I hope—and it'll be a little warmer. Just be ready."

"I'm ready now." A racking cough overtook Charlie's emaciated frame, and he shuddered.

"Sure you are." Owen looked squarely at him. "Don't save any more of your bread ration," he warned. "We've got enough to last us a couple of days, and you'll need all your strength. Promise."

Charlie lifted a skeletal hand. "I promise. But you've got to promise something too. Promise me if I don't make it—"

"You can't talk like that, Charlie. You have to believe we will make it."

"If I didn't believe that, I'd be staying here with the rest of them. But if something happens to me—" he waved off Owen's attempted interruption—"if something happens to me, promise you'll go to Eden. To my family. Tell them in person . . . everything. . . ."

The cough rattled his thin shoulders, cutting off his words midsentence. "Promise," he gasped.

Owen patted his arm. "OK, I promise, buddy."

He hoped it was a promise he would never have to keep.

39

★ ★ ★

Black Thursday

April 12, 1945

Willie fiddled impatiently with the knobs on the radio in the parlor. "That's as clear as I'm going to get it," she sighed, looking over her shoulder at Rae and Drew. Her sister sat huddled on the sofa, her round face bleak and her eyes rimmed with tears. Her handsome husband cradled her in a fierce embrace—he, too, looked as if his world had come to an end. . . .

The radio spluttered to life, the static clearing suddenly.

"To repeat, the president is dead. Franklin Delano Roosevelt, thirty-second president of the United States, died of a brain hemorrhage today at Warm Springs, Georgia. Vice President Harry S. Truman, who will soon be administered the oath of office and become the thirty-third president, has vowed to continue President Roosevelt's foreign policies and bring an end to this terrible war. Meanwhile, the entire nation is in mourning. In Washington . . ."

The voice crackled and broke up as static interfered with the signal, and Willie snapped the radio off.

"What's going to happen now?" Willie slumped on the other end of the couch and wiped her eyes.

"I don't know," Drew muttered. "Truman just doesn't have the experience in foreign affairs that Roosevelt had."

"They should let Eleanor finish out his term," Rae declared solemnly. "What was it she said that day she went down in the mines—'I am my husband's legs'?"

249

Drew shook his head. "She might be his legs, but I doubt that she has his brains."

"What's that supposed to mean?" Willie snapped. "That a woman doesn't have the intelligence to handle being president?"

"Whoa, wait a minute!" Drew raised his hands in protest. "I didn't say that. I'm outnumbered here, remember? I just meant that—well," he stammered, "being president is a man's job. A woman just isn't cut out for it, and—"

"Eleanor Roosevelt seemed to be cut out for a lot of other 'men's jobs,'" Willie interrupted. "She's done more for this country than most of its presidents combined." History was Willie's favorite subject, and she warmed to the discussion, glad for a chance to think about something besides what Roosevelt's death might mean to the war effort. "Who was it that visited the soldiers overseas? And championed the cause of the Negro troops?" Willie shifted and fixed Drew with an intense look. "You, of all people, should appreciate that."

"I do appreciate it," Drew said, "and I'm not implying that Mrs. Roosevelt is anything other than a bright, energetic, noble woman. She has had a profound impact upon this nation, and apparently a great deal of influence with her husband. But a lot of people think—"

Willie cut him off with a wave of her hand. "A lot of people *don't* think," she muttered. "They believe, without thinking, that a woman couldn't possibly run this country. But my opinion, for what it's worth, is that Eleanor Roosevelt has been running the government for years—or at least has had a significant part in it."

"The power behind the power," Rae interjected. She put a hand to Drew's face and stroked his cheek. "After all, that's what an equal partnership in marriage is all about, isn't it, darling?" She asked the question so sweetly that Willie had to stifle a laugh. "I know you believe in that."

"Of course I do." He sighed and pulled his wife close. "And I hope President Roosevelt was a wise enough man to appreciate his wife. But that doesn't change what's happening. Truman is president now, and I doubt he will ask Eleanor for her advice on how to run the country—or end the war." He shook his head. "What I'm most afraid of, I guess, is that Roosevelt's death will give the Germans and the Japanese the edge they need. It's sure to boost their morale, at the very least."

Silence descended over the room. Willie considered Drew's words, and a knot of apprehension twisted in her stomach. Why, she wondered, did everything seem to happen all at once, like a huge storm cloud descending over their world? Daddy's death, then Mama's, and now Roosevelt's. Outside, spring was well on its way—the redbuds were coming out, azaleas were budding, and the daffodils were already in full bloom. Rae and Drew were settling in at the farm, and life was beginning to rouse in Willie's soul once more. The contrast made today's news seem all the more bleak.

Suddenly, like a puppy with a flea biting its tail, Rae jumped up and tugged at Drew's hand. "Come on," she said to Willie over her shoulder. "Drew, get Daddy's truck."

"Where are we going?"

"Into town—to the cafe. Everybody's bound to be gathered there, and I think we need some company."

The knot in Willie's stomach relaxed a little, and she nodded. Yes, Rae was absolutely right. The Paradise Garden was where they needed to be.

★   ★   ★

Rae peered through the windshield of the pickup truck. The sign on the door said CLOSED and black bunting draped the doorway, but the lights were on and strains of piano music drifted out into the cool night air. Drew parked the ancient truck to one side and got out, rubbing his lower back and muttering about getting a car with some springs in the seat.

"I told you you wouldn't like being poor." Rae kissed him on the nose as he helped her from the cab. "We can't afford a new car."

"I don't care about new," he answered. "I'd just like something that didn't come off of Henry Ford's original assembly line."

"It got you here, didn't it?" Willie slammed the door on the passenger's side, and it bounced on its hinges a couple of times before it caught.

"Just barely." He grinned and offered an arm to each of the women. "Shall we go, ladies?"

Inside, as Rae had predicted, Thelma was serving coffee and apple turnovers to Stork and Madge Simpson, Bennett Winsom, and Olivia Coltrain. Ivory was at the piano, playing a background of somber blues with Mickey in his lap.

"Hey, y'all come on in." Thelma motioned them inside, and Stork got up and pulled another table over. "We've been expecting you—or at least hoping you'd come." She poured more coffee and set another plate of turnovers in the center of the table. "It's awful, isn't it?"

Rae nodded. "We couldn't stand being alone out there at the farm. We needed some company."

"Looks like you came to the right place." Bennett Winsom shifted his chair over to make room for Drew and Rae. Willie sat on the opposite side of the table next to Madge.

"How's Mickey?" Willie asked Madge, and Rae leaned over to hear the answer. The discovery that scarlet fever had left the little fellow deaf had been another in a series of difficult blows, all of which came in a two-week period right around January fifteenth. The Ides of March was nothing compared to the Ides of January. Somehow, they had gotten through it all—Mickey's illness, Stork's crisis of faith, the death of Rae and Willie's parents. Now the president's passing. Things had to get better—they could hardly get worse.

"Just look at him." Madge pointed. Ivory had switched from blues to jitterbug, and Mickey gleefully bounced on the old man's lap in time to the music.

"But if he can't hear the piano—" Willie gave Madge a puzzled look.

"We're not quite sure how much he can hear—if anything," Madge explained. "The doctor thinks that, as young as he is, he'll adjust fairly easily. He may be able to hear some of the notes, or he may just be responding to the vibrations."

"Not hearing doesn't seem to be bothering him very much," Rae commented.

Madge smiled and shook her head. "Children are remarkably adaptable. It's the parents who have the greater adjustment to make, I'm afraid." She cast a loving look at her husband. "Michael is wonderful with him. He's found a book on sign language, and he's teaching me and Mickey as he learns. That child is amazing, I'll tell you. He's learning the basic signs faster than I am—it's like a game to him. And I think he's beginning to read lips, too. He certainly understands when I tell him no."

"That doesn't surprise me," Willie said in her schoolteacher voice. "He was already beginning to talk. He's very bright." Rae's eyes followed her sister's gaze as she looked over at little Mickey, who was laughing out loud as Ivory tickled him with one hand and fingered the keys with the other. "How old is he? Two?"

Madge chuckled. "Michael and I jumped the gun, Willie, but not by that much. He'll be one on Saturday. But he is big for his age—big and smart. Too smart, I'm afraid, for his mother."

Rae watched Madge's face closely and saw no trace of embarrassment or shame with the mention of the baby's untimely conception. It was good that she could joke about it, even briefly. No doubt Stork's acceptance of God's forgiveness had a lot to do with Madge's ability to relax.

Rae looked around the cafe. "Seems kind of quiet around here without your mother-in-law, Madge."

"Yeah," Willie put in. "She was the life of the party."

Madge tried—unsuccessfully—to keep the grin off her face. "Yes, it's too bad she had to leave so soon." Madge rolled her eyes. "But speaking of parties, we're having a birthday party for Mickey on Saturday afternoon, and you're all invited." A cloud passed over her face. "Heaven knows we need something to take our minds off what's going on in the world."

What's going on in the world. That last comment snapped Rae back to reality, and she looked around the cafe. Drew and Bennett had their heads together, engaged in conversation, and Olivia was sketching on a paper napkin, talking animatedly about arrangements for Libba's wedding reception while Thelma nodded. It all seemed so normal, so ordinary.

Ivory stopped playing suddenly, and Mickey's high-pitched giggle rang out over the hum of conversation.

Yes, Rae thought. Life went on. The world might be falling apart around them, but even in the midst of darkness, there was hope. Music. A child's laughter.

★ ★ ★

Bennett Winsom watched the passionate deep blue eyes of the young man who sat before him. Andrew Laporte was much more than a pretty face, that was certain. The man had a bright mind and a quick wit and a nobility of soul that warmed Bennett's heart. As he listened to Drew talk about his dreams for his legal career, his heart leaped with anticipation.

"I won't go into details," Drew finished, "but I found out my father was engaged in some business dealings that weren't quite ethical—at least by my standards." He gripped his hands together on the table and looked into Bennett's eyes. "All I've ever wanted to do, since I first entered law school, was help people who couldn't help themselves. My father thought I'd be seduced by the prospect of financial success." He shook his head. "Maybe I'm crazy, but I don't care about money, Mr. Winsom. The only thing that will ever give my professional life any significance is doing what I feel called to do—working to make life better for ordinary people."

He paused and ran a hand through his hair. "I guess . . . well, I was wondering. . . ." He stammered to a halt and shrugged his shoulders.

"You were wondering if there was some way we might work together?" Bennett prompted.

Drew brightened. "Yes, sir. When Willie told me you intended to stay, to practice law here . . . I mean, I know I'm young, but I was second in my class in law school, and—"

Bennett patted his arm. "You don't have to sell yourself to me, son. You're just the kind of man I'd choose for a partner."

"I think I could be a lot of help, sir, if you don't mind my saying so. I've got a lot of energy, and if you could use an assistant—"

"Hold it, hold it," Bennett said sternly. "I didn't say anything about an assistant."

Drew's face fell. "Oh."

"I said *partner.*" Bennett grinned as the light of understanding dawned on the young man's handsome face. *"Full* partner."

"Partner?" Drew repeated, blinking.

"How does *Winsom & Laporte, Attorneys-at-Law* strike you?"

"It strikes me just fine," Drew gulped. "Only . . . how much will it cost to set up a practice? I don't have much money."

"Neither do I, son. Sounds like an equal partnership to me." Bennett slapped Drew on the shoulder and sealed the agreement with a firm handshake. "There's an empty storefront on the square that we can get for almost nothing." His eyes drifted to Olivia Coltrain, still in discussion with Thelma about their children's wedding. "I happen to know the owner quite well."

Drew's eyes followed the direction of his gaze. "Not Coltrain's Hardware?"

"No, no—the empty store next to it. Much smaller, but quite adequate for our purposes. Apparently Libba's father had an option on the place, thinking to expand, but he died before he could do anything with it. Olivia—ah, Mrs. Coltrain—held on to the property, and when I decided to stay, offered it to me. It won't cost much, and there are some benefits to keeping it in the family." He laughed. "At least you don't have to fight with your landlord, and if the rent's a little late, well . . ."

"Not to mention other fringe benefits," Drew chuckled. "Such as having an attractive widow lady right next door."

Bennett heard the remark, but it took a minute or two for his mind to process Drew's implication. Did the boy think that he and Olivia . . .? Impossible.

"Nonsense," he scoffed. "Now, back to business. You need to get your credentials in order as soon as possible. And get your tools dusted off— we'll need to build partitions for a reception area and three separate offices. You do know how to wield a hammer, don't you?"

"Yes, sir. I'm a fair carpenter—nothing fancy, but I can put up a wall that won't fall on your head."

"Good enough."

"You said three offices?"

"That's another issue we'll need to talk about. I don't know right now what my son will be doing when he gets out, but he's talked about going to law school. Would you be opposed to *Winsom, Laporte, & Winsom*—not right away, of course, but eventually?"

Drew gave Bennett a dazzling smile. "Opposed? I should say not! We'll need to put in a ramp from the street—" he paused and frowned—"just in case, you know. And make sure the doorways are extra wide. Maybe a counter and low bookcases in one of the rooms—"

Bennett smiled wistfully as Andrew Laporte went on talking about plans for turning the store into legal offices. When Link had talked about getting his law degree, Bennett had never envisioned him practicing from a wheelchair. But Drew was right, of course—it was wise to prepare for that eventuality.

Suddenly Drew fell silent, and Bennett felt the young man's eyes on him. He looked up to see the handsome face contorted in a frown. "Something wrong?"

"I need to ask you a question . . . or at least to tell you something that might make a difference to you," Drew hedged.

"Speak your piece, son."

"Well, I—you need to know, Mr. Winsom, that I believe we have a problem in this country that is going to come to a head sooner or later. Now, integration's not a popular idea in the South, but as a Christian I don't think we have the option to oppress other people and treat them as second-class citizens. I know a lot of people justify segregation by using the Bible, just like they justified slavery in Lincoln's day, but I don't subscribe to that kind of interpretation." He paused and took a deep breath, and Bennett waited for him to continue. "The time is coming—maybe not tomorrow, but eventually—when this issue will explode and people will come out fighting. I intend to be involved in the fight, and I'll be fighting for equality, for voting rights. If you have a problem with this, or don't want to take the risk, tell me now."

Bennett looked at the table and suppressed a smile. Drew Laporte was an intense young man, full of fire for righteous causes and the plight of the underdog. Not many like him left in the world, Bennett mused—men who would walk away from a promising and profitable career to practice grass-roots law in an obscure little town. He liked this boy—liked him a lot. Maybe this was one other reason, among the hundred or so he had already identified, why God had brought him here and directed him to stay.

"I have one insurmountable problem with what you have said," Bennett said deliberately. "One thing I cannot accept."

He watched as Drew pulled in a shaky breath. "What's that, sir?"

"Stop calling me Mr. Winsom," Bennett said with a grin. "And drop the *sir,* or the deal is off."

★ ★ ★

Thelma looked at the clock: It was just after nine. Ivory had stopped playing. Mickey lay asleep in his mother's arms, and Stork sat beside Madge with one arm around her shoulders and his other hand around the baby's little fist. Drew and Rae leaned on the table with their hands entwined, and Willie sat between Madge and Olivia, stroking Mickey's hair.

For the dozenth time that night, the voice on the radio intoned the news that the president was dead.

Thelma turned the radio off, and a profound silence engulfed the cafe. No one spoke or moved, and Thelma suspected that, although not a syllable was uttered, all of them were praying, in their own way, for their nation and their leaders, for an end to the war, for a return at last to a normal life.

She felt a warm, strong hand enclose hers, and she looked up to find Bennett Winsom smiling at her.

"Look around," he said quietly. "We're all here together—family, friends, and loved ones." He shook his head in wonder. "What miracles it took to get us all here together! We're not here by accident, but for a purpose. God has plans for us, my friends, plans that cannot be thwarted even by a national disaster of this magnitude."

The serenity in his voice and the peace in his touch washed over Thelma like a soothing balm.

"We've all had a lot to grieve over in past months," he went on in his rumbling baritone. "Death of family members, loss of loved ones, shattered dreams." He nodded toward Stork and Madge. "But that little boy in Madge's arms gives me hope. He's a survivor, just as we all are. And no matter what happens, we can sleep peacefully in the Everlasting Arms, just like Mickey is sleeping now."

Deep in her soul, Thelma felt it—the peace Bennett Winsom was talking about. And as she watched the faces of the others, she could see that they felt it too.

Black Thursday had come and gone. They had survived. And they would continue on, trusting God to be there in the midst of their uncertainties.

Somewhere beyond the walls of the cafe, out across the rolling hills and flat Delta farmland, church bells tolled for the leader who had gone to his eternal rest. But in Thelma's mind, they rang for her and her loved ones as well. Not a death knell, but a call to live on in hope. There was business to attend to, after all—a partnership to establish and a wedding to plan and a little boy's first birthday to celebrate.

40

★ ★ ★

Striking a Blow for Rosenfelt

Charlie's heart sank when he took his place in line and saw the smirking SS officer pacing back and forth in front of the prisoners' roll call. *No, he* thought glumly, *not more propaganda.* He ducked his head to avoid meeting the officer's steely gaze, and his hand instinctively went to the scar on his cheek where the man had struck him months ago. Surely the officer would recognize him.

The strutting Nazi paced down the line and back again, stopping in front of Owen Slaughter. He thrust his swagger stick under Owen's chin and lifted his head. "Hah!" he sneered in his broken English. "You still here, stupid friend?" He laughed into the chilly morning darkness. "Not dead yet? Too bad. Maybe I kill you, put you out of misery." His eyes cut to the side and fixed on Charlie. "Or maybe I kill him."

Dear God, Charlie prayed frantically, *don't let him react.* He pleaded silently, as if Owen could hear him. *Keep your mouth shut, Slaughter.*

The Nazi pushed the head of his stick against Owen's windpipe. "You learn your lesson, eh?" Owen said nothing. "Good." He tapped the stick against the side of Owen's head. "You learn good, even if you stupid." He withdrew the stick and slapped it against his high jackboots, then turned as if to go. But suddenly he wheeled around and spat full in Owen's face.

Please, God, Charlie begged.

Owen didn't move a muscle. He just stood there with the Nazi's spittle running down his cheeks and made no move to respond, not even to wipe it off.

One side of the officer's face turned up in a half smile. "You learn good," he repeated.

With an exaggerated goose step, the Nazi strode back to the front of the assembly. He stepped onto a wooden crate so he could be seen by all and turned to face the prisoners.

"Americans!" he shouted. "I bring you news from home. Your Jew-dog president, Herr Rosenfelt, ist dead."

A murmured gasp ran through the crowd, and the Nazi bellowed for silence.

Propaganda, Charlie thought. *It can't be true.*

"You think the noble German people lie to you?" the officer yelled. "See for yourselves." He held up the front page of a newspaper—an American paper, to all appearances, although Charlie couldn't read the masthead. The banner headline, in bold black letters, proclaimed, **ROOSEVELT DEAD.**

"Do not bother to deny," the Kraut officer went on. "Ist newspaper from your city of Chicago." He pronounced it Shy-ka-go. "We have ways of obtaining such information." He shook the paper above his head. "Herr Rosenfelt's brain exploded," he said with a sinister laugh. "Too much Jew propaganda."

The bitter taste of bile rose up in Charlie's throat, and he swallowed hard. If this was true . . .

"Ist true," the SS officer continued. "Und now the Fatherland will be triumphant, as der Führer has predicted." He tossed the paper to one side and pointed his swagger stick at the prisoners. "Any man who wishes to come to the victor's side will be welcomed in Deutschland," he said. "All others will join the Jew Rosenfelt in death."

The Kraut stood there for a moment, his steely eyes boring into the faces of the captives. At last he picked up the newspaper and shoved it under one arm. "Heil Hitler!" he shouted, then stalked to his waiting car and sped through the gates.

★ ★ ★

"Is it conceivable he's telling the truth?" Lieutenant Colonel Effington asked as he scanned the faces of the men gathered in the common room of the barracks.

His eyes lit on Charlie, who shrugged. "I don't know, Marsh," he hedged. "The newspaper looked real enough, but I was too far back to see much except the headline."

"I got a fair look at it," Tiger Grayson put in. "But I ain't that familiar with Yank newspapers."

"I was pretty close," Owen Slaughter said. "If it wasn't real, it was a good copy."

Grayson turned on him. "Like you'd know squat about American news-papers! If you didn't have your dog tags, you wouldn't know your own name."

"That's quite enough, Grayson!" Effington snapped, and Owen raised an eyebrow in Charlie's direction. Maybe Marshall Effington did have a back-bone, after all. Maybe this would be the final straw, the circumstance that would convince him they had to attempt an escape—and quickly. The Kraut officer had said that anyone who didn't come over to their side would be killed, and it was anyone's guess whether that meant tomorrow or a month from now.

But apparently the RAF officer only had enough spine to stand up to the likes of Tiger Grayson. "Whether it's true or not," he was saying, "doesn't affect us. The war effort will continue, with or without Mr. Roosevelt. We still have Churchill, after all. The Allies will win this one—that much we know. It's only a matter of time."

Only a matter of time? Owen cringed inwardly. If he heard that simpering phrase once more, he thought he'd scream. He cast a pointed look at Charlie, who nodded and mouthed the single word *tonight*.

★ ★ ★

The barracks was silent as death. The guards had locked them in for the night, and except for the familiar sounds of snoring and the occasional scuttle of a mouse across the bare wood floors, nothing stirred.

Charlie was awake when he felt Owen's hand on his shoulder. Without a word he rose and retrieved his meager supplies from under the thin mattress. He slipped into the common room behind Owen and put his mouth to the man's ear. "Are you ready?" he whispered, stifling a cough.

"As ready as I'll ever be," Owen whispered back.

"God be with us," Charlie murmured, making the sign of the cross over his chest. It was only the second time in his life he had ever done that—the first was on board ship right before they landed in Normandy. Now, as then, it gave him a little comfort.

"Amen," Owen muttered.

With his homemade knife in hand, Owen led the way to the door of the barracks, where it was a simple matter to jimmy the latch from the inside— there was enough space between the boards to see out into the darkness of the compound.

He gingerly opened the door. Except for a rising half-moon and a few scattered stars, darkness engulfed the camp. There was not a guard in sight.

"Where is everybody?" Charlie mouthed the words in the dim light.

From some distance away, laughter erupted, and Owen pointed. Behind the main building, a handful of burly Germans swayed drunkenly as they passed a bottle around the circle. "Celebrating the demise of President Rosenfelt," Owen hissed. "Lucky for us."

Charlie opened his mouth to protest that luck had nothing to do with it, but this was no time for a philosophical conversation. He followed Owen around the back of the barracks, flattening himself against the dark wall. When they were safely hidden behind the building, he breathed a ragged sigh of relief.

"That way," Owen said, indicating the spot where the outer fence came closest to the woods. Keeping low to the ground, they scuttled across the open space and arrived, breathless, at the fence line.

Charlie looked up. It was doubtful he could make the climb, given his physical condition, and even if he could, the coils of razor wire that spanned the top of the fence were a powerful deterrent. "I don't know, Owen—"

Owen stared at him. "Do you think I'm an idiot?" He pulled a small pair of wire clippers from inside his jacket. "We're going under, not over."

"Where'd you get those?" Charlie breathed, feeling for the first time as if this might work.

"Don't ask." Owen flattened himself to the ground and pulled Charlie down behind him. "Just keep still."

Charlie buried his face in the dirt and hardly dared to breathe while Owen grappled with the fence. In a minute or two—it seemed like forever— Owen whispered, "OK, let's go."

Charlie looked up. Owen had made two parallel cuts in the bottom of the fence, with just enough space between so that they could lift the fence like a flap and slip through on their bellies. Once they were on the other side, they could bend the flap back into place, and unless the Krauts were looking closely, they'd never know the wire had been cut.

"Come on." Owen bent the flap up and Charlie flattened down on his stomach. All he could see on the other side was dark woods looming before him. Then, halfway through the opening, he heard a sound that made his blood freeze.

"HALT!"

Charlie swiveled his neck around to see Owen standing next to the fence, face-to-face with a German guard who held him at bay with an unsteady rifle. The Kraut, obviously inebriated, was scratching his head, trying to figure out what they were doing out here in the middle of the night.

Owen didn't give him a chance to think for long. With a mighty lunge, he drove his homemade knife through the guard's chest, and the man fell with a shudder, pinning Owen against the wire.

"Get on through!" Owen hissed. Charlie scrambled to the other side, and Owen threw the dead guard to the ground. In a flash Owen slid through the opening and turned back to the fence. "Help me drag him," he whispered over his shoulder.

"Why?" Charlie asked, transfixed by the dumbfounded expression etched into the guard's face.

"We can't leave him here," Owen muttered in an exasperated voice. "They find him, they'll come looking for us."

"Oh." Charlie bent down and helped Owen drag the corpse through the opening, then watched as Owen retrieved the Kraut's rifle and bent the fence wire back into place.

"Don't just stand there," Owen said through gritted teeth. "Get his pistol and his ammunition."

Charlie complied, shoving the pistol into his jacket and buckling the guard's ammo belt around his own narrow hips. But, thanks to the meager diet of the prison camp, he was a lot thinner than the bulky German. The heavy belt slid down his legs onto the ground, and Owen shook his head. He grabbed up the belt, nearly tripping Charlie in the process, and slung it around his shoulder. "Here, take the rifle and come on." Then Owen began to move, dragging the dead German by the collar of his heavy coat.

"We'll dump him here," Owen said when they came to a small ravine about thirty yards into the woods. "The Krauts won't be able to see him from the fence, and by the time they find him, we'll be long gone."

Once the dead guard was disposed of, they increased their speed, going deeper into the woods. Charlie began to wheeze and cough, and Owen relieved him of the rifle.

An hour or so into the woods, Owen slowed their pace and listened for anyone coming behind them. Except for the occasional rustle of night creatures and the hooting of an owl close by, no sound broke the silence of the night. No baying hounds or running feet or shouting.

Owen exhaled a long breath. "Let's take a break," he suggested, helping Charlie sit down on a fallen log. "Are you hungry?"

"I could eat," Charlie answered quietly, taking the bundle of supplies out of his jacket and handing Owen a piece of bread. He fumbled with the parcel for a moment, suddenly overwhelmed by the enormity of their undertaking.

"Something wrong?" Owen asked around a mouthful of dry bread.

"It's just—well, I'm sorry I froze on you back there."

"It's all right," Owen said, slapping Charlie on the leg. "Don't worry about it." He began to chuckle. "I wish I'd had a picture of you with that ammo belt falling down around your knees. Looked like something out of the Keystone Cops."

Charlie's mind latched on to Owen's last comment, and he peered at his friend's face in the darkness. "You remember the Keystone Cops?"

"I guess I do," Owen mused. "I remember this one scene in particular, where they kept falling out of the car."

Charlie started to laugh, but the action made his lungs contract, and a round of coughing seized him.

Owen leaned over and gripped Charlie's knee. "You feeling all right?"

The coughing subsided, and Charlie nodded. "I'll be fine. I couldn't believe my eyes, the way you took out that Kraut guard."

Owen shrugged. "He was drunk and slow. Otherwise we'd both be dead."

"Still, you did it. Roosevelt would be proud of you—if he's still alive."

A shadow passed over Owen's face. "I don't remember Roosevelt," he murmured. "Was he really Jewish, like that Nazi officer said?"

"I don't know," Charlie answered. "And I don't really care. He was a good president. If he is dead, it's a great loss."

Owen raised his chunk of bread in salute. "To you, President Rosenfelt," he said with a grim laugh. "Wherever you are."

41

★ ★ ★

In-Laws

The wards at Kennedy General this morning reminded Libba of a funeral home. No one moved who didn't have to, and when people did, they slipped soundlessly along the corridors with eyes downcast and heads bowed. No one spoke or smiled, and even necessary business was carried on in a subdued murmur. Through the window she could see the flagpole, where the banner of the nation drooped at half-mast. Even the spring winds had died.

Libba tried to move quietly along the tiled hallways, but every click of her heels against the linoleum floor echoed back to her. It seemed sacrilegious, almost, to make any sound at all on a day like this—a day of mourning, a time of nationwide grief and uncertainty. Libba's very happiness made her feel like a heretic. While the country kept silence for its fallen leader, she was on her way to plan a wedding.

The doors to Link's ward were shut, and they creaked on their hinges when she pushed her way through. Hans Amundson's bed was empty. He had been discharged, and he and Marlene were in the process of setting up housekeeping in a small rental house near Overton Park. Stevie Sutton would be leaving by the end of the month to take a job as night-shift manager at the Kellogg plant. New faces appeared on the wards, of course—wounded soldiers came and went—but Libba knew few of them. Everything was changing, and her life was moving on with the tide.

Libba found Link sitting in his wheelchair at the foot of his bed, staring morosely at the black-draped framed photograph of Roosevelt that hung on the far wall of the ward. She kissed him and then stepped back to look into his eyes.

"Are you all right, sweetheart?"

"Yeah, I'm fine," he muttered. "It's just so hard to believe that he's really gone. He's been a fixture, you know, for so many years. Not everybody liked him, but almost everybody respected him. A lot of people pinned their hopes of winning this war on that man—" he nodded toward the picture— "and now—well, I just don't know."

Libba put an arm around his shoulders. "From what I hear in the news, the war effort is making good headway—especially in Europe. Maybe it will all be over soon."

Link nodded. "I hope so. I'd hate to think that this—" he motioned toward his legs, covered by a hospital blanket—"was all in vain."

"It wasn't in vain," she said. "It brought you home, didn't it? It brought us back together."

He smiled and reached up to take her hand. "Yes, it did. Any price would have been worth that."

Libba stroked his cheek. "Our parents are probably waiting for us. Are you ready to go?"

Link took in a deep breath. "I suppose. For some reason I'm nervous about this."

"Planning our wedding? Relax, darling. It won't be as bad as you think. And you'll only have to do it once."

"It's a good thing. Are you sure we can't just elope and get it over with?"

"And miss all those great wedding presents? Not on your life. I've got my eye on an absolutely stunning set of china." Libba winked at him. "Besides, having a real wedding makes a man realize that marriage is serious business."

"That's not a lesson I need to learn," he said, pulling her down for a kiss. "I can't imagine living my life with anyone but you."

★ ★ ★

When they reached the commissary, Link's father and Libba's mother were already there, waiting at a corner table. Despite the atmosphere of gloom that pervaded the hospital, they were smiling and chatting over coffee like two old friends, like . . .

Like a husband and wife.

An unexpected jolt of pain shot through Link when the thought penetrated his brain. He didn't think his father had any designs on Libba's mother, even though she was still attractive, in a middle-aged way. Surely

Dad would have told him if anything of that sort were in the works. But his father was a handsome, available man, and he deserved some personal happiness in life.

Link barely remembered his mother, yet witnessing the easy companionship between his father and Olivia Coltrain made him feel betrayed somehow. And betrayal rapidly transformed itself into irrational anger. This was *his* wedding for heaven's sake—his and Libba's. They should be the focus of this discussion, not . . . whatever was going on between his dad and her mother.

"So, how long have you been here?" he snapped as Libba wheeled him to the table.

His father looked up with a confused expression. "Only a few minutes. Long enough to have a cup of coffee." An uneasy pause stretched between them. "Is something wrong, Son?"

Link felt Libba's eyes on him and shook his head. "Sorry. I guess all this is a little overwhelming."

Obviously his father interpreted "all this" to mean the tragedy of President Roosevelt's death. "It's a terrible blow to the country, I know. But we'll get through it; you'll see."

Link started to correct his father's misunderstanding, then thought better of it and shut his mouth. No point in raising an issue that might not be an issue at all, and certainly not one he was prepared to talk about.

He rolled his wheelchair closer to the table. "What's the agenda?"

Olivia Coltrain couldn't contain herself any longer. "I talked with Thelma about having the reception at the Paradise Garden. She's going to take care of all the food, and Stork and Madge will help with the decorations."

"I'm going to ask Willie to be my maid of honor," Libba interjected. "I assume Stork will be your best man."

"I guess so," Link mumbled. He couldn't keep his eyes off Olivia Coltrain's hand, resting lightly on his father's arm, and for a moment the anger flared up in him again. But his eyes were playing tricks on him. As he watched, he began to see something else—himself and Libba, middle-aged and comfortable with each other, sharing a cup of coffee and talking about the events of the day. All his uneasiness faded, and he smiled.

Libba gave him a strange look. "Where are you, sweetheart?"

Link came back to the present with a start. "Just . . . thinking." He took her hand and gazed into her eyes. "We're going to have a wonderful life, you know that?"

"Of course we are, honey." She patted his hand. "But not if we don't get this wedding planned."

★ ★ ★

Thelma sat behind the counter pretending to read the newspaper, but it was full of gloom and doom—projections and speculations about what Roosevelt's death would mean to the war effort and to the nation as a whole. Thelma was concerned about the nation, of course, but right now even the prospect of total annihilation couldn't hold her attention.

All she could think about was Bennett Winsom, who was presently seated in the back booth with Olivia Coltrain.

Thelma let her eyes drift up over the edge of the newspaper. Bennett had thrown his head back and was laughing, and Olivia was wiping her eyes with a napkin. Some private joke, no doubt—maybe a joke at her expense. Thelma fiddled with an errant strand of hair, then looked at her work-roughened hands. Olivia Coltrain could afford to get her hair done at the beauty parlor every week and get a manicure. The hardware store was doing better than ever, and rumor had it that Robinson's life insurance had been sufficient to keep her in style for the rest of her life. Not that Olivia was wealthy, but she was at least well enough off that she didn't have to slave her life away cooking in a two-bit cafe and wiping down tables from morning till night.

Olivia was a lady.

From deep in her memory, something pushed its way to the forefront of Thelma's mind—a line from a play, she thought, something she had read back in high school. Shakespeare, maybe. *"Beware of jealousy . . . it is the green-eyed monster which doth mock the meat it feeds on."*

Tears sprang to Thelma's eyes, and she lifted the newspaper to hide them. It was high time she faced the truth about herself. She *was* jealous. Jealous of Bennett Winsom's attention to Olivia Coltrain. Jealous of Olivia's position, her status, her money.

It was a nasty feeling, and Shakespeare—if it was Shakespeare—was right. Jealousy ate you up from the inside out. It made you dissatisfied with your lot in life and ungrateful for the blessings God had given you. It made you want to be something other than what you were.

The way Thelma desperately wanted to be a lady.

If only she had a little more class, a little more sophistication. A little more education. If only she could afford to have her hair—which had gone prematurely gray during the year after Robert Raintree left his farewell note on the screen door—professionally colored instead of doing it herself out of a henna bottle. If only she had the wherewithal to buy her clothes in a fine Memphis department store instead of picking them off the rack in that dumpy little shop in Grenada. If only she could wear those sweet, feminine pumps rather than these old-lady lace-ups, which gave her needed arch support for being on her feet all day but had absolutely no style. If only . . .

Thelma stopped suddenly and laid the newspaper on the counter. She wasn't accustomed to such negative feelings about herself and her life, and giving voice to them, even in her own mind, made her distinctly uncomfortable. Besides, something else, some other voice besides Shakespeare's, was trying to get through, but she couldn't hear it clearly.

She waited.

At last the whisper came again: *Would you be someone other than the person I have made you to be?*

Yes, she thought with a trace of belligerence, *I would.*

Would you? Would you insult the Giver by failing to appreciate the gift?

Gift? What gift? The gift of being an undereducated, homely woman whose entire life was spent behind the four walls of this dingy little cafe, listening to other people's problems? The gift of loneliness? The gift of discovering that she was in love with a man who clearly wanted—and deserved—a fine lady instead of a broken-down old waitress?

Love is always a gift, the voice in her spirit said. *Love is never wasted.*

Deep in her soul, Thelma knew it was true. She was not alone. She was not unloved. The Lord had given her a family in Madge and Stork and little Mickey and the friends who made the Paradise Garden their second home. And even the love she thought she had wasted on Robert Raintree had come back to bless her in the end, for his rejection had cast her into the arms of God.

But was the other part of it true—was she, honestly, in love with Bennett Winsom? And if she was, what on earth could she do about it? She had nothing to offer a man like that. Even if she had money and leisure time and fancy clothes and professional hair color, what difference would it make? She would still be Thelma Breckinridge underneath it all. She would never be able to change enough to attract a man like Bennett Winsom.

Thelma folded the paper and looked down at the front page, which bore a picture of Eleanor Roosevelt and a story about her accomplishments as First Lady. As if seeing the woman's face for the first time, Thelma realized suddenly that here was a woman who would be a strong contender for the homeliest female on the face of the earth. And yet no one thought of her that way. Her soul, her commitments, and her compassion for others made her the most respected—possibly the most adored—woman in the world. Nobody cared what she looked like. Nobody minimized her accomplishments because she had a weak chin and buckteeth.

Thelma sighed. What needed changing was not her hair color or her wardrobe, but her attitude. Until Bennett Winsom had walked into her cafe on Christmas Eve, Thelma had been happy and carefree and acutely aware of her blessings. She had a loving family and faithful friends and a life of meaning and purpose. None of that had changed. Only her perspective was different—she was focusing on the wrong things.

Well, it was high time she got her feelings back in line with reality. Bennett Winsom or no Bennett Winsom, she couldn't afford to be anyone but the person God had created her to be. And she wouldn't waste any more time being ungrateful for the life God had given her.

She was herself, and that would have to be enough.

★ ★ ★

"And so," Bennett said to Olivia, "before we left the hospital, Link drew me aside and asked me whether or not there was anything . . . ah, developing . . . between you and me. Can you imagine?"

Suddenly Bennett realized how that sounded, and he began to backtrack. "Not that it's an unthinkable idea, of course. I mean, you are a very attractive woman, Olivia, but—"

"Never mind," she soothed, patting his arm. "I know what you mean, and you haven't offended me in the least. I just think it's so funny, Link's assuming something like that. Just because we get along well doesn't mean that we—" she lifted her eyebrows—"well, you know."

She leaned toward him and lowered her voice. "I want you to know, Bennett, how much I appreciate what you did for Libba today. That was her biggest concern about the wedding—who was going to give her away. It was so thoughtful of you to offer."

"It was something I very much wanted to do, Olivia." He smiled into her eyes. "I already think of Libba as a daughter, and I consider it a great honor that she would allow me to escort her down the aisle."

"You are aware, I assume, of how things were between Libba and Robinson?"

Bennett closed his eyes and nodded. "She told me. I must admit, I was shocked and saddened by what I heard."

"So was I," Olivia said. "I knew Robinson was a self-centered man who felt compelled to control everybody within his reach, but even I was shocked that he went to such extremes." She paused and smiled wanly. "Libba needs a father—a real father. I think you're the perfect candidate."

"Well, thank you, m'lady." With mock formality he picked up her hand and kissed her fingers lightly. "You're not so bad as a mother yourself."

Olivia laughed and pulled her hand away. "We're being watched."

Bennett looked over to where Thelma was sitting behind the counter with the newspaper. "Thelma? Certainly not. She's too noble to spy."

"Noble, is she?" Olivia gave a wicked little laugh. "That's another reason it's ridiculous that Link should ask if there's something going on between us. It's clear you only have eyes for one woman in this town."

Bennett felt his neck beginning to burn, and he fiddled with his coffee spoon. "I don't know what you're talking about."

"Don't play coy with me, Bennett Winsom," she said. "I can read you like a book. If there's anyone in Eden who strikes your fancy, it's Thelma Breckinridge."

"That obvious, huh?" The warmth crept up his neck into his ears.

"To anyone who has eyes to see. And just for the record—" she took a sip of her coffee—"I think it's absolutely wonderful."

Bennett snapped to attention. "You do?"

"Of course I do. Thelma is a fine woman. She's loving and compassionate and has a heart as wide as the Mississippi. I don't think there's a soul in this town who hasn't been touched by her in some way. You could do a lot worse."

"I don't know . . . I sense some reticence in her. I've talked to her, of course, and everything I've seen about her convinces me I want to get to know her better. But she treats me like . . . like a friend."

"Friendship is a good start. If I had married someone who was a friend first, I probably wouldn't have gotten into the kind of marriage I ended up with."

"But friendship isn't enough. There's got to be—" Bennett stopped, groping for words.

"Passion? Romance?" she supplied.

"And—for me—spiritual substance," he added. A wave of nostalgia washed over him, and he sighed. "My wife, Catherine, was not a beautiful woman, at least not as some people define the word. But there was so much to her—so much inner beauty. She was my equal, my partner. She was strong, and she challenged me to grow—especially in spiritual terms. I see those same qualities in Thelma. And for the first time in almost twenty years, I believe if I'm not careful I might find myself falling in love again."

His gaze wandered to the counter, where Thelma sat looking down at the newspaper. Before he could check it, a smile crept over his face.

"It's too late for being careful," Olivia chuckled. "In Ivory Brownlee's words, I think you done fell."

42

★ ★ ★

The Good Samaritan

April 15, 1945

Owen Slaughter awoke to the sound of Charlie's coughing. He stripped off his jacket and put it around his friend's shoulders, helping him to sit up.

"Easy, buddy. Take slow, deep breaths."

The two men had spent a full day and two nights in the woods, sleeping in snatches and walking until Charlie could walk no more. So far they had been lucky, and it hadn't rained. But this morning Owen could see heavy clouds hanging just above the treetops, and if they didn't find shelter soon, they were going to be in deep trouble.

A cold spring wind whipped Owen's shirt and made him shiver.

"Here, take it back," Charlie wheezed, attempting to remove the jacket. "I'll be fine as soon as we start moving."

Owen pushed Charlie's bony arms into the sleeves of the coat and patted him on the shoulder. "You need it more than I do. Do we have any bread left?"

"Just a little." Charlie handed him the last crust of hard brown bread. Owen broke it in half and handed Charlie the larger portion.

"This do in remembrance of me," Charlie murmured under his breath.

"What?"

"The Last Supper. Right before Jesus died, remember?"

"No, I don't remember," Owen snapped. "But nobody's going to die. Got it?"

Charlie ate his bread solemnly, and Owen looked around. There had been no sign of pursuit, and that made him nervous. Where were the Krauts? Were they so stupid—or so incompetent—that they didn't even bother to look for two escaped prisoners and a missing guard? Had they really made it, or was there a trap waiting for them somewhere up ahead?

"It's going to rain, Charlie," Owen said. "We've got to find some shelter."

"April showers bring May flowers," Charlie said in a singsong voice.

Owen shook his head and reached over to feel Charlie's forehead. His skin was flushed and hot, and his eyes had a glazed look. April in Germany was a lot colder than April in Mississippi. If they got caught in the rain—

Suddenly Owen felt a shiver run up his spine, but it wasn't from the early-morning chill. Where had that spark of memory come from—April in Mississippi? Azaleas blooming, daffodils swaying in the wind, the white flash of dogwood trees along a wooded roadside. . . .

He closed his eyes for a moment, and his stomach knotted. Charlie must have told him about spring back home in Eden. That's it. It was Charlie's memory, not his own.

He raised his head, and his eyes fluttered open to the sight of dark clouds closing in above the trees. "We'd better go, pal. We need to find someplace to get out of the rain."

"It's not raining." Charlie held a hand palm up and stared at it as if waiting for the first drops to fall.

"But it will be soon. Come on."

★　★　★

Charlie stuffed the last of the bread into his mouth and struggled to his feet. His head felt fuzzy, and the burning behind his eyes blurred his vision. But he kept going, doggedly following Owen Slaughter's lead. They had made it out of the prison camp and come this far, and he wasn't about to let his friend down if he could possibly help it.

Owen was already a few yards ahead of him, and Charlie increased his pace to catch up. His legs weren't working very well, though—they seemed weak and rubbery, and his feet didn't want to do what his mind told them to do. Once, when he thought he had stepped high enough to clear a fallen tree trunk, he stumbled and fell headlong into the underbrush.

Owen turned back and came to his rescue. "Are you all right, Charlie?" Again Owen put a hand to his forehead—checking, Charlie supposed, for fever. He did feel hot and tingly, but it wasn't a bad sensation. And Owen's gesture reminded him, strangely, of his mother, leaning down over him when he was sick. He could almost feel the cushiony softness of the big feather comforter in his attic bedroom, could almost hear the rain pinging like marbles against the tin roof. . . .

Charlie tried to focus. He wasn't at home, wasn't in his bed, with his mother bringing him chicken noodle soup. He was in a forest in Germany with his best friend, who at the moment looked extremely worried.

"I'm OK," he muttered thickly. His tongue felt swollen, and he couldn't make the words come out right. "I just falled . . . fell, that's all."

Owen reached out a hand to help him to his feet, and suddenly, as if from a great distance, the sound of a barking dog came to Charlie's ears. But it couldn't have been very far off, judging by Owen's reaction.

"They've found us. Come on!"

Owen jerked him upright and set off running with Charlie in tow. It was hard going, through the undergrowth and around trees, down ravines and back up again. Charlie's heart pumped as if it would burst, and his lungs struggled for air. For a while he kept going, matching Owen almost step for step, until at last he could go no further. At the top of a shallow gully his wind gave out and he fell, coughing and wheezing, into the pit.

Owen slid down beside him. "Breathe, Charlie!" Owen commanded, thumping him on the back. "Slow, even breaths. Like this."

Charlie shook his head and tried to speak, but all that came out was an uncontrollable spasm of coughing.

"You can do it, Charlie. Relax. Slow and even."

Again Charlie shook his head, and this time pointed over Owen's shoulder. With a look of absolute terror, Owen turned.

At the crest of the rise stood a huge German shepherd, its hackles raised and its teeth bared in a silent growl.

★ ★ ★

Owen's heart sank. To come all this way, just to be captured again. Now they would be killed for sure—if the dog didn't get them first.

But the animal didn't move. It just stood with its feet planted and its head thrust forward, watching them. Owen started to move, just a little, and the dog snarled.

"OK, OK," he soothed, keeping his eyes on the animal as he felt with one hand for the rifle. In his haste to come to Charlie's aid, he had dropped it, and now he kicked himself for being so stupid. In their present condition, neither of them was a match for this powerful, muscled creature. With the rifle, he could have dropped it in its tracks before it had time to lunge.

He cut a glance at Charlie out of the corner of his eye. The man was sitting upright, staring with wide eyes at the dog, his lips moving soundlessly. Had he gone over the edge, or was he . . .

At a rustle of leaves and the sound of footsteps, the dog's ears flicked backward, but still it didn't move.

"Führer!" a voice commanded. *"Setz dich."*

The dog sat. Within a few seconds, a tall, bearded figure appeared at the top of the gully with a rifle slung under one arm. *"Ach du lieber!"*

We're dead, Owen thought miserably. He turned and helped Charlie to his feet, then faced their captor and said in halting German, "We surrender."

The man threw back his head and laughed out loud. With a flying leap he jumped into the ravine beside them. "American soldiers?" he roared. "Ha! You escape from stalag, no?"

"You speak English?" Owen stammered. "How—who—"

"You no speak so good yourself," the man chuckled. He doffed his cap and clicked his heels together, a motion that made a soft rustling sound in the wet leaves. He turned and called to the dog, who instantly leaped down and stood, grinning and wagging his tail, beside his master. Owen took a step backward and shielded Charlie with his body.

"He not hurt you," the man said, reaching down to stroke the dog's ears. "His name ist Führer."

"Führer?" Owen repeated stupidly. "As in Herr Hitler, der Führer?"

"Ja," the man said with a grin. "Der Führer ist a dog, no?"

In spite of himself, Owen smiled. He felt Charlie's hand on his shoulder and said, "I think it's all right, buddy."

"Und I—" the man replaced his cap and lowered the rifle to his side—"I am Fritz Sonntag. These woods ist mine." He thumped himself proudly on the chest.

"Yours?" Owen frowned. "I thought all this belonged to the army . . . you know, property of the Reich."

Fritz turned up his lip and spat angrily into the dirt. "The Reich takes what it wants from the German people, and gives nothing in return." He glared at Owen. "All this—woods, pastures, everything—belongs to Fritz Sonntag. The Brownshirts come, build railroad track, fence, shacks for prisoners. Call it a stalag." His lip went up in a sneer. "I call it garbage."

The sneer faded, replaced by a sly smile. "You watch." He turned to the German shepherd. "Führer!" The dog came to attention. "Heil Hitler."

The animal lifted his lips and began to snarl. Fritz laughed. "You see? I teach him truth."

"But you're—" Owen faltered—"you're German."

"Deutscher ist not Nazi," Fritz said curtly. "This—" he motioned back

273

over his shoulder in the direction of the stalag—"they call it 'the glory of the Reich.' *Nein.* The glory of the Fatherland ist the people. Good people. Good, God-fearing German people."

Charlie stepped forward and held out his hand. "I'm Charlie Coltrain," he said. "This is Owen Slaughter."

Fritz nodded. "You escape, no?" He eyed Charlie. "You too skinny to be regular soldier."

Charlie nodded. "When we heard your dog, we thought we had been discovered." He ran a hand over his face. "I prayed."

Owen turned and stared at him. "Is that what you were doing, Charlie? Praying?"

Charlie nodded. "What did you think I was doing?"

Owen started to say, *I thought you'd gone loony on me,* but he caught himself in time. "I didn't know."

Fritz grinned. "You pray, I come," he said. "God send me. And Führer."

"God's got a strange sense of humor," Owen muttered, "to send a Führer to fetch us."

"Ja," the German agreed. "Gott ist pretty funny sometimes." He looked up as thunder rumbled in the distance. "Storm coming fast," he said. "You come with me."

"Where?" Owen retrieved the lost rifle from the gully and fell into step with Fritz. Charlie trailed a step or two behind.

"Not far. Two, three kilometers. That way." He pointed. "You stay in my barn. Out of the storm."

Owen grabbed the man's arm and wheeled him around. "We can't do that. If the Germans—the soldiers, that is—find us, you and your family will be in danger. They'll kill you."

Fritz shrugged and resumed walking. "Führer ist my family. I take risk."

Owen grabbed Charlie's arm and hauled him along. "We can't let you do that, Fritz. Your life is at stake."

Fritz pivoted toward Owen and fixed him with an intense look. "Your friend pray, I come. God owns my life like I own this land." He lifted a bushy eyebrow. "Some things worth dying for."

★ ★ ★

As they made their way through the woods with Führer in the lead, Charlie felt a little strength coming back into his body and hope returning to his heart. He was still feverish, and he had a hard time keeping up, but at last they were going somewhere. And Fritz Sonntag was, indeed, an answer to prayer.

The German was a huge man with legs like pillars, a broad barrel chest, and a ruddy face half hidden by a light brown beard. Charlie always expected that, if he ever did see an angel, it would be some kind of pale, ethereal creature with wings and a halo of light. If Fritz had wings, they were hidden under his drab brown hunting jacket. And there was no halo, unless you counted the wild strands of blondish hair, thinning across the top, that flew out from the sides of his head.

But Charlie had prayed, and Fritz Sonntag had come. If he wasn't an angel, he was close enough to satisfy Charlie.

As the woods gave way to a clearing, Fritz paused at the base of a tree to pick up a dirty burlap sack. "Squirrels," he explained, hefting the bag in one hand. "Dinner."

"Squirrels?" Owen frowned. "But we didn't hear any shots. If you had been hunting, we—"

Charlie silenced him with a nudge. "Don't ask."

Owen shrugged, and together they followed Fritz across the clearing and over a stone bridge that spanned a rushing stream. On the other side, a small stone cottage nestled against the trees, flanked by a sturdy wood-and-stone barn.

"You come." Fritz motioned them toward the barn.

Inside, the place smelled of fresh hay and horseflesh. A massive bay gelding, seventeen hands high, nickered softly as they entered. Führer went straight for the stall and barked softly, and the horse bent down to nuzzle the dog. A long-haired calico appeared at the edge of the hayloft overhead, surrounded by a litter of tiny, round kittens. She stood rubbing against a post, emitting a rumbling purr.

"Führer thinks he is horse," Fritz laughed. "Or maybe Kaiser thinks he is dog." He pointed upward at the cat. "Das ist Liebchen."

Charlie smiled, marveling inwardly that this peaceable kingdom could exist in the midst of the war and destruction all around them.

"You follow," Fritz said, putting a hand to the ladder and motioning them to climb into the loft. Owen helped Charlie ascend, one rung at a time. Liebchen and her kittens waited for them at the top of the ladder, twining around their legs and purring. One of the kittens, a soft gray with a white spot on its nose, attached itself to Charlie's pants and clambered up his leg to perch on his shoulder.

"Das ist only boy cat in Liebchen's litter," Fritz explained, scratching the kitten under the chin. "He like you. You name him, yes?"

A warm rush filled Charlie's soul, and he nodded. "Can we call him Charles?"

"French name, Charles?" Fritz grinned. "Good. Deutsche cat with French name. I like."

★ ★ ★

Owen watched as Charlie set the kitten gently onto a mound of hay. *Charles*—the little boy whose life Charlie had saved in the woods in France. Now, perhaps, that courageous deed was being rewarded. If he could just keep Charlie warm and dry for a few days, maybe his cough would subside and he would get better. Maybe . . .

"Come, come! Schnell!" Fritz was standing at the back wall of the hayloft, motioning to them. The wall held a collection of farm tools on hooks—a hand scythe, a leather ox yoke, a two-handled saw.

"You stay here. Be safe."

"We really appreciate it, Fritz. At least here we can be dry and out of the weather." Owen turned to Charlie. "We can sleep on the hay, all right? We'll stay for a few days until you get stronger, then—"

"Nein, nein!" Fritz protested. He pulled on the ox yoke and a door swung back to reveal a small room about ten feet wide and twenty feet long. At either end of the room, the roof sloped downward at a steep angle.

"A hidden room!" Owen exclaimed. "A false wall?" He stepped away from the door and surveyed the hayloft. Everything seemed intact—an ordinary loft filled with mounds of hay and assorted tools. Inside, beyond the fake wall of weathered wood, a row of neatly made cots lined the walls. At the center of the room, a sturdy square table held an oil lamp, a washbasin and pitcher, and a stack of clean towels. In the far corner, the edge of a chamber pot was just visible behind a wooden screen.

"I make myself," Fritz said proudly. "You like?"

"It's wonderful," Owen said. "Perfect."

"Soldiers never find people here." Fritz pulled back the door and started to go in, but Owen stopped him.

"What people?"

Fritz smiled. "People getting away from soldiers. All kinds. Yellow stars. Pink triangles. Little girl with—" he tapped his forehead with one finger— "slow mind. A priest who spoke against the Reich. A Lutheran pastor—my pastor. One time, a Hitler youth who ran away. Everybody. All God's children."

A wave of realization washed over Owen as he considered Fritz Sonntag's words. This simple, brawny woodsman had been hiding fugitives from the Nazis. How many, and for how long? And more important, why? Why would a man like this—a man obviously Aryan, who was himself in no danger from the Reich—voluntarily risk his life to help others?

As if he had read Owen's mind, Fritz drew him inside and sat down on one of the bunks. "I have brother," he said. "Older brother, named Kurt. My brother leave home, go to city to work. He meet beautiful woman—good woman—named Leah. She is one-quarter Jewish. But to Hitler's mad dogs there ist no such thing as part Jew. All Jew, all die."

He sighed and ran a hand through his beard, and Owen motioned for him to continue. "Kurt and Leah marry, have beautiful baby daughter. Then the soldiers start to come. Leah does not look Jewish, so they do not bother her at first. But her family—ah!" He shook his head. "They will not leave, but they give her money to go. Kurt and Leah take their baby and move to America."

"Your brother lives in America?" Owen glanced at Charlie, who had slumped down on one of the bunks and was staring at Fritz. He had tears in his eyes, and his hands were clenched in front of him.

Fritz nodded. "They go to Minnesota. To a place named after a German city called Ulm—no, New Ulm. Many Germans there. They are safe to raise their children. And happy, except—"

"Except what?"

"All Leah's family—Jews and part Jews—the soldiers take to Dachau."

Owen frowned. "What's Dachau?"

Fritz shuddered. "Dachau ist camp."

"Like the prison camp, you mean? The stalag?"

"Like, and not like," Fritz murmured. "Camp for killing Jews."

A chill ran up Owen's spine. "The death camps."

"You know of these?" Fritz turned wide eyes on him.

"We heard rumors," Owen answered. Charlie began to cough a little, and Owen looked up. The tiny gray kitten Charlie had named Charles was in his lap, burrowing under his arm. Tears were streaming down Charlie's face as he stroked the soft fur. "We hoped it wasn't true."

"Ist true." Fritz cleared his throat. "So, you see why I help. For Kurt and Leah. In memory of Leah's family."

Owen laid a hand on Fritz's arm. "Maybe they're still alive. Maybe—"

Fritz shook his head. "I go there once. Outside the gates, away from the camp. I see the smoke rising, smell the burning flesh. I know."

"But the war will end, Fritz," Owen insisted. "Those camps will be liberated, sooner or later—"

"For Leah's family, liberation has already come."

"You mean heaven?" Owen looked at him. "But you said they were Jewish."

A light came into Fritz Sonntag's blue eyes, and a faraway expression filled his face. "Do we not serve the same God?" he murmured. "I am Christian, but I say *kaddish* for them. Others may disagree, but I believe they are free."

43

★ ★ ★

The Death of Saints and Tyrants

May 2, 1945

Owen Slaughter awoke before dawn to the sound of Kaiser moving restlessly in the stall below him. Quietly he groped for the table, lit the oil lamp, and went to Charlie's bedside to check on him. This had been his morning ritual every day for the last two weeks. And every day he found Charlie weaker, his breathing more labored.

Shortly after Fritz had taken them in, Charlie's fever had shot up again, no doubt from his exposure in the woods and the general deterioration of his health in the prison camp. Fritz had done everything humanly possible to help, feeding them with nourishing stew from the game he shot in the woods, providing extra blankets, even riding Kaiser to the nearest neighbor, five miles away, to get fresh milk and a few eggs.

But nothing seemed to help. Charlie tried, but he couldn't manage to eat enough to build up his strength, and now the racking cough and fever were accompanied by nausea and diarrhea. Even if Charlie wanted to eat, he couldn't keep much of anything down. Fritz said he had seen it before. They called it influenza, and Charlie, in his weakened condition, had no resources to fight it off. If he could hang on until it ran its course, he might be all right. All they could do was wait and hope . . . and pray.

This morning, as Owen watched, Charlie stirred restlessly in his sleep. His skin was clammy and sallow, with two feverish spots of red on his cheeks. Every now and then he would thrash his head about, muttering unintelligibly.

Owen wet a rag with cool water and placed it on Charlie's forehead. His eyes fluttered open, and the sight of Owen seemed to calm him. He quieted down, and within a minute or two he slipped back into sleep, his breathing shallow and wheezing.

Owen slid to the floor next to Charlie's bunk and tried to pray. He wanted to ask God—if there was a God—to spare his friend's life, to make him well again, to get them out of Germany and back to Eden, where Charlie belonged. But the words wouldn't come.

Charlie believed in God, believed that God had saved his life and given him the strength to go back to the front and do all those heroic things. Fritz believed, enough to put his own life in danger for the sake of strangers. Owen wanted to believe. Maybe, in the past where his memory lay hidden, he had believed. All he felt at the moment, however, was fury—anger at the injustice of the situation, rage at his own helplessness.

The God Charlie and Fritz believed in was an omnipotent Deity, capable of intervening in people's lives and powerful enough to make a difference in their circumstances. But God had not seen fit to heal Charlie or to help them escape danger. . . .

Or had he?

Charlie prayed, and Fritz had come.

Charlie would probably say it was a miracle—all of it, right down to the fact that they had been incarcerated in the same prison camp. Owen didn't know much about miracles, but he had to admit that meeting Charlie had been a lucky break for him. In their barracks, only Charlie had understood what it was to be "crazy," to have no past and no memories. Only Charlie had befriended him. And because of Charlie's friendship, Owen had found hope. At least enough hope to risk an escape instead of waiting for the liberation that might never come . . . or might come too late.

Owen fished in his pocket and came up with the dog-eared picture Charlie had given him at Christmas. The gift of a family, of a place to belong. He held it up to the dim light and traced with his finger the tiny faces of the figures on the front porch of the farmhouse. William Coltrain and his wife, Bess. Were they dead, as Charlie believed? Or did they still wait for their only son to come home again?

Mabel Rae, the sister who, according to Charlie, would probably end up as an old maid. Short, round, and a little on the dumpy side, she had a wide smile and laughing eyes. And Willie.

For some reason, Owen always paused when he came to Willie. The picture was so small that he couldn't see much of her features, but every time he looked at her photograph, he felt a tiny shock—almost like recognition. Like he really knew her.

It was ridiculous, of course. He couldn't know her—he had never met her.

Maybe someday, if they got out of this mess, he'd get to meet Willie. And he was pretty sure from what Charlie had told him that he'd like her a lot. She was a down-to-earth girl, practical, reliable, the rock of the family. He could almost envision walking up onto that rickety front porch, looking up at her, and hearing that low, sultry voice—

He was letting his imagination run away with him again. Charlie had never said what Willie's voice was like. It just wasn't the kind of detail a brother would tell about his sister, even if he noticed it. She probably had a high-pitched, annoying southern drawl, the kind of voice that would shatter glass and make pigs squeal. If he ever did get to meet her, he'd better be prepared for the worst.

A noise below him startled Owen back to the present. He stuffed the picture into his pocket, crept to the door, and opened it just a crack. Before Owen could catch him, the little gray kitten scampered into the secret room, jumped onto Charlie's cot, and settled on the pillow next to his head, purring. *Ah, let him stay,* Owen thought. He wasn't causing any harm. And Owen would be back in a couple of minutes—just enough time to find out what was going on.

Leaving Charlie and the kitten, Owen blew out the lamp and slipped through the door.

★ ★ ★

Charlie heard a pulsing rumble, muted and far away, like the sound of motorcycle troops. He was standing on a road in the scorching noonday sun, and he couldn't move to save his life. He tried to dive into the ditch for cover, but his legs wouldn't carry him. He just stood there, waiting for them to come.

Then, over the crest of the hill, he saw something—men marching, advancing toward him. Waves of heat shimmered off the road and distorted his view. He couldn't tell, from this distance, whether they were friend or foe. As they drew closer, he squinted into the summer sun and made out a bedraggled, exhausted company of Allied forces, and at the head of the column, standing upright in a jeep, an arrogant-looking officer in a helmet, holding a swagger stick at his side.

At first Charlie thought it was the smirking SS officer from the prison camp, but this man was wearing khaki, not black—an American uniform. A general's uniform . . .

Patton!

Charlie was seeing his own company marching through Sicily.

Then, without warning, he was with them, in ranks, marching. Following Patton to his glory—or to destruction.

281

"No!" he screamed. "There's an ambush up ahead!" But no one heard him. As if he had never shouted, they just kept marching, marching. The general was yelling back to them about being real soldiers, about not giving up no matter what the cost, and the column kept right on moving, following the jeep into the heart of Messina.

As they rounded the last curve into the village, a man stood on the side of the road, motioning to Charlie. The man wore faded overalls and a white shirt, and his boots—farmer's boots—were dusted with a layer of red earth. Was it . . . could it be. . . ?

Pop?

Charlie broke ranks and drew closer. It was his father, but he looked different somehow. Peaceful. Much younger, with smooth tanned skin and a full head of hair. His arms were taut with muscles, and his smile revealed a full set of even white teeth.

Charlie's father held out his arms, and Charlie rushed into them, sobbing. His dad patted his back and held him close, and Charlie felt like a little boy again . . . except that he couldn't remember ever having his father comfort him this way.

"It's all right, Son," his dad said. "It'll all be all right."

"No, it won't," Charlie mumbled against his father's chest. "This is where it happens, and I can't stop it. A boy is going to be killed, blown to bits, and I—"

He stopped. Even now he couldn't tell his father the truth: that as a result of this ambush he ended up in the hospital, a victim not of shrapnel but of shell shock. He shuddered, and he felt his father's hand on his shoulder.

Charlie looked up. Pop was still smiling. "We know, Son," he said simply. "We know all about it—about everything. And we're not ashamed—we're proud of you."

"But how—"

"We know, Son," his dad repeated. "We know how you rescued little Charles and his brother and sister. We know all you did on the beach at Normandy, and how you were captured, and what you've done for Owen Slaughter."

Charlie sagged against his father's chest. "I'm tired, Pop. I can't do any more."

"I know, Son. It's almost over. Just one more thing, and then you can come home."

"I can't stop what's going to happen, Pop." Charlie looked over his shoulder, where columns of khaki-clad soldiers still marched through the July heat toward Messina. "I tried to tell them, and they wouldn't listen. They can't hear me."

"Just one more thing," his father repeated, stepping back. "Then come on home. Your mother is waiting to see you."

"Mom? Where is she?" Charlie reached for his father again, but he retreated into the distance, toward the horizon. Charlie could barely make him out now, a tiny figure in blue denim with one arm raised, pointing Charlie back toward the ranks of soldiers marching on the road.

Then he was gone.

Charlie turned and dashed blindly toward the front of the column, frantically trying to reach Patton and the jeep. He ran like a man possessed, passing the marching troops and leaving them in his dust. But it wasn't enough. Just as he drew even with the jeep, he looked to one side and saw a flash of white in bushes beside the road. Like sunlight reflecting off a bayonet . . .

★ ★ ★

Owen crept to the edge of the hayloft and looked down. Fritz was there, with Führer at his heels, standing in the doorway of the barn. The sun was barely up over the horizon, casting a glow through the door and bathing Fritz and his companions in a reddish light.

Owen squinted against the glare. Unless his eyes were deceiving him, Fritz Sonntag was sharing his morning coffee with three men in German army uniforms.

Two of them seemed very old—stoop-shouldered, one with gray hair and the other, when he removed his cap, almost totally bald. The third, a small, slight youth, shifted from one foot to the other like a nervous teenager on his first date. His eyes flitted around the barn and up to the hayloft, and Owen drew back with a smothered gasp. He was just a boy, and the pistol at his hip seemed strangely out of place for one so young.

So, Fritz Sonntag had deceived them. He had kept them here, all this time, only to betray them to the Germans. Owen should have known better than to trust a Kraut. They were all the same—all of them Nazis out to rule the world—

"*Achtung!*" the boy said, pointing toward the loft.

"Owen?" Fritz called softly. "Ist you? Come down, if you please."

Owen sighed. Well, he probably should have guessed it would come to this. So much for God's being interested in what happened to him. So much for the idea that someone like Fritz really could exist, someone who truly cared about other people more than himself.

He swung a leg over the ladder and began his descent. "How much reward are you getting for us, Fritz?" he snarled over his shoulder. "If that's your real name. Or is it Himmler?" He turned and faced the foursome. "It better be a good bounty. You've fed and kept us for two weeks."

Fritz handed him a cup of coffee and gave him a puzzled smile. *"Guten Morgen,* my friend. How ist Charlie dis morning?"

"Not well." Owen snatched the coffee from him. "He'll probably die and save your friends here the trouble of killing him." He glared at Fritz. "I won't make it that easy on them."

Fritz shook his head. "What ist he talking about, Führer?" he said to the dog. Führer wagged his tail and went over to put his nose in Owen's free hand. In spite of himself, Owen scratched the shepherd's ears. It wasn't the dog's fault that his owner was Judas incarnate. He was just a poor dumb animal.

"Ah!" Fritz went on, tapping a forefinger to his head. "You think that because my friends here are in the uniform of the Reich, they are enemies?"

"What else am I supposed to think?" Owen stopped petting the dog and held out his hands. "I'll go quietly. Just don't let them hurt Charlie."

Fritz began to chuckle. *"Nein, nein,"* he said jovially. "Take a good look at them, Owen Slaughter. Two grandpapas und a Kind—a little child."

The boy began to protest, rather loudly, that he was no child. Owen didn't catch all the dialogue, but he understood enough to know that Fritz was soothing his ruffled feathers.

"But that one's got a rifle," Owen said. "With a wicked-looking bayonet."

"The army has—how you say? Conscripted—ja, conscripted every man in the village too young or too old for the regular troops. To keep peace, you know? They get new boots und a warm winter coat. And in the case of these three, they help me get my friends out of danger and across the border." He pointed to the bald man, who smiled and nodded. "Das ist my Uncle Helmut. The other two are Rutger Klein und his grandson Dieter."

"You mean they're friends?" Owen gaped. "They're not here to kill us?"

Fritz patted Owen's arm. "I would not betray you, my friend. No one ist going to die today—except perhaps der Führer."

Owen reached down and gripped the shepherd's neck. "Führer is going to die?"

A confused expression passed over the German's bearded face; then his countenance cleared. "Not Führer the dog. Führer the *mad* dog." He grinned broadly. "Our friends have brought us good news. Herr Hitler ist dead."

Owen's mind spun. "How? When? Are you *sure?*"

"Army rumors ist re . . . reliable," Fritz said, groping for the right word. "He killed himself, like the coward dog he is, in his bunker. Him and that

Eva Braun woman. Two days ago." Fritz addressed the dog. "Heil Hitler!" Führer began snarling and barking, and both Fritz and Owen laughed.

Fritz clapped Owen on the shoulder. "Helmut, he says the American troops are already in Deutschland, moving this way." He raised his coffee cup in salute. "To the liberation of the Fatherland."

★ ★ ★

Charlie awoke in a fog from his fitful sleep. His head pounded, and his mind swam with heat and pressure. His pillow was soaked with sweat. Beside him, a small gray cat stirred and stretched, pressing against him to be petted.

A little sunlight filtered through the cracks in the wall, enough for him to see that Owen wasn't there. What had happened?

With great effort he swung his feet over the side of the cot and tried to stand; but his legs wouldn't hold him, and he collapsed in a heap on the floor.

Where was he? He couldn't remember. He only remembered the dream, and the vague notion that he had to do something—something important. He tried to take a deep breath, but his lungs seized up and sent him into a fit of coughing. He lunged for the pillow and pressed it over his mouth. He had to be quiet, very quiet. . . .

He shook his head, blinked, and tried to clear his vision. There! Very faintly, he could make out the outline of the door. He had to get to it, had to get out, to—

To do what? Charlie didn't know. His mind was fuzzy, and he couldn't concentrate. But it was important; he knew that much.

He crawled to the door and pushed it open. The bright light of morning stabbed at his eyes, blinding him. His stomach lurched, and he gagged, but all he brought up was water and bile. Still he pressed on, across the hay-strewn wooden floor, until he came to the very edge of the loft.

He was in a barn of some kind. He could hear people talking—in German! Charlie peered over the edge. Below him stood five men—or was it six? His eyes wouldn't focus. Everything kept moving, getting smaller and less distinct. His head pulsed as if it would explode any minute, and he began to sway. Then, suddenly, everything snapped into view.

Owen was surrounded by three Kraut soldiers—one wielding a rifle and bayonet. Their dog—a killer, probably—stood next to Owen, guarding him. The fourth man, the one not in uniform, had one hand around Owen's neck and some kind of weapon—a hand grenade, maybe—in his other fist.

The heat behind Charlie's eyes caused the scene to shimmer. He had to do something while he still had a chance.

Suddenly a shout rang out from below: "Heil Hitler!" The dog went wild, snarling and trying to attack Owen. Owen's captor raised the hand grenade.

Charlie's mind wouldn't tell him what to do, but he didn't need instruction. Owen Slaughter was in danger, and nothing else mattered. He only had one chance. If he did it right, he could take out the guy with the grenade and the Kraut with the bayonet at the same time.

With a feverish roar, he gathered all his remaining strength and leaped from the loft, hurling himself toward Owen's attackers. Tears sprang to Charlie's eyes, and through the blur he saw it all as if in slow motion—Owen's mouth forming the word *no,* the Kraut soldier lifting the bayonet, the German shepherd pushing the bearded man out of harm's way. . . .

Then everything went black.

44

★ ★ ★

Future Perfect

The Coltrain Farm
Near Eden, Mississippi

Willie Coltrain pushed against the porch floor with one foot, and the swing creaked gently on its chains. She looked out over the cotton fields and sighed contentedly. Amazing, the transformation that took place each spring when the fields began to show green. No longer did the farmland stretch to the horizon in an endless flat sea of depressing brown and gray. New life was budding, in the land and in Willie's soul.

"It's pretty, isn't it, when the sprouts start coming up?"

Rae pushed through the screen door with two cups of coffee in her hands, and Willie slid over to make room for her on the swing.

Willie took one of the cups and sipped the coffee, watching the steam rise into the cool morning air. "There were times this past year when I thought I'd never get through it all," she murmured, half to herself. "Losing Owen and Charlie, and then Mama and Daddy."

Rae nodded. "I know it was hard, Willie. I'm sorry I wasn't here to help."

"It's all right." Willie patted Rae's hand and looked into her eyes. "I understand. You had your own life to live, your own path to follow. I'm just glad your path finally brought you back to Eden."

"So am I. And I think Drew is, too. Finding out about his father was hard on him, but he's so much more at peace now. I suspect he's relieved."

"He and Bennett Winsom are really hitting it off, aren't they?"

"I don't think there could be a more perfect partnership," Rae said.

"They've got big plans for that office of theirs. Did I tell you there's a chance Link may go to law school and join their practice when he's done?"

"The Coltrain dynasty." Willie grinned. "Only without the Coltrain name. Give us an inch, and we'll be on the social register before you know it."

"Yep." Rae affected an exaggerated drawl. "I can hear it now: *Them uppity Coltrain girls don't know how to keep in their place. That's white trash for you—thinkin' they're good as ever'body else.*'"

Willie laughed. "We've always been as good as everybody else, my dear sister—only nobody knew it."

"We knew it." Rae dissolved in a fit of giggling. "They just wouldn't listen when we told them!"

Rae's infectious mirth overtook Willie, and she laughed until the swing shook and the coffee spilled and tears ran down her face.

When the laughter subsided, Rae put her arm around Willie. "It feels good to laugh, doesn't it?"

"Uh-huh." Willie swiped at the coffee stains on her apron. "Some mornings while you were gone, Rae, when Mama and Daddy were so bad, I didn't think I had the strength to get out of bed. But the world keeps on turning, spring comes again, and just look—there's new life everywhere."

Willie gazed across the expanse of front yard, where the azaleas were in bloom and the pink-and-white dogwood trees along the roadside lent their delicate color to the morning. When she turned back to her sister, a strange light emanated from Rae's face, and she had her hand spread across her stomach.

"Yes," Rae whispered. "There is new life everywhere."

Willie stared at her sister. "You mean—"

Rae nodded eagerly. "How do you feel about being Aunt Willie?"

"I feel—" Willie groped for words. She was stunned, and in the back of her mind, a bittersweet longing tugged at her heart. She wished it could have been hers—hers and Owen's. But she didn't say so. "I feel wonderful, of course. How do *you* feel?"

"I feel absolutely . . . radiant. Isn't that the word everybody always uses for an expectant mother?"

Willie nodded. "And you look it, too. You're sure, now? How long has it been?"

"Two months. I wasn't sure until a few days ago, and I still have to go to the doctor. But I was always on a schedule like clockwork. I'll have the test, of course, but I don't have much doubt."

"Another bunny bites the dust," Willie quipped. "You've told Drew, I assume?"

Rae laughed and nodded. "This morning. He was thrilled—tore out of here like a crazy man to tell Bennett. He'll probably end up in Grenada, buying everything in sight." She gave Willie a quizzical look. "His mother sent us quite a sizable check—to 'get us started,' in her words. Drew . . . ah, he wants to do some renovations to the house, to make the small bedroom upstairs into a nursery. I told him I'd ask you if it was all right."

A knot formed in Willie's stomach. Despite her joy for her sister, despite the new life that was coming to her own soul, she had the sinking feeling that life as they had known it was changing, moving on, leaving her behind.

"I've been thinking," she began carefully, "about going back to teaching next fall. Now that we've got the land leased out to the Stewarts, I won't have the burden of running the farm. Maybe I could get Charity Grevis to rent me our old apartment, and—"

"Willie!" Rae interrupted. "How can you even think about leaving?"

Willie looked up and saw tears standing in her sister's eyes. "I just thought that you and Drew should have the place to yourself, to fix up however you want, and now with the baby coming and all . . ." She trailed off miserably.

"We wouldn't think of it," Rae said in a clipped voice. "Drew and I already talked about it. If anyone leaves, it will be us."

"That doesn't make any sense." Willie frowned. "This big old house needs work, and I don't have the money to put into it. Besides, it's a great place to raise children. So much room and—"

"Yes, so much room. Plenty of room for all of us, I'd say." Rae narrowed her eyes. "Willie, tell me the truth now: Do you really *want* to leave?"

Willie shifted uncomfortably under her sister's gaze. She had never been able to lie to Rae, not even a little. "No," she murmured. "But it seemed the most logical—"

"It's completely *il*logical," Rae snapped. "Look, Willie. You get along with Drew, right?"

"Of course."

"And he adores you. We both want you to be a part of this baby's life, and not just on a part-time basis. We'll do a little remodeling, create some private space for you, and for us and little Bubba here—"

Willie chuckled. "No way. Not if you're going to saddle my nephew with the name Bubba."

"Who said it was a nephew?"

"Well, no niece of mine will be called Bubba, either."

"Willie! Where's your sense of southern heritage? It's the white trash way."

They both laughed, and Rae went on. "That's better. Now, as I was saying before I was so rudely interrupted, we'll foot the bill for renovations—we'll use the money Drew's mother sent."

"That doesn't seem fair," Willie protested.

"All right, let's talk about fair. Who stayed here and took care of the farm, and Mama and Daddy? Who nursed Daddy through his illness? Who worked her fingers to the bone until all she got was bony fingers? Who, I ask, has *earned* this house?"

"Well, when you put it that way—"

"Aha!" Rae nodded decisively. "So, my dear sister, this is *your* house."

"Wait a minute. I thought it was our house."

"OK. Have it your way. It's ours. But all discussion of your moving out is off-limits. Agreed?"

Willie looked into her sister's eyes and smiled. "You mean it, don't you?"

"Of course I mean it."

Willie set her coffee cup on the porch floor and drew Rae into a hug. "Thank you," she whispered.

Rae returned the hug, then pushed her sister back to arm's length and scowled at her. "Nonsense—don't thank me. This is the way it's supposed to be. Now, let's plan. You can take Mama and Daddy's room—it's the biggest."

"That's absurd. You and Drew should have it."

"Are we going to argue about every little detail?"

Willie chuckled. "Probably."

"Well, listen to reason before you get your stubborn little mind set," Rae countered.

"No, you listen to reason—my reasons. Mama and Daddy's room is right next to the small room you said Drew wanted for a nursery. I may be the doting aunt, but I'm not going to be the one getting up at two in the morning to change diapers. And if that child has a mouth and a will anything like her mama's, she'll be screaming bloody murder at all hours of the day and night."

"Babies do that," Rae admitted.

"So, I'd rather have the bedroom at the other end of the hall."

Rae brightened. "You know, you could take both those rooms, and we could cut a doorway between them—maybe double French doors. You could have a sitting room—a whole suite!"

"A suite," Willie mused. "Yeah, them dirt-farming Coltrains is comin' up in the world."

"We can take that big walk-in closet and add a second bathroom."

"But what about the kitchen?" Willie asked.

"What about it?"

"Mama always said no kitchen is big enough to accommodate two women."

"That's ridiculous," Rae scoffed. "We've been cooking in that kitchen together all our lives."

"I'm not worried about us, Sister. But what about your husband? He'll be living here too, you know."

Rae began to laugh and couldn't stop for a full minute. "Our 'equal partnership' ends at the kitchen door, Willie. When it comes to cooking, Andrew Laporte is the most traditional of men. He wouldn't set foot in the place if it were on fire."

Willie gazed out over the budding landscape and leaned back in the swing. "This is going to work, isn't it?"

"Of course it is," Rae answered confidently. "Nothing's ever stopped the Coltrain sisters yet."

★　★　★

"A baby?" Bennett Winsom jumped up from the table and encircled Drew in an exuberant hug. "Congratulations, son! Thelma! Thelma, come out here!"

Thelma appeared from the kitchen, wiping her hands on a dish towel. "What's going on?"

"My new partner is having a baby. Break out the cigars, Thelma."

Thelma put her hands on her hips and looked at Drew, who felt a hot flush creeping up his neck. "Well, I'm very happy for both of you. This should make medical history."

"No, no." Bennett shook his head. "I mean, Drew and *Rae* are having a baby."

"Thanks for the clarification," Thelma laughed. "It eases my mind some, I'll have to admit."

"Thelma, stop it." Bennett flushed and clapped Drew on the shoulder. "Where are those cigars? We have to celebrate!"

"Sorry, boys, no cigars," Thelma said. "But I do have a couple of slices of apple pie back there. On the house."

"Bring three," Bennett called as Thelma went back to the kitchen. "And some more coffee, please."

Drew watched Bennett's face in amazement. He had never in his life seen a man this excited about someone else's baby. He himself was thrilled, of course. But on the drive into town he had begun to think about the responsibility, and by the time he pulled up in front of the cafe, he was completely overwhelmed.

"What's it like? Having a baby, I mean," he asked when Thelma had returned with pie and coffee. "I'm excited about it and all, but I'm a little scared, too."

"A *little* scared?" Bennett prompted.

"Terrified. It's so much work, so much responsibility. So much—"

"Commitment," Bennett supplied. "Isn't that right, Thelma?"

Thelma shrugged. "Don't ask me. I've never been a mother."

It took a minute for this to sink in, and Drew stared at her. "I keep forgetting you don't have children of your own, Thelma. You seem like the perfect mother."

Thelma held up a hand. "Correction. I seem like the perfect *grandmother.* I happen to subscribe to the play-with-them-until-they-cry-and-then-give-them-back philosophy."

"You do not," Bennett protested. "You adore little Mickey Simpson, crying or not."

"Mickey never cries." Thelma lifted her eyebrows as if she had made her point. "He's the perfect child." She smiled fondly. "Besides, Mickey is different. Special."

Drew was amused, listening to their good-natured bantering. They were so comfortable with each other—it almost reminded him of himself and Rae. Wait a minute, he thought. Was it possible something was developing between Bennett and Thelma?

Nah. Impossible. Bennett was at least as old as Drew's father, and Thelma couldn't be much younger than his mother. They were old enough to be grandparents, for heaven's sake.

Still . . .

"Can we get back to the subject?" Drew interjected, uncomfortable with the direction of his thoughts.

"Of course." Bennett winked at Thelma and settled back in his chair. "We were discussing—"

"Fatherhood." Suddenly Drew's heart sank, and he didn't know why. He should be happy. This was supposed to be one of the most joyous moments of a man's life. "What if I turn out to be a rotten father?" he blurted out.

Bennett stared at him, as though dumbfounded by his question.

"I mean," Drew went on, "I don't know anything about babies. I might do OK with a son, once he's old enough to be interested in fishing and playing ball and stuff like that. But a baby? I'd be afraid to hold it—afraid I might do something to hurt it. And what if it's a girl? What if—"

"Get a grip on yourself, boy," Bennett said with a laugh. "You'll learn."

"But how? Do they expect a fellow just to know these things? I never had any little brothers or sisters, never spent any time around children."

"Drew," Thelma soothed. "You love Rae, don't you?"

"Of course I do." The words came out defensively, and he winced. "You know I do."

"And you'll love your son or daughter, too. Trust me. You will. Just relax."

Drew took a deep breath and thought about it. Imagine, a little person, born out of his and Rae's love for each other. Completely dependent upon them for love and care and nurture. A round little chubby-cheeked girl with her mother's laughing brown eyes and captivating smile. A little dark-haired boy . . .

Suddenly Drew realized that the cafe had grown quiet, and he looked up to find Bennett and Thelma watching him with questioning looks.

"Sorry. I was just . . . thinking."

"Thinking about your son?" Bennett asked.

Thelma slanted a glance at Bennett. "Or daughter?"

"Yes." Drew nodded.

"You'll be a fine father," Thelma said, patting him on the arm. "Can I give you one word of advice?"

"Please do."

"If it's a girl, teach her how to fish. If it's a boy, make sure he learns to cook."

"All right," Drew agreed, then frowned at her. "Why?"

"Because the best talks I ever had with my father were on Saturday mornings with a fishing pole in my hand," she said. "And any man who can bring his wife breakfast in bed will have a happy woman for the rest of his life."

45

✦ ✦ ✦

The Second Time Around

Paradise Garden Cafe

Thelma Breckinridge peered through the service window at Bennett Winsom, alone in the booth he usually shared with Olivia Coltrain these days. He had his head bent over a yellow pad, and papers were spread all over the table.

Thelma picked up the coffeepot and made her way toward him, feeling both hesitant and a bit self-conscious. She couldn't help it. She had prayed and struggled and agonized, but she simply couldn't free herself from her feelings for this handsome, compassionate man. And she didn't understand it. If the Lord intended for them to be just friends, why wasn't God taking away these other feelings, as she had asked so many nights lately? Asked, begged, pleaded. But still she felt a rush of pleasure when Bennett came into the cafe, and she wanted to be near him, to see the light in those warm brown eyes, to brush his hand, ever so slightly, as she reached to pour his coffee. . . .

"You'd better get that office of yours in shape soon, or I'll have to start charging you rent."

Bennett looked up, a confused expression on his face. Then his countenance cleared, and he smiled—a smile like sunrise over the Delta, a smile like springtime. Thelma's heart lurched, and her hand shook as she filled his coffee cup.

"Thanks, Thelma. Sorry I was so preoccupied." He stacked his papers to one side and motioned to the opposite bench. "Do sit down."

Thelma shook her head. "I don't want to disturb you. I was just bringing you a refill."

"Please.' His eyes held a look of—what was it? Desperation? Longing? "I'd like to talk to you for a minute, if you're not too busy."

Thelma fought against the tide of emotions that rose up in her. She wanted to be here, close to him, and she wanted to run. She wanted to shout at him, to shake him from his blindness, yet she found herself tongue-tied, like a shy schoolgirl. Surely her feelings for this man were emblazoned across her face like a banner headline on the *Commercial Appeal*. A part of her wanted him to know, and another part wanted to hide those feelings, to protect herself from being hurt again.

"Thelma?"

Miserably she settled into the opposite side of the booth and avoided his gaze.

"Is anything wrong?"

"What do you mean?" she asked, still looking down at the table.

"Have I done something to upset you?" He reached a tentative hand across the table toward her. She drew her hands back, evading his touch. "You seem so—I don't know, so distant the past few weeks. Except for the other day, when Drew Laporte came in with his news about Rae, you've hardly given me the time of day."

Thelma pulled in a shaky breath. "Don't be ridiculous, Bennett." She struggled to keep her tone light. "You've been busy; I've been busy. There's nothing wrong. Honest."

He smiled again, patting the table where her hand had just been. "All right. I'm not trying to pry, you understand, but if there's something you'd like to talk about—"

Thelma suppressed a laugh. As if she could talk to Bennett Winsom about her feelings for Bennett Winsom! No, this was something she'd just have to deal with on her own, between herself and God. Surely the Lord would eventually get around to answering her prayers, and life could get back to normal.

"I've . . . I've been a little worried about Ivory," she hedged. It wasn't a lie; she had been concerned. But it wasn't the whole truth, either.

Bennett seemed relieved. He pulled his stack of papers in front of him and sorted through them. "Well, let me ease your mind a little. I've received an extension on Ivory's taxes until June 15. That breathing room will give us time to find out who's behind this scam and look for a way to break the contract. Drew's going to do the legwork, and I have the utmost confidence in his ability to ferret out the truth." Bennett grinned. "He's a good man, and he's had a little experience in dealing with this kind of problem."

"No kidding?" Thelma said, glad for the change of subject, for a chance to set aside her tumultuous feelings. "He's so young, I figured he would just be getting his feet wet."

"In many ways, he is," Bennett answered. "But his problems with his father's business centered around something similar. He didn't tell me details, of course, but I got the general idea. Some kind of unethical dealings with people—poor people, mostly—where Drew's father and his cronies were getting rich off folks who couldn't defend themselves and for the most part didn't even understand they were being taken." Bennett smiled, his affection for his new young partner obvious. "He's a good man, Drew is. His first priority is people and doing what is right by them. He'll be a successful lawyer, I have no doubt, but probably not a wealthy one."

"Like you," Thelma said.

"Thank you for the compliment," Bennett said graciously. "I certainly hope that my life—both as a lawyer and as a man—reflects that kind of integrity."

"You sure do in my book," Thelma murmured, getting lost in his eyes. Suddenly she realized what she had said and jumped up. "I'd better get back to work."

"Do you have to?" Bennett's eyes scanned the empty cafe. "There's nobody here but us. I'd like to talk to you."

"The lunch crowd will be coming in soon," she hedged. "And Madge—"

Bennett looked at the clock over the counter. "It's nine-fifteen, Thelma."

"Oh. Well, I still have a lot to do. I'm making a meat-loaf special, and you know how long that takes."

"How long?" He captured her hand and grinned at her.

"A long time. Hours. My meat-loaf special is . . . well, special."

"I'm sure it is," he said. "I know you are."

Flustered, Thelma reached for the coffeepot and sloshed coffee all over the table. He grabbed for his papers, and she snatched a towel out of her apron pocket and began trying to absorb the spill. But it was too late. Coffee spread across the table as if it had a life of its own, soaking the bottom layer of notes and, when Bennett lifted them up, dripping onto his white shirt and tie.

"I am so sorry," she said over and over again, mopping frantically. "I am such an idiot."

"No, you're not." Bennett held up his wet papers, and she blotted them dry as best she could.

"Did I get it all?"

"No." He pointed at the tabletop. "There's a little over here."

She reached across the table, balancing herself with one hand, and he put his hand over hers. "Thelma?"

She could feel heat and color rising up her neck, and she tried to pull away.

"Thelma, look at me."

She looked, and his gaze held hers as if a cable of iron stretched between them. Thelma felt as if her heart were out there on that wire, dangling in thin air, exposed and vulnerable. But in the depth of his eyes she saw something else, something she dared not name.

"There's a little bit here, on my tie." He guided her hand to the spot, but his eyes never left hers. "And here, on my shirt."

Thelma held her breath as she leaned toward him.

"I've been trying to tell you something for several days, Thelma, but you won't ever light anywhere long enough to listen." His voice was quiet, compelling. "I never thought this would happen to me because no man deserves to be happy twice in a lifetime. But—" he raised his head until his face was inches from hers—"I love you, Thelma Breckinridge."

Thelma's knees buckled, and at this angle, leaning over the table, there was no place to go but into his embrace, into the kiss she had dreamed about since Christmas Eve. His mouth pressed against hers, and she could feel his warm breath on her face. For a second or two she held herself rigid, hoping and praying this wasn't just a dream. Then the reality of what he had said took hold in her mind; He loved her. Bennett Winsom loved her!

With a passion she had never known before, Thelma returned his kiss and felt his lips, gentle and seeking, merge with hers. A flame shot through her veins, and tears welled up in her eyes. When she sank weakly back into her side of the booth, she was crying in earnest.

Bennett held on to her hands as if he would never let go. "What did I do?" he asked, obviously worried. "What's wrong?"

"Nothing's wrong." She shook her head. "How could anything be wrong?"

"You're crying."

Thelma smiled through her tears. "Women always cry when they're happy, don't you know that?" Laughter bubbled up in her, and she gripped his fingers. "Men!"

"Does that mean—?"

"That I love you, too?" Thelma nodded. "Of course I love you. I've loved you since the minute you walked through that door on Christmas Eve. I just didn't think I could ever be fine enough or educated enough—"

He reached across the table and placed a forefinger on her lips to silence her. "Not another word."

"But—"

"No buts." He gave her a look so tender, so accepting, so inviting that all her doubts and fears vanished. All but one.

"Bennett, I have to tell you something."

"Tell me everything," he whispered.

"I'm not . . . not the woman you think I am. A long time ago, when I was young, my life was, well, not pleasing to God. I did a lot of things I'm not proud of, and—" She paused, groping for words. "I—"

"You had a reputation for being, shall we say, not quite pure?"

Thelma nodded miserably. "I figured you ought to know what you're getting, in case you want to change your mind."

Bennett looked intently into her eyes. "I know all about it."

"You do?"

"Olivia told me about some of the things you've been through. And I know exactly what I'm getting. I'm getting a woman whose capacity for love and understanding amazes me. A woman whose relationship with God challenges me. A woman whose spirit and mind enthrall me. A woman whose past has long ago been wiped clean." He got up, slid into the booth beside her, and put his arms around her. "You are the woman I have waited for ever since I left my grief for Catherine behind. You are God's greatest miracle in my life."

He kissed her again, and Thelma felt the burden of the years lift from her soul. "We'll need to take it slow," she murmured in his ear. "The last time I trusted a man, it was Robert Raintree, and he left me with nothing to show for my love but a note pinned to my screen door."

"Robert Raintree was a fool," Bennett murmured in a husky voice. "And the only note from me you'll ever find on your screen door is the one that says, *I love you.*"

46

★ ★ ★

Hero's Homecoming

May 6, 1945

Owen Slaughter sat in the tiny bedroom of Fritz Sonntag's stone cottage, keeping watch. It was nearly dawn.

For the last hour or two, Charlie had been sleeping fitfully, his rest interrupted by bouts of delusional raving. Fever raged through his body, spreading outward from the angry bayonet wound in his left shoulder. Fritz had cleaned and dressed the wound the best he could, but when the bleeding had finally stopped, infection had set in.

Two days ago, Charlie had become coherent long enough for Owen to piece together what had happened—at least partially.

"I saw Pop, standing on the road. He said there was something I still had to do," Charlie had mumbled groggily. "When I saw the Krauts, I knew what it was—I had to get them." He reached up and patted Owen on the cheek. "You're alive—you're all right. I didn't panic, did I? I got them."

"You got them, Charlie," Owen sighed. He wasn't quite sure how Charlie's father figured into the equation, but he was pretty certain that in his fever Charlie had interpreted the scene in Fritz's barn as a threat—German soldiers surrounding Owen, ready to kill him. Unaware that the Germans were Fritz's friends, Charlie had thrown himself onto the bayonet to save Owen.

"You're my good friend," Charlie said, his voice thick with pain. "My best friend. Had to keep the Krauts from getting you."

"Good friend," Owen muttered to himself. "Stupid friend."

Charlie had raised up then, grabbing Owen by the collar and pulling him down. "Promise me," he rasped. "Promise you'll go home and tell my family face-to-face. Tell them how I died. Tell them—" he let go and sank back onto Fritz's bed—"tell them I'm not a coward."

"Of course you're not a coward," Owen soothed. "You're a hero. But you're not going to die. Do you hear me? You're going to make it."

"Go home," Charlie mumbled, shutting his eyes. "They'll be your family, too—you'll see. Tell them. . . ."

Without another word he had faded into an exhausted sleep and hadn't been awake since.

Owen bathed Charlie's forehead with a damp cloth and watched him closely. Every now and then his eyes would open, but he obviously wasn't seeing anything. It was getting worse by the day, by the hour. With a sinking heart, Owen realized that his friend couldn't hold on much longer.

"Ist getting worse, no?" Fritz's subdued voice came from the doorway.

"I'm afraid so," Owen said without turning around. "He thought—" His words strangled on tears, and he cleared his throat. "He thought your friends were going to kill me. He thought he saved my life."

"Ja," Fritz said. "Ist a brave man who would die for his friend."

"But it's such a waste!" Owen snapped, his anger flaring. "He didn't have to die—he would have gotten better. He would have been all right."

"Maybe, maybe not," Fritz mused. "He was very weak. I do not know where he found strength to do what he did. But I do know this—the greatest love a man can have ist to lay down his life for his friend."

Something stirred in Owen's memory, and his head snapped around. "I've heard that before. Where?"

"Ist the word of our God," Fritz answered simply. "Jesus said it—und Jesus lived it. He sacrificed himself for others—for all of us—like your friend Charlie here. But there ist a difference." He came and laid a gentle hand on Owen's shoulder. "Charlie's death ist for noble cause—to save one friend, best friend. Christ's death saves all people, to make them friends of God."

Friends of God. Owen thought about that for a minute. Charlie was a friend of God, and his death was the ultimate sacrifice a man could make. Owen's only response to God—at least as far as he could remember—was anger at the injustice people suffered. He knew, although he wasn't sure how he knew, about Christ's death, the Innocent One dying for the sins of all. And it had seemed like a mockery to him—the worst injustice ever perpetrated. Yet Fritz spoke of the event as if it were a great gift—a gift of love.

"I go pray for our friend Charlie," Fritz said, squeezing Owen's shoulder. "We will talk later."

Owen sank back into the chair. A heavy weight in his chest made breathing difficult, and his stomach knotted. Charlie, he realized with a sudden terrifying certainty, was going to die. The only friend he had known. The only person on earth with whom he shared any memories at all.

An unutterable loneliness engulfed Owen, a dark emptiness that reminded him of the early days when he had first turned up in a German prison camp without knowing who he was or how he had gotten there. Until he met Charlie Coltrain, he had no hope at all. Charlie had befriended him. Charlie had shared his memories, his family, his life. Charlie had given him a reason to live. What would his world be like without Charlie? And—an even more disturbing concept—what would his life have been if he had never met Charlie in the first place?

Then Owen's mind seized upon an ironic thought. From everything Charlie had told him—about Messina, about the shell shock, about the hospital and the landing at Normandy and the battle experiences, Charlie by rights should be dead already . . . dead, or in some nut ward back in the States. The man had been prepared to die—indeed, he had sought death. And yet he had lived.

Was it possible that God had protected Charlie Coltrain, brought him back to sanity, kept him alive, even brought him to the stalag, just for Owen's benefit—so that Owen wouldn't have to face the emptiness alone? Instinctively, without hesitation, Owen knew what Charlie's answer to that question would be. And he also knew that Charlie would do it again, gladly, for the sake of his friend. For Charlie was, as Fritz had said, a brave man. A hero.

Yes, it was unfair. Unjust. Unthinkable. And yet strangely encouraging, the idea that God might care that much about a man like Owen. A man with no past, no memory—

"Slaughter?"

Owen's head jerked up. Charlie's eyes were open, and he reached weakly in Owen's direction.

"I'm here, buddy." Owen gripped the bony hand and blinked back tears.

"It's time," Charlie rasped. "Time to go . . . home."

Owen leaned over his friend and strained to hear the words. "Home?"

Charlie nodded. "They're all waiting. It's over. I have to go."

A strangled sob broke from Owen's throat, and he held on tight. "No, Charlie!"

"Yes. Promise me—" His words dissolved in a fit of coughing, and he winced in pain.

"I'll go to Eden, Charlie. I'll tell your family everything. I promise."

Charlie shook his head. "Not just that," he wheezed. "Promise me . . . you'll come too."

Owen took a ragged breath. "Where, Charlie?"

Charlie lifted his hand and pointed upward. "Home." He smiled. "It's OK, pal. I'm fine now. No pain. . . ."

"Hang on, Charlie," Owen pleaded.

Charlie's eyes cleared, and he fixed Owen with an intense look. "No," he whispered. "Let me go. It's time."

Owen's heart lurched, but he nodded. "All right, Charlie." He smoothed a hand across Charlie's forehead. "I'll miss you. You're the best friend a fellow could ever have."

A smile touched the corners of Charlie's lips. "Tell Willie and Mabel Rae . . . I love them. And I love you, Owen. I'll be waiting . . . for all of you. . . ."

His hand dropped to the rough blanket, and the light went out of his eyes. With a final heaving rattle, Charlie Coltrain breathed his last.

For a long time Owen sat there, holding Charlie's hand. At last the skin grew cool and waxy under his touch, and Owen's tears subsided. He closed Charlie's eyes, stood, and walked numbly out into the spring morning.

★ ★ ★

That night, just as the moon was rising, Fritz and Owen buried Charlie in the glade beside the stream. Fritz prayed, committing Charlie's soul into the hands of almighty God, and Führer sat at Owen's heels, pushing his muzzle into Owen's hand and whining softly.

"I will carve a wooden grave marker tomorrow," Fritz said as he laid a large rock at the head of the grave. "If you will tell me what you wish engraved."

Owen stood staring at the photograph of the Coltrain family, straining in the dim light to make out the tiny figures. "What?"

"Ist something special you wish on the grave marker?"

Owen thought about it for a minute. "Yes," he murmured. "Let's put, *Charlie Coltrain—a hero who gave his life so that others might live.*"

"Ist good." Fritz nodded approvingly. He patted Owen on the shoulder as he turned back toward the cottage. "You are blessed to have so good a friend," he said. "You will see him again—of this I am certain."

Owen followed at a distance along the path that led to the little stone house in the woods. He wasn't so sure Fritz was right about seeing Charlie again. But something in him desperately hoped it was true.

47

★ ★ ★

Hollow Victory

May 8, 1945

Owen stuffed his gear—what little there was of it—into the rough burlap sack Fritz had given him. He glanced in the small cracked mirror that hung in Fritz's bedroom, then looked down at himself. In the coarse breeches and tunic and Fritz's brown hunter's jacket, he could easily pass for a German woodsman or farmer. At least he hoped so. With the help of Uncle Helmut and his friends, Owen was going to try.

The plan was for Helmut, Rutger, and young Dieter to escort Owen down through the Black Forest to the Swiss border. There were roadblocks all along the way, of course, but somehow Dieter—who was obviously more resourceful than Owen had given him credit for—had managed to get his hands on forged transport orders. When they got close enough to the border, Owen would go on by foot over the mountains into Swiss territory.

Fritz's hearty stews had put some muscle back onto Owen's bones, and he had sufficient food and water for three days. Still, it would be a hard climb and a dangerous escape. He was acutely aware of the possibility that he might be joining Charlie sooner than he had anticipated if his identity was discovered.

Owen was scared, and he murmured a halfhearted prayer for help. If only they weren't challenged. . . .

He peered out the window toward the barn. Dawn was just breaking, and he wondered if he would ever again see a sunrise without remembering Charlie's death. In some ways the events of the past two days seemed like a blur, some vague memory out of the distant past. But when Owen saw the rising sun streaking the eastern sky with red and blue and purple, a fresh wave of pain assaulted him. He blinked back tears and looked again.

Right on time, as promised, a tarp-covered truck with a swastika painted on the side approached the house. Helmut and his friends. The vehicle bucked and shimmied on the rough dirt path leading up to the cottage, then shuddered to a stop just outside the barn door.

Owen grimaced and shook his head. It would be a rough ride, but it was better than walking. Better than—

Something was wrong. Helmut had jumped from the truck and was running toward the barn, shouting and gesturing. When Fritz appeared, he waved his arms and shouted some more. Owen grabbed his bag and headed out the door.

When he skidded up beside Fritz and asked what was going on, Fritz motioned for him to be quiet. Helmut continued his tirade, now joined by Dieter and Rutger. With all of them speaking at once—in German, of course—Owen couldn't figure out what was going on. Finally Fritz held up a hand for silence and turned to him.

"There will be no escape today," he said. "Ist over. Troops coming this way."

"Troops?" Owen parroted. "German troops?" His insides turned to jelly, and he grabbed Fritz's arm.

"Nein," Fritz chuckled. "Helmut brings word—Allied troops coming into Germany. Ist over, my friend. The Reich ist surrendering."

The hairs stood up on the back of Owen's neck, and he ran a hand through his three-week-old beard. "Surrender?"

"Ja." Young Dieter smiled and clapped him on the back, and in halting English said, "Ist gute news, ja?"

"Ja," Owen said miserably. Two days. Charlie had missed the liberation by two lousy days.

★ ★ ★

At noon, a haggard and weary-looking lieutenant stood shaking his head in amazement. "How long did you say you'd been here, soldier?"

"Almost three weeks," Owen answered. "My buddy Charlie and I escaped, and Fritz here hid us out in his barn." He sighed deeply. "Charlie didn't make it. He's buried over there—" He pointed toward the clearing.

"And you say three Kraut soldiers helped you, too?"

Owen nodded. "Two old men and a youngster. They were going to escort me across the border into Switzerland, but you guys showed up just in time. They won't be harmed, will they? Or arrested?"

"We'll get their names from your friend Fritz here. Don't worry." He jotted some notes on a clipboard. "You were at the labor camp twenty kilometers north of here?" He pointed toward the woods.

"That's right. You've been there already, I assume?" Owen chuckled to himself. He could imagine Tiger Grayson's reaction when they saw each other again. No doubt Tiger would flaunt his idiocy in his face—going to all the trouble of escaping when liberation was just around the corner.

But the lieutenant didn't crack a smile. "What's left of it."

Owen's heart constricted. "What do you mean?"

The American looked at him. "I'd say you and your buddy got out just in time. Apparently the Krauts got wind that we were on our way and that a surrender was imminent. Rather than give up as prisoners of war, they took off. They're probably scattered all over this sector of Germany by now, hiding out. But they left a pretty grisly mess behind them." He exhaled heavily. "Burned the barracks to the ground, with every last prisoner locked inside. We got a mess of bodies over there, I'll tell you. I doubt we'll ever figure out who was who."

All the blood rushed from Owen's head, and he gripped Fritz's arm for support. The world spun, and his knees buckled. The last thing he remembered was the face of the American soldier peering down at him.

★ ★ ★

Owen came to in Fritz's bedroom. Führer had two paws on the bed, licking his hand and whining. The American sat on a stool next to him, and Fritz stood in the shadows of the doorway.

"You OK, Slaughter?" the officer asked. "Sorry about breaking the news to you that way I wasn't thinking that you might still have buddies in the camp."

"Not buddies, exactly," Owen said, sitting up. "But it was a shock." He rubbed his eyes and swung his feet over the side of the narrow bed. "It just hit me all of a sudden that Charlie and I could have been there. Charlie died anyway, of course, but—not like that." He shuddered. "I guess we were pretty lucky, all things considered."

Owen caught Fritz's eye and saw just the glimmer of a smile.

"Or maybe somebody was looking out for us," he corrected.

"If I believed in stuff like that, I'd say there was a battalion of guardian angels around you," the lieutenant said. "To escape in the first place, and then to get away, and to survive—it's nothing short of a miracle. Too bad your buddy didn't make it."

"Yeah," Owen muttered. "Too bad."

"Fritz has been telling me about Charlie," the lieutenant said, looking at his clipboard. "He sounds like a real hero."

Briefly Owen sketched what he knew of Charlie's exploits—being wounded on the road to Messina, rescuing the French children after the Normandy landing, keeping his sergeant alive in the woods, and—with only a little elaboration—attempting to save Owen when he thought Uncle Helmut and the others were about to kill him.

"I'm going to see that he's recommended for several medals," the officer said. "The Distinguished Service Cross, for sure—maybe even a Medal of Honor. It won't bring your friend back, but it may give some comfort to his family, knowing what a courageous man he was."

"Right," Owen said dully.

"Can you tell me where those should be sent? And yours, too, of course."

"Mine? I didn't do anything."

"You escaped from a German prison camp. You took care of a wounded buddy at the risk of being discovered. That's outstanding heroism in my book."

Owen raked a hand down the side of his face. He didn't feel like a hero, and he didn't want any stupid medals. He was just a man with no memory, with no place to go, with no past and no future. He just wanted his best friend back.

"Send them to Willie Coltrain, Eden, Mississippi."

"Is that his father?"

"His sister," Owen corrected. "I'm going there myself. She probably thinks he's been dead for a long time. She needs to be prepared before a bunch of medals just show up."

The lieutenant nodded. "The army will notify the family, of course, but it's good that you'll be there. I'll send a flag along with you."

"A flag?" Owen repeated stupidly.

"Well, we can't send him home for burial," the officer said. "Unless you want to exhume the body and—"

"No!" Owen closed his eyes to shut out the unwelcome image. "Let the poor man rest in peace."

"Fritz Sonntag will take good care of him," Fritz said softly from the doorway. "The memory of Charlie Coltrain will be honored in Deutschland."

Owen smiled. Fritz was a good man, a noble man. A friend.

"So," the lieutenant was saying, "we'll get you out of here and get your discharge paperwork under way. Get you a bath, a shave, a few days in Paris, and you'll be a new man."

"Paris?" Owen stared at him.

"Most guys take a few days in Paris en route—you know, kick up their heels, have a little fun. You'll have a lot of back pay coming."

Owen puzzled for a moment. Obviously this lieutenant expected him to know what Paris was, and to be excited about going there. But he hadn't the faintest idea. The only places he consciously knew were the German prison camp and Fritz's humble cottage. The only people he knew were Charlie, who was dead, and Fritz, whom he was leaving behind.

For a minute or two he considered staying with Fritz. This was a peaceful place, a safe place. But he had promised Charlie he would go to Eden.

"You say I'm going to be discharged?"

"That's right, Slaughter."

"So I'm a free man?"

The lieutenant frowned at him. "Well, yes, but—"

"Then forget this Paris place. I'll go straight home, if you don't mind." He looked over at Fritz, who stood stroking his beard with one hand and scratching Führer's ears with the other. "And in honor of my friend there, I'll keep the beard."

★ ★ ★

The sun was setting as Owen stood with Fritz and Führer beside Charlie's grave. The marker, handsomely carved by hand out of a thick plank of oak, was a masterpiece. Owen had spelled out the words for Fritz, and watched as it was carved and set in place, but it still moved him now as if he were seeing it for the first time. Tears filled Owen's eyes as he gazed at it in the waning light:

> CHARLIE COLTRAIN
> d. 6 May 1945
> A Hero
> He gave his life
> so that others might live.

In the center of the plank Fritz had carved a cross, entwined with lilies, and below it, in German, the words, *Mit Gott . . . With God*.

"I wish I had a camera," Owen muttered to himself. "They should see this."

Fritz reached into his pocket and pulled out a folded sheet of paper. "Ist

307

drawing I do before carving," he said, thrusting it into Owen's hands. "I keep for you, in case you want."

"Thank you." Words failed him, and he extended a hand toward Fritz. "Thank you for everything."

Fritz took his hand and drew him into a bearlike embrace. When he finally let go, his cheeks, too, were wet with tears. *"Danke,* my friend. Go with God. I pray for you."

Owen squatted down to Führer's level and looked the German shepherd in the eye. "Heil Hitler," he whispered, and the dog lifted his lip and growled. "Good boy!" He massaged the animal's ears and accepted a sloppy kiss across the side of his face. "You two take good care of each other."

"Auf Wiedersehen," Fritz said as Owen gathered his burlap bag and stood.

Owen shrugged. "They're waiting for me."

"Ja, ja," Fritz said. "You go."

Owen turned and walked slowly across the stone bridge, pausing one last time to look into the laughing waters below.

"I come to America, I look you up!" Fritz called after him.

Owen waved. "And I'll find Kurt in Minnesota and tell him you're fine."

Führer barked, and Owen cast a final glance over his shoulder. The image burned into his mind: Fritz Sonntag, standing like a mountain beside Charlie's grave, one hand lightly stroking the tall oak marker—and the dog named Führer lying in the gathering dusk with his head resting where Charlie's chest would be.

48

★ ★ ★

The Gathering

Paradise Garden Cafe
May 8, 1945

The sign on the door said CLOSED. But inside, the celebration was well under way.

Link's father held the door open while Libba wheeled Link through. A barrier of paper streamers in the doorway parted for them, and the crowd in Thelma's place whooped and hollered in greeting. Across the front of the counter was taped the banner headline from the *Commercial Appeal: VICTORY IN EUROPE!*

It had been more than a year since Link had last laid eyes on the Paradise Garden. A knot formed in his throat as memories of his times here with Stork and Owen leaped into his mind. Those were good times, innocent times. So much had changed.

And yet so much remained the same. Ivory out at the piano, playing swing tunes and grinning. Thelma stood behind the counter pouring coffee. Stork and Madge were dancing in the center of the cafe, where the tables had been pushed back, with little Mickey between them. Drew and Rae and Willie waved to him from a side booth. Within seconds everyone came over and surrounded Link, hugging him and clapping him on the back.

Stork plopped Mickey down in Link's lap and squeezed his shoulder with one hand. "Welcome home, buddy!"

"Thanks. You know, I've missed this place. I didn't know how much until just this minute."

Madge kissed him on the cheek, and Drew came over to shake his hand. "I hear we may be getting a new partner before long," Drew said, smiling broadly.

Link nodded and tickled Mickey in the ribs. "Looks like it. I've been accepted to law school at Ole Miss, and we'll be moving down to Oxford in June, right after—" he grinned up at Libba and saw her blushing—"right after the honeymoon."

"Hey, hon, it's about time you got here!" Thelma came out from behind the counter and gave Link a big hug, then went to stand beside his father. She looked different somehow. Younger. Light radiated from her face and softened her features. It was amazing, Link thought, what love could do.

And it was also amazing that he felt not a touch of jealousy on his mother's behalf, as he had when he thought that his father was interested in Olivia Coltrain. This budding relationship with Thelma Breckinridge was right, so completely right that Link could feel nothing but happiness for his father and the woman who was becoming so important to him.

"How's my soon-to-be son-in-law?" Olivia Coltrain appeared out of no-where and leaned down to hug him, wafting a scent of expensive perfume in her wake.

"I'm just fine, Mrs.—" Link stopped suddenly. "What shall it be? Olivia? Mom?"

She flushed a little and patted his hand. "What are you most comfortable with?"

"Mom, I think," he said decisively.

"Then Mom it shall be." She drew up a chair beside him and sat down. "I want to thank you, Link, for the joy and love you've brought into Libba's life. I won't give you the standard motherly warning about taking care of my daughter and making her happy because you've already done that. I just wanted you to know that you are a gift from God to her—to all of us—and I'm very grateful for you."

Link closed his eyes and wrapped his arms around Mickey, who still sat in his lap playing with his uniform buttons. Then he opened his eyes again and gazed around at the people gathered together in this place to rejoice over the Allied victory in Europe. These were the people who made Eden, Mississippi, home for Link. This was not just a celebration of military victory. It was a celebration of love, of family. He belonged here.

His mind cast back to the very first time he had come into the Paradise Garden Cafe a year and a half ago, on his way to his new assignment at Camp McCrane. How alone he had been, and how miserable! He was certain that naming the place Eden was some kind of cosmic joke. This town was too small and insignificant for the map—even God's map. But Ivory had played the piano for him. And Thelma had fixed him breakfast—his first taste of grits, as he recalled—and offered him friendship and hope, her henna-dyed hair extending out from her head like a halo.

Yes, despite Link's doubts, God had been in this place. God had been with him every step of the way, even during those horrible dark days on the front and in the hospital after he was wounded. It was no accident that he had stumbled upon Hans Amundson's little Bible on the beach at Normandy. God had done that and then miraculously brought them together as friends, brothers, in a hospital thousands of miles from that spot. God had given Libba back to him, even though his own stupidity had nearly cost him the relationship . . . twice.

Gratitude welled up in Link as he watched these people, his family, laughing and talking and celebrating. He was, indeed, a man richly blessed.

★ ★ ★

Thelma came out of the kitchen with a huge tray of sandwiches and set them down on the counter between a platter of turnovers and the enormous three-layer coconut cake Rae Laporte had baked for the occasion.

"All right, everybody!" she called above the din of music and laughter. "I think we're ready to eat."

Gradually the noise subsided, and everybody gathered around. "We've got quite a spread here, folks—and everybody's contributed. Rae, our little mother-to-be, baked this huge cake—" she nodded toward Rae, and a round of appreciative whistles and comments erupted—"and Libba's Aunt Mag made her famous cranberry-surprise punch."

Magnolia Cooley, standing next to Olivia, offered a little curtsy and cast a wink in Libba's direction. Libba dissolved into giggles and whispered something in Link's ear that made him laugh as well.

"Maybe there's something Libba would like to tell us about the cranberry surprise?" Thelma cut a glance at Libba.

Libba, doubled over with laughter by now, pointed toward Magnolia. "Let Aunt Mag tell you."

Magnolia, dressed in flowing magenta the same color as the punch, raised herself to a regal height and affected a look of disdain. "The child is demented," she said, lifting one eyebrow. "That recipe has been in my family for generations. It's a closely guarded secret."

"My lips are sealed," Libba chuckled.

Link rolled his eyes. "That'll be the day."

"All right, you two." Thelma turned back to the group. "There's turkey sandwiches and—well, a whole lot of good food."

Bennett leaned over and whispered, "Don't you think we should pray first?"

"I was just getting to that." She squeezed his hand. "Bennett has reminded me that we probably should thank God for all this wonderful food—and for the cause of this little celebration. Since he suggested it, I think he should do the honors."

Bennett reached a hand to Thelma and then to Aunt Mag on the other side. Within a second or two, everyone had joined hands in a circle. Bennett bowed his head and cleared his throat.

"Don't preach, Bennett," Olivia called out. "Just pray."

"Did I say something about welcoming this woman into our family?" He shook his head. "I take it all back."

A ripple of laughter swelled through the cafe, and then everyone quieted down again.

"Gracious God," Bennett began in a low voice, "truly you *are* gracious, and we have much to be thankful for." He went on to enumerate their blessings—the victory in Europe, the safe return of his son, the friendship and love that were represented in this room. With simple earnestness, he prayed for God's continued blessing upon the nation and each of them as individuals. He prayed on behalf of those who had not come home—for Charlie Coltrain and Owen Slaughter, for all who had died in this terrible war, and for their loved ones left behind. Thelma glanced covertly at Willie and saw a tear track down her cheek. But the younger woman pressed her lips together and nodded. Thelma sighed. Willie was still in pain, still missed Owen, but she was dealing with it. She was going to be all right.

Then Bennett prayed in deep gratitude for new life. For Libba and Link's upcoming marriage, asking that the Almighty would be at the center of their relationship and guide them into the future. For little Mickey Simpson and his recovery from scarlet fever, and for the new life growing in Rae Laporte's womb—that their lives would be touched by the love and grace of the Lord.

Thelma listened to his prayer, and her heart overflowed with warmth and joy. She did not know how she came to be so blessed—to be loved by a man with this much passion for God in his soul. She had told Bennett that they would have to take it slow, to give their relationship time to grow and develop. And yet at this moment, hearing him pray, she knew, with a conviction that could only come from God, that this was the person she had been waiting for. Through all the pain of Robert Raintree's rejection, through all the lonely years, God had been at work, preparing her, saving the best for last.

As if he had read her mind, Bennett squeezed her hand. And when he finished praying, he turned to her, and she saw tears brimming over in his eyes. And right there, in the middle of the Paradise Garden Cafe, in front of God and everyone, he put his arms around her and kissed her.

The battle was over. Except for Owen and Charlie, all of them, including Thelma Breckinridge, had come home.

49

★ ★ ★

A Day of Miracles

May 18, 1945

Libba Coltrain stood in the foyer of the First Presbyterian Church and adjusted her veil for the third time. She stood on tiptoe and peered in through the windows of the swinging doors. The pews were filled—almost everyone in Eden had come—and the sweet scent of gardenias drifted out into the hallway. A murmur of voices reached her ears, then quieted as the piano prelude began.

On the podium to the right, Ivory Brownlee sat at the piano, his head down over the keys. From this distance he looked like a true musician in his black suit and white shirt, and he played masterfully. Libba could see the back of her mother's head in the first row next to the aisle, and Aunt Mag's hat with the purple feathers towering above her. Across the aisle sat Thelma, where Bennett Winsom would join her once his fatherly duties were done. In the second row on the left sat Madge. Mickey stood on her lap, grinning coyly and making faces at the people behind them.

Libba strained to see across the sanctuary, but the people on the right side blocked her vision, and one tall candelabra was in the way. She could barely see Stork's blond head, but surely as best man he had everything under control and wouldn't let Link be late. Link was probably sitting up there now, fidgeting in his wheelchair, nervous as a cat.

The main door opened behind her to admit Drew and Rae, followed by Bennett and Willie. She gave Rae and Willie a brief hug, then tugged at the flounced ruffle on Willie's dress. "You look beautiful."

"I look stupid. Why couldn't you have picked a simpler style?" Willie tugged at her billowing sleeves. "I feel like a clown."

"Because it's my wedding." Libba grinned. "You're the maid of honor, don't forget. When you get married, I'll wear whatever horrible concoction you dream up for me—and do it gladly."

"You wait," Willie countered, retrieving her bouquet from Bennett. "If I ever do get married, I'll put you in the most hideous dress you've ever seen."

"You probably will."

There was a pause in the music, and then the opening chords of the processional sounded. Drew planted a kiss on Rae's cheek. "I have to go in the side and take up my position as groomsman. See you up front."

Rae entered first, proceeding slowly down the dimly lit aisle toward an altar illuminated with candles. Willie followed, and Bennett came up beside Libba and took her arm. "Are you ready?"

"As ready as I'll ever be." Libba took a deep breath and clung to Bennett's arm. "Thank you for doing this."

"It's my pleasure," he murmured in her ear. "I'm getting a wonderful daughter, remember?"

The two of them stepped onto the white runner that spanned the length of the center aisle. Ivory nodded to them from the piano bench and began the wedding march. As one, the entire congregation stood to their feet and faced the aisle.

Libba's eyes swam with tears, and through the blur she saw familiar faces and a few not-so-familiar ones, all smiling at her. Friends from high school. Charity Grevis, the postmistress. Richard Benton, who now ran the hardware store under her mother's supervision. Hans and Marlene Anderson, flanked by Stevie Sutton and Nurse Pincheon. Link's big sister RuthAnn, who dabbed at tears and beamed at her. Freddy Sturgis, grinning like the Cheshire cat. Madge and little Mickey, who reached out and grabbed at her veil as she walked by.

At last she came to the front row. Libba withdrew a white rose from her bouquet, offered it to her mother, then bent down to kiss her cheek. When she stood upright again, she turned with a smile and faced the altar.

Link wasn't there.

Tears stung Libba's eyes in earnest as she stared at the empty place beside Stork Simpson. The groom's place. She cast a frantic look at the pastor, who cut his eyes away and shrugged.

Surely this couldn't be happening. She knew Link was nervous, but Mama said all men got cold feet right before their wedding. She hadn't seen him all day, of course—it was bad luck for the groom to see the bride on the wedding day. Or so people said. Apparently it was worse luck if the bride didn't see the groom, especially once the service had begun.

Panic overtook her. She had heard of women being left at the altar, and she always felt vaguely sorry for their humiliation. But she also figured that if the groom was the kind of fellow who would embarrass a girl like that, it was better for them not to get married anyway. Still, it felt different when it happened to you.

A sob rose up in her chest, and Libba whirled toward Bennett and gripped his arm. But he was looking down at her as if nothing was wrong. Smiling, smiling . . .

Gently, he turned her around to face the back of the church. Ivory kept on playing for all he was worth, and slowly the doors to the foyer swung open.

Libba gasped, and everyone turned to look.

And there was Link, on his feet, with only a cane to support him, making his way down the aisle.

A cry of joy ripped from Libba's throat, and she started to run toward him, but Bennett held her back. "Let him come," he whispered. "He's worked for months to be able to do this."

With tears streaming down her face, Libba watched as the man she loved walked slowly down the long runner toward the altar. It seemed to take forever for him to put one foot in front of the other, but it didn't matter. The whole congregation was cheering, clapping, and crying, drowning out Ivory's music with the uproar.

At last Link reached the front and stood next to his father, facing the altar. The pastor cleared his throat loudly, and everyone settled down and resumed their seats.

Link craned his neck around Bennett and winked at Libba. "Surprise!" he whispered, loud enough for all to hear, and everyone laughed.

When the excited murmurs subsided once more, the minister took a deep breath and opened his book. "Dearly beloved, we are gathered together in the presence of God and these witnesses to join this man and this woman in holy wedlock. Who giveth this woman to be married to this man?"

Bennett put an arm around Libba and gazed into her eyes with an expression she had never seen before. But somehow, instinctively, she recognized it: a father's love.

"Her mother and I do," he said in a rumbling baritone. Then he took her hand and placed it in Link's, stepped back, and went to sit beside Thelma Breckinridge.

Libba didn't know how she managed to get through the ceremony without stumbling over her vows. All she could see, all she could think about, was Link Winsom, standing tall and handsome beside her, looking at her with the light of love in his eyes.

At last the pastor pronounced them man and wife, and Link gathered her in his arms for a kiss. Then they turned to face the congregation, and as Libba looked out over the dear smiling faces, she had to bite her lip to keep the tears of joy from overwhelming her.

Through all the days of struggle and the nights of pain, the Lord had been faithful. How could any woman ask for more? A loving husband. A real father. Family. Friends. And the future spread out before her like a glorious tapestry of light and shadow.

She took Link's arm and began the long, slow walk back down the aisle, into that future. There would, no doubt, be other difficult times ahead. But Libba determined, in this moment, that when those times came, she would look back on this day as a testimony to God's presence. A day of miracles. A shining moment of grace.

Epilogue

"Your stop, son. Eden, Mississippi."

Monk Lipkin turned in his seat and looked over his shoulder to the haggard-looking fellow seated on the second row. Monk had been driving this route for years now, and he had let a lot of soldiers off at the Paradise Garden on their way to Camp McCrane. But this guy was different—real different.

He didn't say much, for one thing. Usually they were pretty talkative, especially when the bus was as empty as it was this evening. But except for muttering that he had been discharged and was going home to his family, this one hadn't said two words since they pulled out of the station in Grenada.

Monk could believe he was discharged, all right. He wore a uniform that didn't fit him quite right, and he had a full beard. The army didn't let anybody in active service keep a beard. Maybe he was one of those fellows they had brought back from the German prison camps. Those GIs had had a rough time of it, and this fellow looked like he could fit the bill. He was short and wiry, with curly brown hair and startling blue eyes. But the eyes looked empty, somehow . . . haunted.

What Monk didn't believe was that this guy had family he was going home to. He had never seen a more lost, forlorn-looking soul in all his born days, and Monk thought he had pretty much seen it all. Without knowing why, he felt sorry for the man.

"You getting off?"

The man nodded and picked up his gear—not a duffel bag like most soldiers carried, but a brown burlap sack. He made his way to the front of the bus and mumbled, "Thanks."

"No problem. Take care of yourself, you hear?"

If the man heard, he didn't acknowledge it. He stepped off the bus and

319

stood on the gravel in the parking lot, staring at the door of the Paradise Garden.

Monk shrugged. Well, never mind. If he was in the wrong place, Thelma Breckinridge would steer him straight. She was a good woman, and besides that, she made the best apple pie this side of heaven.

He grinned to himself and shut the door. One of these days he'd get up the courage to ask Thelma out on a date. But not tonight. Looked like she was going to have her hands full baby-sitting this lost soldier.

With a beep and a wave, Monk Lipkin pulled out of the parking lot and back onto the highway. Maybe next time.

★ ★ ★

He stood for a moment on the driveway in front of the cafe, peering in through the window. This was the right place, he was sure of it. If he didn't know better, he'd almost believe he remembered it for himself.

But he couldn't figure out what was going on tonight. The sign on the door said CLOSED; yet the lights were on, and music was playing, and laughter drifted out into the evening air. He could see white streamers across the ceiling and a table in the center of the room with a big white cake.

He squinted and moved to one side to get a better view. A man in uniform sat in a chair, and beside him, a girl in a flowing white dress fed him cake with her fingers. Something stirred in the back of his mind—a wedding?

Yes, that must be it. A wedding party.

He wondered vaguely if the people he was looking for were in there celebrating with the bride and groom. Or maybe one of them had gotten married. An odd sense of apprehension rose up in his mind, but he couldn't explain why.

Maybe he should go away and come back tomorrow. He didn't want to disturb their celebration, and the news he was bringing would surely put a damper on the party. But he didn't know where to go. All he knew was that he had to be here.

He waited for a few more minutes, watching, raking one hand through his thickening beard.

Then he shrugged. It couldn't be helped. If he was intruding, they would just have to forgive him. He was here, and he had to keep his promise, no matter what.

He had come too far to turn back now. . . .

Additional titles by Penelope J. Stokes

FAITH ON THE HOMEFRONT
#1   Home Fires Burning   0-8423-0187-9

FAITH: THE SUBSTANCE OF THINGS UNSEEN
0-8423-1981-6